PENGUIN BOOKS

The Sea Between Us

Elizabeth Smither is a prize-winning poet. Her collection *The Lark Quartet* won the Montana New Zealand Book Award for Poetry in 2000, and in 2002 she was the Te Mata New Zealand Poet Laureate. She has also written two previous novels, *First Blood* (1983) and *Brother-love Sister-love* (1986), and has published four collections of short stories, the most recent being *Listening to the Everly Brothers* (Penguin Books (NZ) 2002).

for Harry & Chris

The Sea Between Us

Elizabeth Smither

PENGUIN BOOKS

PENGUIN BOOKS
Penguin Books (NZ) Ltd, cnr Airborne and Rosedale Roads, Albany,
Auckland 1310, New Zealand
Penguin Books Ltd, 80 Strand, London, WC2R 0RL, England
Penguin Putnam Inc, 375 Hudson Street, New York, NY 10014, United States
Penguin Books Australia Ltd, 250 Camberwell Road, Camberwell,
Victoria 3124, Australia
Penguin Books Canada Ltd, 10 Alcorn Avenue, Toronto,
Ontario, Canada M4V 3B2
Penguin Books (South Africa) (Pty) Ltd, 24 Sturdee Avenue, Rosebank,
Johannesburg 2196, South Africa
Penguin Books India (P) Ltd, 11, Community Centre, Panchsheel Park,
New Delhi 110 017, India
Penguin Books Ltd, Registered Offices: Harmondsworth, Middlesex, England

First published by Penguin Books (NZ) Ltd, 2003

3 5 7 9 10 8 6 4 2

Copyright © Elizabeth Smither, 2003

The extract from the poem 'Carapace' by Gwen Harwood is reproduced by
permission of the author and Penguin Books Australia Ltd.
The extract from the poem 'The Mind Is Its Own Place' by Chris Wallace-Crabbe is
reproduced by permission of the author.
The extract from the poem 'Countries Lodge in the Body' by Paola Bilbrough is
reproduced by permission of the author and Victoria University Press.
The extract from the poem 'Instructions for Living in the Sky' by Philip Salom is
reproduced by permission of the author and Fremantle Arts Centre Press.
The extract from the poem 'Any Time Now' by Allen Curnow is reproduced by
permission of the copyright owner, Jeny Curnow.
The extract from the poem 'My Wish for Land' by Randolph Stow (part of *Stations*
from *A Counterfeit Silence*, Angus & Robertson, copyright © Randolph Stow 1969) is
reproduced by permission of the author and Sheil Land Associates Ltd.

Designed and Typeset by Egan-Reid Ltd
Printed in Australia by McPherson's Printing Group

ISBN 0 14 301859 0
www.penguin.co.nz

A catalogue record for the book is available from the
National Library of New Zealand

The assistance of Creative New Zealand towards the production of this book is
gratefully acknowledged by the Publisher.

My wish for my land is that ladies be beautiful,
that horses be spirited and gentlemen courteous
and all moustaches faultless.

My wish for my husband is that he read Tennyson.
My wish for my daughter is that she be interesting
and capture a million acres.

My wish for my sons is that they be chivalrous,
sun-tanned and tall, and that they bestow on me
perhaps a dozen grandsons.

My wish for my house is that linen be Irish
and tableware sterling, and that the piano
never go too long unplayed.

My wish for myself is that I grow matronly,
straying in dove-grey silk through the roses
under the far far harking of the crows.

'My wish for my land', RANDOLPH STOW

I woke thinking of land –
how countries lodge in the body
long after you have moved elsewhere.

'Countries lodge in the body', PAOLA BILBROUGH

Ouse, Tasmania

Seasons have scoured
this beautiful abandoned house
from which are gone eyes, sinews,
all taken-for-granted gifts.

'Carapace', GWEN HARWOOD

A stranger coming into Maud Betts's General Store in Ouse would have needed to duck his head under rakes and the hems of women's dresses. He would have had to pick his way to the counter across the spotless wooden floor, avoiding sacks of grain and rice and lentils. And when he reached the long counter with its sweet jars and enormous silver cash register he would have wondered how did such a small woman reach down a rake or a summer dress. Compliments – for Maud provoked gallantry – might have sprung to his lips and died there at the sight of a pale fine forehead in which resided a brain capable of mathematics, particularly book-keeping. The darkness threw into relief the soft gold hair, the colour of money, and the serious character-fixing regard which surmised character as well as creditworthiness.

Since Bruce Betts, Maud's husband, had died of a ruptured appendix, she had taken over the store, following what she imagined were his wishes. She had been accustomed to sitting companionably in the parlour with him after supper while he worked on the ledgers, sometimes raising her eyes from her book to drink in his tall bony form, the broad shoulders in one of the shirts brought down – the stranger need not have worried – by a grappling pole. The cost, 4/6, was carefully entered in the ledger. 'You don't need to sew for me, Maudie,' he'd said, 'not when you've got so much on your hands.'

During the quiet times between serving and ordering, shelf-stacking, dusting and mopping the wooden floor, dragging the sacks from their entrenched positions where they clung like crabs, she darted into the long narrow kitchen to chop vegetables for a slow-cooking stew or prepare a pudding. Bruce was a great fan of puddings; no day with a pudding could be counted a failure. For Maud its equivalent was their bed with its fine white embroidered cotton cover turned back and her nightdress and his nightshirt side by side.

At first the ledgers had seemed all she had left of her husband: she took them to bed with her at night and held them against her chest, unopened – she had a longing for hard things. A tear-stained shirt was eventually laundered and hung out in the sun, though she left his pillows pressed against her spine in order to sleep. When she woke she found her hand had moved, thrusting pillows aside, to his side of the bed. The light seeped through the heavy lace curtains: purified and softened, it seemed like the light cast by a white magnolia.

Eventually, propped by pillows, and with a shawl around her shoulders, Maud forced herself to look at columns, figures, suppliers, estimates. Bruce's accounting had been rudimentary but sound: a little refinement, a little leeway, was all she would allow. Father Stanislaus, the Catholic priest, had called, leaving a few holy tracts and suggesting they kneel in prayer together. 'Not in the bedroom,' Maud said sharply, for that is where he had found her, following her 'Come in' like a homing dog. 'If you'll just allow me to get up.'

Shamefaced, he had backed out and waited in the dining room.

'You really should lock your door, Mrs Betts,' he admonished. 'Anyone could. . .'

'There's no one I want now, so anyone's welcome,' Maud replied, hoping he would quickly find a verse and leave. It's all too much or too strange, she thought. The graveside words, each word as heavy as a spade – she had felt her chest ring – or a ceremony swollen with everyone's interpretation. Incongruously, she thought of the loaves and fishes.

'Would you accept a small sherry, Father?' she enquired to excuse her brusqueness in the bedroom.

'Well, since the sun is over the yardarm,' he replied, and for the first time that week Maud smiled. What did it matter what clichés one used or how mixed the source: they were stepping stones. Any port in a storm, she almost said, and stopped herself.

Back in bed, now in her nightgown and shawl, she thought about the ledger entry for the five barley loaves and the five fishes. Had the child with such a substantial lunch, compared to the others, an over-protective mother? The sort who pinned a handkerchief to a shirt or walked you to school? Her own six-year-old daughter, Harriet, would be returning in a few days. It was the one uncontrollable unfathomable thing she had done, its source unknown. 'A month, I want a month to myself,' she had told Emma. 'To mourn,' she added swiftly, softening her countenance to counter the shock she saw rising in her sister's eyes. 'I'll be all right, you know,' she insisted, both sufferer and nurse. 'I just want to get things in order.'

So Harriet, wailing, had been pushed into her aunt's arms and taken off to Guiseford. And Maud, night after night, had peered down at *treacle, rolled oats, bacon, cheddar*. The front door stayed unlocked, and eventually she slept.

At Guiseford Harriet looked up at hams hung from the ceiling, at strings of onions coiled like her own plaits, at lanterns set in the centre of the table in the evening, and her Uncle Jack bending over to light a cigar from the flame. Guiseford was plain but elegant: even her aunt's dresses seemed simpler, looser; her hands, swollen by immersion in stone sinks, hung loosely at her sides as if inactivity was a crime and she was waiting for something to fly to them. Quite often, after a week had passed, that something was Harriet. Emma held the tight compact little body against her and with one large hand smoothed and stroked the flaxen hair. Outside, through the French doors which opened on all sides under the overhanging roof and walkway, the dry fields stretched as far as the eye could see. They rose slightly towards the horizon as if knowing too great a sweep could not be comprehended or comforting, rather like a full stop at the end of a long sentence.

'Conjugal, that's the trouble with Maud,' Emma said to Irene when she visited. 'No wonder Bruce's death has taken her so hard.'

'I suspect Harriet won't remember much of this,' Irene remarked, her eyes straying into the distance, as eyes so often did at Guiseford. The long windows could have been vent holes for arrows or boiling oil in a war of love.

'Children are resilient,' Emma responded, not quite believing it or knowing if she had been conjugal herself before the heavy chores rose up to block disappointment or dreams.

The hams, the onions, the cloth-boiled puddings: what were they but the domestic equivalent of the slaughtered carcass hung from a tree, the blood and the flies? Outside Harriet was making a garden in an old pie dish, snipping heads of stock and making holes with a long nail. She had made a path with dried grass rubbed between her fingers until it resembled chaff.

'I expect we were once,' said Irene, gazing at the distant silhouette of Jack Lascelles on a horse.

'No,' Emma said, and her vehemence surprised her. 'It's supposed to be someone who loves a mate above any offspring. Either you do or you don't.'

'Perhaps you're right,' Irene responded. She was childless so she couldn't answer just yet. It sounded like two chances. If one failed you could have the other.

The vehemence in Emma's voice caused her to reach out a hand.

'Those Americans,' she said. 'The ones who took you to Kuala Lumpur. Do you think they were conjugal?'

'Undoubtedly,' Emma said, and some of the anxiety left her eyes and she smiled.

Four sisters – there were eight in all but four, including Maud, formed a clump in the middle. Four brothers scattered throughout the twelve: older sisters married and gone before the youngest were born, or achieving the status of 'aunts', and youngsters too tiresome to bother with except when they were called upon to help. But Maud, Emma, Irene, Ada were inseparable in the middle. When they left for Melbourne to go into service only Maud, engaged to the son of the owner of G W Betts's General Store, stayed. Why? they asked her. Because it's Bruce, she replied. Once she made up her mind she was immovable.

As for prospective husbands in Melbourne, it was not so easy. At Government House, sharing a room with a vivacious girl called Ginny Boon and rising at 5 a.m. to creep down the stairs to begin the fireplaces – the lift remained locked until the Governor descended for breakfast under covers at 9 a.m. – Irene re-discovered shyness, introversion. She had had to fight for the position: the housekeeper, a formidable Scot, considered her arms too thin for the work required; her glowing references were regarded with scepticism. Several times, with her head inside a fireplace, blacking the back, Irene cried.

Ada and Emma meantime were engaged as a pair by a society doctor: Ada to cook, which she did with great flair, and Emma to supervise the house and the two children. The children were perfect pets: on Friday nights Emma reached down a glass jar of striped boiled sweets and two chubby hands were ceremoniously inserted. Only the boy, Christopher, stirred the sweets about and had to open his closed fist for inspection. And only once were there two gaudy sweets on his palm. A highlight was the nights when Dr and Mrs McManus attended the theatre. Doctor outshone Mrs Doctor in Ada's opinion as she stood by the front door waiting to hand top hat and cane. Mrs Doctor obviously felt she needed to be part of the ceremony, for she stepped up close, wafting clouds of perfume into her husband's face as she straightened his buttonhole: a dark red carnation. Christopher and Petula, allowed to postpone their bedtime, sat on the stairs; one evening Petula almost jammed her face between the railings.

'Okay Ade and Em?' Doctor McManus would ask, giving them a seductive backwards glance as he swung his opera cloak to show the lining: red arterial satin.

Bruce Betts had complained of stomach aches and a pain in his side but he refused to go to the doctor, insisting it was a strain. That Sunday, after mass, he had dug over the vegetable garden, saying it couldn't wait. It took weeks to make the connection between eating and pain: Maud's cooking was a delight; swift preparation and elegant presentation came naturally. Nor did Maud fuss if he seemed off his food for, from a child, she had often elected to spend a weekend day in bed and been allowed. She propped herself on pillows and spread her books about her, she wrote phrases and sentences that appealed in her journal. And when sleep crept upon her she demolished, just in time, the mountain of pillows and lay flat on her back. She repeated the pattern until evening when she rejoined the family and endured its teasing. If Maud had been a doctor this would have been her primary prescription. But when Bruce's pain persisted and he pressed her hand to his abdomen to show its drum-like tautness, 'like you were with Harriet', she felt a cold fear.

But still he would not consult Dr McSkimming or go to the cottage hospital. 'Don't fret, Maudie,' he would say. 'Whatever it is, it will pass.' His family, of course, were like oxen: the men tall and rangy, able to endure deserts and swollen rivers, beating bushfires with wet sacks, subsisting on the meagrest amounts of tucker.

'I think he's really ill,' Maud said to the priest the next time she went to confession, rushing through a catalogue of imagined neglects and overlooked courtesies until Father Stanislaus stopped her and said, 'What is it that really ails you, my child?'

'Can I talk to you outside?' Maud replied. 'Child' jarred her, as if she had never grown up.

'Of course you must get the doctor,' Father Stanislaus said as they stood in the emptied church. Maud had waited at the end of a pew, alternately praying by rote and looking at the sanctuary lamp. 'Get him yourself.'

The very next day one of the Strawbridge twins had burst through the shop door at midday calling for Mrs Betts to go to the school. Through his puffing and wheezing, the bright pink bathing his freckles, Maud gathered that Harriet had fallen and hurt her head. Miss Tole, the senior teacher, had sent for the doctor but since he seemed to be out on a confinement no one knew when he would arrive. Immediately Maud saw her chance of a consultation with Dr McSkimming. 'I won't be long,' she called to Bruce: he was stocktaking in the storeroom and heard only snatches of the conversation. She had thought not of her child but of him; of her determination to bring the doctor to him. And her instinct proved right: Harriet was lying on the grass under the shade of a willow tree, her head supported by a cushion and one of the older girls fanning her with a Japanese fan, part of that month's project display. Harriet's eyes were closed but her breathing was unstrained. A bruise above her temple felt hot to the touch but Maud guessed it would soften and run through a gamut of colours. Yet she felt kindly towards Harriet because at last there was a chance for Bruce. 'Where is the doctor?' she asked Miss Tole, and Miss Tole leaned forward and placed a hand on Maud's shoulder.

'Water,' Maud suggested, stroking Harriet's hair. 'Perhaps she could drink something.'

'We've done that,' one of the children said. 'It ran out the side of her mouth.'

'Well, fetch some more,' instructed Miss Tole. Activity was important on these occasions. Some of the children – there were thirty-five in the school – were already losing interest and had run off to play.

Eventually there was a stir at the gate as Dr McSkimming drove up in a cloud of dust. The children clustered around him and escorted him to the body of Harriet as if he was on a ward round at the cottage hospital. 'No, I haven't brought the jar of sweets,' he said to one of the first entrants who was clinging to his coat.

'Nothing serious,' he said to Maud when the little gallery had been led back into the classroom by Miss Tole. 'A good sleep, for the shock, and keep her off school tomorrow. Check her during the night, but if she seems to be sleeping normally. . .'

'I thought so,' said Maud. 'You needn't have been summoned. But I wanted you to see Bruce. Perhaps we could go together.'

'You can tell me about his symptoms on the way,' Dr McSkimming said.

Two of the larger boys lifted Harriet onto the back seat of the Pontiac. Her eyes opened briefly and she looked up at her mother. 'It's all right, pet,' Maud said. It was the endearment Bruce used. *Goodnight, pet. Sleep well, pet. See you in the morning, pet.*

But when they got back to the general store there was a crowd assembled. Maud and Dr McSkimming leapt from the car.

'We didn't know where to find you,' one of the women wailed.

'I told Bruce,' Maud began, pushing her way through them, inclined to use her fists. The symptoms she had described as they jolted down the hill – nausea after eating, stomach taut as a drum, pain in the side become constant – had been enumerated also by Bruce. Enough is enough, he thought, and in a lull between customers he had turned to the medicine cabinet. A laxative seemed to be the answer. Now he lay on the shop floor, barely breathing, his skin as damp as grass under an early morning dew. Maud flung herself on him, running both hands down his face. 'Bruce, darling,' she called, as if she were beginning to call him back from the dead.

Somehow she was put aside and willing hands lifted him into the doctor's car. Harriet was lifted out, half-asleep. Near death and sleep they passed. Maud went with him, cradling his head. At two o'clock in the morning he was dead.

Young as she was, Harriet had a sensitivity to atmosphere and in two weeks at Guiseford she sensed that her Aunt Emma was unhappy. Not that she would have put it in those terms, in any terms: she simply drew closer to her silent, kind aunt and became her shadow.

'Wouldn't you rather be outside?' Emma would ask as she worked in the dairy or kneaded dough.

'I'd rather be with you,' Harriet replied, and caught a flicker of astonishment before the eyes resumed their normal, slightly guarded but always ready to assist expression. Harriet guessed, as she kneaded a small portion of dough to be set in a small greased tin for herself and decorated with the letter H cut from a spare strip, that Aunt Emma depended on her heavy chores to get her through the day; and that she, Harriet, could lighten the load only to the extent of a pudding stirred or the fowls fed.

In the afternoons, though, there were at least one or two spare hours and then they sat and read: Harriet her *Black Beauty* and Aunt Emma her Palliser novels.

'I like reading about rich people, don't you?' Aunt Emma remarked one warm afternoon when they had dragged two stained and ancient deckchairs under the eaves and were holding their books out in front of their noses as though they were wearing lorgnettes.

'I expect Miss Ellen was rich to own a horse,' Harriet offered. She was nearly at the end where Black Beauty's life improved.

'Rich people have time to think,' Aunt Emma said. 'Not that they always take the chance.' She was thinking of Kuala Lumpur, half-tempted to find the atlas and lay the one exciting episode of her life at Harriet's feet. Then she shook her head at her own foolishness and let her eyes take in the reality that was in front of them: the dry foreground and the rising hills, the earth that would shortly scorch and crack, the firebreaks that would be cut, the smell of eucalyptus when it ignited like a mad woman with her hair on fire. Unbidden, the small animals fleeing and singed came to her mind, their hot paws, rasping breath and eyes unnaturally large. Quickly she turned back to Glencora Palliser who was organising a political weekend and chivvying the housekeeper, who was complaining about the amount of linen.

At night when Uncle Jack and sometimes Leo, the hired hand, came back to the house Harriet noticed the change in atmosphere. It was better when Uncle Jack brought Leo, who was simple but good-natured. The women washed up and the men drank a few beers, sitting in the deckchairs Emma and Harriet had vacated. In the kitchen, her aunt, her face anxious and sadder again, seemed in retreat.

At dinner at the long table with its white cloth turned to hide stains Harriet attempted to interest Uncle Jack, but she was mainly tongue-tied. He was a man who made conversation a test, to see if you could get to the end of a sentence without a failure of vocabulary or logic. Sometimes Harriet felt she was on a swing bridge: there was one at Guiseford and even aged six years and ten months she was still terrified of it. Sometimes, when no one was looking, she approached it stealthily, as if it could hear tremors in the grass, but still it swayed at her first footstep. So far she had advanced five steps before lowering herself onto its plank backbone, opening *Black Beauty* and pretending to read. Since she lay with her head towards solid ground, anyone coming upon her might think she had safely crossed. But even this ruse, she knew, would not fool Uncle Jack if he passed by on his horse, and the thought made her spring to her feet, setting the bridge jangling as if a victim had escaped its jaws.

'I can't think why Maud doesn't need her company,' Jack remarked one night when the pudding plates were being cleared by Harriet. If she couldn't converse, she could clear.

'Ssh,' said Emma.

'Ssh what?' said Jack, stretching back in his chair and contemplating his next move, which would be a cigar.

'It would be hurtful if. . .'

'Rot,' said Jack as Harriet returned, hoping there was something else she could take: a side plate, a teapot. If she had been a dog she would have dived under the table where Patch, the old border collie, saved by Emma's pleading after a life of service, lay his head against Emma's foot.

'It's unwise to be too harsh. There could be. . .'

'I know, I know. Extenuating circumstances. As if the whole world revolved on extenuating circumstances when anyone can see it's the reverse.'

'A brutal ball revolving in space,' remarked Emma, surprising herself. 'A musket ball momentarily prevented from striking its target.'

For once Jack looked surprised. He surmised his wife had been into the novels again or the sun had got to her.

'Good pie,' he said.

And Harriet, unable to bear it any longer, began paraphrasing the last chapters of *Black Beauty*.

When Maud met Bruce she decided she would become a Catholic.

'Turn, do you mean?' Irene questioned her.

The Betts were a long-established Catholic family from Hobart. The thought of Bruce turning, except to her, was unthinkable.

Ada and Emma thought it was due to family pressure. Mrs Betts was president of the Catholic Women's League, a collection of nouns Maud would once have scoffed at – 'League' in particular.

'Is it true their house is full of holy statues and pictures?' Ada asked. The Virgin with a vase of lilies in front of her, a prie-dieu in the bedroom. Praying for what, Ada wondered. More children or less, the ability to see everything as a blessing? Ada had nothing against Bruce personally: he looked like

Chips Rafferty, rangy, sandy, hung on broad shoulders that strained his shirt, tapering, long-legged as a thoroughbred. Ada had not caught sight of his ankles or of any flesh except from rolled-up sleeves or a top button unbuttoned but she was certain his ankles would be as strong as steel. His hair fell forward over his forehead and he brushed it back with his hand. And he bent over Maud, one of the tallest of the family but short to him, as if she was something fine: a flower, a piece of china.

Jane and William Berryman did not fret as much about 'the turning' as did the girls. 'There's nothing to be done, best accept it,' William Berryman remarked. 'If she's got to go to the priest and take lessons, Maud has sense enough to sift it.'

In a sense it was the sisters who 'turned'. Their imaginations ran riot on holy water and confessionals, the power of priests that was somehow connected to the exposed hearts in the chests of statues, sometimes with an arrow or a drop of blood descending. And Maud would be forbidden to cross the doors of any church they themselves might decide to marry in. They were greatly surprised when a week after returning from her honeymoon in Melbourne, Maud went to Kate Strawbridge's wedding.

'Perhaps she's got a papal bull,' said Eileen whose imagination was greatest and ignorance most profound.

'Don't be ridiculous. I don't think the condescension goes that far,' sniffed Ada.

Nonetheless she had been pleased to sit with Maud and join in the plain sunlit Protestant hymns.

In fact Maud felt neither superstitious nor overawed by her 'training'. She did not see it altering her life, no matter what doctrines she gave tacit consent to. (Father Stanislaus who undertook her lessons had a habit – a coward's? – of taking silence for acquiescence.) Mostly, as he murmured about where Catholic emphasis differed from Protestant – the same God, a different, deeper visage – his eyes were fixed on Maud's clear forehead. It was the forehead that made him nervous, as if it might conceal the brain of a scientist. Then he admonished himself that she was only a woman, too deeply in love with her husband and following a more ancient image: Eurydice following the notes of Orpheus. It was her sisters who were agitated and required soothing.

'Must you?' Eileen complained when she was disturbed by Maud's rising at 5.30 a.m. to attend her first mass. 'Won't he love you as much if you go at seven?'

'Or nine or ten-thirty or seven at night. I expect so,' Maud replied in a kindly patient tone that only increased Eileen's fury.

'Then why?'

'Because we're going on a picnic later. Out to Strickland, and this way we can make an early start.'

'And if you missed entirely. . .'

'I don't suppose it would matter too much but I don't want to.'

'So it doesn't matter if you disturb a houseful of sleeping Protestants.'

'It probably matters a good deal. To the Protestants.'

Then she was in the doorway, tying a ludicrous scarf over her wavy abundant hair, making herself up as a Russian peasant street sweeper.

'I expect the Protestants have ways of dealing with it,' she said, turning back with an arch smile.

Eileen made a noise that sounded like *Humph* and threw the bedclothes over her head. Then she rolled herself up tight in them as if they were made of something prickly: a thorn hedge or the spikes of a hedgehog.

If Maud could have talked to her sisters, whose heads she suspected were full of half-ashamed fantasies of nuns giving birth, priest seducers – though Father Stanislaus, only child of a doting mother from Glenorchy and already growing paunchy on the housekeeper's starchy food and his mother's hampers, looked unlikely – she would have reassured them she could not change her character, no matter what catechisms were brought to bear upon it.

'You *are* comfortable with this?' Bruce had asked her, on

that first 6 a.m. occasion when it was still dark and she could hardly make out his figure by the door of Our Lady of the Immaculate Conception.

'Comfortable, yes,' Maud replied.

Even in love she didn't intend to make long explanations. Besides, love, as she experienced it, took all her energy, all her alertness. Just being herself and checking that it was so – that she was not offering Bruce something artificial or counterfeit – was enough. As soon as she could she bought herself a black lace mantilla.

Before Emma turned on her side to sleep her mind produced, like a prodded clue, the childhood prayer, so ridiculous, she felt, in a grown woman lying in a narrow bed with a white quilt washed so many times its continued existence was remarkable, as remarkable as the prayer that kept rising towards her out of the mists of enveloping sleep.

> *Now I lay me down to sleep*
> *I pray the Lord my soul to keep.*
> *If I should die before I wake*
> *I pray the Lord my soul to take.*

The conditional sentence at the end, with its hint of promise or blackmail, and the first two lines with their childish simplicity of sleeping and waking. *Ever and ever, Amen,* her mind said, and she put it aside as a phantom. It was the prayer she had taught Harriet before she took her home to the grieving Maud, who treated her with such diligence and care but, it seemed to Emma, no love.

For two weeks Harriet had slept beside her on a trundle bed. At first she had slept next door: the rooms at Guiseford resembled little cells, and for all the thickness and insulation of stone and the soft light streaming through the French doors, one to a room, there was a rigid quality about where furniture could be placed. The first night Harriet had sat up suddenly and cried out, and Emma had taken her into her room, feeling the little back against hers as Harriet turned to face the wall and eventually sleep. Bone to bone: what comfort there was in that. Admittedly there was a flesh cover but it was the bones that seemed to warm. In graveyards it was adjacent bones one thought of touching or mingling.

By the time she went home Harriet knew the prayer by heart, but she preferred the first two lines and when she said it silently to herself, kneeling against the bed, her hands together steeple-fashion, she stopped her mouth's silent moving then. Silent prayer is best, Emma had told her, once the words were in place.

About Maud, Emma held her tongue. She had tried various phrases: *Your mother is feeling sad but as soon as you are home she will feel better*. Like the prayer, only one half was palatable. Whether or not Harriet was sad, Emma could only imagine she was: she followed Emma about or played close to the house so her aunt was in her line of sight. She is too young to be a Stoic, Emma thought angrily, but there was nothing she could do. The chores, the hours with their demands like working parts, would see Harriet through as they had prevented Emma herself from falling into despair over her marriage. The plainness of Guiseford, the way the light fell warmly on sandstone, the way the kneading bowl stood out, more than a mere bowl, on the scrubbed table, was itself a commentary. Maud might have her mantilla to hide under but Emma believed in the outside world, its ability to speak and nudge, its not-quite indifference: she prided herself that there, if nowhere else, she looked with rigour.

After the dough had been covered with a cloth and set to rise she went to the dresser and took out her diary of her trip to Kuala Lumpur. She had written it each evening when Lillian was asleep. There were descriptions of the railway station with its minarets and arches – she had noted the colours – the tall palms that moved like fan dancers in the wind, Central Market where she and Lillian were accompanied by the Bucksteeds' chauffeur with a disagreeable expression on his face, the glamorous-beyond-imagining Hotel Majestic where Emma could have the fire set by ringing a bell.

Maud spent the first weeks of Harriet's absence sorting Bruce's things, looking for twenty minutes at a time at their wedding photo on the dresser: her high-necked body-hugging satin which opened like a fluted flower at the hem, forming a small train which the bridesmaids, Tilly McSkimming and June Strawbridge, had fussily arranged for the studio photographer. On the edges of the photograph were Grecian plinths, cardboard and painted: Leo Strawbridge, who had come along to make faces at his sister, had knocked one and it wobbled. When her eyes tired and the photo failed to give up some essence – Maud was uncertain what she was looking for – she went to Bruce's bureau and took out a shirt. She pressed it against her face, crumpling the folds, setting the sleeves loose, like a man who has lost his arms and wears his sleeves pinned. She did not cry.

Endure, a voice exhorted in her brain, and she followed it, unflinchingly. She didn't wonder if it was the voice of conscience which had never before spoken in such a deep tone: usually it was a feeble reluctant squeak, or even some legacy from Bruce himself who in the same shirt had lifted supplies into the storeroom. What to dress Bruce in had been an agony: a failure to express his character. 'Not a suit, Maudie,' she seemed to hear him say, complaining of the sacrifice he had made to marry her. When she had finally decided on a dark green Viyella shirt, soft against the skin and buttoned to the neck, she had ironed and warmed it, working on it until it was perfect: not a crease near the cuffs or a seam on the sleeves, the front ironed again at the last, the shoulder seams as flat as the day they were sewn. Then she had hung it on a hanger from the back of a kitchen chair and the sun had aired it until it smelt like bread. She polished his best shoes with the energy it took to wash an entire floor. And now, what did it matter if his grave clothes were dry and aired? There was a dew on the grass every morning and Bruce would be subject to the seasons as he never was in life. The voice that instructed *Endure* seemed to conjugate itself into *Desist* at this point, and she resolutely bent over the ledgers.

Three days after the funeral Maud re-opened the store. Betts's General Store was only the second store in Ouse and Maud could not afford to lose customers. All their careful work of scrubbing and painting, chasing down cobwebs, re-oiling the floor with linseed and clearing the counter top so now the glass jars of sweets sparkled like tabernacles would be in vain if she didn't submit herself to public gaze. She dressed in black, straightened her spine and waited as if she were still receiving after the funeral.

And, of course, the customers returned, coming in twos and threes for moral support, for if death lent a certain distinction, especially a sudden and unexpected death, one was glad it had seized one of the scythes from the ceiling and struck elsewhere and was now hopefully sated. The women, in respect, wore hats and filled their baskets with small purchases: a few bacon rashers, a quarter of a pound of tasty cheese which Maud, counting to ten, for the strain was greater than she anticipated, cut in the back room with the wire cutters. Some brought small posies or cards which it seemed churlish not to hand-deliver. None spoke of Bruce, yet. And none dared to ask if she was managing: the clear high forehead, the hair pulled back as if to test if there was a widow's peak (there wasn't), the simple black dress and the gold crucifix suggested she was.

Father Stanislaus called at the end of the first week and had a glass of sherry in the parlour. It was not his favourite drink but he hardly liked to suggest an alternative. Maud too disliked it, but they sat silently sipping, placing the frail awkward glasses on the lace tablecloth. Father Stanislaus had a slightly myopic look which enabled Maud to gaze at him without offence. It was as if his eyes disappeared or metaphorically rolled over as he sought for something to say: secular or religious, a word of Scripture or a repeat of the weather forecast.

They raised their glasses alternately, like birds pecking. Maud said nothing either. She was beginning to find silence restful.

'The store? You will go on with the store?' Father Stanislaus said at last, as if recollecting where he was.

'Of course,' Maud replied. Perhaps he would talk about the panacea of work but, after directing a sharper glance at her, he refrained. Nor did he, on this occasion, suggest a prayer.

Maud came with him to the door and handed him his hat. It needed brushing. In a few years, if he didn't take himself in hand, he would be an overweight priest in a verdigris suit. Already there was a fleck of sauce on his collar.

'I'll call again from time to time,' he said as he pushed the hat down on his head. No sense of style, thought Maud. She almost replied, 'As you like,' but then, mindful as a new catechumen, 'Thank you, Father.'

On a drenching day at Guiseford when the gutters sang with overflowing cascades and the French doors had descending beads, fascinating to Harriet, Emma took down the shoe box of photographs and looked for the ones of Kuala Lumpur. She was by no means a good photographer but a natural thrift had caused her to consider each view, lining up palm trees or turning the camera on its side to film part of a street. It was important, obviously, to stand at the right distance. Large edifices, small humans, presented a problem: one had to be sacrificed to the other. She held the camera very still, hardly drawing breath, while she pressed the shutter. A second in time: someone handing over ringgits for *ais kacang,* gharries going past and, occasionally, when the chauffeur could be pressed into service, a shot of herself and Lillian Bucksteed. Here was one of them both at the Lake Gardens, Lillian squinting at the camera and holding tightly to her hand. Already she called Emma 'Emee'. 'Take the whole day,' Margaret Bucksteed had said, handing her fifty crisp American dollars. 'And if you or Lillian get tired just come back to the hotel and order something to your room.'

'Would you like a ride in a gig?' Emma asked, after they had walked down Market Street to the Chow Kit Emporium, the chauffeur several paces behind. Emma could feel his resentment on the back of her neck. They had ridden for an hour and Emma had peeled off one of the ten-dollar bills to give the chauffeur to pay the driver. The camera lay on the seat between them; their laps were covered by a rug. Look, Emma told herself. There is no time for anything else. Colours, scents, dust, pollen, the air touched with such a mixture she could never separate the ingredients. A vast mysterious sky, almost like the sky in a novel that hangs over a little group of people (she didn't count the chauffeur who had added his cigarette smoke), the tall palms like pointers; she thought she would remember it always.

'Tell me about the little girl,' Harriet said, when the photographs were spread out chronologically on the table.

'She was a little taller than you,' Emma said, conjuring Lillian's figure, 'and I think she may have grown to be rather plump. Both her parents were large plump people, though they were very commanding.'

When Harriet looked puzzled she explained. Hank Bucksteed Jnr, Lillian's father, was well over six feet tall and Margaret, his wife, was almost up to his shoulder when she wore heels. 'When they came into a room together everyone turned to look at them.' Privately she thought Margaret Bucksteed slightly resembled Eleanor Roosevelt. They were good-natured, used to never being contradicted (their wealth guaranteed that), and if they ever were they looked puzzled. Smaller, lesser people fawned on them, bell boys struggled with their large portmanteaux, meals under silver covers were wheeled swiftly to their rooms. Yet the fuss left them unperturbed, like large creatures unaware of ants at their feet. Emma's references, of a fulsomeness that made her blush when she handed them over, were undoubtedly checked out: Hank Bucksteed Jnr was slow-moving but thorough. But once satisfied and certain that Lillian was happy, they left the two of them largely to their own devices.

'A programme that includes some visits and reading, I think,' Mrs Bucksteed said to Emma. 'A nap in the afternoon. You might like to take one at the same time, if you've been out at the zoo or shopping.' The implication was that the parents didn't wish to be disturbed. Since the first time she consulted

Mrs Bucksteed about Lillian's sore throat and temperature, Emma summoned the hotel doctor at her own discretion. Poor Lillian, she sometimes thought, as the girl's hand slid confidingly into hers. But then she recollected that Lillian would be well protected: there would be private tuition when the trip was over – the trip was being counted as a holiday and Lillian's recovery from a bout of glandular fever the year before; later would come Vassar and a finishing school, and her inheritance would be hers when she turned twenty-one. Yet Emma could not pity herself more, though her employment would end when the ship berthed again in Melbourne. There would be another reference to add to the pile of little deckle-edged pages on which a few lines were scratched by society women's hands.

'We used to go to the zoo quite often,' she told Harriet, turning over a black and white photograph, well focused, though the Sumatran tiger crouching at the bottom was not very clear or perhaps was attempting camouflage. 'Lillian was very fond of the hippopotamus. There was a baby hippopotamus when we were there and she used to find it amusing.'

In two days Harriet would return home and to Ouse school. Her life would take on its routines again, different because her father was gone, but the same. Maud would be abstracted, concentrating on the shop and its book-keeping, kind to her daughter but faintly aloof. Perhaps she is struggling for control, Emma surmised. She had done the same herself when Jack had become involved with Roberta Flett. She had dressed carelessly and let her hair escape from the low knot on the nape of her neck.

'Anyone would think you were a penitent,' Jack had said angrily.

'Wouldn't that require a coned hat?' she had replied, surprising herself, and he had laughed. In those days she had bent over her bread-making as if it were a holy task. How false were all those moments captured by artists: they were the most tremulous of all, as if the very brushstrokes threatened to fly apart. Quite often she went into one of the bedrooms and touched a hand to the thick walls or stood looking out. She knew Jack had chosen wrongly: he had chosen out of an impulse to improve himself, to bring refined touches or refined thought and then found it did not suit, that it bored him. Roberta Flett was the product of boredom, but what hurt most was the feeling that they had had a good time. She saw heads thrown back in laughter; they had met at the races and gone – here she stopped herself, like someone winding a clock – to a local hotel. She touched the cool walls to ward off a force of anger – not hers, which would dissipate under an endless procession of chores, but his. Now she doubted he wandered at all: he concentrated his energies on her re-education, little jolts of insult followed by an occasional word of praise. And she, whose character, in her mother and father's eyes, was so steady and equable, so placid and reasonable – her father had compared her to a lake – was now shy, uncertain and stumbling. What does Maud know, she thought, on the last morning as she sat on the floor with Harriet, packing her case and adding what items she could think of to bring comfort: a book she had enjoyed, the photo of the hippopotamus from the zoo.

At Government House in Melbourne Irene Berryman and her room mate, Ginny Boon, had risen at 5 a.m. and tiptoed down the ninety-six steps to the ground floor. It was not really a tiptoe but they placed their feet on the centre of the carpet runner, careful to make no sound. They sat on the lowest step and put on their shoes. Ginny usually had to be shaken awake; it was fortunate Irene was a lark. Quite often she borrowed Irene's comb and ran it through her hair as they descended, one behind the other.

'Household gods, that's what we are,' Ginny would say, tugging at a knot, then wiping the comb clean on her black apron.

'Don't let Jessie hear you say that,' Irene replied.

Jessie was the formidable Scottish housekeeper, reared on porridge with salt, cold baths, curtainless windows looking out over the moors. Finding kindness in Jessie was like diving for the Loch Ness monster in a bathyscape: it was there but at what punishing depths.

Irene had been selected, on the strength of her wrists, to screw on the hotwater-bottle tops for VIPs. Of course Jessie double-checked. 'I can't think why she doesn't do them herself. She probably tossed the caber as a wee lass,' Ginny complained. Secretly she was jealous that the smaller Irene had been chosen.

'Perhaps she is building me up,' Irene smiled. She was used to Ginny's quick flashes of temper. 'Remember when I first came and she didn't believe my references.'

The hotwater-bottle sealing had been a contest. Ginny had tried and Lola, Marigold, Jocelyn, three other housemaids, as well as Monique, Lady Huntingfield's personal maid who happened to be in the morning room. Irene's sparrow-thin wrists had screwed the cap in so tight even Jessie had been unable to undo it.

'No question, then,' she announced to the little assembly, all rubbing their wrists. Marigold particularly, looked bashful: her hands were enormous.

'The dainty hands of a murderer,' Ginny said to Irene when they took their break.

'Why do you say that?' Irene demanded.

'Delicate and deadly. Don't wrap them around my throat when I'm sleeping, will you?'

At the end of their shift they took the lift to the top floor and climbed the remaining stairs to their attic room. Irene flung the window wide and leaned out to breathe in the cool damp air. Rain-dampened air was almost her favourite scent, along with Lady Huntingfield's eau de cologne and Mrs Lawrence's apple pie. The vast lawns of Government House, the gardens in which gardeners began work at dawn – there was one in sight at present, raking leaves from around the base of an elm, and another with a wheelbarrow just passing behind a stately oak. Tomorrow she and Ginny would have a day off. They would put on their finery – or second-best finery (the best was reserved for big occasions like the Melbourne Cup) – and get the tram at the end of St Kilda Road. They would pass by the guard house and open their purses to show their staff cards. Leonard would call out a friendly warning: 'Don't get into trouble, girls. Don't do anything I wouldn't do.' If Peter was on duty he would whistle and blow kisses along the flat of his palm. Irene imagined them rising and curving when they became airborne, like a stunt plane. They would go to G J Coles for coffee and tiny sweet cakes; they would do Myer's and the shops on Collins Street. And whenever they passed a pair of men their age coming in the opposite direction, Ginny would fall into surprisingly animated conversation with flashing eyes and quick flirtatious glances.

Harriet was returned to Maud and life settled into a new routine, or so it seemed to Harriet. Her mother was quieter, kinder, but also more abstracted. When she packed Harriet's school lunch she leaned on the sink bench and gazed through the window. Harriet waited, wondering if she should suggest lunch money or a Cornish pasty from the store, or taking charge of it herself.

'I could do it now,' she said softly, but Maud didn't seem to hear.

When she became aware of her daughter at her side, standing close but not touching as a more certain or affectionate child might, she closed the lid and asked, 'What is it?'

'I could do my lunch,' Harriet said. Just in time she censored 'from now on'.

'I expect you could,' Maud replied. Another few minutes saved, another chore snatched from her, like a bead from the rosary. The determined energy of the first weeks had gone and been replaced by an abnormal sensitivity to the least remark, the least nuance. She looked down at Harriet's head: one heavy plait and its half-weight twin, the parting like a firebreak that swept the flaxen hair to the right side, leaving the left a mere covering. At night, she knew, Harriet stroked the thick plait before she slept, her thumb moving from coil to coil, substituting each loosened segment with a new.

'I would like to. . .' Harriet began and Maud put down a

palm and stroked the top of her daughter's head. She hardly remembered doing her plaits but she must have: Harriet must have presented herself as she did every school morning and she must have sat on the kitchen stool. 'It feels like milking a cow,' she had said to Bruce, and he had laughed, drawing a finger across his mouth as if the remark might be hurtful. But Harriet had just stood, trying to push her knee bones so they came out the back of her knees. Sometimes, as Maud's practised fingers went down the line of hair, Harriet wiggled her toes and clenched the arches of her feet. Even so Maud was likely to say, 'Stand still.'

With Harriet gone, Maud was free to move from chore to chore, the stepping stones of her day, until, like some grateful animal returned to the safety of its burrow, there was night. As for Harriet, walking slowly up the hill towards Ouse school, there was a sorrow that could be put off only if the Strawbridge boys joined her on the other side of the road – they would not cross the road for a girl – or Katie Kelsey came out of her gate. The Strawbridge twins, under parental embargo, had managed for a week not to call insults or throw small pebbles, but Harriet knew it would not last; she thought she preferred their normal behaviour: boisterous and inconsiderate which could be put down to having red hair. Katie too seemed tongue-tied and able only to discuss school work. They were studying India with its maharajahs and temples, its vast population: what would an Indian child feel if she lost her father? Harriet wondered. With so many people, could one less count? Then she suspected it would. In the playground, a dusty sloping field with goal posts and the shrubland beyond into which they were forbidden to venture because of snakes, the Strawbridge twins proclaimed they were maharajahs and the rest, particularly the girls, lower caste.

'Untouchable,' shrieked Owen Strawbridge, remembering the word. He had snatched a lunch box from one of the younger boys and was pilfering its contents.

'You've got ankles like an elephant and no maharajah has freckles,' Harriet said when the lunch box had been taken back, minus a slice of cherry cake. 'Maharajahs don't pilfer.' But she couldn't be sure. Their wealth was so great and the lower castes so poor.

India seemed as dusty as Ouse: an elephant would have raised the same clouds of dust and hardly left an imprint on the ground.

'I witnessed Harriet give one of the Strawbridge boys a shove today,' Miss Tole said to Maud later that afternoon when she was buying ground almonds and cream and Peak Freen crackers. 'I thought it unlike her. Not that the Strawbridge boys couldn't do with a shove on a daily basis.'

'It's a weary time for both of us,' Maud said, for the first time including Harriet.

'I'm sure I sympathise,' Miss Tole agreed.

'Eight sisters,' said Ginny as they walked towards the St Kilda tram stop. 'I can't believe it.'

'Eight sisters but only four who count. I don't think I can love more than four,' Irene replied, puffing a little, hurrying to catch up. She might have the wrists but Ginny certainly had the legs.

The tram clattered towards them, an old dowager who sat upright on the edge of chairs, or someone who played the harpsichord. Irene loved its harsh music. They eased into a wooden seat and Irene stowed her umbrella at her feet.

'Your mother must have been exhausted,' Ginny said, turning her profile to Irene in a kind of tactfulness. 'No man is going to give me so many children.' Ginny had been reading Marie Stopes. Not that she would mention this to Robert, a young man she had met at a public dance and who seemed to be smitten the moment his arm circled her waist for a veleta. This infatuation on his part had given her confidence to flirt and appear indecisive. 'Men don't respect women who are easy,' Ginny's mother had warned her and, apart from Theresa, a parlourmaid who had got herself pregnant and been sent home, there were women like Jessie to admire. 'I expect high standards of my girls,' Jessie told the new intake, after their uniforms had been issued, rooms allocated, and they were assembled in the morning room. 'When you go out the gates, always remember you work at Government House. The good names of the Governor and Lady Huntingfield are in your keeping. I want no dishonour. . .'

'Sounds like the Montagues and the Capulets,' Lola remarked to Irene as they ascended in the Governor's lift. The Governor and Lady H were in Queensland, paying a state visit.

Nonetheless, walking along St Kilda Road, even the few steps to the tram stop, Irene and Ginny assumed a demeanour above that achieved by mere shop assistants and milliners. They held their backs straight – the way to iron out aches from bending over cavernous fireplaces – and they could have balanced a small stack of books from the Governor's library on their heads.

In spite of the hard work and Jessie's watchfulness, each morning when she woke and gazed around her room, Irene considered herself lucky. She stretched her legs under the white cotton coverlet and listened for the sounds that told her the great house was stirring. Not that Government House could by any means be considered a house. The width of its halls alone could accommodate entire families or trams could rattle, in a subdued fashion, on the carpet runners. The beautiful staircase, designed for slow descents and gracious ascents which had a tinge of leave-taking, was as impressive as altar rails. Even at this hour, when the birds were singing themselves awake in the giant oaks and chestnuts, the gardener's boys would be at work, hoeing around the ornate beds which resembled rich Turkey carpets. If only I could sing myself awake, Irene thought, but even her light soprano would not wake Ginny who lay turned to the wall on her side, blanket and coverlet wrapped around herself like a stubborn cocoon. Each morning Irene allowed herself an extra ten minutes to rouse Ginny. It began with a gentle hand on a shoulder, then a rudimentary back rub, which may not have even been felt, for the bedclothes around Ginny's neck were like a thick collar; finally came a more vigorous shaking. Go away, was the invariable muffled response. I want to sleep. Can't you say I'm sick?

Robert, the young man who had danced the veleta with Ginny and now clapped his palm to his forehead as if overcome by an apparition, struck Irene as a ham actor, full of personality but possibly insincere, when she was introduced to him at G J Coles. But slightly to the rear of him, like a courtier to an unworthy king, stood Teddy McAleer. Not only was he half a head taller, but his eyes were serious, steady, able to look without giving offence.

They looked as if they were considering sentences, Irene thought later. Would this modest young woman be suitable? While Ginny flirted outrageously, trying to attract Robert into such a consideration – Irene surmised there was nothing further from his mind – Teddy, after pulling out her chair, then easing it forward, said hardly anything. But Irene knew something had begun and they would see each other again.

Eight girls and four boys was a family too large by their mother's reckoning, for Jane Elizabeth Berryman was a reader and thinker whose leisure had been snatched away from her. 'I must have had so many girls because I needed domestic help,' Jane said to her husband, unaware that she had no part in the determination of gender. Sometimes she felt it was almost a relief to be pregnant: when the hope that this might be the last, that she might be infertile, that the last occupant of the over-used cot had arrived was dealt a blow, she embraced her husband tenderly at night, consoling him too for another mouth to feed. Were four boys, widely spaced, enough to help manage a farm? Still there was no calling her 'Poor Mrs Berryman, always pregnant', at least not to her face. Tall and always returning to slender after each delivery, she held herself with unconscious pride. Twelve children, how many stars in the sky?

Besides, families of six or eight were not uncommon. But try as she might, with her well-trained daughters and mainly helpful sons – Bernard was a bit of a dreamer, a moocher –

Jane Berryman never, except in old age, cleared a sort of winnowing space for herself, in which to think, to fill a diary with the delicate nature observations she had stored and contemplate the miracles of science. 'Perhaps you should engrave "She never lost her mind" on my headstone,' she said grimly to her one daughter who had remained single and lived with her. What have I been but a strong sleek animal, she asked herself, knowing such thoughts would shock. She knew Ada would choose a poem for her grave.

The disadvantage of such a large family was that the children of it did not know one another. The four eldest became a group, then the four in the middle, and the stragglers. Maud, Emma, Irene, Ada, warmed by the experience above – sisters in hats and gloves, mysteriously incommunicado when there were men in tow – still had a cluster of younger ones to impress. It was nothing to scoop up a wailing child while an older sister swept out the door in a new suit and their mother's fox fur. 'It'll probably be worn out before I get a chance to borrow it,' Irene lamented. She admired the way its teeth closed over its tail. She had held three-year-old Sophie, the worst of the nuisances, up to stroke it, then put her down, wailing. It was as if disaster always came from floor level while in the air she was growing into were scents and powder and veils with enticing polka dots.

Their mother, however, had refused to arbitrate on the fate of the fox fur which was, after all, her possession. It might encircle the shoulders of the next departing daughter; it might end up in the toy box or the sticky clutches of Sophie. Possessions, to Jane Berryman, were of small importance: her longing was for space of mind and if that had to be deferred by so many mouths to feed, so many demands to meet, not least being to maintain the love of the husband she continued to desire, she would ensure their surroundings were as plain and workable as possible. Later Irene would wonder if at heart she was a Georgian: spacious rooms furnished with a very few valuable pieces so being seated was like playing musical chairs, the bare rudiments, though beautiful, in every room. It was the nuisances who spoilt all this and the sisters in the middle who attempted to restore it.

'Come on,' Maud would say, dividing two squallers. 'Let's have a story.' Or Emma would carry someone out into the orchard to touch the blossoms or the small hard apples.

'Look and read' were the instructions Emma had given Lillian Bucksteed when Kuala Lumpur seemed overwhelming and she confessed she didn't know where home was or whether she would recognise it again.

Their father, William Berryman, possessed a trait that seemed to recur in only one son, Rupert, and one daughter, Maud. He had a temper that his wife had long since analysed and, since it was never directed at her, helped him to see as an advantage. For the likelihood of William Berryman's harming anyone or anything was remote: his outlook was naturally optimistic, another mouth to feed never fazed him – he saw a boy chopping wood for the fire or a girl helping Jane. There would be another dress or shirt to sew, of course, for Jane often sat into the small hours sewing. William saw life as a passage and it didn't matter to him how many souls took part: everyone should have their chance. Were he in overcrowded India, being studied at Ouse school, where his children were attempting to draw elephants and imagine maharajahs, he would have approved of the crowds lining the Ganges and using it for washing and burning ashes.

The temper, when it came, possessed him utterly as if he were on fire. Someone had lamed a horse and he leaned on a gatepost to let the fire die down. It flamed from him like one of the hideous statues he had sighted in a Catholic church: the chest laid open to show the workings, as if the heat of the heart had flayed the flesh. 'They should be bandaged,' he said to Maud, half-jokingly, years later when she broke the news to him that she was becoming a Catholic. 'Turning,' she had said. But there is no turning, he thought, from what we are. He sensed she had his temper in a different form: he had seen her become still and concentrated, almost cold, forbidding anyone to approach. Then she returned to something, not so much with delight as reason. Sweet reason. Her brow cleared, her eyes calmly gazed, she offered to perform some chore or service to make up for the time she had been absent.

The horse was soothed and attended to and William Berryman leaned on the gate, feeling the rage that had overpowered him pass into the wooden post. Overhead the sky which had seemed to darken lifted and fresh light streamed. It is not analogous, it is nothing to do with me, he thought. I must never think that, allow myself such foolishness. But there was a sympathy there as well, or if not quite sympathy, a not-quite indifference. He was not alone, and heart lightened – he could feel its degrees – he walked back through the orchard, picking an apple and biting into it, undeterred that it was not quite ripe.

Caroline Talbot, the young bored woman Emma worked for after farewelling the Bucksteeds and promising, after wails and clinging from Lillian, to write – 'You'll write forever, won't you, Emee?' and Emma had nodded and pressed a handkerchief to her eyes too – had left a great mess to clear up in the kitchen. She had wanted to surprise her husband, a stockbroker, who was hardly ever home, with a seed cake and yo yos: 'His favourite when he was a child,' she informed Emma. And now, neither seed cake nor yo yos able to be saved even by pink icing, she had flounced off to lie on her bed. Emma had slowly and methodically lifted the half-scraped bowls from the pools of sieved flour, replaced the butter in its special container in the refrigerator, and set about wiping all the surfaces. The floor would have to be mopped and there was a smear of butter on the kitchen window above the sink. The seed cake could possibly be soaked in sherry and converted to trifle: Mr Talbot would never know the difference. After her labours and hysterics – upstairs Emma could hear the sound of a bath being drawn (at least she had not been asked to do that) – Caroline would be taken out to dinner at a posh restaurant.

Sometimes Emma wondered what had become of Caroline Talbot. She was her last employer before she married Jack. Lillian Bucksteed had written regularly from Boston, tearful letters at first, with little drawings of flowers in the margins, and then Christmas cards that had slowly dwindled. Emma suspected that Lillian had found happiness or at the very least compatibility: perhaps her parents had directed her towards a suitable young man, a banker or an accountant. It was strange that she thought more often of Caroline. Perhaps it was because her own hands were frequently stirring bowls or wiping tabletops, pushing a damp lock of hair back from her forehead as she had seen Caroline do, her face flustered and hot as the seed cake sank in the middle or the yo yos attained the solidity of rock cakes.

After cleaning up the mess Emma had made a batch of shortbread to leave cooling on a rack on the bench, and it was these Gerald Talbot saw as he came into the room, drawn by the sweet buttery scent. 'Another rescue mission?' he had said in a low voice, raising an eyebrow in Emma's direction.

'It's nothing,' she said. 'I thought after a disappointment. . .'

'That's what I'm here for,' he said. 'At least I think that's the reason. But thanks.'

And now her whole life seemed to be clearing up and cleaning, working in the dairy, preparing meals. The hopes of affection – for that is what Emma assumed a passion such as Jack purported to have for her would eventually become – proved false. Jack was like a coin tossed for a wager, slapped down on a sleeve or secured in the dust with the toe of a boot. And maybe he was right, Emma considered. Day and night, light or lack of it: perhaps it was foolish to invest all your hopes in the fringes where light ebbed or tremulously overtook the dark. When something wore out for Jack, he took another tack. He might admire her shortbread, her housekeeping, but he did so with cynicism, the way one might admire a piece of machinery that kept going. 'Haven't lost your touch, old girl,' he would say, but he meant she had. Other women, though he kept the bursts of passion shorter, followed. If she had asked him, he might have said time was running out, women were good for one thing and a man was a fool to tell himself otherwise.

After Harriet returned to Maud, Emma spent most of a day washing the walls of the dairy, stripping Harriet's bed and airing it, washing the fine net curtains. When the curtains were dry she stood in front of the little bureau mirror and draped one of them over her head. A face looked back, astonished and hurt. Her fine bones – 'Emma has the best bones,' her father used to say – looked as if they ached, and her beautifully spaced features that in themselves suggested intelligence were nothing more than a permutation. 'Not quite Miss Haversham,' she thought, for she continued to read every afternoon, lying on an old chaise-longue Jack had picked up at the Hamilton sales, 'but well on the way.' She stayed in front of the mirror, examining her face, for a long time.

Faces seemed to have a lot of dawn and dusk about them, the fuzziness of gradual change. She lifted her chin, and the soft underside was beginning to pouch. Perhaps Jack is just as frightened as I am, she thought, wanting to see everything settled, in black and white. Next week the shearers would come, there would be help in the kitchen and a chance to look at other men, to see if they were like Jack or there were variants. She hung the curtain, standing on a stool, and opened the French door to allow them to billow in the breeze. Then she took down her novel, *Mansfield Park*, and lost herself in the amazing passivity of Fanny Price.

Maud never accustomed herself to the plaster statues, the plaster stations in Our Lady of the Immaculate Conception. Why a chest should be opened to show a heart pierced with thorns she couldn't imagine, unless it was to convey guilt or illustrate a medical condition. Dr McSkimming had a model torso on his desk showing the lungs, bright flattened leaf skeletons. He also had a skull which impressed the children. Father Stanislaus's instructions to Maud took place in the little parlour at the presbytery, a dreary over-varnished room with heavy red velvet drapes. They sat facing one another on fiercely upright chairs, across a gate-legged table covered with a dark brown cloth, thick as a bedspread, with a bobbled fringe. A solemn look was nothing new to Maud, nor was the idea of sacraments. She already felt holy about Bruce. He had held her hand as she pressed the presbytery bell and she had the absurd idea that he was pulling her up from her seat to begin a dance. He had strode towards her at the Strickland dance as if she were the only person in the room, holding out his hand in advance. And she had hesitated, just for a second, as if considering him, though no such consideration existed: she too had known, but because this should be her response.

'You're going to turn then, Maudie,' her father had said, when she told him. A slaughtered sheep hung dripping from a tree and she knew how much killing an animal, even for food, cost him.

'Don't say turning,' she said, walking back to the house with him. 'I'll never turn to anything.'

'Just hold onto that then,' he said, taking her hand. 'Your mother's more upset than I expected.'

'And my sisters, nearly hysterical,' Maud said. 'Sometimes I wonder what they've been reading.'

'Bruce's a fine man, Catholic or not,' William said. 'They'll see that eventually.'

'I won't be decorating my room with holy pictures or starting a novena to convert the family, I can promise you that,' Maud stated.

'I should hope not,' her father replied. 'What's a novena, anyway?'

Now, looking into the slightly evasive eyes of Father Stanislaus, Maud thought of her father with the dead sheep, hung in the macrocarpa tree behind him. She could see their two figures, herself taller, walking over the grass, together in sympathy as if their two hearts were exposed, showing identical markings. 'When I die you will find Calais engraved on my heart,' Elizabeth I had said. And when she died, hers would have 'Bruce'.

For twelve Tuesday nights, before the priest's dinner at 6 p.m., Maud undertook Instructions in the Faith. Bruce walked across the bridge and to the edge of town; sometimes he sat on a wooden seat outside the cottage hospital. Or he turned and walked in the other direction, up the hill and past the school. He and Maud might have children: he tried to imagine a piping voice, a childish form running towards him, arms outstretched. Maud would make a calm mother, he thought. Already he knew all her passion would be spent on him, privately, as if in a sacrament. Even the sacraments, the ones Father Stanislaus was probably droning on about right now in the parlour, would not affect Maud. She might grasp them – he did not doubt her intelligence; she might even make some elucidating remark to show the priest he was on the right track, but her heart remained her own to bestow.

'You're sure I'm not packaged goods,' he had said to her, laughing when she had acquiesced not only to his proposal but to going for instruction.

Her voice had been low but very clear; she would likewise use it for her wedding vows. 'And my package includes doubting sisters you'll have to win over,' she had replied, inserting her hand in his. It felt dry and steady, like a piece of warm wood.

In the presbytery Evangeline, the elderly housekeeper, was fussing over the priest's meal, wishing Maud would hurry up and go. She thought Maud had a sly look, eyes downcast when she opened the door to her, her young man disappearing into the twilight, a hint of laughter on the air. She looked sternly at Maud, sending her an unspoken warning about anticipating marriage. But really she was more concerned for Father Stanislaus. He did little exercise, beyond genuflecting and visiting the sick; he ate heartily, yet his skin stayed pale. Evangeline half-expected one day his mother would arrive to inspect him.

At first Irene had resisted double-dating. She knew it was absurd to hope for anything on a double-date. She had read in a magazine that three times out of four double-dating ended in failure. The article implied that those already blinded by love lost the ability to judge their friends. Love cast a pall as disappointment does.

A pink pall, Irene imagined, as Ginny hurried her along Bourke Street towards the tearooms. She felt her feet dragging, her heart sinking. Lovers would be oblivious of the feelings of others, or wish to use them as an audience. Suddenly she saw the hideous embarrassment of it, as if Ginny had said, 'I can get a man for you too.' And if Ginny hadn't said it, wouldn't it be implied? 'Plenty of fish in the sea, Rene,' her father always said, when one of her sisters bewailed the lack of men in Ouse.

'Slow down,' she said to Ginny. 'Let me get my breath.'

The idea of arriving out of breath was dreadful. They stood for a few seconds looking into the windows of David Jones. Mannequins looked back, gowned, gloved and hatted. Then Ginny consulted her watch and dragged her on. But when they got to G J Coles, Robert and Teddy were not there. They too were looking in a shop window, one that displayed suits and overcoats. Teddy was a snappy dresser or could be when he had money saved; he loved to window shop and plan his purchases. This year he had bought what he considered a classic overcoat, one that would see him right for ten years. He would have worn it this evening but the weather was too mild. He noticed women's fashions too: whether a style was followed blindly or adapted. It wasn't simply a case of money, though quality counted; plenty of men were as blind as women, wearing suits that made them resemble small-time gamblers or petty crooks.

Irene's dark blue wool dress with its white collar caught his eye almost before she did. Her figure was slight though not thin – slight curves on a slight frame; the blue dress flowed modestly from its darted shoulders, a soft white belt clinched the waist. Ginny was more flamboyant. She had added an overblown mauve fabric rose to her shoulder: its wired leaves stuck out at an angle. She reached up to kiss him, after Robert, and he was careful to avoid crushing it.

They sat down on the hard wooden chairs, and silence

ensued. Then Robert recollected himself and made intro-ductions. Ginny piped up and added a short biography. Irene felt she was not sitting there: she was being described like a fictional character, an energetic creature who woke clear-eyed and self-possessed, whose duty it was to shake Ginny awake. No, she wanted to protest, I am more than that. How could a man be interested in such a description, she thought, lowering her eyes, but when she looked up she saw the new man was regarding her intently. Her face flushed and their eyes met. He looked wry, faintly apologetic, as if he too thought the fictional character was wide of the mark. 'Did I tell you how she covered for me one morning. . .' Ginny was saying, swelling her friend into a gargoyle, a little hard dutiful creature without a hope of romance.

Irene and Teddy exchanged only a few words on that first meeting. They sat and watched as Ginny and Robert twined fingers over the tablecloth, as Ginny upset the sauce bottle. 'I hope she can keep house,' Robert said, laughing. 'I hope this is not an indication of things to come.' Instinctively Irene took the folded paper napkins from the little rack and added them to the stain, and Teddy added his. 'Could we have some more napkins?' Robert asked a passing waitress. 'My friend here has had an accident.'

'I wish I could do that tablecloth trick,' Ginny said. 'The one where you give the tablecloth a flick and everything stays on the table.'

'I wouldn't recommend it,' said Teddy.

Irene kept her eyes on her plate. The golden chips, so delicious when hot, were cooling and the battered fish tasted faintly stale. No amounts of salt and vinegar, Worcester sauce, could raise the meal near the standards of Government House. It would be better eaten from a cone of newspaper. If only we could have been walking by the sea, she thought. Then she wondered what she would wear and if her hair would stay in place.

'Penny for them,' Teddy asked. And when she looked up, puzzled, 'Your thoughts.'

Later they had stood at the checkout desk, fussing with the bill. Irene had pulled out the little tapestry purse given to her by Ada: its smallness meant that, even after she had carefully banked most of her salary each week at the Australia and Commonwealth Bank, it still bulged with the remaining coins, the solitary folded note.

Teddy, who had no intention of allowing a woman to pay, was amused by the gesture. 'Put it away,' he said softly.

Gratefully she had slipped the little purse back into her handbag. It was an offer she felt she had to make, however much it went against the mores of the time. In the end Robert had paid for them all with a flourish, declaring it a special occasion: the introducing of two good friends to one another, with who knows what consequences – possibly none, but who could tell: 'Casting bread on the waters,' he said, archly, catching Ginny's eye. It made Irene think of the piles of white bread on the table, near the cruet set.

The words she had been dreading most, though there was no evidence on which to base hope, did not eventuate. Instead of 'I'll be seeing you,' with its certain dismissal, Teddy had simply asked for permission to send a note to Government House.

'Any child will be brought up Catholic,' Father Stanislaus said to Maud at her final instruction, after the Sacraments, Mysteries, Holy Mass, The Papacy had been disposed of.

'Of course,' she said, raising her eyes. It was in her nature to expect the pebble in the shoe, the splinter in the heart, the penalty exacted for love. Besides, she couldn't imagine having a child: it formed no part of her impulse towards Bruce.

Father Stanislaus looked at her seriously for a moment. He knew when a parishioner was not concentrating. But he forbore to elaborate: how often did people acquiesce without seeing the consequences. It might make a sermon: Great Expectations. Paul falling dazzled off his horse, or Peter seeking exaggeration for denial. The wobbling Peter was his favourite.

'Well, that's the end, then,' he said to Maud, and suggested a short prayer.

Awkwardly they both got off their chairs and knelt beside them. His hands sketched a blessing and his knees creaked as he got up. Creaking knees and a tendency now to burp lightly after the housekeeper's over-rich meals.

Bruce was waiting by the side of the presbytery. As the porch light came on he stepped forward from the shadows. But it was not Father Stanislaus at Maud's heels. Evangeline's venomous eyes and tight lips had to be satisfied with a single flung sentence: 'You've kept the Father's meal waiting.'

Three months later, after the publishing of the banns, Maud's baptism and confession – she never got into the habit of confessing: she reasoned her sins and her motives were known and any childish recitation an insult – Bruce and Maud were married at Ouse.

Irene and Teddy had come from Melbourne, crossing on *The Princess of Tasmania* where Irene was amused to notice there was a bridal suite, extraordinarily spacious compared to the tiny cabins. They caught the bus from Devonport to Ouse and gazed at the scenery, the bush that grew to the road's edge. Irene suspected Teddy wanted to live in New Zealand and if she pressed him to stay in Australia he would acquiesce but be disappointed. Was it something about coming from a small country compared to a large? Sometimes, faced with adult decisions, she wished she was a child again, drawing the map of Tasmania in an exercise book. A comforting wide island which she never thought of as small or separate from the rest of Australia. Rather like a joey hung from a pouch, close to the ground.

After Melbourne, with its wide streets, green trams, impressive buildings – nothing in Hobart approached the size of Parliament House or the grandeur of Flinders Street Station which so surprised her the first time she saw it: a fairytale castle, blocking the street – everything seemed faded and dusty. Maud's simple dress with its lace train and cap, her bouquet the size of a large cabbage, were all to be seen in Melbourne too. Dear Maud, Irene thought, cancelling something single-minded in her sister's character: trust her to remain at Ouse and get it right.

Maud held the vast bouquet of white roses and lily of the valley so the flowers and last sprinklings of water did not touch the satin; she walked up the aisle like a creature drawn on strings. Bruce held his head resolutely towards the altar until the last moment, then he turned his eyes like Chips Rafferty at sea, sighting a coast. How did she feel about Father Stanislaus? Irene wondered. Was it like being married by a school teacher? First the instruction and then the performance.

But if Maud felt intimidated she gave no sign. She handed the bouquet to Irene as they went into the sacristy to sign the register. 'She's not thinking of throwing it, is she?' Teddy whispered in her ear. 'I don't know,' she whispered back, resolving not to catch it. Her stomach still felt taut and sore after vomiting on *The Princess of Tasmania*. Teddy had assured her it was the smell of paint – there were paint pots and dust sheets in some of the passageways – but she knew it wasn't that. If they went to New Zealand she would be seasick as well as homesick. The sight of a ship, no matter how regal its title, was enough to set her off.

They came out into the sun and stood in front of the church to be photographed. But Irene could see Maud and Bruce were anxious to be gone. Now it was their turn to go to Melbourne on *The Princess*, negotiating the same decks and corridors Irene had crept along, handkerchief to her mouth. How could a man love a woman who vomits? Once she had vomited over the railing, sensing the people nearby move away as if there was a leper in their midst. She had leaned far out and Teddy had held her, stroking her back when it was over. There was nothing to bring up, just a thin watery bile, like the sea itself. As for the reception, Irene doubted she could eat anything: a piece of dry toast was what she longed for.

Tomorrow, when she was feeling better, she would walk with Teddy over her parents' farm. She would observe their reaction to him, the subtle signs that working at Government House had taught her: a creasing of Jessie's brow when something was not done to her satisfaction, the perfunctory or genuine thanks of a dignitary as they lined up on the gravel driveway to form a guard of honour. You must never initiate conversation, Jessie had warned over and over. 'You must never initiate conversation,' Ginny said in Jessie's Scots burr when Irene shook her shoulders and hissed 'Wake up!' She would tell her mother, while her father was scrutinising Teddy, about the visit of the Duke of York and how she had had to screw on and double-check the hotwater bottles for his bed. 'I don't know where you get those wrists from,' Jessie had remarked when, the next morning, they had each in turn tried to remove the tops. But Ginny had only remarked, 'It'll look good on your reference. It should help you climb the social ladder.'

William Berryman's criteria for judging a man, since he maintained men were the best judges of men and women of women, each sex knowing their own thought patterns, was protectiveness. He meant towards women, a particular woman. What was a man for if not to provide the protectiveness for a woman's nature to flourish in? If William had been asked what he thought this nature was he would have said something vague, like nest-building, producing offspring. He was dangerously close to the birds and the bees, a subject which preoccupied some women but not all. Nonetheless a man without it, even a man who remained a bachelor and expended his protectiveness on a pet, was a man not worth knowing.

Teddy, he felt instantly, had this quality and so, in a different way, did Bruce. Jack, Emma's husband, did not, and it worried him to see this daughter, so firm and chiselled of brow and feature, growing soft and uncertain inside. It was as if her fine bones, high forehead were becoming a shield. Maud had the same forehead, the same perfect hairline, but Maud's eyes were not sad. He had averted his glance from her as she came down the aisle on Bruce's arm. Even Bruce seemed to have his head turned aside, acknowledging a face here, a greeting there.

'Too much in love,' he had said to Jane later that evening. He didn't say it could only come to a bad end: to think it, or even feel the thought forming – resolutely he put the words hovering out of range. It would die down, he told himself. Domesticity would take care of it, or a child. Grandiose houses had the same effect on him: he must ask Irene about Government House when he got her alone. He expected that being fully staffed mitigated the spell – a large house with someone rattling around in it, perhaps with money in a tin under the bed, like bedridden Mrs Fawcett at Lawrenny, was terrible to contemplate. The maids, cooks and housekeepers, the butler brought from England whom Irene had regaled them with in her letters, probably provided company of sorts for the Governor and his wife. Not the sort of company you spoke to, for they had their own class for that, but a company simply of having other bodies about. Even if they had to hide in cupboards or efface themselves. There was a rumour that Lady Huntingfield had instructed her dressmaker to make Irene's wedding dress.

'It seems very kind of Lady Huntingfield,' Jane Berryman said when she was told.

'I have to buy the material,' Irene explained. 'The dressmaker has given me an address and said to mention her name.'

I suspect the words 'run it up' come into it, was Jane's thought, like herself reaching for a leftover piece of material to lengthen a hem. Still, condescension could be taken advantage of by both sides. She had a picture of the tall Lady Huntingfield, more at ease in tweeds or on a horse, being dressed in heavy bead-encrusted satin with a sash and jewels. There would be several fittings, far more than a normal dressmaker would require: Irene would stand on a flat platform in the fitting room while the hem was pinned. All that fuss about matching shoes when only the toes would show. Irene had bought the shoes at Myer's, taking a scrap of material and being emboldened to ask if they could examine fabric and shoes on the pavement. 'What if we scarper?' Ginny had asked, but Irene looked shocked. The knowledge she worked at Government House and was being outfitted by the Governor's wife's dressmaker helped her deal with the assistant.

William Berryman and Teddy meanwhile were walking over the farm. It was not large or impressive but Teddy showed interest in every feature the way Irene showed interest in satin shoes and the long body-shaping darts Mademoiselle Goffette had tacked into her dress. The family cow, the sheep, the dogs, the horses, the abundant vegetable garden: Teddy thought he had never seen what must be a close-to-subsistence holding so well managed. He suspected that William Berryman and his sons must hire out their labour or have a system of mutual help with their neighbours.

'Father has a hot temper,' Irene had told him, but there was no sign. Teddy could see he was being scrutinised and, by the end of the day, he felt tentatively approved. Temper or not, he decided William Berryman was not a man to fear. Jane Berryman was more enigmatic.

'Women need protecting,' William said softly, under his breath, so it would not seem a directive or cause offence. Teddy had offered to cut part of a cord of wood: he felt he needed the exercise. Of course he intended to protect Irene, he thought, half-angrily, as the axe swung and shattered the wood.

'You didn't make him cut firewood to prove himself?' Jane Berryman said to her husband as they sat down to dinner.

'No, he volunteered,' William replied, grinning.

'Then he needs an extra helping,' said Jane, removing a cutlet from William's plate. There were already three on Teddy's plate but he could hardly return it. Dining was not a game of cards.

An odd family, he thought, forbearing to pick the cutlet up in his fingers and gnaw it. A sentimental husband and a wife who doesn't need it. He wondered if all gifts in marriage were so oddly aligned.

William Berryman's fabled temper landed him in serious trouble just once. His old horse, Captain, part Clydesdale, as gentle as a lamb – William could swear he would avoid a daisy if he chose – was retired to the home paddock. The thought of the faithful creature ending his days could bring tears to William's eyes: no one else brought oats, though the children could feed him apples. Every night Captain was the last creature William visited. The old horse moved towards him, in summer or winter: in winter he felt the soft warm breath, the whiskery muzzle before the huge shape came into view. My old locomotive, William called him, and other endearments he made up. Sometimes, when the rheumatism that was spreading in his body like a canker in a tree was playing up, just to lean against Captain was enough.

It was a dark evening in June – 16 June, 1921, William would always remember the date – when Captain did not come to his step. There was a disturbance in the field, a dark swirling, a scuffling, and something that sounded like ragged breath. William set the oat pail on a gatepost, climbed over and crossed the field. His heart beat painfully, adding to the other sounds, sounds that were becoming nightmarish. Captain was at the far corner of the field, backed against a fence, and a young man, crouched, was using a knife. There was blood when William stretched out a hand and touched the horse's flanks. How he tore out the fencepost, for fences on the Berryman farm were well maintained, he never knew. Captain whinnied at his approach. 'I would have done the same if he was a soldier,' William said later, surprising the constable at the Ouse police station. The fencepost came out, trailing wires, and William had beaten the young man until he lay unconscious beside the horse he had attempted to maim. Then William had lain down too – it was the first and only time his rage had felled him. Skip, the young border collie, had found them. The young man, bloodied and aggressive, wanting to press charges, had been taken to the police station, along with William, the knife and the fencepost spattered with blood. But not before William had sent Rupert, the fastest runner, to the neighbouring farm for help and Captain had been given his oats.

William had been held at the police station overnight: the assault was too severe for him to be dismissed with a warning.

Constable Sayer had had to send for advice from the police station at Hamilton. 'Just see to Captain,' William said to Jane when she visited, bringing him supper. He shared the pie with Constable Sayer, who was sorely troubled in his grasp of the law. They sat on the hard bed together and the constable marvelled that William had returned to a small considerate man, one who concealed the strength of ten. The only evidence were the bruises on temple and jaw where the young man, disturbed at his business, had turned on him.

Captain would limp from now on but that mattered less to William than the destruction of his trust. For weeks after – after the case was dismissed by the magistrate on his circuit from Hobart, with a caution – William would spend hours with Captain, talking softly to him, attempting to blot out the experience that had all but destroyed his faith in human beings. The thought of that great patient heart – he clenched his fist to represent his own heart size – made him want to tear out another post from the mended fence. But there were things that did not mend. Limping was nothing: limping for Captain and rheumatism for him. Then he thought of Captain's grave that one day would have to be dug. Near the elm tree, in the uncontaminated part of the field.

Jane Berryman had attempted to reason with him that animals are different from humans, that they are passive in the face of pain, as if they expect it, or expect no help. How often does a sick animal stand stoically by a fence or wait where it is trapped in a bush or bog. By the same reasoning there might be forgetfulness.

'I'm sorry, Jane,' he said, 'I can't believe you. But I'm sorry if I frightened you or the children.'

She assured him he hadn't. She forbore to say he had frightened himself. To the younger children it was explained as a wicked man attacking their father: the wicked man was now in a mental hospital. The bruises on William's face turned yellow and green and he laughed about them. He appeared in the village as usual and was warmly greeted; many of his friends had written glowing letters about his character.

'Undeserved,' he said to David Cumberland at the chandlers. 'I almost went over the top.'

Maud walked with him to feed Captain and put on his cover for the night.

'What goes up comes down,' he said to her. 'It's almost as if rage is rooted in the ground. I felt it run up my body and seize my heart. And then it left the way it came.'

He didn't elaborate that it made him feel whole, that he re-lived the wrenching of the fencepost and the blows that rained from his arm seemed directed by the sky. Just as well I collapsed when I did, he thought. Pride goes before a fall.

Irene and Teddy honeymooned in Melbourne for a week, then they went to New Zealand. It was important to Teddy that his new bride should like his country: he had no intention of living permanently in Australia. He enjoyed the great shearing stations of Victoria and New South Wales, names like Oxley and Yanga, but the harsher wider country did not appeal to his heart. Tasmania was different: smaller, more intimate, apart from the impenetrable bush it was said no man could hack his way through. He liked the Berryman family, especially Emma for whose sake he did his best to get on with the moody Jack. He saw Jack as a man buried under clichés of manliness and opinion so deep the inner man could only be fished for. He did not wonder that Emma might have given up, particularly after Irene confided that Emma had suffered a series of miscarriages.

Irene thought that Emma's suffering then had served only to make Jack angrier and more distant. But she said these words as they were standing on a platform overlooking the geysers at Rotorua, marvelling at the plop and suck of mud flung up as if from a porridge pot. At a distance everything seemed like a story. Her words about Emma or her mother, her father's famous temper, seemed as judicious as any she had ever uttered. Perhaps it was the sulphurous air or the languor following yet another night in a strange bed, an event that had a theatrical quality. Sometimes she looked sideways at Teddy, who always contrived to look innocent, as if he was concocting a plot. A tour of the whole country, starting from Bluff where they had sampled fresh oysters from the wharf, up the long-spined golden and mountainous island which had reminded her of home, to this boiling bubbling place where everything suggested entrails and digestion. The effect of staying in so many small hotels, bed and breakfasts and boarding houses had been to make her uninhibited: near silent lovemaking under scratchy sheets when walls were paper thin and the permanent residents seemed to resent their presence (that was Greymouth) or a vast fire-escape-festooned boarding house (Christchurch) where Teddy hid in a wardrobe and sprang out like the god Pan. By day they were demure sightseers, buying postcards or ingredients for a picnic to eat on the bank of the Avon River or outside Parliament Buildings in Wellington where the statues of statesmen were streaked with bird droppings. And once, Irene forgot where, she watched their two bodies in the mirror doors of a large wardrobe and decided, to her surprise, that they did not look incongruous or ridiculous: more like two loaves of bread.

Eventually, after nearly a month of slow travel, they had come to a small coastal town that was almost a city. It was dusk, and as the road reached the coast a mountain seemed to float over the waves. Irene felt it might be an anchor, like a paperweight. She could never feel totally at home in New Zealand but at least this province, unlike the cities of the plains and estuaries, had definite boundaries. Besides, she longed for a house, however humble, to put their few possessions in; the furniture, stored in Ouse in her father's barn – a Scotch dresser of her great grandmother's was the most precious piece – would come slowly by sea. Also Teddy had promised her they could return regularly to see her family. It was four days by ship to Melbourne and a single night on *The Princess*. Perhaps the seasickness would go away. Looking at the little waves breaking on the beach strewn with driftwood, Irene had doubts. There were huge logs there as well, showing the strength of the sea.

The news that Emma had left Jack reached Irene in a letter from Sophie, one of 'the nuisances'. Even at school Sophie was noted for her essays and fearlessness at reading aloud. Irene and Teddy were now settled in the town so impulsively chosen. It turned out to be surprisingly staid, and overtures from the neighbours were long in coming, with one or two exceptions – a kindly woman had brought freshly baked scones the morning they moved in. The house was nothing more than a hut but the section was large, sloping down into a valley planted with pines. Their furniture, while they awaited the Scotch chest, was apple boxes with cushions for chairs and a packing case for a table.

'I wonder why Sophie fancies herself the family scribe,' Irene thought. Though they were grown, it still seemed a move for ingratiation. And why must she express herself so dramatically. *Emma appeared at Maud and Bruce's shop carrying a small battered suitcase done up with a man's belt*, Sophie had written, and the detail, though vivid, seemed offensive. Why, if it was Maud's shop, had Maud not written? Probably too busy with the ledgers. Irene read the letter aloud, after a first cursory inspection. *She has been staying with Maud for a week. Nothing from Jack until last Friday, after supper, he appeared on his horse, riding up the main street of Ouse.* How irritating she is, Irene thought. Perhaps she imagines she is writing a novel. Horse or not there was no other approach. *Maud, Bruce and Jack were closeted* – here Irene frowned and wondered what her sister had been reading – *in the room behind the shop. Emma refused to come out.*

'Like the suitcase,' Teddy said. 'Good for Emma.'

'I thought you liked Jack,' Irene said, surprised, remembering his efforts.

'I liked him for Emma's sake,' he replied, and then, seeing an uncertain look, 'After you, Emma was my favourite.'

So this is how men think, Irene thought, as she prepared for bed that evening. If a first choice fails, they turn to the next on their list: they profess love but even in an embrace they have an eye over your shoulder. And perhaps, by going down the list, they practise their techniques. But Teddy had not practised: his list had ended with her. Still, if Emma was next, what had she in common with Emma?

All night, with her back turned like a stone wall, despite being stroked, and in the morning the familiar spine pressed to hers, she seemed to go over the differences between herself and her sister. Emma was passive and too accepting: her mistaken marriage to Jack had been a romantic blurring of the truth. Then, rather than fight, she had retreated.

Irene picked up Sophie's letter again and read the expectation that Emma would return to Guiseford; Maud and Bruce, it seemed, had persuaded her to stay for a few days more. *So she won't make the same mistake again, give in to the romantic gesture.* 'Not so romantic,' Teddy had judged, 'to ride a horse through Ouse after dusk.' Then he must have had to turn around and ride back.

When Teddy had left for his work on the building site, Irene sat on the little hard sofa by the living room window. For once plumping up the cushions on the apple boxes seemed unenticing. She found herself thinking of Emma's suitcase, one that had belonged to their father. The leather was almost golden as if, from frequent use, it had weathered and each journey were recorded. It was a small but amazingly heavy suitcase and it held surprisingly little. Perhaps a pressed and folded nightdress, a toilet bag, a novel, for Emma was always reading. But what novel would help in such a situation? She must write to Emma: that would take up a few hours. And she would go on being a little cool towards Teddy, to show him that, top of the list or not, she was never to be so considered.

Emma did return to Guiseford and Jack, but not until she passed a week in Maud and Bruce's company. She had the spare room – the boxroom – that was shielded from the street by thick lace curtains. The sounds of feet passing when she lay on the bed for an afternoon rest were comforting. At night a piece of wood levered the window sash open a few inches and the curtains moved languidly in the breeze that rose before dawn.

Burglars were unknown in Ouse apart from the Giddings' boy who had stolen old Mrs Nuttall's collection of British and Commonwealth stamps. Sometimes a child, standing on tiptoe, attempted to insert a hand into one of the huge lolly jars on the counter while Maud's or Bruce's back was turned. Maud seemed to have eyes in the back of her head, Emma thought, in the odd half hours she stood at the counter while they had a quick meal. She could no more ape Maud's expression or posture, or bring the shop into order under her gaze, as if it were an animate thing, than fly. But she thought, in her pondering way, she could learn something from Maud – something that when she returned, as she had always known she would, would be invisible to anyone else but comforting to herself. That she wanted to learn how to live the remainder of her life from someone whose life was so bound in another's did not strike her. Maud's temperament was so different, her way of dealing with disappointment, though there was none on the horizon, was bound to be different too.

By the end of the week Emma had become remarkably fond of her room, fond of waking at the time the little breeze rose – once there was a sudden shower and she got out of bed to raise the sash higher and smell the damp air. She saw that her sister was ordered, not just in physical things, but mentally, as if she expended energy in a number of areas, like the tiny rooms of a dolls' house. If one part was unsatisfactory – like the day some shelves fell down, just missing a Kelsey child – there were other energies not to be wasted. That night they had opened a bottle of wine with dinner, as if in celebration.

Of Emma's problems with Jack, Maud said nothing. She only brought a fresh posy for her bedside table or saw there was a supply of books, or bustled in with breakfast on a tray.

When, after three days, Jack appeared on his horse, dismounting, it seemed, in slow motion, and knocking three times at the door, Emma was able to see behind the theatrical pose that once would have won her over. His coming in the dark indicated shame not romance, though as Teddy pointed out, he had farm work to do. From behind the lace curtains Emma examined his figure and the way he stood with feet slightly braced, not expecting a blow but prepared. He has never been open, she thought, as Maud let him in. She heard their footsteps leading towards the parlour, knew there would be the offer of a whisky and a cigar. Let me speak to him first, Maud had said. Then Bruce. And then you. It was like being a bride, preceded up the aisle, Emma considered, fingering a piece of the creamy lace. Then Maud appeared in the doorway.

'It's all right. He's agreed you can stay until the end of the week.'

'I'm sorry,' Jack said, when they were left alone, facing each other across a table.

Neither sat, at first; Emma held onto the back of a chair, Jack pointed his cigar towards the carpet as if it were a weapon.

'I just need a rest, I think,' Emma said. And instantly she knew it was a mistake: he was moving away from her again, offended by a lack of spirit, or plain talking. 'At least that is all I am prepared to say at present,' she added.

'That's more like it,' Jack began, but she interrupted him.

'I'm not made in your image, Jack, it's time you realised that.'

Then, because she was feeling shaken, she turned and walked out of the room.

Bruce took ill in spring and by late summer he was dead. Were the days between death and burial a thousand, Maud could not have prepared herself for the sight of the coffin descending between its golden walls of warm clay. Any image of even faint beauty – the soft glow of the soil, the beautifully cut walls – hurt like a pain pressed by an unthinking embrace. Harriet, standing silent and rigid beside her, seemed an affront, for what was the use of birth if it led to this? A flicker of sympathy for her daughter leapt ahead to Harriet's death, a wish, rather faintly held, that Harriet might find some passion to warm her. Find what you need, what becomes your very breath, and have it snatched away from you. Better to be Emma, whose grief-threaded life would have learned to snatch at the effects of light on clay, then light obliterated as the coffin descended, rocking slightly. For a mad moment Maud thought Bruce had raised a fist and struck the underside of the lid; instead the stiff body with its uneven rigor had slid against one wall.

Her sisters had made all the arrangements, summoning the undertaker. It was lucky Bruce was a Catholic so there was no need to consult over the ceremony. His mother had come from Hobart to take her place, shrouded in black veils, in the front pew. Maud thought she looked as complacent as a crow. Father Stanislaus had given Maud to feel now was the time to put the instructions she had hardly listened to into practice. The mass will carry you through, he had said on the evening before the funeral. And how it had hurt: each word made three times more terrible for Maud personally, while her Protestant sisters and mother sat looking around at the Stations of the Cross or the chipped pietà in the foyer. The angels on the altar when the small procession advanced to kneel for communion, Sophie informed her later, had vicious faces. Sophie had very long sight and her eyes had examined the plaster inch by inch.

They came out into the weak sunlight: Maud, Harriet and Mrs Betts first, then the clutch of sisters with her mother in the centre, then the rest of the congregation, personal friends of Bruce, merchants he had dealt with, the busybodies who went to every funeral as if they were estimating them, like a book list. There was Mrs Toogood who did no good that Maud could see but was always airing her black weeds, her black straw hat with hideously over-coloured cherries. The last wheezing notes of the organ – *Jesu, joy of man's desiring,* Bruce's favourite – died away, and they were left with the cold stone walls, the bedraggled willow Father Stanislaus was debating having trimmed, the border hastily and grumpily weeded by the housekeeper. Maud could see a few weeds whose heads had been decapitated.

Maud had wished that Bruce could be buried under the floor of a cathedral: she saw herself returning at night when only the sanctuary light glowed, and stretching out full-length on the flagstones. Instead there was this golden day which the lowering of the coffin had darkened. For the rest of the afternoon she moved like a led creature between patches of darkness and light, the dark connected to the ceremonies: the little procession wending its way through the graveyard, the dark glasses of port at her mother's house, the dark stewed tea which had steeped too long, the dark slices of fruitcake. And the light, the sudden clarity where no ceremony could reach: the wreaths that were dying and taking their messages with them, the blank house fronts, the undertaker's surreptitious signals so the little tray of clay was brought forward for her to select. An hour before she had received the host on her tongue and sipped from the communion cup; now, as though translated to dust, she received and crumbled a lump of clay. It fell on the lilies on the coffin lid, besmirching them. Then she remembered something her father had told her: when he came up before the magistrate he had held his face like flint. Not that he really knew what that meant, he said. He took it to mean imagining his cheeks were marble, immovable, holding the mouth in a firm line. But her father had been terrified he might laugh. His rage had died away, drained into the board floor of the police station where he was giving details to Constable Sayer. It was a miracle that this last and greatest manifestation had evaporated.

At first the shelves and supplies in the store had seemed outlined in this vacant cruel reduced light. Maud would find herself gazing at lemon and orange cordials or golden syrup and wondering why such richness did not bathe the next pyramid in a glow. But the light pressed back, saying It's only chicory essence and fish paste, only pilchards or stoned dates. The tins could have been memorial plaques on a wall.

Bruce's headstone would have to be attended to, but Maud could not think of a verse. She would leave room for herself, an addendum, *Maud Betts, 1906* —. Sometimes she wondered if the quote existed that could summarise their marriage. *Goodnight, sweet Prince; And flights of angels sing thee to thy rest!* Over and over she said it to herself. And sometimes, at night, when she took the ledgers to bed with her and gazed at the figures until they swam, she opened *The Complete Shakespeare* and read a few lines:

> *O, this life*
> *Is nobler than attending for a check,*
> *Richer than doing nothing for a bribe,*
> *Prouder than rustling in unpaid-for silk.*

When she woke in the morning the ledgers had slid to the floor, along with her dressing gown. She had not heard the Shakespeare fall, though it was the heaviest.

Ten months after Bruce's death Irene walked into Betts's General Store and came up behind her sister, causing her to start and upset a pyramid she was building of chicken soup. It was her first solo trip and she had lost four pounds in as many days. *The Princess of Tasmania*, its ludicrous over-sized bridal suite unoccupied while the rest of the passengers huddled together, had been a torture. Surely it was badly constructed, Irene surmised, settling herself away from the smell of paint on the upper deck. The only place she had a chance of survival was with her back against a bulkhead, the wind forcing the nausea back down her throat. She didn't pray *The Princess* would sink – Teddy would be too upset – but she knew she would never please him by attaining sea legs. When she returned to her miniature cabin for the night, her legs trembled and she clung to the wall for support. A kind steward brought her a cup of beef tea.

Irene slid her arms around Maud's waist as she had as a child. They sat in the back parlour drinking tea and listening for the bell or footsteps on the boardwalk floor. There was the amazing news of Emma to take in: after her reconciliation with Jack she had become pregnant. Even their mother, burdened by so many mid-life pregnancies, had not been sympathetic. 'Do you think anything will change? Between Emma and Jack,' Irene asked.

'No, she's become moony,' Maud replied. 'She's too passive and she can't concentrate for long.'

Sometimes Irene thought Emma was an alien species. She would visit her for a few days before she left. In the meantime she was content to feast her eyes on her favourite sister, the one she was closest to in age – a mere thirteen months separated them – and the one she still wished to emulate. There were fine lines around the eyes and across the brow; the skin seemed thinner but the eyes were not veiled or dead as Irene had expected. Maud was not a zombie. Suddenly a memory popped up: she was lying in the soft grass under the apple tree and Maud was bestride her, holding the small tomahawk used to cut kindling. She felt again the bony knees that pinned her, the fury in the spine that pressed her down. Emma, Eileen and Ada had come running, followed by Sophie, one of the babies, who sensed the drama and howled. 'You can say your goodbyes now,' Maud had piped in a clear magisterial voice, 'because I am going to cut off her head.' Maud had been dragged off, fuming, and Irene had flung a cowpat at her sister. It had been their one quarrel and now she could not remember the cause. The bell rang and Maud got to her feet to cut cheese or slice bacon. She is thinner, Irene thought, but, considering everything, well.

At Guiseford the grass was dry and firebreaks were being cut. Jack was falsely jovial, as if this late pregnancy were a masterstroke, but Emma seemed embarrassed. 'I feel like one of those women in the Bible, Elizabeth or Sarah,' she said. The looks she got in Ouse hardly increased her confidence. The matron at Ouse hospital had barely concealed her disapproval when Emma went to book in and have her blood pressure taken. Dr McSkimming had been kinder, guessing it was some kind of reconciliation. Trust nature to hitch herself to a human emotion. After decades of practice he had come to see his patients as pawns to be treated kindly, bandaged when necessary and given bottles of coloured water.

'I'm pleased for you,' Irene said, wrapping her arms around a second sister. 'Truly, I am.'

'Mother's not,' Emma said as they sat down together at the table covered with oil cloth.

'Perhaps it brings back too many memories,' Irene said. 'And now she's so old, she thinks of all the time she might have had.'

Their mother was still reading, holding the book at a distance, but the dream of painting was gone.

They stood at the nursery door together: here at least an effort had been made. The wooden rocking cradle was already made up and a slightly rickety table had been painted. Out through the long French door stretched the view the child would see: a dry garden, grass like blond baby hair, a field with black cattle and dogs running around. The child would learn how many dusty sheep could be supported by an acre. It would identify rabbit holes and see the land ripple with the silhouettes at dusk. Perhaps books on rabbits would be banned; she must remember not to send *Peter Rabbit*. There was the water tank and the old tractor. But also the wonderful land, Irene thought, standing in the doorway, the sweep of it that she never saw in New Zealand. It was what she missed most of all, and new furniture – they had a new table and chairs now, a sideboard for displaying dishes – could not console her. A land that represented human aspirations, even if the chances of any individual achieving them were small.

Irene spent another day helping Maud in the shop before she left. Something in her sister had changed and it was to do with her relationship with her customers. It was hard to put a finger on it. Maud's service to everyone was impeccable, a little reserved, which was to be expected after a bereavement and which those who knew her allowed for. She did not welcome condolences or, if they were still offered, her thanks had a touch of dismissal. Irene thought she was a bit like the Royal family. There had been an incident at Government House when the Duke of York had visited and left a large number of banknotes in his room. Jessie had been summoned by the housemaids assigned to the floor, practically wringing their hands as if they had been accused of theft already, and a great fuss ensued. 'They don't think as we do,' Jessie had said, her mouth grim, for the consequences, if even a farthing were lost, would have meant dismissal. Maud was behaving a little like the Duke of York, who had condescended to depart through a line of parlourmaids and chambermaids, with Jessie at the head. They had curtsied as he shook the hands of some or exchanged a few words with another. 'Thank you for a pleasant stay,' he had said quite inappropriately to Henrietta Smith, a fat girl who had been in her position just three weeks and didn't know which way to look.

Perhaps she is just being scrupulous, Irene thought, observing her sister politely but firmly decline a request for credit from Mrs Cumberland whose husband owned Ellwand Station. Yet later in the morning she saw Maud slip an extra iced bun into a bag for one of the Kelsey children, whose parents didn't have a penny to bless themselves. If Bruce were here, would he chide her? For surely Mrs Cumberland's custom mattered far more than the Kelseys who already had a sum of money on the slate.

Some of the wealthier customers had bristled but none had liked to complain. A few thought of taking their custom elsewhere but Maud's status as a new widow checked them. In every other way, though a Catholic, she was the model of proper behaviour. She was known to keep confidences, even those of children. 'Could I have a word?' someone would begin, and Maud would take them into the parlour and sit them down, leaving the door open the merest crack. Sometimes a child, grubby-faced and bruised, would sob near the sweet jars and be given half a dozen striped boiled sweets and a hand towel to wash its face and hands.

Harriet, perfectly capable of washing her own face and hands and self-rationing sweets, stayed at St Mary's College in Hobart, a school that took all ages, so the youngest girls, like Harriet, almost seemed the children of the eldest. At each level a fresh adornment to the uniform was added, or a fresh privilege. Harriet's weekly letter home was composed on Tuesday evening between 6 and 7 p.m. though girls who finished early could be excused: a minimum of thirty minutes was required.

'Do you miss Harriet?' Irene had asked and Maud had replied, 'Not really. She writes enchanting letters and we have a good time in the holidays.' She didn't say that Harriet reminded her too painfully of Bruce, so she was pleased to honour his instruction that she be well educated. A small life insurance policy she had not known Bruce possessed – it had been taken out by his parents when he was a child – provided the funds.

'I'm afraid your dear sister is behaving rather strangely,' Mrs Toogood said to Irene as she stood waiting for the bus that would carry her to Devonport and *The Princess*. Mrs Toogood looked at Irene from under the brim of her black straw hat. Maud had prevented her putting candied peel, raisins and blanched almonds on tick, especially as Mrs Toogood's purse, when she opened her capacious black handbag, was bulging with notes. 'From now on I am running a strictly cash business,' Maud had said, the sweetness of her tone belying the steel underneath, 'since I have all the books to do myself. I'm counting on my wealthier customers to understand.' Mrs Toogood had seen to it that the news of Maud's eccentricity had spread. She had been observed giving credit to the Kelseys, a thoroughly disreputable family, and even washing the youngest Kelsey's face.

'I think Maud wants to simplify her book-keeping,' Irene replied, remembering her mother's dislike of Cecily Toogood.

'And the simplification seems to only apply to the rich,' Mrs Toogood continued. 'It doesn't seem to apply to the likes of the O'Reillys or the Kelseys.'

'Surely it is a matter of luck who is rich and who is not,' Irene replied, thinking again of the Duke of York's loose change, equivalent to a chambermaid's yearly wage, spread out on the dresser. Or the rows of well-dressed parishioners in Our Lady of the Immaculate Conception opening their hymnals with gloves and listening to the sermon of the good rich young man or the camel and the eye of the needle.

'I can't think Bruce would have allowed it, if he had lived,' Mrs Toogood went on.

'Possibly not,' Irene replied, surprised by a small flare of temper. 'But he didn't, and that's the whole point.'

63

Then the bus had arrived and Irene stood back to allow Mrs Toogood on first. Inside they sat as far apart as possible.

Emma gave birth to a 10lb son at Ouse cottage hospital. She refused to name him Jack Roland Jnr, though Jack appeared on the polished linoleum carrying a bunch of roses. He would be William James after her father, and Jack, hoping for the restoration of something like happiness, agreed.

The two weeks in the cottage hospital were among the happiest in Emma's life. She had the newly decorated room to herself until the last day when Dora Kelsey was wheeled in with a new daughter. The matron fussed and asked if the rumours of Maud playing Robin Hood were true. 'Good for her,' she said, as she crackled out in her stiff uniform. Propped on pillows, holding her son at arms' length as if he were a book she was reading, the days drifted by. Apart from her son, minutely examined, she gave the same examination to a camellia bush outside the window, memorising each leaf and bloom, each glint of sun. Maud brought a beautiful shawl she had worked on in the evenings after the store was closed.

'You know Ouse is full of rumours about you and the shop,' Emma said to her after the shawl was unwrapped and spread out to admire.

'I expect they will die down,' Maud replied.

She was tired, as if she was the inventor of a new theory which had to be endlessly justified. The owner of the rival store, Pettifers, had approached her and asked if she were going out of business. 'If I am you'll see the notice,' she replied. In fact, in spite of a few pursed lips and flouncings out, the shop now seemed to have a different atmosphere. The Kelsey children, unkempt and uncertain, who once hung about blocking the door, now came forward confidently with their mother's list and a small amount to pay off the bill. Mrs Ifield, a widow like herself, whose idea of genteel poverty was excessive neatness of dress and a proud head carriage, now seemed much more relaxed, though she insisted, as if it was a negotiated arrangement, in paying an unvarying amount each week and never allowing her debt to rise above ten shillings. Even, and most surprisingly, Mrs Cumberland, whom Maud knew from the town's grapevine had transferred her custom to New Norfolk for a month, eventually relented and visited to see if noblesse oblige worked. She looked at Maud with the conspiratorial air of another capitalist, one who could rise to eccentricities only conceived by the upper crust.

Father Stanislaus visited and wondered if Maud was applying socialist principles. But she assured him her manner of dealing with rich and poor simply ensured a good cash flow. The poor, however you badgered them, could not produce blood from a stone and, with a few exceptions, were eventually good payers, while the well-to-do, if relieved of their tendencies to procrastination and snobbishness at the start, were free to turn their energies elsewhere. For, to Maud, it did seem a form of snobbery to expend so much energy complaining about exorbitant fees for schools in Hobart or Launceston – Harriet's were always paid on time, whatever the sacrifice – as if the rich must be always complaining about being rich.

'I expect they don't like to mention money at all,' Father Stanislaus said. He was often amazed at the miserliness of the contributions to the plate of gloved hands and fox furs. He remembered his own aunt, Hermione, insisting on a delivery boy bringing home a minute parcel she could have trailed on a string from one finger: the bill would be paid on the last allowable day, three months later. Of course that had been in Hobart. His aunt had shopped only at the best shops.

'But how are you, yourself?' Father Stanislaus asked Maud, after he had finished a slice of plum cake and she had poured him a second cup of tea.

'Tired, most of the time,' she admitted. 'Sometimes I have to catch my breath.'

'You haven't thought of a holiday,' he asked, wondering if one or two of the parishioners could look after the store for a week. Perhaps the rich would be back to having credit by the time she returned.

'I'll go and see Harriet for a few days next term. I've

promised to take her shopping. Ada has promised to look after the store. It'll only be for three days.'

'You don't fear the collapse of your no-credit system then,' Father Stanislaus said, rising and receiving his hat. He might espouse the poor but his gestures remained with the rich.

'No. Mother will come in and sit at the counter. I suspect she will suspend the baker's dozen though,' Maud said, smiling. But perhaps she wouldn't, if they had words first. Her mother was the only one who had supported sending Harriet to boarding school. She had chided those who hinted Maud was cold-hearted. And knowing her granddaughter suffered too, she spent hours writing long letters to her at St Mary's College. Sometimes, when Harriet opened them, pressed rose petals, darker than when the rose was alive, flew out. *I'm sending my love in these petals,* her grandmother wrote, anticipating the spill. Sometimes there was a drawing of an insect or butterfly.

You will have a new cousin, Jane had written to Harriet, *though I suspect his birth will not bring great happiness to his parents.* Her view of grandmotherhood was frankness, however young the grandchild. Besides, Harriet had always struck her as sensible and reflective. *Still there will come a time when age no longer matters and compatibility is more. It is largely a question of temperament.* Few things disturbed Jane Berryman, not her late husband's rages nor the hours, when she was middle-aged, spent sewing for her children. But now she was, to all appearances, really aged, she felt young. *It is not true to say you are as young as you look,* she wrote to Harriet. *There are old children and frivolous old women.* Harriet would get the hint and not send her lavender soap for her birthday. *The qualities you are learning or having thrust upon you at your boarding school, for qualities, I find, are not always external, will serve you well later.*

Harriet doubted the wise words of her grandmother but felt certain of her love. She looked for the minute drawings of flowers in the margins, the flights of fancy where a bumblebee was described as carrying a burden of gossip like Mrs Toogood from Ouse whose legs could hardly move fast enough when she had something to impart. Harriet knew her grandmother intended to make up for her mother's lack of love, which she had explained to her as 'excessively conjugal'. Conjugal in the dictionary meant: *relating to marriage or the relationship between husband and wife.*

Harriet felt she was being strengthened on all sides. Her life at St Mary's had become a pattern: a few close friends, one Presentation sister, Sister Lucy, fresh from the novitiate, whom she loved. Mostly she enjoyed having time to ponder, a characteristic of the Virgin Mary who had a lot to ponder about. And lately, as well as the letters from her grandmother, her mother had begun to write more frequently.

The way Maud described Ouse made Harriet think her mother was detached from it, looking down on it from a great height, the way a soul is said to hover over a body. When Harriet thought of Ouse, which she did sometimes in the evening before the lights were turned off – a small sacrifice because the high windows were curtainless and the sky visible – it seemed to have shrunk into a hollow like the fold in an elbow. The school in its stubbly field at one end, the church and the river and the bridge at the other. There were a few nice houses – her grandmother's for one, two-storeyed, with shutters to keep the noise of the street and the dust at bay. The gate was of wrought iron and her grandmother stood behind it, like Mother Anastasia behind a grille. In contrast, the store was low and one-storeyed; the road curved beside it, as if one could be blown there to buy ice creams, licorice straps and changing balls. Sometimes Harriet, peering from her window, thought she saw it as her mother saw it. Like 'O little town of Bethlehem' which they were practising for Christmas.

Maud, when she stood on a step-ladder to reach the top shelf, sometimes felt a pain under her ribs. Occasionally it extended down her arm. She grimaced, drawing in her breath as she faced the wall, the tins of apricot halves and pineapple rings swimming for a moment; then she turned, smiling, to hand Mrs Cumberland a tin of haricot beans. And at night, sometimes, she pushed a ledger aside and lay back on the pillows as if she were listening. The pain, which passed quickly enough, she regarded with detachment and, the second it struck, calm. Contesting it, as she had at first, made it worse; now she knew every nuance, knew that it depended upon her, upon her heartbeat, momentarily disturbed, to proceed. William Berryman had died of a heart attack when he was in his prime. Still he had always argued that his mysterious rages were the best of him and Maud refused to regret an inheritance that had made her at first the talk of the town and more lately a heroine. She did not accept words as saying anything precise; she had simply carried out something she hadn't known she believed, as her father had, pursuing Jacob Jarowiecki who had maimed Captain. Only last week Mrs Cumberland had come to her and asked her to join the Women's Guild, 'in recognition of your work for the community'. Maud, seeing a refusal would be tactless, had agreed to consider it, though she had no intention. She had no capacity for joining anything, only Bruce.

Nor was the pain frequent, or traceable to causes. A busy day, lifting more than was good for her, often brought a peaceable night, and, if her arms tingled and ached during the day, a few minutes sitting in the parlour allowed it to pass. The only person who was aware of it was Father Stanislaus. He had caught her holding her hand to her chest like a holy statue and led her to the high stool she kept behind the counter. When the pain subsided he brought a brandy from the cut-glass decanter on the sideboard.

'Have one yourself,' Maud said, and he replied, 'I don't mind if I do.'

'You won't say anything,' Maud had said later, and he looked at her seriously and recommended the doctor.

'He can't do anything,' Maud said, sipping the brandy and feeling its warmth fill the vacuum where pain had been, one thing chasing another.

'You mustn't be a fatalist,' Father Stanislaus replied. 'There are sure to be methods of easing what you feel now, actions you can take.' For some reason *as gentle as doves and as cunning as serpents* came to his mind: it could hardly apply to the medical profession.

'We could say a prayer together,' he suggested and Maud, aware that someone might come into the shop at any minute, laughed. The sight of herself and Father Stanislaus kneeling together, herself with a supporting hand on the counter, was bound to be misinterpreted. Still, with the parlour door closed to a crack, they attempted it. Knees bent, they steadied themselves, and a quick Hail Mary was said, gliding over the words so the import was lost and only the aspect of petition remained. A ridiculous prayer, Maud always considered it, like a potted life history: the Virgin gracefully walking one moment, then grossly swollen with child like a ripe fruit, then the rush to ward off death. Father Stanislaus stayed on his knees a little longer when Maud rose to her feet. She left her hand against the table, admiring her wedding band.

One matter Maud did attend to: she wrote more frequently to Harriet. She did not attempt to broach the subject that divided them and which was a mystery even to herself; her intense love for her husband which had allowed little room for her daughter. Harriet, Maud mused, might one day find such a love in herself; it was something one could not know until it happened. It had not happened to Emma, now absorbed in her child, absorbed to a degree Maud considered dangerous, for relations between Emma and Jack had not improved. Then fairness intervened and she wondered if they were not two sides of the same coin. Maud wrote to Harriet at night, replacing the ledgers and balancing the writing pad against an old clipboard. She wrote about Ouse and its seasons, which she thought Harriet might miss, the way the grass changed colour subtly and the wind cast shadows on the paddocks. She asked if Harriet remembered the stubbly field at Ouse school or knew that it was now extended and mowed, and the snakes that were reputed to hide in the long tussocks banished further, though they still gave out snake-bite pills from a tin lid on Tuesdays. Once there had been a tiger snake under the school and Harriet had run home at lunchtime, bursting with the news and how the Strawbridge twins, defying the teacher, were poking at it with long sticks.

I failed to enter her world, Maud thought, lifting her pen and casting about her for the next sentence, the next recollection. She was asking her daughter to read between the lines: it was Bruce who had caught Harriet up in his arms as if the snake had followed her over the board floor, and asked if she wanted the afternoon off school. But Harriet had run back, taking bites out of an apple, practically skipping with excitement. She was in time to admire the snake's carcass and see the severed head. *I have been feeling a little unwell,* Maud wrote*, and I think it is one of those conditions one must bear and make adjustments to, perhaps even modify one's life, like giving up chocolate or eating more vegetables.* And she had written by the same post to Mother Anastasia, a much franker letter, implying that Harriet, at some time in the future – not the immediate future by any means – might need to be sent for or have things explained to. The pain struck again while she wrote, running up her arm, so the arm felt taut like the body of a snake. She set the pen between the folds of the heavy white counterpane with its raised pattern of dots and fleurs-de-lys and waited. Part of her found it interesting: as interesting as a dry stream bed suddenly flooding. She held herself still and hardly breathed: Dr McSkimming had told her there was no need to breathe, air simply flowed between slightly parted lips. There is no one home, Maud's breath told the pain, as it searched and scoured. I am not worth robbing. Then, as suddenly as it arrived, it retreated. The stream bed resumed its dryness; the letter swimming into focus at the foot of the bed could be resumed.

In the shop the Kelsey children asked for a bag of broken biscuits and Maud slipped a dozen current buns into a brown paper bag with the tightly wrapped biscuits at the bottom. Mrs Cumberland, observing behind a rack of dresses, made no comment. Maud had found a supplier in Hobart, and the once outdated racks had plaid dresses for girls with intricate smocking and occasionally a lace collar. She had men's white shirts piled up like meringues and the address of a suit-hire service in New Norfolk.

'You're looking tired,' said Mrs Cumberland, bringing her purchases to the counter, her purse at the ready. 'I hear you've been unwell.'

'A little,' Maud replied, feeling something was owed for a cash transaction.

'Take care then,' said Mrs Cumberland.

Quite gaunt, she said later to a group of ladies at the Women's Guild. Shadows under the eyes, a dress hanging looser about the shoulders. Privately she thought women unfit for strong ideas: their constitutions could not take it. Whereas her own form, in its ginger and white stripes and self-covered belt, swelled slightly year after year. 'The neck,' Adeline Cumberland mused, daintily raising a cup, after the business had been attended to, 'seems to rely on a little extra weight.'

Maud's illness could not be kept from her sisters and the three she was closest to, Emma, Ada, Eileen, excluding Irene in New Zealand, were often at the foot of her bed, dusting the dresser and placing fresh flowers so they reflected in the mirror, bringing soup or little casseroles to be served on a tray. They had arranged a roster for the shop, though it was a source of agitation to Maud. However, she was counselled to rest by Dr McSkimming in a tone that brooked no interference, and now that these childhood guards were back. . . Father Stanislaus visited to bring the sacrament and Maud asked for privacy then, that the door be closed. Emma retreated to the kitchen and banged the dishes about, but Eileen put her ear against the door to try to hear what was being said.

'It sounds like gibberish,' she reported to Ada who was shaking and folding towels.

'She wouldn't like you hovering,' Ada replied, giving a towel a vicious snap, like a sail.

But when Father Stanislaus reappeared they clustered around him in the passage, blocking his way.

'It won't be for a while,' he said, feeling the press of

Protestantism. 'I've given her Extreme Unction. I know she appreciates all you're doing.'

'Extreme what?' asked Emma, when the priest's shadow had crossed the doorstep and Ada had noted the thickening of his waist, probably due to the housekeeper, and the slope, for so young a man, of his shoulders.

'It won't be for a while,' mimicked Eileen, who had been the most savage about Maud's turning. 'As if he has the stars and moon in his hands.' The arrogance of it left her almost speechless. Then, as she took a fresh basket of laundry to the clothesline, she said the Lord's Prayer under her breath. Let the Catholics claim that, she thought, adding the part the Protestants had added so as not to finish on the word 'evil'.

The trouble with lying in bed was not only her sisters hovering, each making their wishes like last chances in a fable, but the emphasis it gave to the least twinge of pain. Maud, normally so active, would have been better pleased to be surprised by it, when it had half-arrived, not waiting for its earlier move. Bed made her restless, which was odd, because in the exhausted days after Bruce's death, it had been a solace. It had seemed like a great bowl of milk or a giant slice of bread, so sustaining had it been. She had inserted herself, leaving his side fastened, and had woken to find herself cocooned and the coverings hardly disturbed.

She could hear sounds from the shop: feet on the wooden floor, voices and the ping of the cash register. It seemed a long time ago that she had attempted her reforms, reforms that she knew would not survive or, if they did, only for a time. But she felt oddly unconcerned about credit and broken biscuits and account reminders sent out each month. The heavy lace curtains hardly moved, though the sash was up; the air was scented with damp, the few heavy drops that had fallen releasing a potent perfume of earth, an anticipation. 'We need the rain,' Emma said, entering with a tray on which wobbled a small crystal vase and a deep red rose.

'I'll call tomorrow,' Father Stanislaus had said, re-packing

72

his bag. She could practically hear her sisters breathing against the door. He held her hand for a moment, then used his free hand to close it. 'I'll say mass for you at midday.' She nodded as she would have to Dr McSkimming.

'Perhaps I could get up this afternoon,' she said as a general statement when the door opened again and her sisters' faces appeared in the frame. They were each struggling to resume an expression: indignation to love, acceptance to empathy, stoicism to some redeeming task, probably another tray.

Dr McSkimming called towards evening and sat on the edge of the bed. He too picked up one of Maud's hands and turned it over to feel her pulse. Then he held onto it, in a hand that was as soft as a woman's.

'I feel as if I am being blamed,' Maud said, and he saw her eyes moisten. 'Blamed for loving Bruce too much, for letting Harriet go, and now my way of running the store.' Her voice was faint but determined, as a person's sometimes is in a confessional.

'You are the most blameless person I know,' said Dr McSkimming. With his free hand he stroked the slightly dry soft hair that met the brow.

'Perhaps I have brought this on myself. A punishment.'

For an instant, Dr McSkimming wished the priest were here, not that he had any time for Catholics or the Catholic faith. All he could say to Maud, as gently and firmly as he could, was that she had lived a good life and he would swear a Hippocratic oath on it.

Father Stanislaus paid one more visit.

'If he says she's going to be all right again I'm going to hit him,' Eileen declared.

She alone stayed in the hallway. 'As if her feet, her hands, her tongue have done any harm in this world,' she had protested when Extreme Unction had been explained to her. Extreme love, she would have said, had characterised her sister.

But both Father Stanislaus and Eileen, when she finally entered the room, found Maud calm. Whatever words had been said or mumbo jumbo applied, she was drifting into sleep.

Harriet had been summoned to the Mother Superior's parlour – a hideous panelled room, so wooden and waxed it reminded her of a hive – and told, in unusually soft tones, that her dear mother was extremely ill and she would be sent home that afternoon. She was asked if she felt she could make the journey on her own or if she would like a friend, or even Sister Bridget, to accompany her. But Harriet could not imagine herself in company with Sister Bridget, the latest novice, who had a serious spotty face and hair that threatened to escape her veil.

'The term is nearly over,' Mother Anastasia was saying, though Harriet was not paying attention. 'You can come back to us next year.'

Then Mother Anastasia had stood up, straight as a poker, for her back never touched a chair back, and taken both of Harriet's hands in her two capable ones, crushing her fingers against a cumbersome silver ring.

The bus wound its way up the island of apples, timber, convict ruins, snakes and tussock, and Harriet, in her uncertainty, tried to visualise, as if Last Things too were an inventory, Death, Judgement, Hell, Heaven; then, more comfortingly, the store, lined from floor to ceiling with tins, sacks on the floor, rakes overhead, the racks of clothing, the bare counter with the massive silver till. *O little town of Ouse,* Harriet thought, for she had been taken from Advent choir practice. *How silently, how silently, The wondrous gift is given!* And then the anxious whispering, and the piano had fallen silent.

Sometimes, as the bus creaked and groaned – she was sitting over a wheel but lacked the energy to move – she thought of nothing at all. But as dusk came on, the words seemed to float and hang overhead and she could have been thinking of her mother.

> *Above thy deep and dreamless sleep*
> *The silent stars go by.*

Melbourne

The mind is a dark
and most solitary place;
throw in a little stone and you hear it
rattling and echoing off steep sides
all the way down

'The mind is its own place', CHRIS WALLACE-CRABBE

'That pot plant needs water. Urgently,' Harriet Betts said into the surprised face of the young man in the Sanitone drycleaners. She couldn't think why she had swerved into the doorway of the shop in Little Bourke Street. It had never occurred to her she might do so as she walked easily along Elizabeth Street; it was not as if she had dry-cleaning to collect or took her custom there. It was something about the light falling on the dusty parched leaves, as if sunlight was the last thing they could bear, the arid pale soil in the bottom of the tub, the carelessness of it, as if the plant were a mannequin. When the young man did not respond – she would not wait to see if a watering can was produced or a coffee cup, half-washed – she turned on her heel in a motion that pleased her, something like an ice-skater, and rejoined the crowd that was strolling in two streams. A tram going past and clanging

75

its bell seemed to applaud her initiative.

'Probably the plant will die now,' she said later to Rosa Prouse. 'Push for something and you set up a resistance.'

'Perhaps you should go past tomorrow and press your nose to the glass. Or you could take my pleated skirt in for pressing.'

But Harriet doubted she had the nerve to follow up her action: in fact the next time she passed down Little Bourke Street it was on the other side. A quick glance through the traffic showed the pot plant had been moved or was no longer there.

I wish to harm nothing, Harriet thought, sitting in the window seat of the house she shared with Rosa, whose bluntness was legendary, admirable, and two young men, Garth Gordon who worked for an advertising agency, and Ross Nyland, a trainee announcer at the ABC whose voice seemed, like Harriet's search for harmlessness towards living creatures, to be striving for a balance.

Through the window Harriet was attempting to improve on the view which was largely telephone lines, insipid suburban gardens and fences, rooftops unharmonious and clashing, unlike the roofs of Venice or Florence. She was reading *Venice Observed and The Stones of Florence,* a book that demanded slowness as if each sentence were a boiled sweet. Still in one of the front gardens there was a flowering jacaranda tree, absurd as a woman in a ballerina-length dress, inching towards the stave-like wires.

Rosa, who came from Strickland, came through the drawing room – a tightly stuffed sofa that looked fit to burst, two cane chairs, a card table and a low oak table that had been made by cutting down a dining table – carrying two art deco mugs. They sat on the worn swabs, still faintly green brocade, and sipped.

'The garden,' Harriet said. 'Perhaps I should make a schedule.'

'Useless,' Rosa replied, dreamily stretching a hand through the open window and plucking a pink hibiscus flower with a long yellow tongue.

'I suppose we could get someone to mow the lawns,' Harriet mused. 'A schoolboy.'

The lawn sloped down and the ancient handmower, discovered under the house, needed sharpening. They could have a house meeting, though the last one had been stilted and ended in making cocktails from whatever was available. But Rosa was not listening. Her profile, turned to Harriet, looked soft, almost cloudy, belying her reputation. For Rosa was famous for an incident that had occurred in Ouse when she was seventeen, beginning her nursing training at the cottage hospital, already setting her sights on Melbourne. She had rebuffed a young man, son of the owner of the local garage, in the most decided terms. And she had not cared that her put-down was all over town. He had come alongside her as she walked between the plane trees that bordered the main street, imagining herself on The Ramblas taking an evening stroll. Behind the shuttered windows – only the Malpas house had shutters or anything like grandeur – duennas kept guard.

'Would you like to go to the Ouse dance with me?' the young man had asked.

Rosa half turned, looked him over, head to foot.

'I'd rather meet an alligator in the dark than go dancing with you.'

'How could you? Be so rude,' Harriet had asked.

'The guy was a sap,' Rosa replied. 'Anyway, a clean cut is better than a lot of broken limbs.'

'Green fractures,' Harriet replied. 'I suppose he slunk off.'

'It was dusk. There was no need to spare anyone's blushes. Besides, I didn't turn my head.'

'What a good surgeon you would have made.'

But instead Rosa worked in an art gallery, where her dark good looks were an asset against white walls and her strong colour sense threatened timid landscapes. Not that The Flying Worm went in for timid landscapes. It aimed to provoke the academicians with their overworked, coolly observed land-scapes and still lifes and the occasional tentative nude in the manner of Lucien Freud, as if the sitter had to be pleased as well. Most of the exhibits were abstract, violent outpourings, barely held together by the unframed canvases; had the canvas not turned a corner and been stapled to a board, the colours might have spilled like a stain across the white walls. The artists were well read but careless in execution, as if they could skip centuries of tradition and begin where they liked.

'It would have made a painting,' Harriet suggested. The trees, the figure slinking away, slightly doubled as from a blow to the solar plexus. A wide narrow canvas, like a narrative.

'You're wasted on that accountant,' Rosa said. Then she uncurled herself from the window seat and went out into the garden.

It was lucky for the flatmates that Rosa gardened. She did not tell them that it frequently took half an hour's delving, rummaging and tugging at weeds before she could begin. Before the scents of crushed stalks and grass or whatever was hiding behind the weeds reached her heart in the same way her words had reached and cauterised the heart of the young man who had asked her to dance.

On weekday mornings Harriet walked along suburban streets until she reached the Victoria Market where she caught a tram. However fresh and pristine the morning, however amazing the colour of the jacaranda opposite, the stall holders were already hard at work, unpacking and setting up. If she had time Harriet bought an apple for her lunch or a bread roll. She wished she had time for a cup of coffee. But Mr Worboys, the accountant for whom she worked, was a stickler for punctuality and seemed to begrudge the fact she was good with figures, as if she had inherited a male brain. Their antipathy, well veiled, was mutual and Harriet was already planning to escape when something better came along.

Mr Worboys was just hanging up his hat when Harriet climbed the stairs of the dark varnished office in Corrs Lane, chosen, Harriet suspected, for location but considered unworthy of refurbishment. 'Well, Miss Betts,' he said, watching as she set her Granny Smith apple on the corner of her desk. 'We've a busy day ahead. A lot of the farm accounts have come in.'

Harriet imagined he could hardly wait for the end of the tax year when the phone rang non-stop and Geraldine, the receptionist, buzzed him constantly for advice about which clients were priority and which less significant ones could be deferred. Harriet almost felt like taking a bite of her apple there and then. Instead she sat at her desk and opened the first pile of folders, ready to add up columns of figures to estimate this year's income against last year's projections. He hires me because I am cheap and unqualified, she thought, inserting a new HB pencil in the pencil sharpener clamped to the side of the desk and giving it a savage twirl so the point snapped off.

Mr Worboys turned his head but made no comment. She might be good at mathematics but Miss Betts was still a woman, with all that implied: flightiness, fidgeting and, though he did not allow the thought, something to do with the cycles of the moon.

In her lunch hour Harriet walked along Bourke Street and looked in the windows of David Jones. Her salary was miserly and she intended after another few months had passed to ask for a raise. If it was not forthcoming she would hand in her notice, for her mother's legacy of skill with book-keeping was not the gift she would most wish to have received. The windows of David Jones were artful, with sections of bare tree to which had been added huge fake leaves in russet colours. Autumn was coming, though the Melbourne autumn, as far as Harriet could tell, was more a diminution than a definite season. Still David Jones and Myer's knew best and already the racks inside were proclaiming the new colours, usually two or three, and the accessories that went with them, the shoes and handbags. Even if one bought nothing and waited for winter to summon forth a heavy coat, the effect was to make whatever one possessed outdated and drab. So instead of going through the wide doors like an acolyte, Harriet walked on, enjoying the real surviving leaves on the plane trees, even if they looked a little tired as though they too could not escape the judgement.

She turned up Collins Street where the buildings were vast and grey and a glamorous hotel flew the flags of powerful nations. A doorman seemed to be controlling a queue of taxis which crept forward to his whistle. Somehow the flags produced not the triumph and esprit de corps that was intended but a sense of isolation in Harriet. She thought of herself as alone, though she imagined some might cite aunts or cousins or even remind her that deceased parents had at least been parents. That she was not one of those faces, indifferent to flies, gaunt to anything but a single expression, that stared from the rural section of *The Age*. Would having old parents have mattered? A black limousine drew up at the entrance of the hotel and a tall woman and a man got out and two small girls tumbled out of the back seat, their clothes replicas of their parents'. Americans, Harriet decided, to distance herself from envy. She had not eaten her sandwiches and she thought she might devote the afternoon to taking small nibbles under the beady eye of Mr Worboys. That would be a worthwhile project for a Thursday afternoon.

Rosa never wasted time staring at the windows of David Jones. She strode right in, head high, and made straight for the newest releases. But she seldom bought more than a basic item: a pleated ballerina-length skirt which could be crushed in the hands and spring up like grass or travel rolled in a cylinder. For a shirt she went to the Menswear Department and bought the smallest size with tails, and a black bow tie. Shirt tails hanging out were not thought of, but in her profession she could ape those who wore white coats. She was greatly taken by the idea of a stethoscope. Anything silver attracted her like a magpie.

Seated at her desk near the entrance of The Flying Worm, a title she considered pretentious, but since it had been dreamed up by the owner, Steffo Castelluccio, it would stay until succeeded by another inspiration, Rosa gazed out at the traffic along Flinders Lane. Her desktop she kept both clear and faintly chaotic; usually a sheaf of just-submitted prints or a pile of invitations lay there, but the impression they could be swept aside at any moment was strong. It was important to look busy and at the same time compatible.

The present exhibition, of intersecting sail shapes laboriously applied by palette knife, with a hint of sky above and sea below, did not appeal to Rosa but sales had been surprisingly good. She had quickly learned it was far more convincing to say very little, so that when she spoke each word seemed deliberate. She walked purposefully but unhurriedly towards the stockroom, which patrons would be surprised to see was a mess, with canvases crowded against the walls and even a few sculptures waiting to be collected. There was a bird bath Steffo had got for a song from an old country house in Red Hill. Its basin was filled with catalogues.

At present there were only two people in the gallery, a man and a woman, whom Rosa suspected were tourists. The woman looked uneasy, stepping up close to the canvases and then back, as if there was a magic point at which all would be revealed. This amused Rosa because the gallery was long and narrow: if the woman persisted, her back would soon touch the opposite wall. The man walked deliberately from canvas to canvas as if essaying what craft lay beneath each design. 'It looks like a catamaran,' Rosa overheard him say to the woman, who was probably thinking of the colour of her curtains or a blank wall. Most of their sales were to the ignorant, attracted by shape and colour. The Flying Worm was known for never offering bargain prices, for it was Steffo's philosophy that low prices produced a corresponding shrewdness in the buyer. And Rosa herself had experienced this, behaving with a certain cruel disdain to the man at the market who kept a stall of old photographs and postcards and pages which he termed prints but were in fact torn from old books.

Rosa got up languidly from her desk, carrying a pile of catalogues. She had a long yellow pencil, newly sharpened, behind one ear, and since her dark hair was scraped back it was a striking colour note. Very casually she stood alongside the woman, as if she too was taken by something in the canvas called *Knife VI*. It was one of the feeblest, and the artist a despicable little man with a face like a hairy rodent. Luckily he lived in the bush and seldom visited.

'I often stop and refresh my memory, though I work here all day,' Rosa said to the woman, lowering her voice as if they were in a conspiracy together.

'He has a fine sense of colour,' she continued when the woman glanced at her nervously and attempted a faint smile.

An absolute pig with the palette knife, Rosa was thinking. The sort of man I would not like to see slaughter an animal. Then she recollected he made a great fuss of being vegetarian. Nuts, roots and seeds, her internal dialogue continued. Berries.

'Very nice,' said the woman, and Rosa had to pull herself back to the present for she thought she had said 'berry'.

Half an hour later *Knife VI* was wearing a red dot, and the couple had been relieved of a deposit, warmly congratulated on their good taste and gently escorted to the door. They had never purchased a work of art before and as they made their dazed way towards Myer's for a cup of tea they could hardly believe their own boldness. For that is what Rosa had so successfully convinced them of: it was bad art, it would never increase in value, but they had been bold to buy it.

At 5 p.m. Rosa closed the door and drew down the blind that covered it. The air of the street soothed her somewhat and men turned to glance at her as she walked along. The yellow pencil was still behind her ear but it was not that that they looked at.

Harriet had decided on Melbourne after her matriculation year. No persuasion of her aunts or Mother Anastasia had been able to hold her. Her mother had given her life to Ouse, Harriet considered, revising her notion of her mother from minute to minute, attempting, now her own character was formed, to understand it. Betts's General Store – everyone considered that it was an unsuitable legacy for a girl – was sold to a man who owned a chain of stores and would not be forced to extend Maud's lines of credit. Not that any mention was made of that when Harriet met Mr Giltrap to exchange signatures and shake hands in the shop parlour he was already mentally redecorating.

Harriet's facility with book-keeping and her ability to type, learned in her last year at St Mary's, would easily secure her a job. She would have a one-way ticket on *The Princess of Tasmania*, unlike her mother who had returned after two weeks.

Of all the aunts, Emma was the most supportive, though her memories of Kuala Lumpur and rich Americans had sunk before the doting love of her son. Seeing her aunt lift Billy, who was too heavy for her and could easily have walked, Harriet felt she admired her own mother more. Reticence is a good heritage, she thought, after *The Princess* had sailed but Tasmania was still in sight. In her handbag she had the address of a family friend; her small suitcase contained a rigorous selection of her clothes. The rest had gone to a charity.

Ross Nayland would not have considered sharing his grand-mother's house at 77 Bouverie Street with two women when she was removed to a nursing home but, as he told Garth, women were natural home bodies. One each, he joked, and we may never need to make a bed or wash a plate. Garth was less certain, especially when Rosa Prouse was one of the women. Still so many women's fledgling careers were just that: a man would appear, and a kind of play and display would be over. In the meantime, hands hovered over typewriter keys or took shorthand (the legs discreetly crossed, the toe pointing towards the floor), arranged things in files, and women sighed, as if a calamity had struck, when the filing cabinet was in disarray.

In the mornings the Melbourne streets were full of young and old men and young women walking purposefully or clinging to tram straps, all lightly – excluding the old men – eyeing one another. Rosa could have told Garth that far from having lowered eyes the older men were the most avid and she was frequently asked to have coffee or dinner or, more inven-tively, to inspect a room where a painting might hang. Rosa struck Garth as making the best use of the time that should elapse before matrimony, whereas Harriet, though attractive in her way, seemed not to have grasped the principles. A short gaiety, a showing of wares, and then settling to support a man's career with budgeting and children and discreet dinners or card parties. These last, for his imagination always leapt ahead in cartoon-like frames or advertising stills, would be intimate friends to whom one would slowly reveal oneself. He did not take it further and consider it a setting for wife swapping, but the idea hung about under the cloth-covered table where legs gently nudged a good hand.

But Rosa forthrightly refused to do any dishes but her own, to iron a shirt in an emergency or even advise on how to remove a stain. She would cook when she felt like it and they could share or live off the leftovers for a few days. But whether this would be on Wednesday or Sunday she refused to say. 'You have a lot to learn about women,' she informed Ross as he followed her down the path on their way to the tram.

When Ross visited his grandmother, surly in his presence but secretly beginning to enjoy herself in her rest home, he did not mention the two women, only Garth whom he described as an account executive. Stocks and bonds were respectable in his grandmother's eyes and she seemed to bestow her blessing. But it was her policy, unconscious or not, to say little about the house in which she had passed her married life: her removal had caused heartache to as many people as possible and there she was content to leave it. Had Ross dared to introduce Rosa, they might have understood one another very well.

After the long-drawn-out hour was up and Ross felt he had gazed at every item in his grandmother's room for more than his fill, he said his ritual farewell, pressing his lips lightly to the two cheeks she turned as if avoiding contact. I hope I don't live so long, he thought, as he walked towards a tram that would take him back to Flinders Street. He thought of Harriet telling the young man in the drycleaners to water his pot plant, and smiled. Rosa had passed it on, probably thinking it the bright spot of a day. He might do something similar, to take away the taste of a life husbanded like his grandmother's. A woman was coming towards him wearing a wide-brimmed hat with a bunch of artificial fruit on the brim. He swerved a little towards her as they came closer. 'Can I say I like your hat,' he began. 'Say what you like,' she replied. Instead of feeling flustered – his grandmother had anchored him in death – he threw back his head and laughed. Then, for no reason, he broke into a run, his tie floating back over his shoulder like a tail.

That afternoon an irate farmer from Moe dumped a sack of bills, receipts, mortgage repayments, insurances in Mr Worboys' front office. Harriet could hear the altercation through the wall: that the government was bleeding him dry as the drought and they could both go to hell. Then the office door slammed and a red-faced broad-shouldered man shot down the stairs. Mr Worboys carried the sack which smelled of fertiliser into Harriet's office. 'Sort this, will you,' he instructed. 'See if you can bring a bit of order to it, then I'll look at it.' At least it was a change from writing bills and reminders.

When Mr Worboys had returned to slam the door of his office, Harriet upended the sack in the clear space on the floor. Rat-gnawed papers and bills perforated by a spike fell out. There were thumbprints on some and something worse on others. When she had them in a reasonable pile she went and washed her hands. She was still squatting on the floor when Mr Worboys came to retrieve his hat and overcoat from the hat stand. There were four piles: Income, Expenses, Improvements, Depreciation; the sack, neatly folded in case the man should reclaim it, was against the wainscot. The order she was bringing seemed miraculous to Harriet, as if she were lost in a dream. Already the client had lost his unpleasant characteristics: the shouting and swearing were signs of distress and fear. She had pulled out of the sack not merely bills and demands but the image of a farm flattened by drought and water rationing, a pale anxious wife and dry-haired children. Even the dog would be subdued.

The next morning the piles of paper were still on the floor and Mr Worboys practically fell over Harriet as he came through the door.

'There's no need to go to too much trouble,' he said, wondering if he'd hired a fanatic.

'I'm good at maths,' Harriet offered, with a bill in one hand.

'Well, bring it to my office later,' he replied, hardly knowing how to look.

When she went to the washroom at noon Harriet glanced at her face in the tarnished mirror. Her eyes gleamed and her hair was tousled. I'm not content, she thought, though at the time she was flooded with contentment.

She marched the papers into Mr Worboys' office and, not expecting a word of thanks, which was wise, turned on her heel.

Garth, two blocks away at Armadillos Advertising Agency in Little Lonsdale Street, was looking out the window of his office just as Harriet, going for a walk in her lunch hour, passed underneath. He waved and then tapped on the glass, and she looked up. He leaned out further, over the fire escape, and called to her to come up.

'Have you eaten?' he asked when she had climbed the stairs and they were standing by the draughting table. 'I can offer you coffee.'

'Coffee will be fine,' Harriet said, aware of other people in the room and their discreet interest.

'Good morning?' he asked, bringing a bottle of milk and a cobalt blue cup decorated with triangles.

'The worst,' Harriet replied. 'I've breached some unwritten law. A woman should know her place. She shouldn't be able to handle a column of figures.' For Harriet had added totals on slips of yellow paper, assuredly a presumption.

'A woman should keep her place,' Garth said. 'That's the way we like it. It makes our own place, however humble, desirable.'

But Harriet was putting the morning behind her and looking down at Garth's sketches spread out on the desk: a bottle that suggested the shape of a broad-shouldered man, except the head was more like a block of wood, and a label containing the slogan.

'It's a tonic,' Garth said. 'A tablespoon a day and you're Tarzan in no time.'

'And will you be taking some yourself?'

'Heavens no. It tastes revolting. Probably full of tar or something. Still, to achieve a body like this. . .'

The body below the block-like head was light-stippled and silky. Harriet ran a finger over the paper.

'That's the idea,' Garth said, approvingly. 'Drink half a dozen bottles of this and women will stroke you.'

'And the head, being so wooden, implies that the body is separate from the mind.'

'Oh the head will have a few light brushstrokes to suggest features. We wouldn't want to appeal only to body builders. It's the idea of what's under the business suit when it comes off.'

'And do women drink the stuff too?'

'Of course. Half a tablespoon for women. You can read that in the small print.'

When Harriet said nothing more, Garth asked if she thought Rosa would cook that evening.

'I can't say,' she replied, looking at her watch. 'I really must get back.' There would just be time to get a sandwich at the little bar where you chose your own fillings. Some days even that seemed too difficult.

Garth came to the bottom of the stairs with her.

'You've gone silent,' he said. 'Was I talking too much?'

'No,' Harriet said, turning to smile at him. 'I think the idea of that tonic, half a tablespoon, has given me strength. I'll see you tonight.'

Lettuce and tomato, she thought, as she walked up Little Bourke Street. Cheese and pickle, cheese and raw onion rings to scent the breath in case Mr Worboys summoned her to his office.

Rosa was in the garden when they returned that evening, weeding around a rose bush.

The scent of 'Abraham Darby', recognised only by Rosa herself, hung in the air. Harriet and Garth came up the path together, panting like dogs.

'You sound as if you need a pat and a rub down,' Rosa remarked.

'Please,' said Garth. Then he raised his nostrils like a hound and made a baying sound.

'What's cooking?' he asked.

'Just some old bones,' Rosa replied, but already Garth was inside the door and racing for the kitchen. He pulled open the oven door, and, overriding the old baked-on odours, the roast dinners of time past – no one had yet been appointed to clean the oven and no one had volunteered – rose the delectable scents of meat and vegetables, a distinct perfume of leeks, of which Rosa was inordinately fond, the roasted fruits of the earth. I should marry this woman, Garth thought, as he raced to tear off his despised tie and splash water on his face. Then, on a commendable impulse, he was out the front door again, tearing a pound note from his pocket, bound for the corner pub and a bottle of Seppelts Great Western burgundy.

They sat around the dining room table and Ross wondered if his grandmother had witnessed such a feast. He considered it unlikely: if she could rise from her rest-home bed she would send them packing into the street. Probably some biblical curse would follow.

Harriet had unearthed a candlestick, and two inches of candle flickered and dribbled like slow tears. In the centre of the table the glorious casserole cooled; Ross had poked about in it for bits of bone from which the flesh had fallen. Not through starvation but largesse, like the prodigal. Rosa held a bone between her fingers as if she was measuring cloth; a dribble of golden oil ran down her chin. For dessert they ate pears and cheese with the rind cut off.

I should propose, Garth thought. He could fling back his chair, fall to his knees and crawl to where Rosa sat in her long skirt. He could seize her hand, lightly coated in oil, and press it to his lips. And for his pains she would probably clock him across the head, the way women did in movies. A sharp slap which required of Cary Grant or Rock Hudson a face of granite. Only the merest surprise was expressed in the disarrangement of flesh. A few seconds later and the same man might be solicitously proffering a silver cigarette case or nursing a flame between cupped hands. There was a lot of standing on either side of cold mantelpieces, or in front of them if a serious statement was required.

Rosa caught him looking at her and raised her eyebrows.

'I feel we are going to be asked to do something,' Ross said. 'Not for nothing does Rosa cook.'

'Why ever not?' said Harriet, and there was a touch of indignation in her voice. Mr Worboys had left a notice on the door of his office saying he was going home earlier than usual and asking her to lock up. She thought he could not bear to offer a word of praise.

Ross cut the remaining piece of cheese in two and then into small squares. He popped them in his mouth as if they were grapes.

'I fell down on dessert,' Rosa said sweetly, 'but I wanted to finish a patch of weeding.'

'Have you ever considered marriage?' Garth asked now he felt safe. He had hoped for a final piece of cheese.

'In general terms, no,' she replied. 'But each candidate would require a response. Are you one of them?'

'And would the responses be individual? Tailored to the man?'

'I presume so,' she replied, and her voice took on a dreamy dangerous tone. 'One would expect to match the tone, the length, the nervousness or otherwise. Even the future of the suitor, his future hopes.'

'Of course,' said Ross, suddenly seeing the wreckage of the table through his grandmother's eyes. 'Isn't that the most awful form of female arrogance? Consigning someone to the B team or the C.'

'Why, I don't know how many proposals you've offered and had rejected,' Rosa said. 'But since you are still in the market I must presume a few. After all, it's the bourne from which no traveller returns.'

'And you make your rejects sound as if they're taking a

parachute jump with a faulty chute.'

'Come,' said Harriet. 'What was really the purpose of the dinner, Rosa? It seems to be some kind of truth wine we are drinking.'

'I'm sorry,' said Rosa. 'The idea of marriage is like a red rag to a bull. I wanted to invite you all to a gallery opening. There is nothing on offer but pretentious people, wine and cheese.'

'Whew,' said Ross to Garth the next morning as they were walking to the tram. 'If that's what it takes to get a decent meal from a female.'

Garth, dragging his feet, had a stomach ache. Flirtation he was accustomed to, but Rosa's remarks had an edge. And it seemed her domestic efforts – a spot of weeding by the front door, a casserole and the table laid – had a purpose. Men were simplicity itself when it came to their mental processes. They simply decided in any given situation what they would reveal: the character could be held far back, but it was not substantially altered, as seemed the case with women. On a bad day such as this, facing a staff meeting and probably reprimands all around, a man could simply limit himself to monosyllables, whereas with Rosa it would have to be a full-blown performance. They spoke about feelings, but their own were often fake. Then he thought of Harriet and was slightly mollified. She sounded as unhappy in her job as he was. But around Rosa, if the same law applied to women as to men, if the dominant was taken as the guide, what hope did she have? At least in the face of doctrine a man reserved something of himself.

Then the tram screeched to a halt and Garth saw that he would have to stand. He looked around at the faces, most of them attempting a morning brightness as if the day could hold something. Only a few older women looked fatalistic, glad of simple pleasures like finding a seat.

The tram seemed to beat its way along the streets, which was odd because the rails were there. Garth rocked and rolled on the balls of his feet and knew he should concentrate. The moment he got to the office he would go to the washroom and take some Alka Seltzer. And at the meeting he would say practically nothing.

Sometimes Harriet got news from Ouse. None of her aunts were great letter writers: they wrote on small sheets of lined paper, which to Harriet suggested inhibition. The subjects were weather, health, and news of people she had practically forgotten. Once there was a letter from Father Stanislaus which filled Harriet with an inexplicable rage. Then she saw the writing was crabbed and he was probably an old man. Nothing remained of the systems under which she had been raised: her mother's acceptance of a church that was foreign to her but which she had accepted so whole-heartedly or passively – Harriet never knew which – that her death had seemed like something prescribed. *I know your dear mother would wish you remembered in her anniversary mass*, Father Stanislaus had written. A little card with a prayer to St Jude had fallen out of the letter and Harriet tore it in half without thinking, like a hound wringing the neck of a pheasant.

Still there were times when the house in Bouverie Street seemed insubstantial, in spite of its clutter and the order she had attempted to introduce. The day after Rosa's feast, when everyone had been hungover or bad tempered, Harriet had had to clear sauce-encrusted plates before she could face a glass of water. She sat on the window seat looking out at the garden where a light rain was beginning to fall. Rosa's patch of weeding was nothing more than a scrabbling in the jungle; already the mignonette was dropping its seeds onto the cleared ground. Her mother's sense of order, though Harriet had only known its effects, had something appealing about it. She would reply to Father Stanislaus, she decided, but it would be a secular card so he should be in no doubt. The nuns, so practical in the main, were inordinately fond of representations of puppies and kittens. Sister Lucy would place a kiss on a drawing of a kitten entangled in a ball of wool.

A door banged and Ross appeared, and shortly after Garth

followed. From Rosa's room there was silence, but Rosa could always sleep in because The Flying Worm did not open until 10 a.m.

In the end only Harriet accompanied Rosa to the exhibition opening. Mr Worboys had been in a sour mood all day, closeted in his office and speaking in monosyllables. Harriet's attempts at initiative had only worsened things. Occasionally now Mr Worboys prefaced a request with a snide suggestion. 'Since you are so numerate, Miss Betts, you might like to . . .' or 'Perhaps if it doesn't go to your head you could . . .' What edifice have I threatened, she wondered. Garth and Ross had both made excuses. Ross was seeing the daughter of a stockbroker, but apart from letting her know he owned property he had no intention of introducing her to Harriet or Rosa. They spent their evenings, when he could afford it, dining out or going to the theatre.

But when Harriet arrived at The Flying Worm Rosa did not seem in need of any support at all. She caught Harriet's eye as she stood just inside the door, looking about uncertainly, but made no effort to detach herself from a group of young men who were standing about smoking. There was a paint-stained tea trolley near the desk, with glasses in rows, so Harriet helped herself to a very thin-tasting red wine that no airing had been able to assist. She took a sheet of paper which represented the catalogue and walked about trying to connect the works to the titles. *Biarritz,* she read. *Venezia, Guadalupe, Qumran. Qumran* was predominantly yellow with mauve and blue slashes.

Eventually Rosa detached herself from the back of the room and came towards Harriet. Her face was excessively animated, her eyes glowed and she looked fervent.

'You will stay,' she said in a low voice. 'You won't go home without me.'

'How long will you be?' Harriet enquired.

'Another hour or two,' Rosa said. 'The owner is going to close up.'

'I won't go without telling you,' Harriet promised, but her

eyes swept the gallery for somewhere to sit and found one spindly chair occupied by a very elderly woman draped in black, with two high spots of rouge like a Pierrette. I could sink to the floor, Harriet thought, as that young man in the corner has done, sinking down as though overwhelmed by the work. The young man was writing something in a notebook. Still she kept steadily on – *Cape Verde, Kosciusko* – trying to find a common thread and deciding only that someone had consulted a gazetteer. Mr Worboys might feel the same about depreciation or current liabilities. Or Garth gazing out the window of Armadillos, seeking inspiration for a purgative.

Eventually she was standing with her toes almost touching the young man who kept writing without looking up. Suddenly he shot a leg out and Harriet was pushed backwards a step.

'I say,' he said in a soft girlish voice. 'Awfully sorry. Just stretching. Care to take a pew?'

So Harriet settled against the wall and instantly felt more charitable. She did not like to reach down and rub her shin, but her back felt supported. From a distance *Samarkand* glowed and seemed to have some purpose.

'What do you think of the titles?' Harriet asked when several minutes had passed.

'Too evocative, too heavy. Too much of a burden like an overladen bee.'

There was another silence, but since they had not been introduced Harriet felt unfazed.

'What are you writing in your notebook?' she asked, slightly turning her head to look at his profile.

'Key words,' he said. 'Sometimes they come to me in places like this. Do you know what rhadamanthine means?'

'That was the poet, Lucien Humfress,' Rosa said next morning. Luckily it was Australia Day and the effects of the red wine could wear off. 'He comes from a very wealthy family, near Hamilton. The first poet in a long line of ranchers.'

'He said he only likes complicated words. That they are the

only ones with truth in them. Anything else is too crude.'
Several times during the evening the poet had written another
word in his notebook.

'You should be honoured he spoke to you. He hardly ever
speaks to anyone. He finds their use of words offensive.'

Harriet racked her brain to recall if she had used anything
above a middle-sized word but she could think of nothing. But
they had both been comfortable to be silent and perhaps the
poet had considered that unthreatening.

'Does he publish much?' Harriet asked, pouring herself
another cup of tea.

'Hardly at all. He doesn't approve of literary magazines
either. I think some of his work has appeared in *Meanjin*.'

'And his parents disapprove?' Harriet asked.

'His father has offered to horsewhip him but his mother
dotes on him. She sends him an allowance.'

'I think he said something about an overladen bee,' Harriet
said, 'but I can't remember in what connection.'

'Well he certainly seems to have talked to you. A whole
sentence is a rarity. You must have made quite an impression.'
Rosa cast her eyes at what of Harriet's figure was visible. 'Of
course you are somewhat flat chested. He may have regarded
you as a boy.'

But Harriet, registering the slight edge of spite, did not rise
to the bait. Instead she got up, stretched herself to her fullest
height, which was five feet three and a quarter inches, and
began clearing the table. Rosa's black and rose-patterned robe,
half a rose to a shoulder, one rose to a breast – there were five
altogether – counting the back, showed a cleavage like a ripe
peach. But Harriet's father, her own Chips Rafferty, since his
real face had now faded, had always counselled her to regard
life as a whole. 'Too many people go for bits of triumph,' he
had told her. Perhaps Rosa was having one of those now.

The day stretched in front of Harriet and she did not intend
to spend it with Rosa who would probably lie about like a
concubine. She thought she just might walk as she had in the
first weeks in Melbourne, like a hunting dog finding its

territory. Then she had walked in all directions, trying to get her bearings, quelling her fears of ever surviving in such a large city. But they were just people, she told herself, going about their business, killing time as she was, trying to pretend they counted, that the surface of the earth was made for them. She had made landmarks for herself: a jacaranda tree, a church steeple, a Returned Services League where red-faced men spilled onto the pavement and someone called her 'Girlie'. She taught herself to look into the faces of the people she passed, just a light unthreatening glance, quickly gliding off, as her mother had looked into the faces of her customers, gauging their ability to pay, their honourableness or otherwise. Her mother was always looking for old-fashioned virtues, Harriet thought. Quite a few people aspired to thrift, but it was hardly major: something like Rosa in her dressing gown, only in reverse. As for the extravagant ones, her mother had introduced the idea of austerity, frowning over some of the purchases, and, if they regarded the frown, rewarding them instantly with extra buns which she pretended were a little stale or pressing a cornet of sweets on a child with a tear-stained face.

The week before Harriet had received a letter from Emma. Billy was coming to Melbourne on a school trip: could Harriet find time to see him, perhaps devote an evening to him. Harriet thought of this as she walked: a thirteen-year-old boy, probably over-indulged as only-children were. Then she amended her thought, for she herself was one. She walked east for an hour or more, tired and sluggish at first, then her feet seemed to find their rhythm and she felt tireless, light. But when tiredness returned it came suddenly. She was outside a suburban church of white wood with a steeple made of overlapping tiles. The door was red and approached by three broad steps. Harriet climbed them as if they were a mountain. There was no one inside, just a light altered by stained glass and stillness. The wooden pews had hand-embroidered kneelers, each signed with an initial. *E.I.B.* Harriet read, before she sank to her knees on one. She did not pray; she imagined she was preparing her knees for the return journey. Then she sat and leafed through the hymn book, trying to recall if she had a favourite. Then, refreshed, she walked for a little while among the twenty or so tombstones that surrounded the church like white leghorn fowls. She read a few inscriptions and noticed not one was unloved.

Billy Lascelles duly arrived on *The Princess of Tasmania*. Harriet did not go to meet him, knowing he had her business address in Corrs Lane as well as her home phone number. When she did not hear anything – the school visit was for a week – she presumed he was happy with his billet and was being shown around.

But on the third day of his stay, late in the afternoon, as Harriet was attending to the day's filing, Billy appeared at the office, cherubic-faced, grim-jawed, and stated he would not spend another night with the Renshaws. The Renshaws, Harriet was informed, were a bunch of misers, he was practically half-starved and he didn't care if he got caned by the accompanying master, Mr Partridge. Mrs Renshaw, Billy went on, sensing Harriet's exasperated sympathy, was a fat cow who never lifted a finger; her repulsive daughters, who were covered in freckles, did the cooking when they got home from school; Mr Renshaw drank and hardly cared what he ate so long as it was some dead animal – though the way the daughters cooked no one could be sure. Harriet repressed a smile, and, as Mr Worboys came out of the office, introduced Billy to him. There were only ten minutes to closing time so Billy might as well wait.

'But isn't there a son?' Harriet enquired when they were walking towards the tram. 'The reason for your being billeted there?'

'Oh he's the worst of the lot,' Billy replied in a confident voice. He had recognised the signs of feminine weakness. 'He's got freckles *and* acne. His head's shaped like an egg. All he cares about are postage stamps.' And he made a noise like someone clearing phlegm from his throat.

Harriet contacted first the family who seemed remarkably unconcerned – simply another mouth at the table – and then the teacher who was decidedly more serious. She assured him that Billy would be safe with her, that he would report for class visits to museums and galleries, and that she would guarantee he would be ready to leave with the class on Friday. But when she put the phone down she felt like the wolf with stones in its belly – that was the effect Billy had – and she remembered that for two days she was working and there would be hours to fill. She made up a camp bed for Billy in her room, shielded by a screen borrowed from Rosa. She would be like a night nurse, lightly sleeping by a patient, only in this case Billy had the cot. Probably, if his speech and mannerisms were anything to go by, he would make hideous noises in his sleep.

'You wouldn't prefer to sleep in the laundry?' Harriet asked, but he said he was used to sleeping with women.

'He could sleep with me, if he likes,' Rosa said. 'I could do with a manservant and they are best trained young.'

'Do you know what the wife of a sultan is called?' he asked Rosa. 'A sultana.'

'It is usually polite to pause a little before giving the answer. As a matter of fact I did know. What's the wife of a pasha?'

They carried on like this for most of the evening until Harriet finally shooed Billy to bed, reminding him of a trip the next morning to the Museum of Applied Science. He had refused to have a bath but promised to give his ears and the back of his neck a lick.

'Don't forget your teeth,' Rosa called. 'A man must have sweet breath.' Tomorrow they would collect his clothes from the Renshaws.

Billy tossed and turned on the camp bed and once, when Harriet eased herself into a sitting position, she saw an arm flung out, the fingers trailing on the floor. He looked defenceless in sleep, the absurdly long eyelashes Rosa had envied resting as lightly as spiders on his flushed cheeks. He breathed with his mouth slightly open, a tiny rim of teeth showing.

Harriet switched off her lamp and lay back, knowing sleep

was unlikely to return. The connection with her family made her feel uneasy; it was like a problem below as well as one above. The problem above was Mr Worboys, who spent more and more time with his door shut. He seemed to be drinking; one morning last week there had been a definite hint of whisky when Harriet took in his morning tea. She could offer to do more but his manner towards her was now brusque. Still, Harriet consoled herself, there were other jobs: perhaps her first choice had been too conservative. She could go to night school or WEA classes. It was ludicrous to imagine the smooth running of the world could be infinitesimally advanced by a novice book-keeper. She looked down at Billy again and with a sigh he threw his whole body into a turn. The little camp bed groaned and rocked, then settled on thin legs.

But in the morning Billy was as bright as a new pin. He stood beside Rosa at the kitchen bench as she squeezed oranges. He set the table in a higgledy-piggledy fashion and laughed when she chastised him. He put brown sugar on his buttered toast and took the top off his egg with a sabre-like stroke of his knife.

'Can you say "The great grey greasy Limpopo River"?' he asked Rosa.

'Certainly,' she replied, 'but not with my mouth full.' Then she repeated it in lugubrious accents. 'It flows into a river called the Krokodil. Did you know that?'

'Of course I did. We're studying Africa this term.'

'What's the plan for today?' Harriet asked.

'Some boring museum and then the Shrine of Remembrance,' Billy replied. 'All dead things. Dead, dead, dead.'

'And you, Billy, are so alive,' said Rosa as she stood at the sink in her rose robe. 'Don't you think they were alive once, those dead things?'

'I suppose schoolboys have always thought this way,' said Harriet, as though they were conducting a duologue. 'A Victorian boy might have despised a water closet but admired a steam train. Didn't worshippers lie down on the tracks before them in India?'

'You mean they got run over by trains?' Billy asked, looking up from pulverising his eggshell. 'They must have been mad.'

'The illustrations never showed that,' Harriet went on, and Rosa nodded sagely.

'Just the approach of the god and the worshippers,' she said dreamily as if the idea could be infinitely applied.

Harriet and Billy left together and took the tram. 'You know where to go,' she said as he waited to climb down. He just nodded his head and she thought there was something numb and defenceless in the gesture. 'See you tonight,' she called.

The idea of hiding under the 'C' class steam locomotive in the Museum of Applied Science came to Billy later in the morning. Mr Partridge had barked at him, 'Don't hang back, boy. Keep up where you can hear the commentary.' The museum guide, obviously put out by a collection of motley boys, was droning on about the inventor of the Thomson Steam Car. 'Who'd want to meet him,' Billy thought. He nudged Carruthers, the boy next to him, and he stumbled into the boy in front. There was a little commotion and a beady stare from Mr Partridge as the group righted themselves. That'll teach them to talk about boilers and condensers, Billy thought. He might dig an elbow into Carruthers, right in the centre of his back like a dagger thrust.

C10 was so like a hippopotamus. Billy laid a hand on its boiler and tried to imagine its heart. A hippopotamus was supposed to possess a turn of speed once it got warmed up by an idea – someone stepped in front of its offspring or obscured its view of prey. It was the work of seconds to slip underneath and then lie down flat on the cool floor. He could hear the footsteps of the little group as they moved away. He thought, with his ear pressed to the floor, there was a faint commotion and Mr Partridge's voice saying something that sounded like 'On his own head.'

In the late afternoon Billy climbed the stairs to Harriet's office. She saw his hair sticking up, making a porcupine shape, where the frosted panel began. His face was grubby and his school uniform unkempt. Getting out from under C10 had proved more difficult than getting under. He slithered out feet first, and then, when the security guard was luckily engaged elsewhere, eased his body out until he seemed to be lying prone to admire the little plaque that was attached. *Built in 1918 . . . the most powerful locomotive in Australia.* If someone came near he was going to say he was a trainspotter. He could write the serial number and the patent number in his notebook. But when no one stirred or shouted at him he got into a crouch like someone looking for a lost coin, and then to his feet. He walked out with a group of old men, avoiding the guard's eye.

Then he used his daily allowance of pocket money to get on several trams: one that went to the zoo, though he didn't get off in case there had been a change of plan and live animals were now on the programme, and another that went along Bourke Street which he remembered was close to Harriet's office. He couldn't remember what Rosa's gallery was called. But first he bought himself two buns with strawberry icing sprinkled with coconut, which he ate sitting on a bench. Several passersby looked at him curiously and he suspected he had coconut crumbs on his face.

'Why are you here?' was Harriet's greeting, hardly appropriate, Billy felt, to the ingenuity he had shown.

'I'll tell you later,' Billy said.

Mr Worboys came out of his office and raised his eyebrows. 'The Tilsey account,' he asked. 'Let me have it when you've got the time.'

'I think you'd better go downstairs,' Harriet said, reaching under her desk for her purse. 'I hope I can trust you, Billy. There's an ice-cream parlour four doors along. It's called Blue Moon. Go in there and have a milkshake or an ice-cream sundae. Don't move. You can make it last half an hour. If you can't, buy a bottle of fizz. I don't want you to stir until I get there.'

At 5 p.m. Harriet came downstairs, heart heavy, and walked along to the Blue Moon. She half-expected Billy to have fled and all the problems that would entail – Mr Partridge, Emma, possibly even the police – but there he was in a cream-painted booth, stirring the last dregs of a sundae as if he hoped to wear away the glass dish.

She saw it was useless to chide; his tiredness was palpable. They sat silently side by side on the wooden seats of the Coburg tram and when they got off they walked in silence. The house was empty and Harriet felt grateful: she shooed Billy off to have a bath and opened a can of spaghetti. She buttered two slices of toast and poured a big glass of milk. He was in bed before Rosa and the others returned, laid flat on his camp bed as if he lacked the energy to turn.

'What a little brat,' Ross said. 'If ever I have children they won't behave like that.'

'I expect they won't,' said Rosa, who had blown in from another exhibition opening with two hardly touched bottles of wine. 'They'll probably be just like you.' Ross was aping his girlfriend's family and becoming more conservative by the hour. He was becoming, Rosa said to Harriet, like some ugly piece of antique furniture, taking up space with its own importance.

'Besides,' Rosa went on, taking off a red beret which she wore at an absurd angle, 'I like Billy. I like him very much. If *I* ever have a son I hope he will be like that. I hope he will squeeze under a locomotive and find his way about Melbourne.'

'It's a wonder he wasn't picked up by the police or a truancy officer,' Ross went on.

'What will you do now, Harriet?' Garth asked.

'I'm trying to think,' Harriet said. She had had a wearisome day and her head was beginning to ache. 'Contact Mr Partridge again, I expect. Find out about the arrangements for getting him home. Take him down to the wharf.'

'Handcuffed, I hope,' said Ross with a nasty laugh.

'Aren't you going out?' Rosa asked. 'I thought you were seeing the fair Gwendoline tonight?'

'Not Gwendoline. It's Gwyneth.'

'It gets worse and worse,' Rosa replied, leisurely lighting a cigarette, preparatory to blowing a few smoke rings.

When Ross had gone, Rosa went over to Harriet and put an arm around her shoulders. 'You look all done in, kid,' she said. 'I'll do it, if you like. Beard the teacher and find out the arrangements. I'll do it in my gallery voice. Just wait until I coat my vocal chords in a little more nicotine.'

So Harriet went to bed early and Rosa brought a glass of warm milk on a saucer. She sat on the edge of the bed, eyes gleaming, and said Billy was to forgo the rest of the programme and be at the wharf to board *The Princess* for the 6 p.m. sailing the day after tomorrow. His behaviour would be discussed when they returned to school.

'I invented some mitigating circumstances,' Rosa laughed. 'The fear and awe of a big city and the effect it might have on a sensitive soul. I told him sensitive souls are often hidden by bravado. I think he bought that. I flattered him by implying he was one too.'

Rosa took the afternoon off – the gallery walls were being painted in preparation for a stock show – and went to the wharf to continue what she considered her unconsummated flirtation with the unsighted Mr Partridge. She found a rather severe man, above average height, with a lined forehead and an expression of long-eroded optimism. But few men could resist Rosa's charms and before long she had tucked an arm through his and led him a little apart from the group.

Harriet and Billy walked the length of *The Princess* – it did not take long – and on to the end of the wharf. The sea was pale grey and choppy; seagulls screeched and the ship's horn sounded.

'I suppose you'll tell my mother,' Billy said, and his voice was low.

'Only a little. Nothing to alarm her. Just that you spent a few days with us.'

'I really like Rosa. And you,' he added hastily. 'I expect she'll help with old Partridge.'

'I expect she will,' Harriet replied, 'but you mustn't always expect it. That there will be someone. There are not many Rosas in the world.'

'I know,' he said, looking at his feet. He wanted to say that he knew Harriet was steadier, but he hadn't the words. 'I'm glad you're my cousin.'

'Me too,' Harriet said. Then she asked, 'Did Rosa sign your autograph book for you?'

Instantly he brightened and pulled it from his blazer pocket. A great deal of sponging and steaming had been required to bring the blazer up to standard. *He was a Rat*, Rosa had written.

> *He was a rat, and she was a rat,*
> *And down in a hole they did dwell,*
> *And both were as black as a witch's cat,*
> *And they loved each other well.*

Harriet's was, and she thought it not inferior or less apposite:

> *How doth the little crocodile*
> *Improve his shining tail;*
> *And pour the waters of the Nile*
> *On every golden scale!*

Mr Partridge made a motion with his hand, *The Princess* tooted a small-scale toot and with a final squeeze of her hand Billy ran forward. Then she stood side by side with Rosa, who blew kisses along her palm. The palm was slightly angled to lift them upward. Mr Partridge waved and nodded.

'We should have brought streamers,' Rosa said. 'I think things will be okay with Mr Partridge.'

Dear Aunt Emma, Harriet wrote that evening. *You may have heard from Billy's schoolmaster, Mr Partridge, that Billy absented himself from part of his class's visit to Melbourne. He stayed with me and was no trouble. I hope there will be no trouble when he gets home. Museums do not suit everyone.* There the pen stopped, as though the artifice was too great; vaguely Harriet remembered her mother had been impatient with Emma. *Billy must be a joy,* the pen wrote, *if a high-spirited one. I'm sure he will remember his trip to Melbourne. Give him my love.* Then she put the letter aside. She would ask Rosa to bring home a card from the gallery. The brief message would look better on that, and Rosa could scrawl her name at the bottom.

Ross had grown more disapproving during the months he had been dating Gwyneth Foyle. Rosa particularly was a target. The gallery, her association with artists, might have been overlooked if Rosa was meticulous in other ways. But the way she had of breakfasting in her robe, her outlandish cooking where his about-to-be fiancée's was classical (she was taking a cordon bleu class), her uninhibitedness – he would never trust Gwyneth with a visit while Rosa was in residence – all aroused his ire.

Rosa responded with sighs and sarcasms, implying he was on the wrong side of a divide. 'Can't you see he wants to sell,' she protested to Harriet. 'A capitalist must start somewhere and it's his grandmother's house. It's the reversal of the old dowry position: the worthy but impoverished suitor needs a small bag of gold as a down-payment. Besides, he's such a fool. He doesn't realise I know Gwyneth. She's been to the gallery and so has her mother.'

Harriet remembered the tall fair-haired young woman the next time she went to an opening. Her amazingly fair hair, almost too pale to be blonde, hung almost to her waist: in the front it was centre-parted, dividing the perfectly symmetrical face into two Gwyneths. 'No face is totally symmetrical,' Rosa pointed out, 'but Gwyneth's comes close.'

The exhibition – portraits – was an improvement on the palette-knife abstracts. Working drawings were displayed on a rough trestle table, and the patrons were invited to pick these up and compare them to the completed work which was mockingly gold-framed. A small glass case, useful for resting glasses of wine on, contained stained brushes and an old palette. It reminded Harriet of a face that had had heavy make-up applied since youth. She looked around for the poet but it was only when she wandered into the stockroom for a rest – the correct phrases in which to admire a painting never came to mind, and portraits, which might have been easier, were no different – that she found him lying up against a pile of old canvases.

'Have you thought up any more words?' she asked him, wishing she too could sink to the floor.

'Words?' he asked, looking suspiciously at her. 'Do you mean word or words? There's a considerable difference, I would have thought.'

'Why, word to begin with, I suppose.'

'That's harder,' he replied. 'A torrent, such as you get yonder'– gesturing towards the doorway where small unconvincing clusters of bodies formed and broke up again – 'is what most people desire. One word in a hundred can hide among them.'

'I'm sure it must be tiring,' Harriet observed, 'to put such a strain on them.' She was beginning to feel like Alice in Wonderland.

'Would you sleep with me?' the poet asked. 'Would you prefer to be asked in French and from a recumbent position?'

When Harriet looked doubtful he gave a harsh laugh. 'I was just trying to show you a sentence that counts. The offer can stand indefinitely.'

'And having made an offer in a few words, you feel satisfied,' Harriet protested. 'What about the other party?'

'That's their business. They can get any collection of words together they choose. They're not rationed, if you haven't noticed. That's the problem.'

'I think the problem's closer to hand,' Harriet replied tartly, looking at the wine glass by his side.

'A refill,' he said, handing it towards her. '*In vino veritas*.'

'I think not,' said Harriet, turning on her heel and disappearing through the entrance towards the first knot of people she met. They didn't seem to be discussing art at all but the races at Flemington.

Rosa was in earnest conversation with a dark-haired good-looking man, and Gwyneth had taken her long silvery mane of hair off, as if it were an exhibit that had been sufficiently shown. A monstrance, Harriet thought, and the word came unbidden from school, as if she was programmed by the poet: a feeling of something cascading like a waterfall or a fish eye that flickered, something milky and imprisoned, like the moon behind railings. It was the influence of the poet whose feet she could still see faintly through the doorway. His body seemed slumped, as if he slept.

'What will you do with him?' Harriet asked Rosa, when the last stragglers were preparing to depart. 'Will he stay there overnight?'

'No,' Rosa replied. 'I'll go and call his brother now. He has one brother who still speaks to him. He'll come and get him in his car if I give him sufficient warning.'

An hour later, the glasses stacked on trays, the lights turned off and the gallery door locked, their little group waited outside The Flying Worm. The poet, lifted at the shoulders by the dark-haired man whose name was Donald, and his feet by Rosa (Harriet did not intend to come closer in case another word came flying towards her), lay stretched out as if on a bier, his arms in their velvet sleeves lightly crossed.

'All he needs is a canna lily,' Rosa remarked.

'Will he never tire of it?' Donald asked. But it was Rosa he looked at.

What will it lead to in the future? Harriet wondered.

Just then a car pulled up and a sober-looking young man got out. There was a hint of resemblance in the features, nothing more. Not a word was spoken. The back door was opened and the limp form was eased onto the seat. A pillow and rug were produced. Christopher Humfress nodded to Rosa before he drove off.

Harriet was intensely curious about the Humfress family and the next time she was at the Carlton library she enquired if there were any books about Australian pastoral dynasties.

A book was produced and Humfress was listed in the index; they didn't have quite a chapter to themselves, being included with other Victorians, but there was a photo of the family home at Wallender and several portraits of bearded and clean-shaven groups on a verandah covered with wisteria. Over the years the vine had grown like an anaconda; Harriet imagined it might seize one of the smaller children and swallow it. It made Betts's General Store and her grandparents' small-holding seem from another world. The great pastoralists, the author implied, were like mariners who rejoiced at the sight of a virgin coastline, like Keats's Cortez. They were men of vision who came to one edge and sought another: an horizon was nothing to fear. Perhaps they only feared another pastoralist, Harriet considered, when she tried to digest two chapters. That night she dreamed of ships that berthed and turned into sheep; the ocean was water and then it became grass.

'Did you ever visit Wallender?' Harriet asked Rosa the next morning. It was Saturday and they were taking coffee in the window seat.

'Only once,' Rosa replied. 'It was a disaster. Lucien was living in a kind of farm cottage, banished by his father. He used to visit his mother surreptitiously. She kept him supplied with food and sometimes he went up to the house and came back with a bottle of whisky.'

But when Harriet asked why Lucien had been banished Rosa could not remember. 'Something to do with art, I expect. The whole family is divided down the middle between art and money.'

'Perhaps that's a little unfair,' Harriet suggested, with vague notions of the pastoralists coming to mind. Someone had to provide the French doors and verandah posts.

'Lucien used to throw wild parties,' Rosa went on. 'I don't suppose the noise carried, but lights burning all night must have been like a red rag to a bull. There was a dais in one room and Lucien's sister used to model for him when he was doing line drawings to accompany his poems. The lines were as minimal as the poems but she didn't seem to mind.'

'Did you meet the father?'

'A huge bluff tanned man. I rather liked him. I only like big men. Bewildered at what he'd produced. But there are two other sons to carry on the tradition.'

'The one who collected Lucien?'

'Studying veterinary science. The other one's at home, managing the property.'

'And the sister?'

'Disappeared off the face of the earth, last I heard. Lucien used to get postcards from time to time, then they dried up.'

'Is that why he drinks himself into a stupor?'

'Oh, I shouldn't think so. It's bound to be more complicated than that.'

Harriet had a way of inserting herself into other people's problems. She saw that herself when she made representations on behalf of a client to Mr Worboys. A woman, abandoned by her husband and bankrupted by him, had come crying to the office, fearful of losing her home. Harriet had imagined representation might be made to the Revenue Department, but Mr Worboys had been curt. Then Harriet had, in her own time, investigated if any supplementary benefits were available; she had surreptitiously made the woman a cup of coffee, which had earned a glare from Mr Worboys. But Harriet had decided she was not responsible for his exits and entrances like Pluto from the underworld.

'Throw yourself on their mercy,' she said to the woman as she accompanied her downstairs. 'It can't be the first time it's happened.'

That sent the woman into fresh sobs and Harriet stood by the open door with her, watching the people pass by.

'Go to the Social Security and pick someone with a kind face. Write down what you want to say. Give them facts and figures.'

The woman looked slightly reassured and Harriet climbed the stairs again, thinking of mercy and how it had to be sought before you could tell if it existed.

Mother Anastasia had been aware of this tendency of Harriet's at St Mary's and counselled her over it. God requires each of us to have an identity, she had said. Losing oneself to find oneself might be fine, but in some people the finding never followed; they never rested long enough to take a sounding. Mother Anastasia might have been concerned if she had seen Harriet on the stairs, climbing up to another empty good deed, for she had determined to pay the woman's bill, earning another reprimand from her boss.

'I find your attitude improper,' he said to her on that final afternoon. 'Interfering, undermining. I'm going to have to let you go.'

'Why feel compulsion about it?' Harriet had answered, surprising herself. 'You've always said there is no sentiment in money.'

'There is none. I'm prepared to give you a reference. And you'll need to work out your notice.'

I expect there'll be something between the lines, Harriet thought as she walked back to her desk. Her face was flushed, and in spite of her pride her heart was racing. Now I am like the woman on the stairs whom I was consoling only a few hours ago. Now we are both to be cast into the traffic.

On the stroke of five she took her coat from its hanger and walked out. She would wait for the reference and then leave. She would ask for it early so she could look for another job.

She couldn't face going home just yet, so she sat in Parliament Gardens near a Moreton Bay fig. A grey statue looked down on her with sightless eyes. She thought of the references her aunts had got when they were in domestic service (only her mother had been smart enough to avoid one): condescending notes in fountain pen on letterhead paper. Letters that reeked of privilege and afternoon dresses, hands that for all their superiority were often ill-formed.

'Good for you,' was Rosa's reaction. Two warm soft arms were flung around Harriet's neck and a face in a green mask with circles where cucumber rings had rested came close to touching.

'You look like an African god,' Harriet laughed. 'I feel as if I am being blessed by a creature that demands sacrifice.'

'I *do* demand sacrifice. And I intend to be sated,' Rosa replied. 'Darling Donald is taking me to the theatre and my beloved flatmate has told her boss where to go.'

'He fired me,' Harriet protested. 'Remember.'

'Because you showed him up for the out-of-date piece of goods he is. He fired you because he's a dinosaur and can't feel the winds of change.' Slowly she began to wipe the avocado off her face as if she were restoring a painting. The flesh underneath was pink and moist as a watermelon.

'Would you like to come to the theatre too?' Rosa asked. 'They often have cancellations. We could ask at the box office.'

'No,' said Harriet. 'A gooseberry or a failure I can bear, but not both together.'

'We'll do something tomorrow night,' Rosa promised.

'What are you going to?' Harriet asked.

'*Waiting for Godot*,' Rosa replied. 'I can't think what I'm going to all this trouble for. Three old tramps. You can see them on Dorcas Street any day.'

Surprising herself, Harriet took two weeks' holiday instead of immediately looking for another job. She told herself these were the weeks she would have worked out for Mr Worboys. 'I should like to have a reference now,' she had told him as she stood in front of his desk. 'Since I am not being dismissed for any misdemeanour.'

'The misdemeanour is in your own nature,' he said to her. 'Still I expect you'll find that out.'

The reference was on her desk when she came back from lunch. *To whom it may concern: Miss Harriet Betts has given satisfaction as an accounts clerk. She shows initiative and a grasp of mathematics unusual in a woman. Her appearance and manner are all that can be required. She leaves with my recommendation.*

I sound a grey creature, Harriet thought, something like a mouse. He has dismissed me by saying nothing more than I am exact. *A grasp of mathematics* sounds vaguely improper, as if I dressed in men's clothes.

Harriet would not go to the office to collect the pay that was owing. Rosa had done that and found a young woman with permed hair in Harriet's place. A muffled conference between the young woman and Mr Worboys had gone on behind closed doors. 'Tell him I won't go away,' Rosa said. She was wearing a particularly dashing hat with a peacock feather. Eventually another envelope had been produced and the permed one had parroted a little speech. 'Mr Worboys says to inform Miss Harriet Betts that he has been more than generous in the circumstances and he expects no further correspondence.'

'You can be certain about that,' Rosa replied, drawing herself up to her full height. 'Tell Mr Worboys Harriet was wasted here. But I expect he already knows that. And if I were you I'd change your hairdresser.'

The following weekend, when Donald was out of town, Rosa insisted on a therapeutic visit to the zoo.

'Imagine living in Royal Park,' Harriet said as they alighted from the tram. 'Going to sleep to the roars of lions and the screams of birds.'

'There are peacocks at Wallender and they sound as if they are being strangled.'

'I thought you just visited for a day.'

'Two days. The car broke down and they put me up at the main house. Lucien stayed down in his studio and I played the young woman who hasn't forgotten the proprieties. Played it rather well, if I say so myself.'

They were climbing a little hill towards the giraffes.

'Of course one never forgets how to use a knife and fork,' Rosa went on.

The necks of the giraffes seemed to cross like someone setting cutlery on a plate; their spots were gravy coloured. Some humans were as haughty, but the faces of the giraffes seemed curiously uncertain, aristocrats without much brain power. 'If you regard the neck as a ruff or farthingale,' Rosa said, stopping to lean over the wire fence, 'the faces are rather like Rembrandts.'

Harriet gazed, certain her friend would go on.

'With Rembrandt, if it hasn't happened already, you always feel that wrinkles and facial hair are going to invade at any moment or the eyes get rheumy or the skin pucker.'

Still the giraffes, for all their worried faces, were very smooth. The baby looked like an ironing board.

'I think you are thinking of the elephants,' Harriet declared.

The zoo had made her tired. So many species, gathered together in concrete pits and artificially contrived wire-bordered spaces with toys and balls, made her long to sweep everything away, to have one giraffe, or a group if that is what they preferred, every thousand square miles. Gathered together they reminded her of the uncertainty of her life.

'Come,' said Rosa, seizing her by the hand. 'The lions are going to be fed. I'll show you what real passion sounds like.'

Harriet found a job at Judd's Drapery and Haberdashery in Church Street. In the same week she enrolled at the Royal Institute of Technology to train as a book-keeper. By day she sat in a glassed-in booth high above the shop floor where women handled bolts of cloth, stretching them out on long wooden benches and cutting lengths with tailoring scissors attached to the counters by silver chains. Vacuous-faced mannequins with impossible figures – at least they did not resemble any of the women who appeared on the floor – were draped with taffeta or Orlon, seersucker or rayon crepe. The money for the transactions winged its way towards Harriet in little metal cylinders lined with green felt. She opened them, counted the change and folded it in the bill which she signed, pulled a lever with a wooden handle and the box whirled back. It was a convention that this aerial transaction of money went un-regarded, as if a cherub flew. Occasionally a child would point up to where Harriet and one of the clerks sat, but generally she looked down without meeting any gaze in return. Between cylinders Harriet attended to the paperwork and at the end of the day she stayed on an extra half hour to ensure the receipts balanced. Judd's Drapery had deliberately stayed old-fashioned, in keeping with the old products it sold: obscure fastenings for brassieres, zips as long as a body, hair cutters for home hairdressing, bridal headgear. And everything that could go with a completed garment was there: gloves, appliqué and rickrack, great boards of buttons under which scraps of cloth were pressed, cottons of every conceivable colour, feathers, diamanté, boas. The floors stayed uncarpeted, like the shop in Ouse, and the manager wore an old-fashioned morning coat like a hotel commissionaire.

There was a For Sale sign in front of 77 Bouverie Street and Ross was complaining about the state of the garden. 'Hire a gardener,' Rosa told him. 'Why should we labour to increase your profit?' The days when Rosa cooked had gone: everyone snacked. Sometimes Harriet carried home a roast dinner in a little covered dish from the nearby dairy. The owner's wife cooked roasts, chicken and pork chops: the meal was like a serving from someone's table. 'Get one for me,' Rosa would call, and Harriet would walk steadily up the street like a waiter bearing a precious cargo. In the morning the dishes were taken back.

Since they were moving and would be hard to trace, Rosa suggested the three of them enter a new art competition, the McKelvey, which was offering a prize of 500 guineas. Garth was enthusiastic, but when Harriet hung back Rosa suggested she could paint some numbers somewhere. 'I can get a canvas,' Rosa said. 'I think I know the size the judges are looking for. We could work on it in the evenings with sheets on the floor.'

It was Ross's sheets they used, and the canvas lay on the floor weighted with bricks from the bookcase which was being dismantled.

'Start with a good slash of red,' Rosa instructed Garth. 'It'll symbolise the bedsheets of Ross and Gwyneth. I know he thinks he's getting a virgin but I know otherwise.'

'It needs to be based on something,' Garth objected, bending his lanky form to peer down on the canvas as if it were a pool. 'Even Turner was based on something.' Wasn't the something more when it was concealed by fog or mist? Didn't one have to cling on then for dear life? Impressionism with extra strain. But to Rosa Garth simply suggested that the street they lived on should be the basis. The jacaranda tree, the bay window with its thrip-infested roses, the piebald look of the lawn, the blue house opposite. Even Harriet could be inserted – unrecognisable of course: a shape carrying the three white dishes she had brought this evening. A white shape, like three white bricks, concealing corn beef, mashed potatoes and cauliflower cheese.

It was not as ridiculous as it sounded and once the basic blocks were sketched in, over several evenings – for Garth was knowledgeable about properties and drying times – Rosa was induced to furnish some Rouault-like outlines: a dark kohl-surrounded eye and another with a mauve iris. Harriet added a series of significant numbers like an addition on a shop-keeper's bill. These numbers were their birthdays – day, month and year run together – and, in another corner, the number of the house, 77.

Prospective buyers of the house were not allowed into Rosa's bedroom: a point of irritation to Ross, but she was adamant. 'Simply say it's the same as Harriet's only larger. Let them peer through the window if they want to.'

'Let them imagine it belongs to Bluebeard,' she said when Ross had departed. 'It'll enable us to stay here longer.'

But a canvas that looked inspired on the floor looked different when pinned to the passage wall.

'How close will the judge stand?' Harriet asked, imagining, in the interests of fairness, a line on the floor.

'Oh they'll move back and forwards,' Rosa said. 'They'll go up and sniff the canvas and touch it with their fingers. Only if it gets into the finals will there be any reverence attached to it.'

Garth thought the elements did not hang together very well.

'Perhaps what it needs,' said Harriet, 'is something like weather. Wind or rain.'

'Brilliant,' said Rosa. 'Let's get it down and give the whole thing a going over.'

In the end they decided on something like mist or gauze curtains. Garth changed into his oldest corduroys and gingerly sat on a few places where a light stroking of white had been added; he wiggled slightly, as if ants had crawled up his legs. Rosa informed them it was the traditional way to do clouds.

Someone knocked at the door but they didn't answer. Three sharp knocks repeated at intervals. Garth put his hand over his mouth to keep his laughter in, Rosa subsided on the sofa with a cushion over her head, Harriet lay flat on her stomach as if examining the carpet for dust mites.

At the Royal Melbourne Institute of Technology, Harriet was in a class of ten men, seven women, including one older woman who had been a private secretary. It was a career Harriet had seriously considered for herself, since her preference for working behind the scenes was as powerful as another's might be to lead. Perhaps there was a category for those who wished to be third, or in the pit where Elizabethan audiences stood to await moments of mirth in high tragedy. To Harriet's mind the position of second was more powerful than the role of king. Her mind wandered off into a daydream as the tutor wrote a list of textbooks on the board. She saw a king, like the king in chess, fall back from a parapet, only just avoiding an arrow. A figure darted from the shadows and dragged him to safety. Or he made a speech and the second passed the stirring words that caused a sea of hands to rise. She turned back to the board and saw that the first assignment had been set: *500 words on why you want to be an accountant and the importance of accounting in society.*

'I guess it's money,' Harriet said to her neighbour, a pleasant-looking older man. 'And whether we want to spend our lives dealing with it.'

'The money of others, the blood of others,' he replied. 'I've always thought there was something medical about it.'

'My mother had a gift for book-keeping,' Harriet said, surprising herself.

'And mine had none at all. She practically bankrupted us.'

'I expect they don't want family histories,' Harriet replied. 'Certainly it's a profession that needs a little romance. The love of money is the root of all evil and only a good book-keeper can save you from it.'

They were at the door now. The corridor smelt faintly of oil and dust and over the exit door a light like a lozenge burned.

'Can I give you a ride?' the unintroduced man asked. Perhaps she would hear his name in next week's roll call.

'No, I'll get the tram. I can hear one coming.'

'I'm Harriet,' she called over her shoulder as she ran, as if she were handing a king the one vital fact he didn't need to know – advance news of a rout, or a treasure ship on fire in the harbour.

The canvas, rolled, and titled *Sgraffito* – 'Let it be pinned like a kite,' Garth declaimed – was taken to The Flying Worm where Rosa filled in the necessary entry forms. One lunch hour she walked along Little Lonsdale Street, carrying it under her arm. It was decided she should deliver it, in case anyone noticed and assumed she had made a discovery. A mysterious expression played about her face as she climbed the steps of the National Gallery, passed under the great columns and, after nodding to the guard and then the clerk at the reception desk, walked through to the Buvelot Gallery. She was in luck, for at that instant one of the judges, a small irritable sandy-haired man in a mustard-coloured suit and black polo jersey, was bending and sighing over a group of canvases spread out on the parquet floor. Others were stacked three deep against the walls, which were white and bare. 'They look as if they are attempting to fly,' Rosa remarked, receiving a hostile look in return; then, taking in her appearance, his face softened.

'Where should I put this?' she asked. 'It seems to go against the grain. It's unframed.'

'Yours, is it?'

'I can't say,' she replied. 'I'm sworn to secrecy.' They had decided on an eccentric spinster and spent an evening coming up with 'Millicent Vavasour'.

'I don't envy you your task,' Rosa said sweetly, laying the canvas at the base of a confused abstract which she felt sure it would knock into the shade.

'There are two other judges,' the little man remarked, and the thought seemed to bring no happiness. 'But I always like to form my opinions first.'

'Good luck then,' said Rosa. 'I have the same problems at my gallery.'

Then, before he could make any rejoinder, she turned and walked out the door. Her feet tap-tapped on the parquet floor and she imagined she remained in his thoughts for as long as the sound lasted.

'How did it go?' Harriet asked when Rosa returned that evening.

'It couldn't have gone better,' Rosa said, throwing her beret in one corner of the dining room and scooping a large helping of Oakhill potatoes onto her plate. 'Were you preparing a feast against disappointment?'

'Not really. I just felt like it. I expected you might just slink in and leave it up against the wall.'

'I only saw one other that was unframed,' Rosa replied. 'I expect that's not a disadvantage. A bad frame can cripple a work.'

'It's a pity you couldn't have taken the bricks as well.'

'That might have consigned it to the sculpture section. No, I guess they will have something to weigh it down. The main thing was to have met one of the judges. I think he might give it a few seconds' more consideration than some of the others. And we do have the colour of his suit in one of the sections Garth did. The piece that's meant to represent the ginger cat.'

The real 77 Bouverie Street was sold and Rosa and Harriet moved to 390 Lygon Street, to a flat above a Chinese green-grocer. Garth had elected to move in with a colleague. Cartons stood in the hallway: Harriet's books and Rosa's clothes. Soon the house was reduced to the rather old-fashioned furniture that belonged to Ross's grandmother. 'How we tarted it up,' Rosa said, stuffing bed linen into a box that had once held a small refrigerator.

'We can live on fruit,' she said to Harriet, the first night above Wu's Greengrocers.

'I expect we'll need to,' Harriet replied. Her salary from the haberdashers was less than Mr Worboys' and there were tuition fees as well.

The flat had two front rooms – one each – which over-looked the street, and a long kitchen which ran across the back. Bathroom and toilet were on a landing, and the toilet was shared with the shop. Mr and Mrs Wu, having lived frugally above their shop for years, had finally built a house of their own. The walls, to Harriet's amusement, were the colours of fruit and vegetables: Rosa's room had watermelon walls while hers were grape. The entrance hall was aubergine, the kitchen pea coloured, and the bathroom a blinding lemon.

'Perhaps they were encouraging themselves', Rosa said, after Garth had departed and they were sitting in Rosa's room. The Wus had left no furniture apart from a kitchen table and chairs and one small, covered chair which looked as if it had been torn to pieces by an animal.

'Where shall we sleep?' Harriet asked. The twenty-two steps were engraved on her brain and with each box load she been unable to stop herself counting.

'I suppose if you woke in a room the colour of watermelon or kale or spinach it focused your mind for the day,' Rosa said.

'Twenty-two steps to the kingdom of vegetables,' Harriet sighed. It was too late now to check out the marts; they would have to sleep on the floor.

Below them they could hear Mr Wu moving softly about the shop, covering the fruit, opening the huge silver till so its emptiness could be seen from the street.

They slept on mattresses on the floor and when Harriet

woke she looked up at an ornate light fitting shaped like a rose. A naked bulb hung from it and she began to plan what sort of lampshade she would buy. The grape-coloured walls would have to be repainted. 'Repainting? No problem,' Mr Wu had said. 'I can give you dustsheet.' Mr Wu had a curious habit of giving a singular when he meant plural; on their first day he had pressed on them a little straw basket: apple, banana, nectarine. Harriet lay on her back, thinking how frail her life felt: the haberdashery where in spite of grumbles everyone seemed focused and she alone had to escape into fantasy, imagining she was Midas as the cylinders whirled towards her from the floor below. Not Midas, because the bill and the carelessly rolled notes were reduced when she pressed the lever to return them. What remained of the money was ceremoniously counted back to the customer, the notes flattened and the silver set down like a pile of buttons. And she was expected to be content with the little piles of money she checked, with her signature on the day's pile of bills, with the day's profit and its comparison with the day before.

Luckily, before she could think of night school, Rosa was awake and they breakfasted on Mr Wu's fruit basket. There was no milk so they had weak tea with lemon and Rosa promised to stock the fridge that evening. There would probably be no mail for days, though they had changed their address at the post office. Reluctantly Harriet pulled herself off the mattress and went to run herself a bath. She felt she was close to tears: each new detail carried a personal reproof – the stains around the plughole and the chain from which the plug had come loose. 'Me fix anything. You tell me,' Mr Wu had said, smiling and bowing as he did to everyone, even if they only purchased an apple. But when she finally descended the stairs with Rosa, Harriet felt her mood lift. Perhaps Mr Wu could be a kind of household god, wise and benign, eversmiling.

'Bring more fruit for ladies this evening,' he said, bowing. 'Everything okay? Make list.'

'Will do,' Rosa called.

'I'm starting to speak like Mr Wu,' she said as they parted to go in different directions.

I'm disorientated, Harriet thought as she walked down Lygon Street. The morning air with its edge of chill would soon die and the heat begin its daily assault. At least we can leave our windows open all night and Mr Wu has a burglar alarm. As it had been at boarding school, her life was made of these 'at leasts'. To others they might have been triumphs: indicators that an illness had broken and there would be future rejoicing. Rosa was like that. Whereas Harriet advanced detail by detail, fully aware that the details were drab, hardly worth recording, neutral witnesses that would remain whatever happened. Maybe she could discover the cause of Mr Wu's optimism. By now she was nearly at Judd's, and the sight of cylinders, like greyhounds waiting to make their first sale, made her think it was probably money.

News that *Sgraffito* had been shortlisted for the McKelvey Prize did not reach Mr Wu's establishment until several days after its announcement. Rosa, who had been careful to conceal any traces, especially to The Flying Worm, was in Sydney; Harriet had the flat to herself for three nights, and on one of them had experimented with sleeping in Rosa's room to see if watermelon walls were more conducive to sleep than grey-green grape. The letter from the gallery had gone to their old address, in spite of Rosa's mail direction, and the box was not cleared until Ross brought Gwyneth to inspect his property. He had hired a man to mow the lawns and tackle the worst of the garden.

'Typical of Rosa,' he said to Gwyneth when his hand encountered an official-looking letter and a pile of brochures in the box. Rosa had been useful to him once as a bohemian but now he had achieved his aim he could afford to be scathing. 'I suppose we should drop it off,' he remarked, holding open the door of his new car. It was these gestures that focused his attention now, for he had never been courteous to women. Holding chairs, rising to his feet as if in the presence of a superior species, must become natural to him. Sometimes he felt he was counting under his breath. So it was a distraction to seek out the shop of Mr Wu and enquire with a raised eyebrow if a Miss Rosa Prouse lived there. He held the rather creased but impressive-looking envelope in front of him as if Mr Wu's English might not be sufficient.

'Very fine lady,' Mr Wu said, bowing. 'Two very fine ladies. Not in. I give message.'

'Give this to Miss Rosa then, will you.'

Mr Wu bowed again and put the letter in his apron. His shrewd twinkling eyes never left Ross's face.

Flustered, Ross fumbled in his pocket and held out a punnet of strawberries.

Mr Wu gave Harriet the letter when she was beginning wearily to climb the stairs. Her mind summoned a little extra energy before she could reach her room and relax. She focused on the fact the windows were open and she would not be assailed by a blast of heat. It had been a more tiring day than usual, with a woman returning ten yards of guipure lace for a wedding dress and demanding a refund. Harriet had witnessed the scene from her box. The manager in his morning suit had been summoned and two flustered assistants had tried to soothe the woman who kept saying, 'It's not my fault the wedding's off.' The pinned-up hair of one of the assistants had come undone and the floor was littered with hairpins. After placating the woman, the manager had turned on Miss Enderby and told her to attend to her appearance and get her hair bobbed if she couldn't control it. At lunchtime Harriet had taken Miss Enderby into the park and sat with her on a bench, peeling and handing her one of Mr Wu's oranges.

'I need the job,' Chloe Enderby said to Harriet, eating the segments as if they were medicine. 'Otherwise I'd walk out the door.'

Looking at the envelope with the National Gallery of Victoria in gold lettering, Harriet's instinct was to recoil. She held it gingerly as she counted the stairs – a habit she could not break – and inserted her key in the lock.

'Man brought it,' Mr Wu had apologised with two bows, for

he had neglected to take the name. 'Tall dark man. Woman waiting in car.'

'You didn't show him the flat?' Harriet asked, wincing at the thought of Gwyneth surveying their small possessions, though now they had two beds from the mart, and a coffee table.

'Never,' said Mr Wu indignantly. 'Never. You private.'

Harriet went to the window and leaned out. The letter in the centre of the table could wait. Down below in Lygon Street crowds were passing on the pavements, though the rusty overhang prevented her seeing how many entered Mr Wu's shop. How tired people looked at the end of the day, Harriet thought. Carlton was a poor suburb and maybe the poor showed their emotions more than rich people. The frustrated mother of the bride had been certain she would be refunded for what was a very unsuitable length of material. 'Don't let Mr Judd see he has upset you,' Harriet had counselled Chloe, but it was already too late. Misery is something that is passed on, one to another. There was a child on the opposite pavement having its ears boxed.

Still, in Harriet's eyes, the street was beautiful. She liked it better than Bouverie Street or even the centre of Melbourne. The telegraph poles, and the tram tracks which glistened when it rained as if they had emerged from the earth like veins. Though they were decidedly unmusical, hearing the trams go past soothed her heart.

Harriet had forgotten the letter by the time Rosa arrived home. Rosa threw her satchel on the floor, shook her hair loose from its Spanish combs and removed her jacket.

'What's up?' she said to Harriet, as she tore the creamy envelope. Then, 'Read this,' she said, one hand held to her mouth. 'We have to get hold of Garth.'

We are pleased to inform you that your entry, Sgrafitto, has been shortlisted for the McKelvey Prize. The winner and two runners-up will be announced at a gala function to be held in the Buvelot Gallery on Friday 8th March, 1963. An invitation to this function will be forwarded to you shortly. The trustees of the McKelvey

Prize offer you their congratulations on your achievement.

Harriet was unceremoniously dragged from the window seat and swept into a wild dance on the linoleum. Rosa, taller, stronger, danced with no qualms, Harriet more like a condemned person. Rosa turned the knob on the radio as they passed and it was playing the very end of Elgar's *Pomp and Circumstance March no. 1*. 'Land of Hope and Glory, Mother of the Free,' Rosa sang and, in the triumph of emotion over sense, Harriet thought she heard Mr Wu's soft steps ascending the stairs and pausing outside their door, listening to hear if he could be of service.

Garth's reaction was excitement mixed with uncertainty, since the idea that one of their staff might have perpetrated a hoax might please his bosses. They were always talking of innovation and entering the world of the client, identifying with his aspirations: the dream of owning a late-model car, a suburban villa, to start children saving by opening their own bank accounts. The prestige of the award worried him, and the searching there would be for the mysterious Millicent Vavasour. Who would they interview? He consoled himself that the likelihood was remote, that the final judge, Sebastian Gwyn Kellough from Perth, would likely detect the traces of fraud, the bogus arrangement of objects, the final obscuring layer and the place where he had sat. He should burn the trousers in the fireplace. In the end he wrapped them and put them out for the rubbish collector. Then, since he was used to calculating the odds, he thought nothing more about it. He bent his head over a mock-up he was preparing for a travel agency extolling the virtues of Honolulu.

Rosa, who was more threatened by being in the art business herself, was reassured when the name of the final judge was announced. She knew him to be a traditionalist at heart, though at pains to conceal it. The eight finalists were on display in one of the side galleries and in the lunch hour she joined the crowds strolling behind the velvet ropes. 'This one is just a mess,' she overheard one woman say, and was comforted.

Harriet, who had least to fear and doubted the staff at Judd's had any interest in art, thought she might be teased about dabbling. At the worst her humble occupation might be remarked on and brought to the attention of Mr Worboys. She was tempted to confide in one of the night-school class, the man called Lewis who had offered her a ride home: the evenings were drawing in and he had asked tentatively as if he were balancing a ride in an overheated car with time to oneself. Nothing, not even partial experience, could make accounting exciting, though their lecturer did his best. And now the worry about the art prize was at the back of Harriet's mind. She dreaded exposure of any kind, the explanations that would be required, possibly a scandal with reporters. What would they say their intentions were: a love of art not an attempt to parody, an attempt to fill in an evening?

Lewis's car was parked under a jacaranda tree and its bonnet and windows were streaked with lavender blossoms. He flung the doors open to cool it down and started the windscreen wipers.

'You look preoccupied,' he said to Harriet. 'Was it Debit and Depreciation?'

'No,' she said, seating herself and feeling her shoe touch something on the floor that turned out to be a pile of newspapers.

'Sorry about the mess,' he replied, when the last jacaranda blossom had been swept aside. 'I can't face the notion of accounting unless there is some great mass to be reduced to order. A client in difficulties carrying ten years' bills on a spike or a widow wringing her hands over a mortgage.'

'Then I have a problem worthy of you,' Harriet replied.

Her telling – he turned the ignition off and more jacaranda blossoms began their descent under the street lights – was as disjointed as he could wish.

'Tell me again,' he said after the first attempt. 'Go back to the beginning. Who had the idea?'

And the second telling *did* seem easier, like a rehearsal for a less sympathetic judge.

'Let me sleep on it,' Lewis said finally. 'I sometimes get ideas during the night.' He looked at her to see if she was taking him wrong but he couldn't read her expression. 'Besides,' he said, putting the car into gear, 'I need to consult a book on statistics.'

At work Harriet witnessed Chloe Enderby being harassed by the boss. From her glass cage, checking stock orders and waiting for the next cylinder to wing towards her, Harriet could look down on the entire floor. She could see the parting in Mr Judd's hair where a line of dandruff was held at bay though enough fell onto his collar to make him nervous. Miss Enderby had been followed into the storeroom by Mr Judd who made an elaborate show of checking his watch. His manner of walking was different, slightly stiff-legged. And he made some kind of remark to another new assistant, Miss Rolfe, on the way. When Miss Enderby emerged Harriet could see at once she was flustered and exerting every last atom of strength to appear composed. But Mr Judd must have excused her from public duties for a while because she disappeared into the ladies' rest room.

'Are you all right?' Harriet asked her that evening when they were putting on their coats.

'Why shouldn't I be?' Chloe Enderby replied. 'And why should you ask? Are you some kind of spy?'

'Not at all,' Harriet replied. 'Though it does amuse me to look down on people's heads.'

'If you want my advice you'll keep your eyes on your job,' Chloe replied, turning her back to Harriet and counting money from a change purse.

So Harriet had lingered in a little teashop near the corner of Swan Street to avoid being on the same tram. She drank two cups of tea from a brown teapot and stirred in more sugar than she usually took. She thought of the overview some novelists took and how, even if you were in a glass box, it was impossible in real life.

Rosa was unpacking little containers from The Golden

Lotus, a Chinese takeaway recommended by Mr Wu. There was a candle in the centre of the table in an old pewter candlestick, paper serviettes with a red dragon in each corner, and chopsticks.

'I don't think I can face chopsticks,' Harriet said.

'Certainly, Madame,' Rosa replied. 'Will Madame accept a spoon and fork?'

'Madame is grateful for this offer of friendship after a tiring day,' Harriet replied, spooning shrimp fried rice into a soup bowl.

'My pleasure,' said Rosa, raising a pink shrimp between two chopsticks. 'Let's keep our problems until we get to the fortune cookies.'

The scent of food, the nourishment of noodles, seemed to fill the room. From below came the last sales being rung up on the till, the screeching of trams, and in the intervals the calls of a wattle bird.

'Does anything matter really?' Rosa asked, re-filling her bowl with chicken chow mein. 'This art exhibition – about which I've had an idea, by the way – or your tedious night classes.'

'The least of the tediums,' Harriet replied. 'I oversaw the manager groping one of the staff this afternoon. Now they both regard me as a spy. I expect tomorrow I'll be summoned.'

'Tomorrow and tomorrow and tomorrow,' said Rosa. 'Let it do its worst. There's always another tomorrow in the wings. Have you thought of that? Twenty-four hours to bear us away.' She pushed the little basket with the two fortune cookies nestling on a serviette towards Harriet. The cookie crumbled and on the thin folded slip of rice paper Harriet read: *Trusting heart is way to happiness*. Rosa's said: *Dragon heart will win day*.

The judging of the finalists took place one week later. Rosa, by that time, had come up with a solution: they, the three artists, would remain anonymous. If anyone had recognised her delivering the rolled-up canvas – and she regretted now the theatricality that had inspired her to dress in beret and black and white striped dust coat – she would say that she had simply delivered the work on behalf of someone else. That someone could be of uncertain age: very old or, more embarrassing, very young, though, if questioned Rosa had decided to hint at someone as old as fifty. Already a figure was taking shape in her imagination: a repressed talent whose circumstances had fortuitously changed – perhaps a small legacy, enough to keep the wolf from the door; a studio improvised at the bottom of a garden. After all, science had such geniuses: exploding out-houses where some experiment went wrong. She woke in the middle of the night and realised she was thinking of Lucien. He had come to The Flying Worm's latest exhibition and interrupted the guest speaker. Lucien, since his own career had failed, saw conspiracies everywhere. Rosa had enticed him into the stockroom with a bottle of claret and he had followed like a lamb. Lucien might be a useful ally, she decided, and his august family name come in handy. 'I'd like you to escort me to the McKelvey Award,' Rosa told him and he opened an astonished eye before subsiding against the wall.

Rosa patted her hair and took around a tray of drinks. The sculptures – for the gallery alternated sculpture and painting – stuck out at awkward angles but made good back rests, for they were made of old railway sleepers and cross-beams from old farmhouses. Some were blackened by fires lit by the sculptor; others had deep gouges like knife wounds in flesh, or showed gaping holes where great bolts had been withdrawn. The walls of the gallery were bare apart from a selection of working drawings and the price list.

Rosa was working on getting Steffo to change the name of the gallery: The Flying Worm sounded too like death and decay.

'Can you think of a good name for a gallery?' she said to Lucien when she came back into the storeroom.

'Orgulous,' he said, lazily opening one eye.

It was strange how Lucien always put her in a better humour.

The chief judge had been interviewed in that day's *Argus*.

His overwhelming desire was to find innovation: not the sort of innovation that comes from adjustment and compromise but a deeper vision. He had quoted Cézanne. That lets us out, Rosa thought happily, thinking of Garth's gyrations and the time-honoured cloud technique. She must see Garth in her lunch hour tomorrow. And Harriet would not object. She had already had one warning from her boss for raising her head above the parapet.

A letter came from Billy complaining about life in Tasmania. *I'm going to die soon if I don't escape*, he wrote, and Harriet suspected that her aunt was included in the things to be escaped from. Instead Billy concentrated on the lack of places to go, the fact that everyone was the same and the consequences if you weren't, the things that amused people in which he couldn't share. *I might as well be tarred and feathered as far as school goes*, he wrote, and his hand was surprisingly firm and decided, seeming to contradict the uncertainty of his mind. *Each master passes on my reputation to the next. I usually have to sit at the front of the class in case I exhibit rabid behaviour and foam at the mouth. If I get a half-way decent mark it gets double-checked and regarded as a fluke.* Harriet suspected Billy was accused of cheating; possibly he had to hold out his hands or empty his pockets. *At home I am just stifled. Mother treats me as if I am about five instead of fourteen.* Poor Emma would be mortified to read it and yet she did treat Billy as a lamb on a religious tract, a creature bathed in light, in spite of scraped knees, mussed hair and a glowering expression. Her aunt was the sort of mother Harriet had longed for as a child, surrendering herself to the child's supreme importance, with always a hand held out to steady, a voice descending into baby cadences. Her aunt had anticipated Billy's every need as a child: it seemed to be a game to guess his wants, to prepare the world for his passage.

One day you should come to Melbourne and complete your studies, Harriet wrote back. She had decided on a bulky letter, worthy of the Victorians. She would describe the art competition she, Rosa and Garth had entered with uncertain outcome, to prove herself not staid; she would describe the street she lived on, the singing trams which, when she retired early after a day in the glass cage, broke into her sleep. *Like violins,* she wrote, *but not the sort played in concert halls.* She used her employment and night classes to discuss the necessity of money. *When I see the little copper containers whizzing towards me they remind me of the Trojan horse with soldiers in its belly –* it had not occurred to her until she wrote it, perhaps she was thinking of toast soldiers – *or some kind of inelegant labouring little boat, rocking on the waves.* Maybe she meant a boat carrying coal or some of the produce of her mother's store – a word like pig iron and the things it might be made into: shovels and scuttles and fire irons.

The night before the McKelvey Prize gala Garth came around to the flat. It was his first visit and his admiration of the fruit-coloured walls hid nervousness. 'We need a plan,' he said to Rosa. 'In the unlikely event . . .'

'In the unlikely event,' Rosa repeated. 'Hold onto that like a blind man's cane.'

'But in the unlikely event . . .' Garth went on.

'I shall say the painter wishes to remain truly anonymous, that she suffers from a nervous disorder, that she comes from a distinguished family who have encouraged her to paint.'

'I feel we should support you in some way,' Harriet said, 'though we are not attending.'

'We'll wait outside in the porch,' Garth suggested. 'Pretend we are the press. Harriet can be a stringer for a women's magazine.'

'Or a relative of the mystery woman. After a day at Judd's I feel as though I have a nervous disease.'

'Have no fear,' Rosa said to Garth when she showed him out. 'We'll improvise if necessary. The main thing to remember is privacy. Millicent Vavasour is a very retiring creature.'

'Isn't it strange how a fictitious character assembles,' Harriet said. 'I can almost hear Millicent's voice, faint with a slight complaining quality, as if no one of good family should be plagued like this. I imagine at some time there was a period of sickness and she developed an iron will. Mother Anastasia was like that: she spent years lying on her back with a spinal injury. She just smiled sweetly at any girl who attempted to cross her.'

'You know,' Rosa said, 'I am quite looking forward to it.'

'Me too,' said Harriet, and she realised she was. 'Garth and I can go for a walk if we get tired of hanging around.'

Chloe Enderby was sobbing in the women's cloakroom when Harriet went to her locker in her ten-minute tea break.

'Keeping your eyes on your work are you, Miss Betts?' Mr Judd remarked when he came into the glass cage. He did not bother to lower his voice, so the two accounts clerks, eyes fixed like forensic scientists on ledger book and receipts, could hear.

'As much as is consistent with my job,' Harriet replied, a little surprised at her boldness. 'I can't be expected to account for the movement of my eyes every minute of the day.' Now she had gone further, prompted by who knows what inner demon.

'Keep this up and you'll be getting your notice,' Mr Judd replied, and this time his voice was lowered and menacing. 'I'm warning you.'

'He's a pig,' one the clerks said when Mr Judd was out of range: they could look down on him walking the floor, putting a hand on the shoulder of Miss Rolfe as he passed.

Chloe was sitting on a bench in the locker room, wiping her eyes.

'Why aren't you having a tea break?' Harriet asked.

'Because I feel like staying in here,' Chloe replied. She looked defiant, as if anger could account for her flushed cheeks.

'Is it Mr Judd?'

'I can't say. It's more than my job's worth.'

'Aren't you engaged?' Harriet enquired. She had memories of a cake and congratulations a few months earlier.

Silently Chloe held out her left hand. An inexpensive but pretty ring graced her third finger.

'It's lovely,' Harriet said. 'Are you sure I can't get you a cup of tea?'

'We need my salary,' Chloe said. 'We're saving for a deposit. I don't know what to do.'

'I'll think of something,' Harriet said, and her mouth was grim, like the edge of a coin.

'You won't do anything?' Chloe pleaded. 'It'll just make it worse.'

'I promise,' Harriet replied, and she held the hand with the ring. 'I really think you should have some tea before you go back to your counter. Let me come with you. I'll ask Mrs French to cover for you for ten minutes.'

'Miss Enderby is feeling indisposed. I am just going to take her to the staffroom for a cup of tea,' Harriet said to the large motherly woman who was on gloves and buttons, bridal headgear. 'Then she'll be right down.'

'Does she want to go home?' Mrs French asked, and Harriet noticed the slope of her bosom and wondered what sort of brassiere was required to hold it in place.

'No. Just quarter of an hour,' Harriet replied, and smiled her thanks.

There was no sign of Mr Judd as they walked to the tearoom together, Chloe blowing her nose on her handkerchief as if calico and muslin had given her hayfever.

It's not my role, Harriet thought, but I've stepped into it. Somehow it fitted. She made a strong cup of tea with two sugars. She did not ask about sugar or strength and Chloe did not complain. Then she led her down the stairs again to the safety of covered buttons, belt buckles and underarm pads for afternoon dresses.

Garth and Harriet stood by the imposing steps of the National Gallery and watched the crowd pour in through the big wooden doors. Harriet, if she had not been tired from a day at work, could have named the fabrics: crepe de Chine, matte jersey, hand-painted silk.

'How do I look?' Rosa had asked. 'Do I pass?' and Harriet

had admired the emerald satin cloak with a huge bow at the neck which Rosa wore over her trusty black dress with the soft glitter of jet. Rosa's hair was pulled back ballerina-style, as if no surprise announcement could increase the astonishment of her features. Her makeup was heavier than usual, her lipstick darker.

'Do not fear, darlings,' she told them when she left them under Boehm's statue of a nude St George slaying the dragon. 'I know the judge and he's a reactionary through and through.'

'How long will we have to wait?' Garth asked. He admired the great grey stone edifice with its long narrow windows but why were there no seats? 'Let's walk,' he decided.

So they took the wide path that led around the great building. Lights blazed from the windows, even those devoted to humble activities like restoration. We are meant to be intimidated, Harriet thought, and those inside must feel it. The judge holding the audience spellbound after the complimentary speeches are over, the close-pressed perfumed bodies hardly able to breathe. And the artists would be there too, fighting to control their faces, ready to come forward, fingering speech notes from a pocket, or looking disdainful if their name was not called. Harriet shivered suddenly, thinking how Rosa must be feeling.

But Rosa was enjoying herself. Lucien stood, or rather swayed, beside her and, since they were not against a wall, she held his elbow. The introductions were long and tedious, almost chiding, as if those who had taken such trouble with their appearance needed their status reaffirmed. Rosa's cloak, splendid to walk in, felt uncomfortable when she stood. Cloaks are made for movement or throwing at someone's feet. If Lucien fell over she would swiftly fold it into a pillow. This image of herself took up most of the remainder of the director's speech. As the patron of honour got up, Lucien groaned audibly and the feet behind drowned him out with little shuffling sounds. Suddenly Rosa thought of a use for the cloak: she could put it over Lucien's head. She put a gloved hand over her mouth to stifle a giggle, and at that moment Lucien slid to the floor, knocking a glass of champagne from the man beside him and thrusting the man in front forward.

Harriet and Garth, who were standing by the great doors, saw a guard run along the hall, and a few minutes later Rosa appeared leading a little procession consisting of herself and the prone body of Lucien Humfress between two guards. A little wave of sound was stifled by the closing doors. Inside the master of ceremonies had called for a short break.

Lucien's family name had been mentioned; the awards would resume in a few moments; more silver trays of champagne were carried in, and some took advantage to change their position, loosen their collars or slip out of their shoes. Some even moved to the long windows to look out, but there was nothing to see.

Rosa's emerald cloak blended with the darkness as she loosed it from her shoulders and tenderly lifted Lucien's head.

'Propugnation,' he murmured. 'Hagiolatry.'

'I'll call a taxi, Miss,' one of the guards offered. 'If you'll just wait here. I presume you know where he lives.'

'I know where art lives,' Lucien murmured, trying and failing to rise. 'At the bottom of a well.'

When Lucien was safely deposited at his flat, Rosa, Harriet and Garth drove to Mr Wu's. A green light glowed in the shop, accenting the green felt on which the fruit lay; flowers drank in their buckets. A jar of Chinese fortune cookies stood by the big silver till. *Happiness will come at unexpected time* was on the one Harriet had received a few days before, when she was buying leeks.

The phone was ringing as Rosa fumbled with the key.

'Who is Millicent Vavasour?' a voice asked when Garth picked it up. 'We need a profile for tomorrow's *Argus.*'

'I'm sorry. You have a wrong number,' Garth replied. 'This is Wu's Greengrocery.

'Who is Millicent Vavasour?'

Later he was to congratulate himself on having a circular conversation. For there was no reply to this question. He held the receiver to his ear and jumped when it was slammed down.

Sebastian Gwyn Kellough admitted in an exclusive late-night interview with the Argus *that he had taken as much of a risk in his judgement as the mystery artist at last night's gala at the National Gallery. Before a glittering crowd of socialites and art aficionados, Mr Gwyn Kellough announced the winner only to discover that the 'artist' is possibly a pseudonym. Whoever 'Millicent Vavasour' is, and this paper suggests a recluse, one in an honoured Australian tradition, Mr Gwyn Kellough considered that the boldness of the judge should meet the boldness of the winning entry. He cogitated long and hard before settling on* Sgraffito, *passing over works which were accomplished, recognisably of one school or another. The runner-up,* Werribee *by J. Moncreiff is, said Mr Gwyn Kellough, a fine adaptation of the Fauve technique with landscape overtones. But* Sgraffito *goes further. It sweeps away the detritus of our lives – domestic architecture and still-lifes, the natural though circumscribed environment of urban existence – into an abstraction that is equally and competitively powerful. One of its greatest appeals is the fact that it allows the viewer to participate in this journey: recognisable elements not merely remain, they impart to their mortality a kind of tenderness. One example of this, Mr Gwyn Kellough explained, is the yellow teapot poised on what could be a windowsill yet already transmogrifying into the street beyond or the desert of the interior. Mr Gwyn Kellough's decision has been harshly criticised by several Friends of the National Gallery. See* Letters to the Editor, pg 14.

It was Rosa who dealt with the editor of the society page of the *Argus* and who was mysteriously vague – she soon perceived the need to be little more than that, and the interviewer would provide the rest – about Millicent Vavasour.

'I am beginning to get quite a picture of dear Millicent,' Rosa confided to Harriet, who marvelled at her bravery. 'Rather tall, thin, straight up and down figure, probably driven to art by a father who did not find her desirable enough to tease or warn her about boys. Perhaps there was an old barn on the property where she went to read novels.'

By day Rosa was assailed at The Flying Worm by more enquiries. Women's magazines were interested in what a lady artist might wear, but Rosa convinced them they should concentrate on clothes for an art opening instead, and they seemed relieved to abandon dust coats and long cardigans. In the rare quarter hours she had to herself, Rosa plotted the months ahead. She had discovered a gift for strategy, and reflected there were military men in her family, including, far back, a general.

Harriet was the perfect confidante and they spent evenings sitting side by side or leaning out the window looking into the street. Conversations with a landscape, Harriet thought. Years later, stemming from this, she would wonder if the best conversations didn't take place with words directed not at a person but at a view, like arrows whose falling was out of sight.

The McKelvey Trust had written to Rosa asking her to contact Millicent Vavasour for the handing over of the prize money. 'I shall stall them for a month or two and then it'll be confession time,' Rosa said. 'Interest in Millicent will have died down by then and she can be left to simply fade away.'

'Like Miss Haversham in her bridal gown,' said Harriet, trying to sound light-hearted. Still her job at Judd's could not last much longer. It was becoming pure poison.

'You, Garth and I will go up those broad steps together and meet the gallery director. I shall arrange an appointment beforehand. I expect it will last some time.'

'The poor judge.' And this time Harriet did feel amused. 'How will he feel?'

'Privately I shouldn't like to vouch for. Publicly he can talk about a new trend. Works by more than one hand.'

The first term of night classes was coming to an end. The second term would be more serious and, in the third, exams. Yet Harriet was no longer certain what she wanted. Occasionally she went for a coffee after class with Lewis and some of the others.

'Will this matter?' she said to him one evening. 'That in life one balanced the books or died with everything paid up. It's not a serious virtue.'

He looked at her for a moment before replying.

'What serious virtue do you want?' he asked, keeping his voice low, for the words sounded harsh.

'The cardinal virtues. Last things. I don't know,' Harriet said. 'Take Mr Wu, our landlord. He only sells fruit and vegetables yet he seems virtuous and content.' In the last week Mr Wu had asked permission to give Rosa and Harriet the leftover flowers on Friday nights. Now the flat was filled with bowls of anemones and carnations.

'Is it so hard at work?' Lewis asked, and was amazed to see a flash of anger in Harriet's eyes. Quickly he asked her to name the cardinal virtues.

'Prudence, temperance, courage, justice,' she recited and was instantly back at St Mary's.

A silence fell between them, as if they had walked between tombstones or thrown their accounting texts from a high building.

'My mother was a kind of Robin Hood,' Harriet went on, when fresh coffee had been brought. 'I don't know whether she realised it. Extra sticky buns for the poor. Whole biscuits inside bags of broken ones. Usually gingernuts.'

'Would you like something to eat?' Lewis asked. 'Is this art business still bothering you? Can I give you a ride home?' Would you like to marry me?, he almost added, slipping it onto the list. He tried to think of his virtues besides the ones enumerated: stolidness, a plodding endurance, pessimism masked by attempting to help others. He needed someone with real worries. Then he thought sadly of the age difference.

They walked out into the still-mild air. Stars shone above Latrobe Street and behind them someone raised a chair onto a wiped table. Probably this moment their cups were being dowsed in soap suds.

'You'll come back for more?' he asked. 'Profit and Loss. Though you wouldn't like it on your tombstone.'

'Harriet Betts, book-keeper' she replied.

On the drive home through quiet streets they composed suitable modest inscriptions: *moderately liked husband of, martinet wife of, conformist, social climber.* Restored to equilibrium, Lewis ventured a comradely handshake.

At Armadillos Garth saw Rosa walking below and beckoned to her. She indicated he should come down, and he took the stairs two at a time.

'Everything fine?' he asked, slipping an arm through hers as they continued walking. He thought of them as the Three Musketeers. Rosa would be D'Artagnan and himself Portos.

'It's all over between me and Donald,' Rosa said. 'He couldn't accept my involvement in what he considers a fraud.'

'They're delighted at the office,' Garth replied. 'They're thinking how they can use it. Garth Gordon who can fool art critics.'

They walked into a long dark coffee shop with glass-topped tables and chairs with animal-print cushions. Garth queued at the espresso machine, which was the dominant feature of the room, like a steam train. The coffee came in dark brown cups.

'I'm waiting for the third thing,' Rosa said, when Garth had settled the tray by his chair. 'Perhaps I'll lose my job.'

'Harriet is expecting to lose hers,' Garth said, and then felt his tactlessness. Concentrate on the woman you're with, his mother had told him. Women don't need much: small gestures and attention.

He put his hand out and covered Rosa's, but it could not lie flat because of the enormous perspex ring she was wearing; he left his hand there with his middle finger arched.

'I wouldn't have minded a quarrel,' Rosa went on. 'It's not as if he gave me a ring or anything. He just systematically withdrew. It was like watching the tide go out, a little more each day.'

'I read a novel like that,' Garth said. 'What was it called? *The Winslow Boy.* The woman was in love with a soldier. As soon as she started acting on her kid brother's behalf – he'd dishonoured the Navy or something – he legged it. All braid and no honour.'

'I suppose it's the hours I put in listening to his problems: whether he should go into music or art. His mother wants him to go to the Conservatorium.'

'He didn't by any chance have an entry in the competition?'

'I believe he did,' Rosa said, and her eyes were full of enlightenment and astonishment. 'I believe that's the truth of the matter. And it's quite true, it does set you free.'

Mr Wu brought up two leftover bunches of anemones and a big can of lychees. 'You girls have trouble,' he said. 'Need treat.'

He hovered in the doorway and Rosa patted his shoulder. 'You're a good friend, Mr Wu. We are lucky to have you.'

The lychees were as delicate and elusive of taste as the anemones were bold and comforting.

'Perhaps Mr Wu has heard about the money,' Harriet said, laying aside her spoon. 'Perhaps he associates it with trouble.'

'Obviously he's very wise,' Rosa said. She too was not in the mood for lychees.

A few days earlier the McKelvey Trust had paid out £175 each to Garth, Rosa and Harriet. The judge had stood by his estimate of the work, saying it was not his role to investigate the artist or artists, to adjudicate on the use of a pseudonym. The press had made much of what were, in fact, sparse clues. The three had produced, by design or accident, a work that had parallels with work being produced in Europe. Privately he doubted he would be asked to judge an award again and was considering writing a paper about the whole affair.

On a Saturday morning, six weeks after the glittering evening, Garth, Harriet and Rosa had climbed the broad steps of the National Gallery, entered the magnificent doors and been directed by a guard to the director's office. The cheques, in plain envelopes, were handed over, a brief speech made, and they walked down the steps again. It was unheard of wealth; Mr Wu had reason to be concerned.

They sat on a bench in Russell Street and looked at the traffic; Rosa slit her envelope and pulled out the cheque: there was nothing else inside, not even a compliments slip. It was drawn on the Commonwealth Bank of Australia.

Autumn brought new colours to the city and new fruit and vegetables to Mr Wu. He appeared more stooped and climbed up the stairs more slowly with a bunch of navy blue irises. Leaves swirled down, and people passing changed colours too. Some persisted longer in light clothes; at Judd's the bolts of cloth darkened: mauve and grey and burgundy were the fashionable colours. A small piece in the *Argus* noted that the Trust had paid the prize money to the three creators of *Sgraffito* and the matter was considered closed.

'I'd like to see you in my office after closing,' Mr Judd said to Harriet on the Friday following. A canister was winging its way towards her, and a small boy attached to his mother by reins was looking up and pointing. Harriet, looking down, met his eye, as bright and shiny as a brown button. Mr Judd darkened the doorway and she had not been aware of his presence.

The cleaners with their wide brooms were moving between the aisles when she made her way to his office. She carried her coat over her arm, and her paisley Viyella scarf.

'I may as well come straight to the point,' Mr Judd said.

Harriet remained standing, tightening her calf muscles and straightening her spine. Clerks in London, Garth had informed her, often had trouble with their winter coats; their pale bent shoulders could hardly support the weight of winter wool.

'Go ahead then,' said Harriet, and her voice was firm. She sounded like her mother correcting Mrs Toogood when she demanded to know why the broken biscuits were not broken.

'I always found you impertinent,' he went on, eyeballing her. Neither would sit. 'And now this art business. It sounds like a cheap fraud to me. Several of the customers have made comments. They don't like the mickey being taken.'

'I imagine not,' said Harriet. 'Especially if they are dressed from Judd's.'

'And what's that supposed to mean, may I ask? Are you some kind of anarchist?'

'Do I look like one? I should be flattered.'

For a wild moment Harriet wished she could deck herself out in everything in the shop: brocades and satins, sequins and feathers, a bridal headpiece of pearls and netting, fake boa sold by the yard. She could be pinned into it like a store mannequin.

'I don't want you here,' Mr Judd shouted, and his tone was blustering. 'You're a bad influence. A woman who can forge art.'

'I assure you it was quite original, as the judge said in his summing up.'

'Then why did you hide behind a false name?' he asked, looking triumphant. 'Tell me that.'

'Because we all hide behind a false name of one kind or another. Perhaps yours is respectability to cover your attentions to young women on the staff. If my art hasn't gone unnoticed, neither has your philandering.'

'Get out of here. Before I lay my hands on you.'

And Harriet had turned on her heel, calves as taut as steel now, and marched out. She heard his movement behind her and half-expected a blow to land between her shoulders. She felt heat as if his face burned. A middle-aged woman, pushing a broom by the button counter, turned to look at her and move the broom aside.

I am contaminated, Harriet thought.

'I'll send what's owing on.' His voice followed her, and then she was in the street. Something about putting it with your other ill-gotten gains but she could not hear the exact words.

A tram, gliding to a halt, bore her away.

Rosa wrapped her arms around Harriet the second she caught sight of her face.

'I left some things in my locker,' Harriet said into Rosa's shoulder.

'I'll get them for you. It'll be a pleasure.'

'There's some salary owing too.'

'Another pleasure.'

'You think life should be nothing but pleasure?' Harriet asked, releasing herself. Rosa's face swam in front of her; then she realised she was responsible for some of the smudges.

'I'll make some tea, we'll look at Mr Wu's customers, and you can repeat as much of the dialogue as you remember.'

'The dialogue, yes.'

Harriet went off to clean her teeth and brush her hair. She half-filled the basin with cold water and dashed it on her face.

A true friend always wanted to hear dialogue.

Unknown to Harriet, Rosa's position at The Flying Worm was also under threat: the woman who greeted you at the desk and whispered prices in your ear and the woman who was part of a dubious prize was a difficult combination in the art world.

'If only five years had passed,' Steffo Casteluccio said. 'Then you could be pointed out as an art radical.'

'And in five years,' Rosa objected, 'I could have returned to my perfect disguise, giving nothing away, smiling mysteriously like some Melbourne Mona Lisa.'

'Precisely,' Steffo said.

'And yet on the walls,' Rosa went on, feeling warm, and grateful that her skin was not the type to blush, 'we applaud the brave risk-takers, the breakers of new ground, the provocative. How very enlightening.'

'Don't take it personally,' Steffo said, detecting anger nonetheless. 'We must simply think of a strategy.'

'Well let me know when you've got something in place.'

Rosa turned away, walked firmly on the polished floor which gave back a glow like patent-leather shoes, and went into the stockroom. She lifted canvas after canvas from its fellow and let it fall back, for the stockroom was more like the real world where art was treated with disdain. Looking down she saw there was one of Lucien's. It was from his 'Green Nudes' period. Green, he had explained in the catalogue notes, was the tint of light on flesh. It seemed to Rosa it was also the colour of decay, the green before someone was violently ill, the green of a fractured bone. *If this is what they do when the wood is green* came to her mind but she couldn't remember the source. The backs of the canvases felt dry and listless. Rosa straightened her back, washed her hands and started to make the morning coffee. She would bring a cup to Miriam, who had taken her place at the front desk, with a demure expression, as if five years had already passed.

Harriet thought she might spend the next morning, or even the whole day, since it was her possession, in bed, but to her surprise she felt invigorated. She bounded into Mr Wu's shop, after Rosa had departed, and bathed her eyes in the fresh colours of broccoli, aubergines and red peppers, and in the gloriously jumbled bunches of gentians and alstroemerias in the big iron buckets. I'll always arrange flowers like Mr Wu, she decided, and it seemed she had discovered something profound and at an early hour. She intended to spend part of the day revising for the book-keeping exam in two weeks' time but first she might go walking or tram riding.

'You look better, Miss Harriet,' said Mr Wu, lifting apples from their wrapping paper and giving each an extra polish on his apron. Harriet marvelled at his energy, a slow fire like that of an apparently sleeping animal, for Mr Wu stood on his feet the whole day except for a brief respite when he drank green tea.

Harriet rode on the Coburg tram, sitting passively on the wooden seat, regarding everything with the slowly strengthening interest of a convalescent. She watched the bodies going to work, looking as if they were under some command not willingly received; an artificial eagerness lit some faces, especially of the young women, who had stood before mirrors applying makeup. The men's faces were neutral, their defences based on the set of a jaw or a carriage of the head. How private we are, Harriet thought, as the tram shrieked to a stop and a new crowd forced themselves on board. Beside her a young blonde woman strap-hung. Her eyes gazed with the soft intensity of someone admiring a shop window but her only view could be a segment of street and other bodies.

At lunch time she bought a packet of sandwiches with mixed fillings, an apple and a soft drink. She sat on a green bench in Flagstaff Gardens, and when an elderly woman, clutching an assortment of dirty plastic bags, perched on the end of the bench Harriet turned her head and looked into her face. The hands in their unseasonal fingerless gloves delicately arranged the bags at her feet: there was a kind of gentility that reminded Harriet of one of her aunts. The sort of woman, she thought, who would wait to be spoken to, though that must have been in another life. The marshalled bags could have been children. Slowly Harriet ate one of her sandwiches. Then she passed the greaseproof package towards the woman. 'Would you care to join me?' she asked.

In the afternoon Harriet wrote a postcard to Billy. *Come to Melbourne when you are older. I am jobless at present – not to be emulated – but I am taking a few days off. I love this city: in the press of my concerns I had forgotten to see it. One day I shall show it to you properly. This is the Victoria Market which you would love.*

On the way home she walked past Rosa's gallery. There was no sign of Rosa and there was a new woman sitting at the desk. Harriet didn't feel dressed enough to go in and ask.

She had talked to five strangers and been cheered by the kindness of strangers. 'Take care,' one had said, and another, 'Look after yourself.' Perhaps they had guessed she was un-employed, that the pace of the city had fallen from her and, though she walked almost as briskly, she was loitering.

The book-keeping exam was approaching rapidly and each afternoon, when the flat was quiet except for the ping and slide of Mr Wu's silver till, Harriet studied for two hours. But she found it hard to concentrate: whatever her mother had found absorbing in mathematics escaped her. She guessed there were two parts, like an equation: the secret rewards of the columns of figures at night when the accounting books were spread out in her parents' room, unchanged after her father's death, and her mother's guardianship by day. For years Harriet had not been able to think of her mother with more than a faint affection; now, looking down with swimming eyes at double entry and net assets, she imagined her as a kind of female Solomon. Would she have offered to divide Mrs Kelsey's disagreeable baby, Seamus, in half if he didn't stop squalling and hand half to Mrs Cumberland who was childless? Harriet put her hands to her temples, closed the books and peeled a mandarin. She ate the segments as she walked downstairs. Mr Wu had pushed a bucket of tiger lilies out onto the pavement and their scent followed her for three or four paces and then stopped. A dog turd would do the same, Billy had pointed out. Nevertheless to be assailed was better than nothing: perhaps her mother had felt this in the evenings in the quiet room with her accounts. The scent brought back the heaped bouquets at her mother's funeral, but she shook them off – everything must fail, was designed to, after a certain number of paces.

When her feet led her to Judd's, Harriet went boldly in and bought a piece of dark red velvet from the remnant bin; she tapped on the window of The Flying Worm and Rosa came to the door and embraced her. She tore a corner of the brown paper parcel tied with string – Judd's would countenance nothing else – and the rich colour showed through.

'A cushion, I think,' said Harriet.

'A waistcoat and fez,' said Rosa.

And then there was something to tell. Just before she left, Garth had phoned and invited her to the advertising agency ball.

Auckland

Extraordinary things happen every day
in our street only this morning
the ground opened at my feet
without warning

'Any Time Now', ALLEN CURNOW

Billy Lascelles came to Melbourne in 1968 to study at the university. He thought he wanted to be an engineer. Perhaps it was the Derwent bridge that stayed in his mind, lying flat as a hair ribbon across the smooth River Derwent. Though harbour was at the end of the bridge, and arrival, crossing it felt like an escape. His mother had anguished at his leaving but he had assured her the University of Tasmania did not amount to much. Not that he knew this for a fact but Emma had no evidence with which to contradict him, no idea of courses offered or the status of professors. For her he had painted a picture that at once demeaned her – an idealistic society of equals, a dialogue that might be expected among angels or some cerebral neutered creatures – and left her feeling inferior, as if she had not supplied him with some essential nutrient. His father's indifference he expected. There was no scope, even if the floods came, for a bridge at Guiseford. Fire and drought were more likely. 'A bridge to nowhere,' was Jack's laconic comment, for Billy gave no guarantee that he would ever return to the farm to which he was heir.

'Perhaps I can make my fortune,' he said to his mother on the last day when he allowed her to supervise and fuss over his packing. 'This place could do with an injection of capital.'

'You sound like Dick Whittington,' Emma said.

The bed on which his clothes were spread out had been there since childhood; his shirts with their collars neatly pointing and their buttons done up lay on an old white bedcover washed so many times it was a wonder it still held together: fine threads showed and part of the scalloped edge was torn. A heavy suitcase with not much space inside had been brought down from the top of a bureau and lined with fresh paper. Socks curled into balls – his mother had shown him how to do that: three sections of the top rolled against one – lay in a little mound.

'It'll take the best part of a week to enrol,' Billy said. 'I hear it's as complicated as finding your way through a maze.'

'I hope you meet someone then,' Emma replied. She was thinking of someone clutching a piece of string, or a sort of conga, hands on waists and feet moving in unison. Perhaps that came later, a drinking song.

The case was closed with keys that had been found at the bottom and, for extra safety, a leather strap. It didn't quite match, but a man need not be conscious of his luggage.

The Princess of Tasmania was still lumbering between Devonport and Melbourne, the same cramped wallowing tub he had taken his school trip on, pressed elbow to elbow with boys leaning over the rail, Gus Turkington being sick and the wind blowing the sour liquid back in their faces or onto their maroon blazer sleeves. Turkington never made it up after that: no one wanted to sit beside him or discuss an exhibit in a museum.

Billy went up on deck immediately after depositing his suitcase in a four-berth cabin, the cheapest: he could not be fussed for one night. There was another man there and they skirmished lightly for bunks. He leaned over the rail and looked back on the island which was fast disappearing. *If you want to put another person on you have to take a sheep off* was the old joke. Or it could have been an apple: posters of huge apples, roughly the shape of the island, had started appearing, especially as most visitors docked at Devonport. Perhaps they expected to walk through a grove of apple trees or see apples everywhere when they tottered to the waiting bus. Yet apples, from Billy's observation – he had an observation about most things but not a lot to connect them to – apples were notoriously hard to locate in the thick foliage, as if each was guarded by a leaf. The world was so different from the way it was portrayed: apples the size of a human face on a poster – *Come to the Apple Island.* He thought of his mother then, the way he had ladled on the notion of failure as if it were her fault Guiseford was dry and arid and Ouse had no intellectual stimulus and only one cinema showing outdated movies that might have been in a time warp. He knew he was abandoning her to something she had been or been becoming before his birth, something resigned and irritatingly stoical which would only increase his father's annoyance. He saw his parents as two dried pods together, hardly able to rescue farm or house, eating skimpy meals and barely speaking. Perhaps his mother would not even set the table now he was gone.

Billy's first plan, after enrolment and securing his place in Ridley College – he had a place saved, dependent on showing up by a certain day – was to look up his cousin Harriet. And he also thought and wondered about Rosa, whose seductiveness seemed to have grown over the years. Probably she had only condescended to him, gauging what was necessary for a schoolboy, for he was beginning to realise that a woman sophisticated in one sphere might be capable of infinite variations. Probably she gave him a mere flick of her talents: his grubby face, looking up, with his back lengthened and embryonic shoulders pulled back, as if the blades were trying for wings, had occasioned a deep analytical look that had thrilled him to his soul. And he longed to think of more daring exploits than hiding under a steam train at the museum. Still it was the wrong way round: a man did not want rescue by a woman, and rescue it had been. He had behaved reasonably well in the years following, mainly to please her.

So he trailed patiently through the enrolment procedures, queuing good-humouredly even when they told him he was in the wrong line, listening to the exaggerated sighs and chatter around him, the near hysteria of some of the girls, the bluffing of the boy-men fresh from protected colleges. His room, when he found it, was pleasantly impersonal and shabby, as if its stone walls had received endless layers of cream paint. Holes had been gouged for pictures, and tape had left snail-like tracks. The small wardrobe with its jamming door looked beaten, though its golden body was still standing. But there was a decent long window, and outside a yellow hibiscus: one of the flowers was pressed against the glass.

Billy put his case down on the bed: he could unpack later. The books he had purchased, Hoff's *The Analysis of Structures* and Durelli, Phillips and Tsao's *Introduction to the Theoretical and Experimental Analysis of Stress and Strain*, he placed reverently on the desk. Daunting formulae flashed past as he flicked the pages. Perhaps he was making a mistake, as his father had informed him in no uncertain terms: he was in love with escape and had transferred his liking to a symbol.

He pulled the rickety chair, unsuited for long periods of sitting, up to the desk and took out a postcard to send to his mother. A few words about safe arrival, an easy crossing (the image again), a brief parole of his room. The only other chair had threadbare patches on the arms and the springs in the seat were gone. It could be worse, he thought. There was Harriet to re-claim acquaintance with, and news – even a morsel, he felt, would satisfy him – of Rosa.

Harriet, in the last month of pregnancy, took her heavy body into the garden of the house in Cotham Road and contemplated the washing line and the washing basket. There had been no time for Garth to hang the clothes this morning, and she had assured him there was nothing heavy, only a few towels and pillowcases, a shirt and underclothes. If there had been sheets or bedcovers he would have flung them roughly over the line for her to ease out and peg. 'I'll make it up when I get home,' he called, tie floating over his shoulder like a propeller as he dashed around the side of the house, over the rough paving of the path which he warned her about on at least a daily basis.

The towels, the tea towels, the individual socks seemed to take ages; Harriet pressed her palms against the flat of her back, leaned back as if her palms made a wall. There was a low straggly lillypilly hedge which Garth had promised to remove: it was next in line after the path. White puffy clouds were hurrying across the sky; already the wind had twisted a pillow-case, and a corner of a towel was caught on a peg. Footsteps were coming around the side of the path. Harriet put out her hand to lift the clothes basket. When Billy caught sight of her, she had the wicker basket over her belly, like a Roman soldier under a shield. Slim, delicate-looking Harriet. She held the basket out towards him, base up, and he thought he would need arms ten feet long to embrace her.

'I'm already embraced,' she said to him later, when they were seated at the kitchen table with a yellow teapot between them. 'It's like having something leap and tackle you. Something that's taken into your skin.'

'Flesh of my flesh. It's very literal, isn't it?' Billy remarked, glad part of the mound was out of sight. He thought they should have nude pregnant statues in museums so men could walk around them, examining them at their leisure, like women were supposed to do to the statue of David. When you confronted one in real life you hardly knew where to put your eyes. He had stepped back from the hard embrace and concentrated on Harriet's face. There were violet shadows under her eyes, and her skin seemed both damp and taut. He told her about enrolling and orientation week, exaggerating everything: the all-night session of vampire movies he had sat through, mindlessly eating popcorn and staggering into the dawn street as if he too had risen from a tomb. Now he thought he would never see another offspring of *Nosferatu*, nor would their tricks work again. As the vampire had fastened his teeth on a white throat Billy had wondered about finding a dentist in Melbourne if it was not covered by student health.

'Due in three weeks,' Harriet said, as if the question hung between them. 'Garth is taking his annual holidays. Poor darling doesn't know what he's in for.'

'I guess not,' said Billy. Did anyone, ever? The white throat of the young woman lying there like a Burne-Jones in the artfully disordered sheets; one hand was even turned palm upwards, exposing blue veins. Whoever wrote the script had allowed time for the vampire to gloat.

'And Rosa,' Billy asked. 'Do you still see her?'

'She's away at present but she is going to be godmother. Just in case she never has any, she says.'

The thought of Rosa having children had never occurred to Billy: it came as a shock. An image of her filling a doorway, dressed in furs, carrying parcels, came easier. He could not tell Harriet it was Rosa who had made the difference when he was a schoolboy, not her.

'She's working at The Windsor,' Harriet went on. 'After the scandal with the art prize she couldn't keep her job at The Flying Worm. She stayed for just six months. She tried a few more galleries but they were all closed to her. I think they were scared we might start painting again.'

It hadn't mattered so much for herself and Garth: the advertising world regarded hoax in the same league as coax. He had shrugged off his minor celebrity with a mock-modesty that did him no harm at all.

'Did you know Rosa worked for Mr Wu for a few months?'

Donald and Rosa had split and she was between jobs. In that period she had prepared beautiful meals.

'The Chinese guy?' Billy asked.

'Dead,' Harriet replied. 'Rosa found him one morning lying on the floor.'

Not for the first time she thought birth brought thoughts of death. A bucket of spider orchids had spilled and Mr Wu's trouser legs were wet. And Rosa, with so much grief in her life, had lain down on the floor beside him and sobbed.

Twenty minutes, she had explained to Harriet that night. Twenty minutes before I called the police. She had lied about the time, made it seem she had just arrived for work. Two buckets of flowers were already on the pavement; probably the orchids were next. A wild impulse to surround Wu's body with fruit and vegetables, to cover his face with the pink tissue in which individual apples were wrapped, overcame Rosa. Instead she wiped her face with a piece of the tissue, holding the apple in one hand – Granny Smith – then set it back on the tray. She went to the door to let the policeman in, and since she was so obviously in shock and Mr Wu so obviously dead, few questions were asked. Billy did not ask too many questions about Rosa: Harriet's form seemed a reproof when she rose from the chair and brought a plate of biscuits. He would see Rosa again; he might even go to The Windsor and enquire for her. He could not expect anything, but his heart rose.

Back in his room he completed a wall chart for his lectures and seminars. He opened his mother's present, *The Story of Engineering* by J K Finch, and read a few paragraphs of the introduction. Engineering was a high calling and the author invoked the great feats of the Romans, the aqueducts that still functioned, the daring works of Isambard Kingdom Brunel. But Billy's spirits did not lift at this as they were supposed. He had known a welding textbook invoke something similar: knights in stifling masks which they lifted to peer out with scorched eyes. His mother's incessant reading and this father's scorn of it had left him suspicious of words.

Nor did his first lectures fill him with confidence. Engineers, it was well known, had an apish reputation: their behaviour in capping week, when they went about beating their chests and terrorising females, meant for most of the year they were shunned. Billy, with thoughts of Rosa circulating in his head, was abstracted as laboratory, drawing office and class-room work was outlined and the chalk began its scratching on the blackboard. They poured out into the corridors and the noise reverberated off the thick walls and rose up the stairs. Would any of these faces make a Brunel, Billy wondered. It was what had drawn him to engineering in the first place: those designs that not only showed the workings but gloried in them, rivets as ornaments, girders and struts, parts not to be concealed but to celebrate the clean and clear thought that created them. His childhood book had had a photograph of Brunel's suspension bridge at Clifton. Now, back in his room, which was already beginning to feel like a cell, he consulted a leaflet that had been poked under his door. *The Melburnian Debating Society*, it read. *The Debating Society is desperately in need of new brains.* It brought back an image of the vampire films of the week before. *Next month's debate will be: Is fascism dead and is it nurtured by universities? The meeting will be addressed by Dr Amos Goldfarb, a well-known Jewish scholar and commentator, who has worked for the Jewish Documentation Centre.*

Harriet's delivery, when it came, was a fiasco. She could laugh about it later: the students in white coats surrounding her, since the Queen Victoria was a teaching hospital and she had presumably signed something; the obstetrician, a tall thin man, so ascetic-looking it seemed he could have nothing to do with sex: something to do with the extreme cleanliness of his skin, the fastidious way he inserted his hands into the gloves held out to him. The nurses who attended her, indifferently, sprang suddenly into a solicitude so false and fawning Harriet had a furious desire to protest. They had been unable to contact Garth at Ogilvy & Mather, and when he eventually arrived, tie streaming, damp hair clinging to his forehead, Harriet was back in the ward, asleep.

'A typical primipara,' Dr Jago had said in a voice as dry as leaves. 'And you may notice Mrs Gordon beautifully exhibits the butterfly mask. I think you remarked on that, Nurse Golightly,' turning his head slightly towards a pretty blonde nurse who blushed fiercely. 'Never underestimate a nurse.' And when the first child had crowned, a tight wet ball of fuzz that Harriet could not see though one of the energised nurses had offered a mirror, and the shoulders had eased themselves through; when the cord had been clamped and the specialist was turning away as if receiving applause, there had been another wave of pain, and it was not the placenta at all but a twin.

'Hidden,' Dr Jago said later, when the boy and girl, eight minutes apart and forever contesting superiority, were laid in their plastic cradles, swaddled as if they were already being punished for fooling the great specialist. And Harriet, too tired to protest, had gone along with it, almost as if it were her fault, that some constriction of organs, some personal irregularity had been to blame. But no one in the surrounding coterie had laughed until Dr Jago did.

Three weeks later, when Harriet was home again and the twins were miraculously asleep, curled together in a position she marvelled at, Rosa arrived, arms full of presents. She took one look at her friend's pale face and tossed the presents onto a chair. A few small squeaks issued from a parcel.

'You look all in,' Rosa said. And when Harriet just nodded, she wrapped her arms around her, feeling how soft Harriet had become, how oddly frail.

'It's their being twins,' Harriet said later, as if this was the heart of the problem. 'Everyone, including Garth, is so pleased, as if I've performed a card trick. Two for the effort of one. One of each. A pigeon pair. And now you'll stop. I can see it in their eyes.'

Experience had taught Rosa to say nothing in the face of grief – it was Harriet who had listened over and over to her laments about finding Mr Wu, until finally she had come to the conclusion she was mourning the entire human condition.

'Is it having to do everything twice?' Rosa asked when the kettle had boiled. Her parcels were the only tidy thing in the room.

'Not really. Garth helps and we bathe them in the evening.' Their names were Susannah and Samuel. Talcum flew everywhere and the air smelt like a hothouse. 'It's their completion in each other,' Harriet said. 'You've seen the way they sleep together. Perhaps the mother of twins always feels like a servant.'

'Only if she treats herself as one,' Rosa said briskly. She was trying to blot out her behaviour at the hotel in Brisbane. A few drinks in the bar, after a day poring over brochures and consulting with tour guides and hotel managers, and it had seemed natural to join Simon Frater for a whisky in his room. They had stood at the window looking down Alice Street as the street lights flickered on. Fireflies, Rosa thought, as Simon's arm encircled her waist. She shook her head to clear her mind of the rest, the scuttling along the corridor in a borrowed bathrobe, avoiding the dinner dishes under their covers.

'Billy called. He said he wanted to see you. In that evasive way men have.'

'Not too evasive,' Rosa replied. 'Another candidate for disillusion.'

Life at the university soon settled into a pattern. Leaves started falling from the trees; the students from the hostel made contact and light friendships over noticeboards, endless cups of coffee in the battered common room where the chintz covers needed washing. A ginger cat named Maximus was evidently a resident and took it in turn to sample the beds. To have Maximus on your bed was considered a piece of luck, like carrying a rabbit's paw.

Billy's first marks, in spite of his love of Isambard Kingdom Brunel, were little above average. He had imagined himself being discovered, not in his first year, which was unrealistic, but perhaps towards the end of it. The hand on the shoulder, the passing on of a significant glance from the professor whose gown was dusted in dandruff and chalk. Instead they sat in a tiered lecture theatre and Professor Blekinsop rasped through his notes as if knowledge at Section I was hardly worth imparting.

'So he hasn't thrown any chalk yet,' Todd Simpson re-marked to Billy as they walked along Grattan Street. That was the charm of it: learning and the real world so close. Simpson was repeating his first year in Structural Engineering because of illness the year before. 'He gets a movement in his shoulders before he lets fly. It's like seeing an old bat come to life.'

'What's his aim like?' Billy asked, because Professor Blekinsop showed minimal movement in all parts of his anatomy, like a creature who has been electrocuted and is conserving himself.

'He used to play cricket,' Todd said. 'Last year he hit a student in the eye and it had to be hushed up.'

'Something to look forward to,' Billy remarked. Perhaps that would be his distinction.

A direct hit to the heart.

Anna Gregor was crossing the quad at Auckland University on her way to her anthropology lecture. The little quad was raised, with stone walls that looked as if they had been laid by hand and then weathered for a century. Just after enrolment week a stage had been erected there and Richard III had paced the boards, leaping onto the grass when he cried, 'A horse! A horse! My kingdom for a horse!' The stage had been hung with banners produced by the Art School. Anna's mind was on the great apes she was studying, their bonding patterns, their patriarchy (for apes were undeniably patriarchal), and what this could mean for human society, separated, it sometimes seemed, by a mere veil. Her lecturer, Dr Loeb, had the rounded shoulders of an ape and the same deep broad chest. She would have to ask for an extension for her essay, but she felt reasonably confident. Dr Loeb had a weakness for blondes, and tears – perhaps like a great ape – reduced him to tenderness. If all else failed she thought she could hurl herself at his chest and beat her hands against it, minding to be feeble and saying in a low tremulous voice, 'I need more time for my primatology essay.'

In the event the extension was granted without any histrionics. Dr Loeb was standing in the doorway of his office, collecting essays from a slot fixed to the door. Anna waited until he turned, and simply blurted it out. His eyes, under their very bushy brows, looked into hers for a second. She thought he had the sharp appraising eyes of a senior male gorilla – the alpha male would be Professor Hunnibal, Head of Department. Perhaps, since the extension was so readily granted, Dr Loeb regarded her as an adolescent female, not yet worthy of his attention.

The real reason – that Dr Loeb was in the middle of an affair and behind with his marking – could not occur to Anna. She walked back, between the library and the registry, and crossed into Albert Park. Here there were no signs of apes, only a kind of harmless colonialism: a statue of Queen Victoria who nonetheless looked dyspeptic – as Anna crossed the path behind her, she noticed the Queen's dress bunched at the back over commodious hips; a cannon as white and useless as marzipan, and a mild white solider on a pedestal.

Anna shared a house in St Georges Bay Road with two other students. It was the worst house in a good street and one of the best located. It had a view of the sea and mangroves, a delightful elevation. The walls were peeling and the window frames warped but a verandah along one side, furnished with cane castoffs, was delightful to sit in. Anna had contributed a maidenhair fern and a peace lily. It was there she sat on a chair padded with cushions to read about the great apes. The way they had of building daily nests reminded her of bed-making, which was in short supply in the flat.

Her own principles of feminism were in sharp contrast to the hierarchy of the apes, yet whenever she closed the book with its photograph of the gorilla seen from the rear, his massive shoulders straddling both covers, with droplets of water adorning the fur, she felt the inappropriateness of including such sentiments in her essay. The female apes were thoroughly domestic and watchful, in the way of subdued women. They had energy not for war or territory but for their social positions. Secretly Anna wished she might discover a female tribe in which a different order prevailed, surprising Dr Hunnibal who seemed to regard the apes as avatars of human behaviour. So many people in the Anthropology Department seemed to be adorned with a bone pendant, an ivory tooth, or to wear, in the case of Associate Professor Grice or Dr Fernando, dangling earrings made of raffia or feathers.

Anna put the book she was reading on the floor, cover uppermost, so she could still look down on the shoulders of the gorilla and the droplet of water on his blue-black fur. She balanced her pad on her knee and wrote: *The patriarchal nature of the great ape society should not be seen as either forerunner or analogous to human society. The enclosed terrain, inhabited by the great apes, protected their communities from disintegration.* Dr Loeb would not accept this. Not for the first time Anna, who was liable to flights of fancy, marvelled at the difficulties of academic writing. Each sentence must lend weight to the one that followed and be made secure by the one before. Sometimes it reminded her of an obscure state in Central Europe, cut off by forests and mountains from language contamination. No one outside their borders could understand them, but it was considered purity.

The back door slammed and there was the sound of a load of books being set down. Anna picked up the gorilla by his spine and inserted a marker in the chapter she had been reading.

Rosa and Billy met in the lounge bar of the Windsor Hotel in well-upholstered chairs with heavy silver coffee pots and jugs between them, a bowl of sugar lumps and silver tongs. The Windsor prided itself on tradition and a slower time than that which operated outside in Spring Street. Billy felt instantly at a disadvantage. He wore a pea jacket, and his hair, freshly washed, combed, then combed down again by his hands, felt unruly. And Rosa had assumed command in a way he did not quite like, as if she was showing the workings of the great hotel to him like someone showing the parts of a watch. Of course she must go behind the mahogany doors which swung open and softly closed, keeping what lay behind them secret. The receptionists in their smart dark green blazers would occasionally turn on their heels and glide through a door. Billy wondered if their expressions, all polite concern and polished competence, hushed voices when presenting a bill, stayed the same on the other side of the door or did they put a hand to a forehead and allow their posture to sag. He had these distracting thoughts because Rosa had changed.

Her hair was still dark and she wore the same perfume – at least Billy thought it was the same perfume that, wafting over him as a schoolboy, had so enchanted him with the notion of being in the presence of an exotic creature. But somehow Rosa seemed less knowing; once he caught her looking at a fine marcasite watch on her wrist.

'Hotels are where people land up,' she was saying, lifting the coffee pot and pouring refills for them both. The pot seemed to hold just the right amount. 'Don't let the appearance of wealth fool you. There are quite a few people here who are washed up.' Last evening in the Grand Ballroom she had witnessed one of the thrice-divorced regulars send a cocktail to a young unaccompanied businesswoman who was trying to read a paperback Perry Mason at her table. *The Case of the Caretaker's Cat*, Rosa had read as she passed by, indicating with an imperceptible gesture to the head waiter that the young woman was not to be pestered.

'It's a good idea not to leave your key on the table,' Rosa had said in a low soft voice as she passed the table, and the young woman had looked up and blushed.

'Your studies?' Rosa was asking, as Billy still took in her appearance, piece by piece, for later analysis. Had her face thickened? Her figure? He had been short then, and the Rosa, deliciously scented, who had hugged him after his escape from the Museum of Applied Science, had enveloped him. Something like coming on the clouds of heaven.

'I'm just going to be average,' he said, and it suddenly seemed his defiance in leaving Tasmania had been nothing more than that, and now the impulse was gone a different kind of reckoning was in place.

'Why think that?' Rosa asked. Though it was a thought she had had about herself.

Simon Frater came through the lobby, saw her talking to Billy, raised a questioning eyebrow. She looked more intently at Billy then, noting the circles under his eyes, the lost expression in them.

'We could meet,' she said. 'Away from the hotel. We could go on the river. Somewhere there is a chance to talk.'

'As long as it's not *The Princess*,' he said. 'It's the lamest duck I've ever been on.'

'Me too,' Rosa said. 'It's not like sailing off on the back of a swan.'

She came with him to the big glass doors, their glass so dazzling you had to be sophisticated to get through. One of the doormen slightly raised his top hat, letting a triangle of light onto his head. There were so many cars pulling up, taxis being whistled, it was hard to speak.

'I'll arrange a time,' Rosa said. 'I think I'll write to you. That's probably best.'

But when Billy walked along Spring Street, away from marble and mahogany, red carpet and chandeliers, potted palms and shaded lamps, the air felt sour. It's not the real world she's in, he thought. Then he braced his shoulders, told himself it was a concentration of exhaust. But he felt better when he was under shabbier awnings again.

Anna found the postcard on an earthenware plate in the St Georges Bay house. Never, afterwards, could she forgive that it was a postcard, its message clear to any eye. To be fair, she doubted if it had been scrutinised: there were other letters on top, a gas bill and a brochure about having your house chemically washed. *Restore your residence to mint condition* read the green writing across the envelope.

Afraid it's over, Denzil Gibbs had written, in black ink, in the sprawling script with the trawling y's he affected. She looked at it, eyes blurred, and it formed the word *raid*. Denzil had always prided himself on his bluntness: the contrast between an engineer and an architect, which his brother was. *I'm sorry,* the card went on, free now to soften the blow, now that the earth had been pounded and the piles driven in. *Sorry* felt like a bird passing overhead, an insignificant sparrow.

Automatically Anna shuffled the letters as if she were scooping her hand into a rock pool: there was one for Juliet, surely familial, the envelope was so densely packed, and something for Kirsten that looked like a dentist's appointment. No one else had a postcard. She turned it over, for it had been lying message side up, and it was the Old Engineering Building, the University of Melbourne, meaning it had come from the university bookshop or a stand by some coffee bar. She could not bring herself to pin it on her wall; instead she stuffed it into the bottom of her underclothes drawer.

Some nights Rosa slept at The Windsor. Her work as assistant conference organiser to Simon Frater, the conference manager, meant long hours, especially in autumn and winter when the flow of conferences was at its height. Something about rain and cold seemed to drive hordes of dark-suited men and an increasing number of women, classic suits enlivened by a silk blouse or an edge of lace overflowing a flat pocket, in through the doors, shaking umbrellas and stamping their feet. The warmth of the hotel, the huge bouquet of fresh flowers on the big round rosewood table, the bellboys in their dark green jackets with gold buttons, surrounded them. At the reception desk Rosa stood, clipboard in hand, elegant fountain pen at the ready, to indicate the way to the Winston Room or the Canberra Room. She would have checked that fresh coffee was waiting, and carafes of water, and that the long tables, so like a wedding banquet, had the look of largesse to come. What this largesse was to be – the fruits of their brains written in various coloured pens or the delicious buffet which would be wheeled in at midday – she was not sure. Certainly at the beginning everyone seemed to be favouring brains. Several of the men declined coffee as if their adrenalin levels were sufficiently pumped up, and some of the women took only a glass of water.

Rosa made her welcoming speech, wishing them fruitful deliberations (some of the men smiled and a woman ran a comb quickly through her hair), assuring them of her availability at all times. The final day often had a banquet at which the brains seemed in abeyance and the hesitant coffee drinkers polished off bottles of champagne.

Simon Frater had invited her to make his suite her own and some nights she spent with him. Rosa sensed their liaison was already in decline; she could tell this because the courtesy between them had increased. Simon had a wife in the suburbs and a child attending a private school. Rosa herself was in the process of paying off a small apartment in Gertrude Street: the whole apartment was not much larger than one of the luxury suites.

She looked out at Parliament House and thought about writing to Billy. He is surprised at the change in me, she thought, but then men always were and it was women who were the realists. That afternoon, trying on a pair of dress slacks in Myer's she had noticed veins behind her knees, the beginnings of what would be splotches of colour swimming up through the skin. Soon parts of her body would be in purdah. But the thought did not alarm her; it only amazed her that the veins had been there all this time, unseen.

She sat at her desk and took out a sheet of the hotel's stationery. It was meant for a few words, a modern billet-doux.

Dear Billy, she wrote, in her bold rounded sloping hand. *Let me take you out on the river.*

At the end of the first term Anna flew to Melbourne. The offending postcard was in her handbag. *Afraid it's over* had been turned so many ways in her mind she could no longer decipher its meaning. Was being afraid the condition of the writer, shown in the determined but slightly nervous handwriting, like someone signing a death warrant, not with their best signature but an approximation? Did being afraid instantly become the state of the recipient, handicapping their future with a dead weight? Now the card was in the pocket of her handbag, along with her Visa card in case there was an emergency, and a slim folder of traveller's cheques ($100), enough for a room or a bed and breakfast; there might even be enough for a little therapeutic shopping. But when the plane landed in what looked like bare brown fields at Tullamarine and she was on her way to the city in an airport bus, Anna felt her courage desert her. When she was finally set down in Collins Street she took her small overnight bag to a coffee shop and ordered a pot of tea. She sat at a table overlooking the street and tipped in a flood of sugar from a faulty dispenser. She sat at the table for a long time, gazing at a plane tree whose trunk, protected by a grille, disappeared into a hole in the asphalt. Somewhere, far below, must be the earth and stones, and further still, a source of water. Then she took a tram to Parkville.

Billy, returning from his structure and mechanics tutorial and a few beers with Simpson, was surprised to find a small woman slumped in a chair near the phone booth in Ridley College. He instinctively averted his eyes until a large sniff caught his attention.

'Do you need money for the phone?' he asked.

'No.'

'Is it out of order?'

'No, but you are.' She couldn't say where the comment came from: Denzil Gibbs's embarrassed face, his reluctant admission of her to his room, his accusatory stare at her hand luggage as if it contained a mortgage, children, curfews.

'I'm sorry,' she said, looking up. 'I just need to be left alone.'

'The common-room chairs are more comfortable,' Billy said, but instead of walking the few steps to his room, he stayed.

An hour later, Billy and Anna were sitting in the Chinese equivalent of a greasy spoon: a preponderance of cabbage and cabbage stalks, an excess of steaming noodles. Billy wondered they didn't charge for the steam which hovered, white like an exhalation, in the air above the blue and white fish-patterned bowls.

Anna's luggage was beside a small but not lumpy bed in a private hotel (dinner on request: a communal dining table; a few orchestra players sometimes contributed their status). They had declined dinner and now they were at the Wing Wah Chinese Restaurant and Anna was regretting egg noodles which had a tendency to hang like wet washing.

'Do the partridge thing,' Billy said. At least the Chinese did not stint on the napkins. 'St Teresa eating partridges. "When I pray I pray and when I eat partridges I eat partridges." I shan't think any the less of you.'

So they had gone through almost a whole container of pink paper napkins, which they left crumpled in the cabbage-scented water at the bottom of their bowls. Anna thought they looked rather like camellias, especially the napkins that were damp around the edges. She declined to open the fortune cookie which came with the green tea. Instead she began to tell Billy about gorillas.

Harriet bathed one twin and then the other. Even when one was replaced in the bassinet the other seemed to be twisting its body towards a vacancy. 'Lie still,' she told Samuel, placing a hand on his chest while she raised the talcum powder to sprinkle over his creases. She knew her meditations on two-ness were unworthy, especially as everyone else considered twins a triumph. 'One of each,' visitor after visitor had chanted, as if the thought had just occurred. Only having to go through it once, although Susannah had been born almost as an afterthought. Dr Jago had made her feel a special case: a second child almost concealed by the first was a miracle that even he had been unable to detect. Or perhaps, and when this thought occurred Harriet chased it away or pondered it until its folds and crevices disappeared – she was smoothing Susannah's stomach now, massaging the folds at the top of her legs, checking that the creases were thoroughly dry – like her mother she was uncertain about the whole thing. Samuel lay over her shoulder in case there was another pocket of wind – of the two he was the more prone – his head, with her hand supporting, swivelling like a beacon towards his sister. Harriet lay him down beside Susannah, on his back, and his body, which a moment before had been tense, relaxed. Like two Egyptian mummies, she thought, putting the bath trolley, a converted tea trolley, to rights. Faint sighs and gurgles rose from the double bassinet, a settling of which she had no knowledge.

When the twins were asleep Harriet went into the kitchen and made a pot of tea. She took the teapot, the milk jug and her cup out onto the verandah, leaving the hall door open. The neglected garden, admittedly small, looked back at her; the grass was going bald in patches and a type of flat weed making advances. Still it was less depressing than the back garden in which a solitary swing hung from an apple tree. When she had drunk the first cup Harriet upended it on its saucer and turned it three times in a clockwise direction. Tea-leaf reading had been her mother's parlour trick. Sometimes there would be a parcel on its way, or a palm tree shape would promise an over-seas journey. Brown tea-leaf birds flew towards the cup's rim but Harriet could not recall their meaning. A desire for flight, a portent? Rosa had visited, bringing another assortment of twin gifts: two koala bears, two sunhats, two fabric books.

'I think I'll take Billy out on the river for a night cruise,' she said, helpfully holding Samuel. 'River light is flattering and I can tell he is disappointed. He didn't expect a loosening of the jawline,' she added, peering at herself in the bedroom mirror, 'or these permanent bags under my eyes.'

They stood side by side examining their faces, Harriet holding Susannah over her left shoulder and Rosa with Samuel over her right.

'Do you suppose we are twinned as well?' Rosa asked, turning away. Harriet's eyes were as shadowed as her own.

'When will you go? With Billy?' she asked later when the twins were settled in their ancient embrace, sharing an air pocket.

'When I can get in touch with him. I'll send a note to his hostel. Sometimes I wonder if he's really studying.'

Then she had swung her legs up onto the sofa, pulled a

cushion or two behind her head, crossed her arms over her chest and gone to sleep.

Billy was not much interested in the male gorilla but he found Anna Gregor surprisingly entertaining. Nobody less gorilla-like could be imagined. Anna was petite and flawless; one looked in vain for a blemish or a less than perfect eyebrow. It was true her eyes were still puffy, and when they walked along Royal Parade she wore dark glasses. Perhaps she found the mountain gorilla society secure in spite of guards and poachers. He thought of the gorillas making fresh nests each night and let out a guffaw.

'What are you laughing at?' Anna asked, and for a second she lifted her glasses off her nose.

'Fresh nests,' he said, and then he really was laughing, bending over and clutching his chest. Any minute now and he might drum it with his fists. Just in time he pulled himself up and began to talk of student flats, unmade beds and smelly linen that a gorilla would have taken in hand.

He put out a hand, and gently and hesitatingly Anna allowed hers to be encircled. A gorilla paw, Billy thought, but now the laughter was tamped down as if he were concentrating on a task. The task of bed-making. The hand in his did not move: he could feel the fine bones, the way they lay side by side. What am I doing? he thought. His stomach was full of cabbage stalks and noodles; he was walking holding the hand of a woman who was in love with gorillas. The streetlights were coming on. In the window of Anna's hotel he could see the glow of a pink lamp.

Two nights later Billy and Rosa sat side by side as the ferry pulled away from Princess Walk and made its way into the middle of the Yarra. Rosa was aware her best profile was towards Billy if he turned his head; otherwise it was a position for soliloquies, conversations without eyes. Still she sensed change: no longer were the changes in her face being scrutinised; she need not raise her chin slightly or straighten her shoulders after a night spent with Simon Frater. Perhaps Billy will talk to me, she thought, and I can tell him about my life, for she needed a sympathetic ear, even to a disguised problem. The river was flowing at a great pace and the ferry seemed to just glide, despite the beat of its engine.

'I'm thinking of leaving Australia,' Billy said, his eyes on the river like a navigator. 'I'm thinking of going to New Zealand.'

'Whatever for?' Rosa asked. 'Why would one go there?'

'I've got an aunt there,' he said, smiling. 'She met a New Zealander.'

'What are you saying?' Rosa asked. 'You've met one of the natives?'

'Something like that,' Billy replied, and Rosa saw there would be no conversation including herself, no veiled discussion of adultery in which she might ask for a young man's perspective.

'What about your studies?' she heard her voice saying. 'What about engineering?'

'My father will regard it as another bridge to nowhere,' Billy replied, fixing his eyes again on the river as if to sight a bridge would confirm it. 'I don't imagine engineers are much different in New Zealand. I can transfer to Auckland University. I've made a few enquiries.'

For quite a while Rosa did not reply. She lowered her head and closed her eyes; the breeze from the river stroked her face. Later they could go below and have coffee and something to eat.

'Tell me about the native,' she said.

Auckland was a revelation to Billy, starting with St Georges Bay Road. Its long slope to a glimpse of blue harbour, its feeling of being at a height (which it was, but for a long time his sense of the terrain was uncertain) the Norfolk pines and pohutukawas, and the houses which wore wooden skirts. The Auckland Harbour Bridge was nothing on Sydney, of course; Anna told him it was called the Coathanger and its structure was certainly utilitarian. Its gradual curve might well have held a coat, its approaches represented sleeves. The Parnell Rise, with its shops painted in lollipop colours, the sedate churches that stood on its summit, the butcher that sold the best veal – all these enchanted. And the light was different: knife-sharp some days, on others faintly softened with a promise of depth behind. Anna took him on the ferry to Devonport; they sat leaning against the fo'c'sle, eating bread rolls and cheese, and Anna bought a sea-green scarf in a craft shop.

Billy settled in quite easily in the university's Engineering School; his fellow students, among whom there was a sprinkling of women, though they shared the universal reputation, seemed milder. On his first day he had been paired with a sandy-haired young man who introduced himself as Witherspoon and seemed to have nothing against Australians. On a stand outside a bookshop Billy selected another postcard for his mother: *One Tree Hill.* He wrote another anodyne message but added where he nearly ran out of space: *Don't worry.* Perhaps she would read it as aggression, as she had read his leaving: *Don't add to my guilt by worrying.* But if he could have seen his mother he would have noticed changes. Emma was thinner and the bones of her face showed more prominently, but she had come to terms with living in a space between her two men. She had even become more tolerant of Jack, whose dislike of his son had not abated. And she had embarked on a serious reading programme, the whole twelve volumes of Proust, of which she had previously read the first two: nothing much remained but a tone so languid and leisurely it was like dissolving a chocolate on one's tongue. And with her new loss of appetite, though she busied herself for Jack's evening meal, she walked for miles, once through a field with a bull who turned to confront her but did not advance.

Billy, however, was in love. The image of himself that Rosa had given him when he crawled tousled and defiant from under the steam locomotive in the Palmer Hall burst into flower: he felt bold enough to deal with anything – a horde of male gorillas, if they operated in hordes. At least he felt like an alpha male in waiting. This new confidence affected his studies. For the first time he scored a B. But Anna, who was also taking a single English paper on the Romantic poets, would not allow him to see her too often. The house at the end of St George's Bay Road was often glowing with late golden light on its boards as he walked towards it, the shrubs in the garden catching the light on their leaves. He bought a bunch of violets from the greengrocers on Parnell Road; he could feel the stems dripping through the purple paper. And it seemed Anna was becoming almost as starry-eyed about the poet Keats as she was about gorillas. When she pushed Billy away she quoted to him something called Negative Capability. 'The ability to be in uncertainties, mysteries, doubts, without any irritable reaching after fact and reason,' she explained, but Billy couldn't see what she was driving at.

One evening they ended up talking about tuberculosis. Hours later, when he walked up St George's Bay Road and turned down towards the city where the glamour of Parnell turned to commerce and squat factories, he wondered how it had come about. He hadn't liked to ask if gorillas got tuberculosis or why she kept on about someone finding a spot of blood. It seemed easier to hold his tongue. These absurd sympathies he wanted directed towards himself. Suddenly he found himself remembering Rosa, sitting beside him on the ferry. Probably she had had a tiring day and the trip was a concession to him. He had hardly looked at her: a glimpse of her tired face and he had turned away. Yet the image he had replaced her with was partly her doing. Using people as building blocks, he thought angrily, as he loped down Emily Place, so unlike Parnell it could have been its wicked twin.

Anna's paper on the Romantic poets – she had chosen poets rather than novelists, thinking of the time involved, and that poems were compact – was more absorbing than she expected. It was true the poems, the four famous odes by Keats, some selections of breathless Shelley, hardly anything of Byron whose name endured but not his work, were mainly short, but the lecturer, Dr Edgcumbe, could not resist adding details which were the more potent because little background reading was required. Dr Edgcumbe wanted them to approach the work from a modern viewpoint while at the same time she provided images of nightingales and death. Keats's desire for a thicker skin, Shelley's heart being plucked from a pyre. Would anyone today sit under a mulberry tree and be half in love with death or drink melancholy as if it were claret? Anna thought she might begin like a child with a primer book by quoting:

> *I stood tip-toe upon a little hill,*
> *The air was cooling and so very still,*

which turned her mind back to the gorilla harem and their nest-making which was fastidious and begun long before nightfall, using leaves and branches warmed and aired by the sun. I have chosen concentration instead of expansiveness, she thought, half-angrily, wishing she had taken the Victorian novelists paper instead. There at least she could have rested among the furniture, or let her eye glide over descriptions of dress or manners or the preparations for a political house party.

There was a knock at the door and the postman held out a small registered parcel for her to sign. It was the ring she had left in Denzil's room at Melbourne, that had skidded across the surface of the dresser and fallen behind it. She had said something: 'You might find a use for this' or 'It might come in useful.' Since the postcard her fingers had become thinner and it flew from her hand as she pulled it off.

A little card read: *I'd like you to keep this. Sell it, if you like, or keep it for the memories.* Anna took the ring over to the light and held it up critically as if she was the owner of a pawnshop. A small modest stone, whose simplicity had pleased her and which she had rushed to praise. But smallness could mean two things: a fragment of some ungraspable whole or a splinter falling back, bound for annihilation. At the last lecture Dr Edgcumbe had tantalised the class with *Bright Star* and Fanny Brawne's unopened letters in Keats's coffin. Anna's sympathies were with Fanny: carefully choosing her words, not being literary herself, and lapsing probably into common sense and measured cheer. Occasionally, she imagined, returning the ring to her sandalwood box with her mother's pearls and a few old-fashioned brooches, there must have been a sentence rising above the rest of which Fanny was justly proud.

But the day was too fine to spend on either great apes or Romantic poets. The estuary gleamed in the distance, even the leaves of the half-submerged mangroves, which were stealthily colonising the mudflats, glowed. Later she would take Billy on the *Kestrel* to Devonport and they would eat in a little bistro that served lamb shanks and stuffed aubergines.

The twins, now waddling, tottered towards Harriet together, and she circled each with an arm. I could hold something between my teeth, she thought, for she felt pinioned by them. They pressed their bodies against her sides like two little warm sacks. When she lifted them she assessed her balance. Then they were back in the double buggy and they were passing under the plane trees. They were trees that made Harriet think of misery: pomaded with thin spikes shooting from their stumps, the trunks peeling like old stucco or a face swollen with tears.

Now Billy was in Auckland, Harriet found herself thinking of Emma. Perhaps twins in the end might prove a blessing. There would be no obsessive love to hurt both ways, so both were stifled. At least, she consoled herself, my mother was independent. She forgot that her mother had loved her father most; forgot herself at boarding school, mothering discreetly augmented by nuns. She would write to Emma, confess how stifled she felt, make light of it, for she felt a letter should impart information or entertain. In return Emma might confide in her.

One of the twins, Samuel, the more assertive, was wailing and she stopped and picked up a plane leaf and handed it to him. Instantly Susannah's hand reached out and seized a corner. I should have called them Shylock and Portia, Harriet thought. Will they go through the world demanding synchronicity, equal shares? Rosa was coming to stay for a few days while Garth was at a conference in Adelaide. The twins were sleeping through now; there would be a chance to talk.

With the milk and bread and a copy of the *Bulletin,* Harriet turned for home. A simple trip to the dairy and it felt like a day's work. In a few years she might work from home, do someone's books. But even then her heart didn't lift. You can have years of vague unhappiness, one of the nuns had told her, and then it will lift. She came to the gate and took out an electricity bill, a pile of junk mail and a letter addressed to Garth with the logo of a hotel. She put two cushions on the lounge carpet and propped the twins there with their bottles. Four placid eyes gazed steadily in her direction, seeing and not seeing.

Auckland grew steadily on Billy as his engineering grades improved, as Anna permitted him more and more of her time. They had stood on the deck of the *Kestrel* and Billy had found her abstracted, but later, walking by the shore on the way back to the old corrugated-iron terminal, she relaxed. There were groups of people, mainly elderly, out walking, taking dogs for a last constitutional under the palm trees. There were boats lining the shore in various stages of repair, and the last shallow surges – too small to be called waves – sucked on the pebbles like someone drinking tea. Devonport seemed like an island and wasn't: from its steep steps and gentrified villas you could look down on playing fields; there was a kind of golf cart which picked up passengers on the way to visit the extinct volcano. And the university was smaller: perhaps a Melburnian would have considered it inferior.

Away from his country, Billy could evaluate his interest in engineering, see it was not just an escape, a bridge he had built in his head, as his father would have it. Not that he was likely to get the chance to design a bridge any time in the near future. But he realised he loved structure, as his mother loved novels and considered them useful. She would have seen the Coathanger's rush-hour traffic, pitiful by Melbourne standards, as so many strung words. And he felt, though he didn't mention her to Anna, free of Rosa and the imaginings that had occupied his mind since the fourth form. At a distance he could feel grateful to her, unaware of an element of condescension in his attitude, as there had been in hers. Why would a sophisticated woman scoop up a young boy under her wing unless it were pity or a chance to test her powers? Sometimes, when the view in front of him excited him, he thought it was kindness; at others it sprang from something too murky to investigate. Auckland was the present and if the natives thought it merely a series of sprawling villages around a city centre with no heart, he was prepared to give it a chance. The little overlapping verandahs of Queen Street, the great and somehow deserted space the main street ran into, the Town Hall sitting at its odd angle as if it were aping the Ile de la Cité and no one was paying any regard, and, at the other end where the harbour stretched out, an equally blank and seedy set of streets, warehouses and newspaper offices. Soon he would buy a second-hand car; he could see himself spinning along Gillies Avenue. Most of all he wanted to coast from the top of Hobson Street down towards the ocean or wait at the lights on Wellesley Street East with its view of the library with its blue mansard roof, a true touch of France.

And now, in the true present, the ferry was pulling away from the Devonport wharf and he was walking with Anna, one behind the other, around the deck of the *Kestrel* on the port side. They sat on a cream-painted wooden bench, pressing their backs against the wood. Billy's stomach was full of mashed potato and lamb shanks; he felt he could hardly bend. If the ferry goes down, he thought, I shall sink like the wolf with the stones in its belly. He saw his body being recovered from the floor of the ocean, lamb shank bones in his stomach. Anna, who had eaten only pumpkin soup, would float. But he thought, standing up to excuse himself, asking if he could return with a brandy and having a hand waved in refusal, that he would die happy. They could even go back and forth on the *Kestrel* until the last trip, holding hands or standing side by side watching the ocean surge and smack against the hull, carve and scatter into a wake, and then resume. The *Kestrel* was steady, that's what made it so likeable. No nonsense. Billy staggered slightly at the bottom of the stairs. On the way back he stopped at the little nautical bar (draped nets and lobster pots, a dried starfish or two) and bought himself a brandy.

That gorilla society is patriarchal is undeniable, Anna wrote, and then lifted her head as if she were a female gorilla checking her options. These would depend on her position in the harem, her desirability, her temperament. Perhaps she would sit patiently grooming someone while her mind darted about, as women's minds were supposed to do while they sewed or knitted. *The male gorilla*, she went on, *nonetheless has possibly greater burdens.* Obviously this sentence would not meet any academic criteria; probably it would have to be removed. *Type A behaviour is a feature of all but a small subset of male gorillas and these, in human terms, might be regarded as either wise or eccentric.* She was falling into the trap of anthropomorphism which was worse than confidently judging history from your own perspective: gorillas had no need of human categorising or even observation.

The week before there had been a wine and cheese get-together for Dr Loeb's seminar class. It had taken place in the Anthropology Common Room, unchanged for the occasion, with the same outdated *National Geographic*s and *The Savage Mind* strewn about and the chairs higgledy-piggledy as if a group of animals had just vacated a clearing. The cheeses had labels inserted in them, which seemed odd because they were hardly exotic. There were flasks of red and white wine, the red rather sickly, and some carafes of orange juice.

Billy had come to collect Anna and stood in the doorway unnoticed until she spotted him and came over carrying a paper cup of claret.

'Why are they wearing bones around their necks?' he asked when he had her to himself in a corner.

'Not all of them,' she said defensively.

Dr Fernando was wearing a primitive crucifix and Dr Peek, the newest member of staff, was unadorned apart from some whale's teeth earrings.

Someone had struck a few chords on the piano and Dr Fernando and Associate Professor Grice, who imagined their relationship was secret, stood with their hips touching, gently rubbing together.

'The men look like apes,' Billy said, when they had eased through the crush in the doorway and were running down the stairs. 'All those open necks and hairy chests.'

'The engineers are no better,' Anna protested. 'The anthropologists might look like apes but the engineers behave like them.'

They were at the bottom of the stairs now, and Billy reached out a hand. 'Better to be than seem,' he said.

'Suit yourself,' Anna said.

Rosa spent more and more time in her apartment in Gertrude Street. She had been supplanted in Simon Frater's affections, as she knew she must, by a young telephonist. Privately she knew her days at The Windsor were numbered. Often, after a sleepless night, she scrutinised her face in the mirror and wondered how long her efforts would work. Cold water and patted cheeks, moisturiser and then the careful layering of concealer and tint – *line minimising*, it said on the bottle – the outlining of lips with lip pencil, the pulling down of eyelids to add a dark line surely suited only to a young animal. Sometimes she pursed her lips into the shape of an air kiss – popular at the hotel – and saw six short lines and two long ones, like tram tracks, deepen.

On her days off Rosa dressed like a peasant woman, in baggy trousers and an old shirt. She air-bathed her face and did not blow-dry her hair. Though there was only a patio and a small front garden bisected by a brick path, she plunged her hands into whatever soil she could find: a border, the base of an umbrella tree where she had planted bulbs, in her terracotta pots. On Mr Wu's anniversary she took down her *Origami for Beginners* and made a crane. Then, hoping the neighbours were not watching, she made a small pyre of leaves and twigs and set fire to it. She thought of all the banknotes Mr Wu had accrued in his frugal life and which had gone to a niece in Sydney. The niece had appeared and bowed politely when Rosa offered her condolences; she had not wanted to talk. And occasionally Rosa cooked aubergines stuffed with mince and garlic and tomatoes and ate them on her patio, with a glass of wine. Sometimes she thought of Billy, studying in Auckland, and how completely she had lost him. She ran her fingers through her hair and felt a leaf entangled in it: if Billy could see her now, his disillusion would be complete. Yet she had been prepared to forgive him his disillusion, to be a guide, to fade from view, if only he had permitted her. But after the first appraising unflattering stare he had hardly lifted his eyes to hers on the ferry.

If my knees creak when I get up, Rosa thought, I shall know I am done for: fit for the glue factory. But there was only a small click which could have been the gate. And a car was pulling up and a familiar face getting out. A changed face: it took her a moment to recognise Lucien Humfress. Rosa felt in her hair for the leaf, failed to untangle it, and walked through the hallway to meet him.

'You look like a hag,' Lucien said when she'd opened the door.

'You don't look much better yourself.'

He had a cane, speckled, some kind of bamboo. He was thinner, his face paler than she remembered. In each cheek there were two vertical grooves.

'I've dried out,' he proclaimed as he stumped along the hall. 'So don't tempt me with the grape or barley.'

'And is it worthwhile?' Rosa asked.

'Not really. Is that leaf in your hair on purpose?'

'Still the artist, I see,' Rosa replied, but she got up and went to the bathroom, extracted the leaf and ran a brush through her hair. She spread moisturiser on her face and concealer over the worst places. She put on some red lipstick. She brought the leaf back in her hand.

'A leaf falling always seems like fate,' Lucien said, tucking the leaf into his breast pocket. 'I wondered if you'd like a spin?

I've got my inheritance in a lump sum and signed away my soul for more. So the first thing was a decent chariot.'

'What are you going to do?' Rosa asked. She meant the rest of his life, which, from his appearance, might be truncated.

'Paint again,' he said. 'Soberly get at it, if there's anything left. I'm taking life classes again. Learning to draw from scratch.'

They sat with the coffee between them and it felt companionable. How many times had she lifted his frail shoulders out of a gutter, or taken hold of his feet? And once she had carried one end of a Turkey carpet in which he was rolled, feebly protesting and half-singing to himself. She could faintly remember the house: two storeyed with a long verandah room, glassed in. He had slept through the interminable dinner courses under the table, together with a King Charles spaniel. There was enough air in the carpet of course; it was lightly wound.

Harriet, Garth and the twins were walking along Harp Road. Harriet held Susannah's reins, Garth Samuel's. Unseen by the twins Garth's hand held Harriet's. He knew she was unhappy, depressed even, and didn't know what to do about it. Rosa's visit, full of false cheer and daily outings, had not helped. Looking back, Rosa's energy seemed to have a manic edge. Perhaps there was just a time in women's lives when they were unhappy, Garth thought. But he sensed it was something to do with the twins, who were now moving apart as far as their reins would allow and then almost colliding again with paroxysms of giggles. It was true they were self-sufficient: even when they fought they turned to make up at the same time. A single child would have been easier, demanding involvement on both sides. And it seemed he had failed Harriet too. A slight anger made him squeeze her hand harder until she withdrew it. He was in line for promotion; two large accounts had come their way in the last year and his designs were attracting attention. He was rumoured to have an eye for trends: using native animals, not in the old condescending way of a chimpanzee's tea party, but as intelligent sensate beings, was something fresh. 'You're on to something,' his boss at Ogilvy & Mather had told him, and Garth had felt himself straightening his tie and squaring his shoulders before he sloped back to his desk. Perhaps he could use the twins, take them off Harriet's hands? Or was there some work he could encourage her to begin at home when the twins were asleep?

They had reached Straddy Park now with its expanses of grass, sloping hills and ovals.

'I'll take them to the playground,' Garth suggested, taking hold of Susannah's reins as well. 'Give you a rest.'

There were eucalypts on the rise that ringed the park. Designed for watchers, Harriet thought, as she walked towards them. A place not to partake but to be on the edge, to watch life passing, other people's lives, while contemplating the smallness of one's own. She settled herself and allowed her eyes to take in the pavilion, the barbecue area. The twins had their reins off now and were racing along the walking track. How straight their backs were. Like swans, all poise above the surface and churning paddling legs. Garth ran behind them, an easy lope, their reins hanging, doubled, in his hand.

Anna found she was becoming fond of John Keats. *The Romantic Poets and Their World* was not an overly demanding paper: a pass was all she required. Still she was drawn to the image of a young man, over-sensitive, who longed for an extra layer of skin to survive in a world of casual cruelty, a short young man who might rear up. The trouble was Keats, gorillas and Billy were becoming mixed in her mind, as they were all ongoing. 'Patriarchal structures in gorilla society' seemed to take as much daily effort as Keats's attempts to write a poem on scraps of paper. She turned her head and looked out one of the long windows at a glimpse of scudding clouds. Billy had pointed out how fast the Auckland clouds moved, how much it rained.

'Would you beat someone who was torturing a kitten?' she asked Billy as they were walking along High Street on their way to Simple Cottage, a favourite student eatery where the helpings were large and the prices low.

'How do I know?' he replied, rather irritably. 'I'd have to catch sight of the kitten first, I guess.'

'Keats and this butcher boy kept at it for about an hour,' Anna persisted, allowing Billy to go ahead because in certain sections High Street pavements were narrow. Its mix of warehouses, eateries, art shops and lanes descending to Queen Street made it her favourite street. She stopped for a moment and pressed her nose against the window of the Swedish silversmith to admire silver cylinders strung on thick black cord. Billy had gone on and was crossing the street. Anna hurried after him, and a piece of flying newspaper tangled around her feet. Inside Simple Cottage the windows were steamed up and a smell of cabbage and tofu and bean sprouts rose from the servery. We might be in Madrid, Anna thought happily, seeing the hunched backs of students in their tatty clothes, a young woman in a black panne velvet skirt lifting her chopsticks in fingerless lace gloves.

On the way home they must keep an eye out for kittens. And, if he wished, Billy could stay the night. Reading when Billy might stay the night or go back to his flat – they hadn't quite decided on co-habiting yet – was almost as difficult as understanding Keats. *Thin-skinned,* Anna had written in her notes, and yet without thin skin would the poems have existed? Or the kitten?

Rosa and Lucien drove out of Melbourne towards Werribee. Just a spin, Lucien had said, but the Porsche ate the miles and soon they were in the country. Rosa, low in the passenger seat, thought how exhilarating it was and at the same time how endlessly impractical. A good part of Lucien's inheritance was gone on a car he could not even sleep in. A car thieves would desire.

'What happened to the studio?' she asked, shouting to make herself heard above the wind.

'Razed to the ground,' Lucien shouted back. 'Like the prodigal's pigsty. Only the chimney left standing.'

As if in illustration they were passing flat parched fields with a few cattle grazing. Eventually, just when Rosa thought they might make Geelong, Lucien turned the car into a driveway and turned off the motor.

'It's more an animal than a car,' Rosa remarked.

'Driven by a human that's less than an animal,' Lucien replied. 'But I hope to get myself back into condition. Some sort of condition. Just to spite my father. If he'd been an aborigine he'd have pointed a bone.'

'So you go away from him in a chariot.'

Rosa's heart sank, as if symbolism was an ever-expanding pool. You threw a stone in and the ripples spread out: familial at first, full of hate and pain and unrequited love, and then myth made up the deficit. Hadn't she felt something similar, surrounding Mr Wu's body with his own flowers? Australia was like it too: cities that seemed civilised, and then vast plains like something else, gardens mocked by desert. How Lucien's father would have been vindicated by the purchase of the car. Another such folly and the inheritance would be gone.

'I'm going to set up in a cottage somewhere. I thought a worker's cottage. That'll be a nice contrast with Wallender. I thought you might like to come and join me.' He turned his head slightly, as if his neck was in a harness as he said it, and Rosa too turned her head towards the window.

'No,' she said. 'I won't live with you, Lucien. But we might come to some arrangement.'

'Anything will do,' he said cheerfully. 'I'll leave it up to you.'

Harriet's family doctor had recommended her to a psycho-analyst, a Viennese woman in her seventies, Dr Oona Bibescu, who had more or less retired but occasionally obliged a colleague. Dr Bibescu and Dr Franks had worked together when she first arrived in Melbourne; he had used her himself at times when his life lacked perspective.

'Things cannot be fixed,' she had told him, 'but we learn to see that they are parts of ourselves. We learn to take them with us.'

Dr Bibescu had an odd attitude to success. In the most vaunted qualities she often saw failure. She had convinced Dr Franks that his good humour, the way he strode into his surgery with a nervous patient, as if his confidence was enough to effect a cure, covered uncertainties that were far richer. And as he grew older his equilibrium, as she had suggested, faltered: he learned to listen more to his patients, even to let the patient attempt an unscientific diagnosis.

'I wish you would have a word with this young woman patient of mine,' he had said to her on his ritual Thursday night visit when they were sipping the sickly liqueur that she preferred. 'Having twins has disturbed her in some way. She needs someone to talk to.'

So Dr Bibescu had been persuaded to see Harriet for one hour a week on a Tuesday evening. Luckily they did not live too far apart. And after the first session Dr Bibescu had offered to drive Harriet home in her ancient Morris Minor.

At first Dr Bibescu – 'Call me Oona,' she said to Harriet, who sat on the edge of a wingback chair in Dr Oona's front room – talked about her own life in Vienna. She talked, almost casually, about a stratified society in which knowing your place brought, or was supposed to bring, a prescribed happiness.

'The front steps of the houses were immaculate,' she told Harriet, 'scrubbed every morning by maids. The door knockers shone so you could see your face in them. You could even check if you had a smut on your nose. As a young girl I often used to quail standing before one of those front doors.'

Harriet listened patiently, failing to see the resemblance between Dr Oona's life and her own. 56 Cotham Road had no knocker and, if it had, it would not be highly polished.

'The women wore corsets,' Dr Oona went on, 'but outside the air wore corsets as well. Here, let me show you a photograph of my sister and myself in our hats designed to keep the sky off.'

The photo was sepia toned. Harriet wondered if Dr Oona kept it handy for each new client, then she dismissed the thought: Dr Oona gave no impression of falseness, rather of a person who had earned the right to say whatever she thought. The hats on the two little girls might have been designed to protect them from tropical heat or hail stones – Harriet could just make out shadowed eyes and unsmiling mouths.

She looked quickly across at Dr Oona and their eyes met. Dr Oona smiled. 'You're wondering how I've become what I am today after seeing me in that hat?'

The first session did not last much longer than that. Dr Oona scooped up a shawl that was hanging over the back of her chair, located the car keys in a dish full of paperclips, coins and marbles, and led the way to her little Morris Minor. 'I call him Gustav,' she said. 'After Jung. None of them really knew anything about women, only that they were a necessity.'

She backed the car out into the traffic in a swift unhesitating movement and Harriet clutched hold of a little strap. 'Next time we'll talk a little about twins. A most interesting subject, as I'm sure you know. Being gifted with a whole world requires great courage. But I am sure you possess that.'

And Harriet, when she was let down outside her gate, aware suddenly of the overgrown state of the front garden, the untrimmed shrubs, acknowledged that she did feel better. She went indoors and kissed Garth who complained she tasted of pears.

Anna and Billy sat in Albert Park. Billy leaned against the trunk of a giant banyan tree, in a space made by its roots which were breaking through the ground like giant tentacles; Anna sat between his legs, leaning back. It was far from comfortable and Billy, after a suitable interval, planned to suggest they risk their spines and move onto the grass where other students lay or draped themselves, and a few sat gazing at open books. On the paths that crossed and circled the grass there was heavy traffic: groups of twittering Malaysian students, girls in threes and fours, even a cluster of engineers. When he saw them Billy shrank deeper into the shade of the tree. And a few yards away, oblivious of statues and passersby, a young woman stretched out flat was surrendering her mouth to a crouching male.

'What are you thinking?' Billy asked.

'Of that Seurat painting of bathers on the river bank,' Anna replied, for she too was amazed at the range of intimacies in front of her – in her case a couple folded together like spoons while a mere foot away a bespectacled student smoked. Suddenly she stood up, brushed down her skirt and extended a hand. 'Let's move onto the grass,' she said. But once they were on their feet they walked instead, around the path and past the cannon with its paint thick as marzipan. A white soldier with a face from another age looked on.

'Have you seen the Queen from the back?' Anna asked, thankfully settling her books.

But Billy didn't reply; he had a mechanics lab in a quarter of an hour. They parted near the floral clock.

'Twins,' Dr Oona said to Harriet on their second Tuesday, 'are a complete world.'

Harriet, leaning back in her wingback chair, was relieved that sessions with Oona consisted mainly of listening. She did not know that even her movement on the chair was noted, though in a kindly fashion.

'Do you feel that?' Oona asked, immediately challenging Harriet's repose.

'I suppose so,' Harriet replied unhappily.

'And you feel guilty at not being overwhelmed by such a gift? A gift beyond your imagining. Perhaps even beyond your deserts.'

When Harriet could think of nothing to say – an image of a Christmas box came to mind, a life-size doll her parents had given her when she was six, a doll that could cry when its body was tipped – Oona got up and put a record on her old-fashioned turntable. It was Mozart's Quartet in D. Then she re-filled their glasses with Csaszar.

'I want you to think, Harriet,' she said gently. 'You are intelligent, and intelligence is the best way to get out of a maze. Of course there is blundering and trying to hack one's way through. But if we think, we have not only an answer but something for later.'

And Harriet, inspired by the music in which thought could be heard, thought and repetition, but thought going on, told Oona spontaneously about the hateful doll with its porcelain skin skilfully painted to imitate a blush, its thick golden hair and the hairbrush that came with it, and her hatred of it so intense she had to turn her face away from her parents. And though she had played with it sometimes to please them, it had stayed mainly in its box beneath her bed.

'Left to themselves,' Oona said dreamily, as if the doll was of no consequence, 'I believe children would often choose something insignificant for themselves, or something that would soon be battered or misshapen, a soft toy with askew features, an eye hanging from a thread.'

'Because they don't wish to have competition,' Harriet said softly.

'Indeed,' said Oona. 'We want to love but we want to reduce what we love too, to make it manageable.'

Slowly Oona led the talk back to twins. She wanted Harriet to see her fear was natural. Twins *did* exclude the mother. But Harriet had been excluded before, Oona surmised, and grief had a way of mining old channels. Underground passages, Oona thought, for part of her therapy was to go into a reverie of her own. Escape passages, sometimes, used in times of crisis and boarded up. Then something causes them to re-open; a flash flood pushes memory along them. Lucky or unlucky, Oona could never decide. But everyone had them, these hollowed-out prepared places where grief had done its initial work.

Rosa had agreed to help Lucien search for a place to live. It was not easy. Lucien had no concept of his own oddity; he had learned nothing from being tossed into gutters blind drunk or being lifted by the shoulders so his feet flailed like a marionette's. Really he needed a bodyguard. There was the car to be considered too: it could hardly be left on the street. It would be better if he didn't live entirely alone, and yet solitude and rest were the only things likely to restore him.

Sometimes Rosa wondered if talent would out, or if it would not be easier for Lucien to simply give it away. If he was careful with his remaining capital he could live frugally. The car, if he didn't crash it, could be sold.

None of these problems bothered Lucien as they drove through the outer suburbs, looking for land agents' signs. Or even a place that charmed, for he was quite capable of trying to persuade someone to sell. An old lady who might surrender her house to him while she removed herself to a rest home in the manner of a lord moving into a gatehouse.

At the end of the day they drove back to Rosa's apartment and Lucien fell asleep on the sofa. Rosa cooked supper and shook him awake. At the table he peered into the water glass she had set beside his plate as if an incantation might turn it into gin.

'Next week,' Rosa said firmly, 'we'll see about AA.'

But she weakened and let him stay on the sofa.

Dr Loeb strongly objected to Anna Gregor's conclusions to her essay on 'Male Patriarchy and Primacy in the Primate Society'. When Anna went to collect it, knowing it would be cross-hatched with minute writing in red ink, like the scratchings of some small animal, there was an envelope addressed to her. *Miss Gregor,* it read. *Please see me about your Patriarchy essay.*

So now she stood in front of him, one of the lesser females, waiting her turn to groom a male low in the pecking order. Eventually her resigned posture wore him down and he invited her to sit on a low chair. Her eyes were level with his bone pendant, a vee of chest hair darker than the hair on his head.

'I understand,' he began, sarcastically, 'that it is almost impossible for a young modern woman not to be infected by notions of equality between the sexes, but we are dealing here with great apes to whom the concept is foreign. Utterly foreign. And I must point out to you that conclusions taken from human society are not transferable. We cannot bring about changes in another society simply by wish-fulfilment from our own.'

'I was not attempting to do that,' Anna replied.

She was shaken, of course, because she felt her observations about female gorillas were sound. Why should one society not evolve as much as another? Even now the gorillas were probably being peered at by parties of tourists and patrolled by rangers with guns.

'You were indeed attempting to do that,' Dr Loeb went on. 'It's not the first instance of a personal agenda being slipped into a discipline where it has no place.'

'But since we are talking about societies . . .' Anna began.

'If you are implying that anthropology is somehow a less august subject than physics or botany, then I think you should reconsider your degree. As a special favour, because your work has been satisfactory, I have refrained from marking this essay until you have a chance to reconsider. The summary is almost pure fantasy and I am allowing you to rewrite it. I'm prepared to grant you a week from today.'

So, in the end, like the lowest servile female, Anna had accepted the essay back and agreed to return it in the specified time. But her cheeks burned as she crossed the quad and she half-thought she might go in for a spot of counselling. But that was for women who needed the pill or had VD. Instead she came out on Princes Street in front of the Clock Tower and crossed into Albert Park. She kept away from the normal paths and walked across the grass and behind the band rotunda until she came to the little plaque to a music student. Women's desires are like music, she thought, and the reeds at her feet rustled as the breeze moved through them. A line of leaves ran like a kite-tail across the grass and then settled. She passed the leaf sweeper, Michael, who was prone to epileptic fits and whose helmet had perforated holes. If he fell to the ground in front of you he was to be watched over but not moved. But at the moment he was happily deployed: a wheelbarrow, a rake and a sack of leaves, and heaven knew how many sackfuls to come.

Rosa and Harriet sat in the front room of 56 Cotham Road, drinking coffee. The twins crawled about amidst a pile of blocks and hardly needed any attention. Harriet's visits to Oona were over; in fact Dr Oona had suffered a slight stroke, been admitted to hospital overnight, and then returned home. On her last visit she had counselled Harriet to keep a journal. 'Nothing daily,' she had said. 'That tires the heart and wearies the spirit.' Instead she had suggested Harriet emulate the seasons. In winter the twins would be mainly indoors since the effort of dressing them both in waterproof gear, boots, hats and mittens would seem prohibitive. Dr Oona had talked about Plato's idea of the divided soul, of male and female halves that attempted to join. She had suggested that the detachment which Harriet felt guilty about could in time become a virtue. 'Children do not wish to be smothered,' she said. 'A parent can do a child a great favour by a strategic withdrawal.' As for Harriet herself, Dr Oona suggested she take the first steps towards making a whole, analogous-to-the-twins world of her own. 'Not immediately,' she said, when Harriet looked startled, 'but a beginning.' And when Harriet could not imagine what this world might be, Dr Oona suggested a programme of reading or some correspondence courses or simply learning to sit still and listen quietly to music while the twins slept. All this was being expounded to Rosa, who wondered if she needed a reading programme herself, something along the lines of: *How to get over an affair* or *How to live with the artistic temperament*.

'I think I feel envious,' Rosa said, when a second cup of coffee had been poured and the twins had crawled into another room, still without complaint.

The week before, without consulting her, Lucien had bought a quite unsuitable cottage in nearby Nicholson Street. 'As small as Klee's cupboard,' he had said, triumphantly, when Rosa had been taken on a tour. It was a very truncated tour, for the front door led to the back like an alimentary tract. Lucien's expectation that she should be full of praise for his ingenuity had put her in a sour mood and she almost felt like asking to see his bank statements. Still the back garden was nice and there was a carp pool with some surprisingly large carp glimpsed among the water lilies. Rosa suspected they had simply gone on growing, unconcerned, while the garden was neglected or the cottage changed hands. And as she stood with Lucien on the front verandah he had told her the best bedroom would henceforth be known as Rosa's room.

'That's all I have to show for my life,' Rosa said. 'A designated room, an apartment I've outgrown, a half-hearted career. And now, on offer, if I choose to accept, a rescue mission, a mother's role without reward, and occasional rides in a sports car.'

'I think there's some brandy,' Harriet said, getting to her feet. And there was a half-full dusty bottle of Napoleon. They drank it out of tumblers, letting the fumes rise in their nostrils and the heat warm their throats.

'Half full or half empty,' Rosa mused, noticing the level. 'Volumes could be written on it, whole societies divided, wars fought. One might even commit hara-kiri for such a cause. Or make god-like images covered in gold.'

'I'm supposed to be writing a journal,' Harriet said, 'but I haven't begun yet. *The Journal of a Depressed and Recovering Woman*. It's meant to be a kind of therapy.'

'What isn't?' Rosa replied, but she sounded more cheerful. For, suddenly, as the brandy spread its warmth, she recognised there were things still to come.

While the female gorilla may exercise some judgement in the selection of a mate, and research suggests qualities besides virility and rank may be considered, the society remains patriarchal. Anna paused with her pen in her mouth, tapping her teeth. The patriarchy of the Anthropology Department, ruled by Professor Hunnibal with Associate Professor Grice and Dr Loeb as his cohorts, and Drs Fernando and Peek, being female and therefore subservient, was inviolate. Any male anthropologist would fight to the death to retain his supremacy, however brilliant the work of a female colleague. Dr Peek had had a paper accepted by the *American Journal of Physical Anthropology* but no one had

shouted her a drink in the Buttery where the male anthropologists gathered on Friday evenings, their bearded faces
leaning together like a war cabinet. Anna had gone there once
in search of Dr Fernando when she was urgently required by a
family member: they had walked along the wide corridor,
together glancing in at the ranks of high-backed chairs, the low
tables, the art works, and the alcove where the latest journals
and papers were laid out. Dr Fernando had seemed not to
regard the crisis that had summoned her as serious; she had
raised a hand to the male anthropologists as they passed the
Buttery, and been nodded to in turn.

Should Anna say something about the subset of male
gorillas whose political skills were more highly developed, a
group someone had referred to as 'the navel-contemplation
guys'? These in fact did rather well in the breeding stakes,
being able to distinguish real from perceived threats. But Anna
did not know if Dr Loeb held this view or whether he saw
himself as a Type A gorilla, always on the lookout for snubs,
having to groom Professor Hunnibal whose position he
coveted.

She thought back to the day she had chosen anthropology,
for the truth was, when she came to the university under
pressure from her parents, her mother in particular, she had no
idea what subjects she wanted to take. 'It doesn't matter what
you study,' her mother had told her, 'it's just important to be
there, to take part.' Two laughing girls with a trestle table full
of pamphlets promoting anthropology had persuaded her.
Now she realised they were atypical and possibly, since she
never saw them in the department, they had dropped out. But
they had made it sound like fun. Later in the day she had
enrolled in English. She thought it might be an antidote:
literature and the origin of species. She could feel she had
covered both options.

Harriet, meanwhile, was writing in her journal. *I saw the twins
crawling through a doorway when Rosa was here and realised the
truth of Oona's words. I can think myself privileged and let go,*

knowing they have each other. As they passed through the doorway
they looked like two parts of a train, an engine and carriage. Samuel
will always dominate, I suspect, but Susannah will be so close
behind she will not feel it and his boldness will be supported by
having her at his shoulder. Perhaps they will only be truly
themselves when they are together. Oona didn't mention what
separation can mean to twins, she was only concerned at my
separation. I am feeling calmer.

Harriet put her pen down: she was at home with figures,
not words, and her thoughts turned to what she might be able
to do in the evenings to bring in a little money. Dr Oona's time
might be replaced by a night class. There were thoughts of her
mother in the background but she would not record them: her
journal would read like a Nursing Mothers' Association
manual. Thoughts of herself too, leaning on her elbows at one
of the high windows at St Mary's in Hobart, looking across the
lawn at the black figure of Sister Lucy as she glided swiftly
towards the chapel.

Billy received regular letters from his mother which he
answered with postcards: The Clock Tower, Queen Street, the
Floral Clock in Albert Park. From time to time Emma
mentioned her sister, Irene, who lived in New Zealand. But
Billy was an expert at not replying; the blank side of his card
was a series of linked clichés which he thought she expected: his
health (fine, as always, even if he was recovering from a
hangover) his diet (she once asked if he was eating vegetables:
yes, if you counted a few lettuce leaves as greens or the twice-
weekly meals at Simple Cottage) the weather, a universal non-
sequitur – the endless drizzling rain to which Auckland was
prone, the swiftly moving clouds which resembled the yachts
on the Waitemata. By the time these had been gone through
there was just room to wish his mother good health in return
and to pass his greetings to his father who, of course, never
replied.

Billy suspected his mother could not be happy: her letters
contained so little of interest – what was happening on the

farm or to the rest of the Berrymans. He did not know that Emma was perplexed by the independence and self-interest of this new generation, even though her life was more constrained than her son's. She had added a few words about her sister to stir his interest, in case he should consider a visit. When he thought of Guiseford at all, he thought of worn things: an old deckchair with discoloured spots, walls darkened by cigar smoke, a stubborn adherence to old ways that had made the place a museum.

But if Billy did not know his Australian, now New Zealand aunt, his aunt knew of him. For Emma, sensing her son's writing style would go on resembling a drawbridge, wrote frequently to her sister. Irene, after regular trips home in the early years of her marriage, was now settled. But the settling had not been easy. The little seaside town, which had attained city status, was conservative and faintly unwelcoming. A kindly woman in the same street had become a friend, tentative at first and then welcoming whenever Irene wanted to borrow anything: a cup of sugar, an egg. Sometimes Irene borrowed a teaspoon of baking soda and returned it the next day with a little extra added just to have the chance of talking to this woman whose name was Adelaide.

'I knew you didn't really want to borrow anything,' Adelaide would say later, when they were comfortably taking tea in one another's kitchens. And when Irene's two daughters were born, Adelaide who had had one child, stillborn, became a kind of surrogate mother. Angela, the eldest daughter, was quiet and serious like Irene but the younger, Minnie, was volatile and difficult. Angela was the subject of much speculation between Irene and Adeline. Her passivity seemed to provoke Minnie, and Adelaide guessed she needed a response before she could regain her equilibrium. Yet Minnie was capable of great sunniness and humour and her obligingness, when she was in the mood for it, knew no bounds.

Irene felt for Emma, now cut off from Billy. 'What do you do with the postcards?' she wrote, and Emma replied she had almost a shoebox full. But she had ceased to hope for anything from them and returned to reading novels, as if some character by Trollope – she was reading the Palliser novels for the third time – might give her a clue. But dispossessed or discarded mothers were not the subject of novels: there was something agricultural about knowing your place and stepping back, something like seed heads and husks and flowers left too long in a vase so the water turned rancid and the vase slimed with green. In human terms it might mean an adjustment in dress, a locket at the throat or long sleeves: Emma's saving virtue, though she did not know it herself, was an ability to meander among a range of thoughts, though she seldom found one that was satisfactory.

Billy, meanwhile, was sitting with Anna on the sloping lawn of the Auckland Domain, listening to a jazz concert. The night was clear and cool and the clouds that he might mention in his next postcard were moving in front of the stars. The band was highly amplified and there was a tradition, in the last bracket, of the audience getting up to dance. Further down the slope young children were rolling over and over in the grass. Anna had brought a thermos and two lines – Billy guessed they were lines – of ham and chicken sandwiches cut in triangles and skewered with a long wooden skewer, something she had seen in a Parnell cafe. It seemed an endless trouble to Billy, but he plucked them off, one at a time, and popped them in his mouth, holding the skewer between his fingers.

When the last bracket began he pulled Anna to her feet and spun her about. She complained her legs were stiff, but he pulled her back and forth towards him and away. They were on a little slope and his grip on her waist was firm. He felt he was in love with her, but her head was full of gorillas and anger at her tutor for whom she'd had to rewrite an essay. He had fallen for a woman who had returned an engagement ring to another man and now hid her vulnerability as best she could.

The last blaring discordant note faded on the air and there was a shower of applause. Billy kept his arm around Anna's waist and she pressed her palm against the small of his back.

Then they sat down to get their breath back before rolling up the rug.

I know Billy has a girlfriend, Emma wrote to her sister. She doubted Billy was in contact with his aunt or his cousins. *It was the reason for him leaving his studies in Melbourne.* Another postcard had arrived that morning – the Auckland War Memorial Museum – but there were no words about dancing on the grass or walking home under the stars with an empty hamper. *The rain has stopped, temporarily,* Billy wrote, as if this could interest his mother.

He has behaved like a kangaroo, Emma thought, one of the huge red kangaroos fleeing from a bushfire. When Billy was a child they had made up stories about the kangaroos. *In their pockets they carried the mail: the small brown kangaroos carried the letters and the big red ones the parcels.* Often they shot across the road in pairs, vanishing into the spindly bush.

Emma got up from the table, abandoning her letter, and went to see if they had any books about New Zealand animals. But there was only the old Everyman encyclopedia with one volume missing. Under 'Flora and Fauna' she read: *The only pre-European mammals were the Maori rat and the now extinct dog, but there were also native bats. The native plants are numerous and include many peculiar species.*

Emma left the encyclopedia on the table beside her letter and went to stand at one of the French doors. It was raining today in Ouse; she could hear the gutters running and the flow of water in the drains. In the distance she could see a man in an oilskin riding a horse. After Irene had married and gone to New Zealand and Maud had died, Emma had felt abandoned. She had felt grief burrowing in her, like the water which was now swelling the lawn and creating a tiny meandering stream. It was no distance at all but the clear water persisted in aping a river, with loops that almost doubled back on themselves.

I must write cheerfully to Irene, Emma thought, taking up her pen again. Adeline Cumberland had visited and invited Emma to join the Ladies' Bridge Club. And she had bought a brown paper parcel tied with ribbon. 'Something my foolish cousin sent from New York,' she explained when a black silk dress with full-blown pink roses was revealed. 'She still thinks of my figure as girlish . . .' Emma had demurred, over bridge and the dress, putting her hand up to check her untidy hair. But the silk dress reminded her of Kuala Lumpur, and clearly it could not fit Adeline. She enjoyed embellishing the scene for Irene. *I expect one day Billy will arrange an introduction,* she wrote, finally.

Postcards are well and good, she would explain – dealing with Adeline had made her feel firmer – *but I am tired of views of Auckland. I feel I know it by heart. I would prefer a photograph of you.*

Leaning over the rail of the *Kestrel* Anna shredded 'Male Patriarchy and Primacy in the Primate Society' and scattered the pieces into the lace-like wake. A seagull swooped down, thinking it was bread. *I have considered your conclusion,* Dr Loeb had written in his bird-scratch hand, *and am prepared to award you a B. Be aware in future that conclusions must be based on scholarship and field results. Anthropology is no place for romantic self-indulgence.*

'Shouldn't you keep it?' Billy asked but Anna simply shook her head.

The wake behind the *Kestrel* was endlessly filling itself in: if Dr Loeb had been leaning over the rails he too might have disappeared. Anna would have thrown a lifebuoy but it would have fallen short. His arm would come up in a last gesture and she would turn her back.

Anna and Billy stood at the little bar and drank a brandy. Then they climbed up on the port deck as the city came into view. They passed ships tucked into their berths like old whales; the water under the barnacle-encrusted wharves glowed sapphire green; another crowd was assembled to cross the gangplank, some pushing bicycles. And behind the wharves, once Quay Street was crossed, lay a strange hinterland of warehouses and press offices, seedy and slightly frightening. Here Anna doubted she should have torn up her essay. Then she recollected that Dr Loeb would have recorded her grade. If she had made an error in judgement, it was better that it was gone. But she would not admit that. It was easier to think of Dr Loeb as a not particularly gifted ape, unprepossessing even to females who might accept a wimp. Whatever she wrote now would not find favour with him.

Billy was thinking that Auckland, apart from the ferry buildings which he admired, looked best from the sea. It could never compare to Melbourne of course, nor hope to reproduce that richness of tone, of tradition and faint decrepitude. He missed the green trams that made the air waver and the leaves of the plane trees shiver. And there were buildings in Melbourne of a size unconceived of here. But from the sea he admired the smaller treasures spread out, the little volcanic hills, a spire artfully placed, not through design but because there was nothing else near. There was the University Clock Tower set in trees they would shortly be walking under, trees that were shedding and filling the deep gutters in Princes Street and blowing like congas in Albert Park. The leaf-sweeper with his barrow, sacks and rake would have his hands full.

They climbed up through Emily Place, leaving the depressed sad streets behind, and cut through a little park with a statue. They parted near the library.

In Melbourne Harriet was writing in her journal. *Twins: a voyage*, she had inscribed on the inside cover. Perhaps when they were older she would show it to them. Then she thought it unlikely: they would be unaware of her struggles. Possibly, and the thought seemed strange, they had problems of their own. Susannah might feel Samuel was always in her head, sensing her moods so her thoughts were not her own. Later, when they were separated by continents, premonitions might bring them awake in the middle of the night; they might never be free of worry. And what of those who carried an embryonic twin, a fossil that never developed? There had been such a case in the *Age* recently; an operation to remove a cyst had revealed a tiny perfectly formed twin, like the smallest Babushka doll. And there were advantages to herself; Harriet could see that now. Her life could be freer, as her mother had wished her life to be. Garth had suggested that a hobby class replace the visits to Dr Oona. Next month she would be taking Watercolour for Beginners.

For several minutes Harriet couldn't think what to write. Then she thought of a ship, turning to rescue someone who has fallen overboard. She thought of *The Princess of Tasmania* lumbering across Bass Strait. *I think*, she wrote, *there is a period of hopelessness and floundering that is essential. It is unlikely a ship could turn immediately: the one in the water must manage as best she can. It relies on someone else's sighting – in my case Dr Oona – and even when the ship comes into view again rescue is not certain.*

Looking back, Harriet could see that Dr Oona had come alongside her in a wingback chair. It was likely that Dr Oona was in her chair this moment, patiently bearing the paralysis in one arm and down one side of her face. *To accompany someone is all we can do,* Harriet wrote, as if she had turned into a therapist herself. Then one of the twins let out a cry and she got to her feet.

Rosa meanwhile was nursing Lucien. It was only bronchitis but he gave the impression of death. Each night she walked to the cottage in Nicholson Street with bags of grapes and mandarins, new mixtures from the chemist. She lifted his head onto a pile of pillows and he opened his mouth for the plastic spoon like a nestling. When he felt better he sat up against the pillows and drew her in his sketch book.

'Be sure you add a red cross to my apron,' she instructed, feeling like Florence Nightingale.

'Just sit on the end of the bed for a minute,' he pleaded, and she sat for half an hour, her face growing stiff as a corpse, her hands heavy and useless in her lap. She was almost too tired to think.

Several times he had suggested she sleep on a camp bed by his side, so if he needed her he could touch her with his hand.

'And have you breathing over me,' she replied. 'No thanks.'
When she was too tired to walk home, she took a taxi.

In a few weeks he had roughed in a series of paintings, his first works in oils for ten years. They were to be called *Nurse*.

If Anna had no hope of winning Dr Loeb's favour – he had singled her out in the lecture theatre with a mock bow, and used her as an example of flights of fancy – her essay on Keats had achieved an A. She had chosen not one of the famous odes or story poems but a sonnet a child might understand: *On the Grasshopper and Cricket*. Perhaps she had been affected by Dr Loeb's criticism and lost her nerve, choosing something she could easily comprehend:

> *The poetry of earth is never dead:*
> *When all the birds are faint with the hot sun,*
> *And hide in cooling trees a voice will run*
> *From hedge to hedge about the new-mown mead:*

Was it easy to write like this, she asked in her essay. Was it tiredness, as the birds were tired, that made the words come easily, each word at ease among its fellows, with no strain? And the seasons, she had written, were like a toggle, so the poet who seems at one moment outdoors and the next by the stove imagines the insects' songs as interchangeable. Keats is a drowsy poet, longing to sink into a half-awake doze where images are freed from constriction.

Well done, Dr Edgcumbe had written. *You have chosen wisely and shown some original thought.* A shy smile had been exchanged as Anna walked out of the lecture theatre. She walked along the corridor and down the stairs to the ground floor. Her second choice poem came into her mind:

> *I stood tiptoe upon a little hill,*
> *The air was cooling, and so very still,*

Billy was in the University Bookshop, revolving the postcard stand as he waited to make a purchase. He selected a view of the *Kestrel* with Devonport in the background for his mother, then changed his mind and chose one of Rangitoto instead. On the last weekend of March he had gone with a group of students on this climb so easy it was derisory, in tramping terms. Anna had declined to come and Billy, for once, was glad to be on his own. It was a curious rigid kind of island with paths as prescribed as an athletic track. Though it looked romantic from the ferry and the landing stage was promising, they were soon climbing on a surface like a skin condition, black and uneven, punishing if you did not have tramping boots. One of the girls was wearing sneakers and Billy waited beside her when she stopped to catch her breath. There was nowhere to rest. On both sides of the path the rock rose in peaks: no one, man or animal, could be expected to walk on it.

'Don't you have any boots?' Billy asked.

'I'd be wearing them if I had,' the girl replied. 'Go on, if you like. I'll just be five minutes.'

But he had waited, letting his unfitness be taken as gallantry, holding his hand out for the girl to stand up.

'I waitress most nights,' the girl said. 'My feet are sore.'

It was ridiculous, he hadn't asked her name and the harsh landscape would have made it seem important. There was something operatic about the place, as if their dialogue could have been set to music.

'What are you studying?' he asked as they climbed higher, concentrating on the track now, the view which was likely an illusion.

'I'm at Elam,' she replied. 'I'm majoring in sculpture.'

'And this is like climbing one,' he said, but there was no responding smile.

They walked on, side by side, and then in single file as the track narrowed. And finally, when they caught up to the others, there was a summit, grasses and flaxes, soft undulations and the city looking towards them. A soft wind flowed over their heads and over the island; seagulls swooped and called. They stood reading the sign and looking down on the beautiful ocean. On the way down the girl walked with someone else.

I climbed this, Billy wrote to his mother. *The surface was horrid like hell but it was heaven when you got to the top*. His mother would ponder this sentence for days, for, though banal, it was unlike anything he had written before.

Unknown to Billy, Anna too was pulling back. The nights they spent together in the St Mary's Bay house – there was an agreement that one of the 'Do Not Disturb' signs Kirsten had stolen from de Bretts when she worked there as a waitress meant an overnighter and no surprised looks at breakfast – were cosy rather than passionate. A single bed that creaked, and a selection of stuffed toys, including a gorilla, moved onto a chair, induced an innocent quality as if they were both wearing flannelette pyjamas and had been tucked up by their mothers. At any moment Anna felt there might come a knock at the door and hers would appear with a medicine glass and a spoon. The mattress was too narrow for anything inventive and because of the thin walls in the old villa Anna refrained from making any sound above a whimper.

Billy's flat had a double bed with a rubber mattress but after one visit she had declined to make another. The other engineers had greeted her with leers and comments about her figure, as if they were tossing a ball about and she was not in the room: one had run his tongue over his lips. She had been too scared to meet them at breakfast, even though Billy assured her the other rooms were similarly occupied and no one thought anything of her staying. She had put on her slacks and jersey and coat and gone to stand on the front porch to wait for a taxi. Billy, half-frustrated, for it was usual to present a woman in triumph in the morning, had remained in bed rolled in his week-old sheets. Still, some of the women encountered at breakfast, if the term could apply to such a scrabbling for food – old cornflake packets rattled as if they were castanets, burnt heels of toast and a scraping of Rose's Lime Marmalade labelled *The Property of Boz. Hands off!* – were hardly delectable.

The taxi driver turned and gave Anna a long stare as she settled into the back seat. Let him say something, she thought, her hands clenched inside her coat pocket. But a look from a man was so often enough: they specialised in looks which, in their estimation, did as well as words. Billy had withdrawn when she bent over to kiss his forehead, slightly turning his head so she had kissed his hair instead. She had turned the doorknob softly (heavy white porcelain – the house had some redeeming features) and walked along the dark hall, carrying her shoes in her hand. If I were a man, she thought, I would have slammed the door, and none of the sleeping bodies, accustomed to tiffs, would have stirred.

She had patted her hair down on the porch, though, as she stood waiting. Then she reflected she had behaved in a way no female gorilla ever would, separating herself from the protection of a male, even a male who was kind to her, who might even, given time, be one of the navel-contemplation guys, able to undertake a bit of parental care. For she didn't doubt Billy was protective. But is it enough? a voice asked. Isn't protection always a kind of power, an assumed weakness on the part of the protected? The taxi moved swiftly along the deserted streets and Anna wished she had a fur coat. Then when she cried a tear could fall on her shoulders of fur, like a drop of rain on the coat of the mountain gorilla.

I'm sure your relationship with Billy will resume in time, Irene wrote to Emma. *I am sure there are fallow years.* She was having one with her youngest daughter, Minnie. She was half-tempted to describe Minnie's behaviour to her sister but she did not believe that confession was good for the soul. Teddy was en-amoured of Minnie, her wild spirit, her frank way of speaking which took no regard for anyone's feelings. Whenever Minnie opened her mouth Irene wanted to cover her face with a handkerchief. Only last week Teddy had found her lying on the sofa with a lace handkerchief over her face, like Jane Austen, hiding blotched cheeks. 'What is it?' he had asked, lifting the handkerchief off. 'Minnie again?' But rather than elaborate, for it always sounded petty, she had got to her feet and gone and sponged her face, combed her hair and applied fresh powder.

Minnie's crimes might fill volumes but taken singly they resembled an auction catalogue. Angela, on the other hand was calm – too calm, in Teddy's opinion – studious, content to spend hours in her bedroom, surrounded by piles of books.

Irene lifted her pen after writing *fallow* and tried to remember if it was the word she wanted. She thought of an old history lesson at Ouse school, not that the subjects were as divided as they were now, and in any case Mr McKenzie had taken them for everything: maths, spelling, composition. Fallow field would have been an afternoon subject, for the afternoons were lighter, devoted to other lands and reading, silent or aloud. A fallow field that was left to lie untouched for a year, that could be gleaned for last pickings and was then out of bounds. There were no boundaries on the huge fields of medieval England; perhaps those labouring in one of the productive fields looked towards the fallow field with longing.

I think they need to separate themselves from us, Irene continued, *and we must let them.* Then she recollected herself and wrote about New Zealand. She would not say she had never settled, because she had turned her mind to it, the way Maud had to the General Store. But she suspected that homesickness ran deeper for Australians when they were transported. Which was odd, because everything showed them as more confident, less dissembling when it came to rules. How long it had taken to be on terms to borrow the first cup of sugar, to cross a threshold for a chat.

Angela and Minnie had been to Tasmania with them just once, when they could still get half-fares. They had disembarked at Melbourne and a man had come forward to help with their suitcases. He had touched his hat and smiled at Irene. He had seized a suitcase in each hand and led them to the taxi rank. It's wonderful to be home, Irene thought, smiling with pleasure. But Teddy had been angry. 'He might have scarpered,' he said. 'How could you tell?'

Dr Oona woke in her house in Melbourne and felt her left arm tingle, pain move up and down her side. She pressed her right hand against her left shoulder, urging the pain to abate. Stumbling against piles of books in her office, she reached her desk. Harriet's number was on her blotter and a note saying *Follow up call.* The clock under the green shade showed 3.27 a.m. She should call an ambulance, make her way – but here the pain came back again, as if it had simply reached the end of a journey, paused and begun its return: for a moment Dr Oona thought of Viennese trams with the driver changing ends, the conductor turning over the wooden seats so they faced in the direction they had come. Instinctively she dialled Harriet's number. A male voice answered and as the pain faded to gather itself again she gave her name, asked for an ambulance to come, for Harriet to be told.

It was easier to crawl, she decided, less distance to fall. By the front door with its stained-glass panel – fleur-de-lys in twelve small panes, alternating rose, emerald and cobalt blue – she waited to pull herself to her feet. A knock came on the door as she fumbled with the catch. It was the ambulance men. And by the hedge Harriet, a dressing gown over her nightdress, was getting out of her car.

'Revenge,' Dr Oona said to Harriet when she visited her later in hospital. 'Perhaps I was getting revenge on my patients and you were the nearest name. It's a far deeper motive than we understand.'

Harriet who had not been allowed in the ambulance and who had driven thankfully home, sat on a chair lower than the bed. Dr Oona's face had sunk and lines that had been held at bay by plumpness and vivacious expression had gained ground. Victorious, Harriet thought, as if they had been waiting in the wings. Her own face had crowsfeet, and two lines ran across her forehead.

'I'm sorry for calling you,' Dr Oona went on but she was not looking at Harriet. Instead she turned the plastic label on her wrist to read her name. The curtains around the next bed were drawn: they had a pattern of faded yellow roses.

'Do you mind being in here?' Harriet asked.

'Not at all,' said Dr Oona, and this time her eyes met

Harriet's. 'All I need do is breathe. Everything is done for me. I feel as though I am surrendering.'

Harriet walked along the polished corridors to the entrance. Dr Oona would be home in three days. 'I won't ask you to call,' she had said as they parted. 'I'll retire properly this time.'

Poor Keats, Anna was thinking as she walked across the little grass quad and then took the path that led past Old Government House. *If Poetry comes not as naturally as the leaves to a tree it had better not come at all,* he had written. Her essay, which had attempted so little, an essay about five feet high, the poet's height, still gave her pleasure. And now she had his letters to dip into. *Lord! a man should have the fine point of his soul taken off to be fit for this world.*

She walked around the back of the old wooden building where rows of rubbish bins were being filled with scraps for pigs. A few wasps hovered. The roses in the little rose garden had their soil ruched as if one of the gardeners had just forked it over. She crossed the lawn where the grass never seemed to grow very long and went out through a little wicket gate.

At Simple Cottage Billy was waiting, drinking carrot juice.

'Hoo-ha! Hoo-ha! Hoo-ha!' chanted the Engineering haka party as they marched around the perimeter of Commerce. Faces looked down from the top floor of Anthropology.

'A day for staying indoors,' remarked Dr Fernando.

'Perhaps one of their buildings will fall on them. Like Jericho,' Dr Peek agreed.

Between the chants the engineers smote their chests, ape-fashion.

'What about those literature appreciation classes we gave them,' Dr Fernando asked.

'Nil effect,' said Dr Peek.

The last stragglers, a crude banner between them and cardboard clubs in their hands to strike at anything that appeared, had now disappeared around the side of Anthropology but the chants still reverberated.

Dr Loeb was lecturing on anthropomorphism, giving it the full benefit of his sarcasm. But Anna was not there. She had an appointment at Student Counselling. She wanted to know if being rescued by a man (Billy) was a ground for love or just obfuscation. The counsellor was obviously tired and surprised by such an abstract enquiry. Finally she had offered a prescription. If you are on the edge of a cliff and someone desires to interpose his body between you and the cliff edge, it is love; to press his body against yours and force it over the edge is hate. 'These are only illustrations,' she added. 'The desire is the important thing. In reality the person on the cliff edge would decide for themself. The other person, whatever their desire, would not reach them in time.'

'Thank you,' Anna said, pulling on her gloves, as if they might offer protection.

'Hoo-ha! Hoo-ha! Hoo-Ha!' Louder came the chant as she turned towards the library. A few people were scattering in the path of the sound. The leaf-sweeper, pushing his barrow and rake towards the park, looked up. Still Anna paid no heed: she was imagining pale bodies at cliff edges, a push in the small of one's back, a sense of venom. It was an impulse only, but how could anyone know how another thought? And then, as though she had been watching a street uprising from a doorway and just stepped off the kerb at the wrong moment, the bodies were upon her. 'Hoo-ha! Hoo-ha! Hoo-ha!' The library steps were close by and Anna thrust out her hands to send the nearest engineer over an invisible cliff. She was propelled backwards and nearly fell against a low stone wall. Then her elbows were seized.

'A woman who dares strike an engineer,' a deep voice said. 'What's the punishment for that?'

'Let go, you ape,' Anna shouted, striking at the chest of one. She might have been hitting a drum.

'She might almost be spirited enough,' one of the marchers said, and a huge meaty arm was thrown around her neck. Then, kicking at her captor's shins and trying to keep her balance, tears of anger in her eyes, Anna was dragged down

Kitchener Street to begin the Engineering haka party pub crawl.

Billy was in the Engineering Library, checking worked solutions for a problem in reinforced-concrete design. He heard the engineers go past but didn't look down. Anna would regard them as apes and he could think of no counter-argument. It's tradition, he would say. But engineering had lost its glory decades, probably centuries, ago. No one cared about the workings any more, no one admired the way things were joined. All they were left with was a crude chant and breast-beating. But he couldn't eat humble pie. When he next saw Anna he intended to defend them.

Anna, at this moment, was seated on a bar stool in the Queen's Head. Her tears had dried while the engineers, hoarse from shouting, were calling for handles, yards, chasers.

'Something for the mascot,' someone said, and a shandy was placed in front of Anna.

'I'd prefer brandy,' Anna said.

'Captives have no rights,' said the meaty one whose arm had been around her neck. His face was pockmarked like an old worn-down cog.

I'll humour them for a while, she thought. Then I'll say I need the bathroom. There's probably a narrow window with louvres I can remove and an alley outside with dustbins. I'll leave my bag on the bar as surety.

But surely there would be no need for such subterfuge. One engineer was already on the floor, prostrate after skulling a yard without drawing breath; another was chundering in the gutter. 'Gentlemen, gentlemen,' the barman was urging. 'I know it only comes once a year. . .'

'They've kidnapped your girl,' someone told Billy when he emerged from the library. At first he couldn't take it in: there was such pleasure on the face of the messenger.

'The engineers. The haka party. They've taken her off somewhere.'

'They went through the park,' someone else, grinning,

volunteered. 'Probably on the way to the Queen's Head.'

Then Billy was running. Past the blurred floral clock, the fountain, the lawn where the leaf-sweeper staggered and clutched his wheelbarrow. When Billy was out of sight, leaping down the steps three at a time, the leaf-sweeper fell and began one of his fits, his protective helmet rising and falling, striking the grass.

There were two bodies in the gutter now and the publican was on the phone, calling the police. Billy seized the first handful of rugby jersey he could grip, bringing its wearer close to his face. 'Where is she?' he asked through gritted teeth. A yard glass fell to the floor and shattered.

'Hiding in the toilets,' someone suggested.

But when he flung the women's toilet door open – for a few moments his eyes blurred and he couldn't read the symbol – there was no one there. He cleared his throat loudly and called Anna's name but neither cubicle was occupied. A pile of paper towels overflowed a wire mesh basket and the basins were slimy with soapsuds.

There were sirens outside and the sound of running feet. Billy leaned against the wall and waited. When he finally made his way down to the bar, treading gingerly over broken glass, he was given Anna's handbag.

'Haven't seen the lady,' the barman said. 'What is it with engineers?'

Anna meanwhile had climbed back into Albert Park, up the stone steps on which someone had written *Nipple Nee Nee Ya Ya*, and was sitting at the base of an ancient oak. She missed her bag sorely, for she longed to run a comb through her hair. Several students climbing the path looked at her oddly and then averted their eyes.

I stood tiptoe upon a little hill, she thought, but the second line had vanished. When she had recovered a little she would go back down the hill and ask if anyone had seen her handbag. She might even go into the little rest room from which she had escaped, not by removing the louvres, for there were none, or climbing onto rickety dustbin lids, but by simply following the corridor until she came to a small and greasy kitchen with an outside door. She had walked in the other direction, head lowered, but the students lying in the gutter were too preoccupied to notice. One was attempting to crawl across Queen Street on his hands and knees and some hooting cars had come to a stop.

And Billy, burning with zeal, his heart on fire like one of the hideous statues in the church at Ouse, was making his way up another set of steps towards the cannon. All he held was a woman's handbag, slightly the worse for wear, but he could have been carrying a pike, a sword, a drawn bayonet. He climbed the steps three at a time, unaware he was stretching his legs. The leaf-sweeper was still on the grass, surrounded by a group of students. Billy pushed a few of them aside, looked down, diagnosed sleep, and ordered them to move on. Send me any more problems, his heart said. Problem solving, he could see now, was like parting the waters. Secretly he wanted a brawl while the energy lasted, to give and receive blows, and receive energy from them. Before he knew it he was standing under the statue of Queen Victoria, handbag in his hand like a dispatch case. Tall palms looked down like bearers and the park suddenly resembled a Victorian drawing room. Then he recollected that Anna had always found the rear view of the Queen poignant, and he stood looking up at the marble hips, the commodious folds of her gown.

And there, waving from behind a tree, was Anna. He crouched down on the ground beside her and went to put his arms around her.

'Wait,' she said, taking the handbag and rummaging in it. 'I'm not hurt. Have you hurt anyone? You look as though you could . . .'

'Thwarted,' he said, as she began rubbing at her face, peering in a hand mirror. And all the time she faced towards the tree.

'Now,' she said, and he pulled her to her feet.

She hugged him as hard as she could but she knew he was not soothed.

The leaf-sweeper was on his feet when they passed. He gazed mildly at them and nodded, and smiled.

The next day Billy encountered Rushbrook, the engineering student who had kidnapped Anna, at the University Squash Club. Billy was drenched with sweat after demolishing his regular partner, Wheeler, a lanky final year whose long arms normally made him formidable. Billy had left him sitting on a bench while he made his way to the showers; they had agreed to meet later at the bar. Though there were other people around, he forced Rushbrook up against the concrete-block wall and pushed the edge of his hand across his windpipe. In no time at all there were arms pulling him off and cries of 'Steady on, take it easy'. Rushbrook, it turned out, when they were face to face with their seconds on either side, squash racquets sloping over their shoulders, had no recollection of taking anyone hostage and forcing them into the Queen's Head against their will. He had spent several hours at Police Headquarters before being released with a caution. After that he had joined up with the pub crawl in Ponsonby Road.

'Don't let me catch you alone,' were Billy's parting words as, still escorted, he made his way to the showers. 'If a cretin like that ever puts up a bridge,' he thought. Later he was called to the secretary's office to explain himself. Finally he sat with Wheeler in the bar, a towel around his neck. They drank tonic water and black coffee. And Billy tried out on Wheeler the theory Anna had expounded of love and hate: to interpose your body between another's at a cliff edge or propel it over with a shove. The trouble was getting the villain to the cliff edge, Billy decided. Wheeler thought it wiser to make no comment.

Anna, though she didn't need to, was reading Richard Monckton Milne's *Memoir of John Keats*. 'His habitual gentleness gave effect to his occasional bursts of indignation, and at the mention of oppression or wrong, or at any calumny against those he loved, he rose into grave manliness at once and seemed like a tall man.' She might read this to Billy; then she recollected he was already a tall man.

In St George's Bay Road Kirsten was moving out and Billy could move in. There was a larger room they could share. I'll read Keats's *Letters* to him, Anna thought. Tell him about the last unopened letters of Fanny Brawne which he wanted placed next to his heart. How poor Fanny must have laboured over those letters, trying to comfort and not raise false hope. And probably attending to her dress, for Fanny Brawne was greatly interested in fashion and related to Beau Brummel.

In High Street Anna stopped outside Second Time Around. There was a vermilion velvet jacket in the window, drop-shouldered, the waist drawn in with a row of fine elastic. Its sleeves ended in ruffs. I might as well begin the way I intend to go on, she thought, though she didn't know what she was referring to.

Billy's anger was gone now, but he thought of it as a gift. His parting from his parents had produced no such emotion; here was something clear and strong. And easily slaked, for he was astonished when a few days later he saw Rushbrook go out of his way to avoid him, to be seen in protective company. That the anger fell back as if it was based on gravel, water welling through it, did not disappoint him. Emotional as he was, he did not like emotion. What had Anna told him about someone fighting for an hour over a kitten? The next time, he told himself, he would strike on the instant, not a day later. He turned on his heel to see no one was looking – he was in Shortland Street – and raised a fist in the air. Bring on the next manifestation, he thought.

Anna had invited him to dinner and there was something new and placatory in her tone. As long as I don't frighten myself, he thought, as he began to climb up Emily Place. I won't allow myself to be overthrown by it, he went on thinking: it was amazing how steps and a statue to people long dead – he was at the little memorial now, its sides covered with moss, and he paused to read some of the names – brought this kind of insight. His mother too had liked to walk in cemeteries. But to have something inside you that burned and stung, and, better still, that died down as suddenly as it came, so, coming and going, you could feel its passage.

He turned as he got to the top of the hill and looked back. He ignored the buildings, nondescript for the most part, like children playing separately with blocks, and let his eye skim over the wide harbour. The *Kestrel* was ploughing its way towards Devonport, skirting the rusted hulks at their berths. A few yachts were tacking and the *Kestrel* would slow to give them precedence. The thought that the *Kestrel* would play by the rules filled him with joy. And Rangitoto glowed with sunlight on its crown.

'Do you realise how close we are to the animals?' Anna asked, passing Billy a plate of crudités. 'Except gorillas do not share their food with others.' She was wearing a fetching new red velvet jacket which accentuated her waist.

'Won't Dr Loeb be pleased. He can relax now, with his bone pendant and facial hair, and I can scrutinise him without fear. I might even give him a copy of *Peter Rabbit.*'

'Perhaps it might stand up in court,' Billy replied, munching on a carrot stick. 'Your Honour, I admit to behaving like an animal.'

'I hope you will. Later,' Anna replied.

She had changed the sheets, wearing her jacket. She had sprayed the pillowcases with rose-water, thinking of gorillas making fresh nests every day, perhaps with a crushed flower or two where their heads would lie. And of Keats admiring a small bright-eyed animal purposefully going about its business.

Later they went and stood on the verandah. The sky was faintly pink towards the city centre. Not a large city but a sprawling one. Above St Georges Bay Road the sky was navy blue and the stars shone like medals. What will become of us, Anna wanted to ask, but she knew it was irrelevant. She remembered an experience she had had as a young girl. She had quarrelled bitterly with her mother, and after she had been sent to bed – not supperless, but early – she had waited until it was midnight and crept out into the back garden. Her prim white cotton nightdress made her feel like a character in a book. She sat on the cool slightly damp grass for a long time, her feet curled up.

After her anger died – it seemed something to do with the night sky – she looked at everything carefully. The wooden fence, the raspberry canes, a tall hedge, a swing with rope handles. No answer came but she could swear, after she had sat there for an hour, that it was not indifference either.

Indian Pacific, Grand Hyatt

Think of a box – and there it is:
six-sided, enclosed. It's empty, of course,
unless you fill it: a naked woman,
three constant friends, a set of wings?
You are what you have made.

'Instructions for living in the sky', PHILIP SALOM

Minnie McAleer swung herself on board Car G of the Indian
Pacific as it waited in two segments at Sydney Central Station.
Like a silver caterpillar cut in half, came the thought that she
had had on her first day, and now could not be dislodged.
Minnie thought of old brains as being like this: her mother
who kept repeating her instructions about life in the big city,
as if repetition did anything but dilute. Still Minnie did throw
a glimpse while her foot was on the plate towards the other
silver half, the lower-status section of the train as it waited on
Platform B. Then she inserted herself, moving her hips like a
cork coming out of a bottle, into the little galley where
someone had left six inches of dark brown soapy water and a
few coffee cups lying on their sides. Pedro, Minnie thought
angrily, but she didn't stop to clear up. She might meet the
young Spanish charmer in the corridor and rebuke him. Not

that it did any good: Pedro Casado regarded any sign of temper in a woman as affection.

There were passengers in the corridor of Car G, bewildered at the curves of the honey-coloured walls, bumping their suitcases against their legs, consulting their tickets to see if this really was First Class.

'The other side of the platform,' Minnie said to a young girl with a backpack who was flattened against a door as a stout woman pushed a suitcase with wheels in front of her. The girl had thrust the ticket at Minnie as she waited beside her. An air of repose, if she could have seen herself, combined with hardly suppressed energy made Minnie very attractive at that moment. At least Pedro thought so, entering at the other end of the carriage and getting straight back into her good books by soothing the woman with the suitcase who was complaining about the size of her First Class couchette.

'Is this all I get for my money?' she demanded. 'Hardly room to swing a cat.'

'You'll find it's very beautifully organised,' Pedro replied, flashing his teeth, which were not as Australian teeth. The woman noticed and her tone softened.

'Look,' Pedro went on. 'Let me show you. On this little table goes your book or your game of Patience when you have had enough of socialising. And here is your wardrobe for your robe and slippers.' The tiny tintinnabulation of a coathanger could be heard within. 'On this little support,' Pedro continued, as if he were already bringing it and calling her name at the door, 'goes your early morning cup of tea. This knob turns on an historical and geographical commentary which is pretty fine.'

By now the plump woman was almost mollified.

'I'll see you in the bar this evening, Madame, and pour you one of my special cocktails,' Pedro said as he eased himself out of G22.

'What do you know about cocktails?' Minnie hissed.

'Practically nothing,' Pedro admitted. 'I leave them to Jimbo. My job is to flirt and soothe and flash my Spanish eyes.'

'You can get your Spanish hands on a tea towel in the galley and clean up that mess you left,' Minnie said sternly. 'I mean it.'

Then, since the corridor was free for a second, she did her sheepdog imitation, moving her hips seductively and anticipating the curves of Car G, so Pedro, looking back, placed his hand over his heart and gave a mock groan.

Three hours later Minnie was serving entrées in the Queen Adelaide dining car. The table lamps glowed yellow in the windows as the landscape withdrew but the faces reflected were not glamorous and jewelled as Minnie required and a certain sadness came over her. The rich tapestry and fine leather, the spotless tablecloths and napkins, the elegant china and heavy silverware, the roses in silver vases on each table, the crammed but perfect look of the tables before the first guests appeared – tonight it was a Swiss woman and a heavily bearded man who had made very little effort with their toilette – suggested a way of doing things, a standard not to be over-thrown. Even the clacking of the rails and the gliding of the train suggested a clicking of the tongue and long skirts sweeping the floor. But the mood of sadness did not last long: the dining car might be glamorous but the galley was as crammed as any out-of-sight Edwardian butler's pantry.

After the second dinner sitting was over, Minnie and Leannah, one of the other hostesses, sat at the rear of the Queen Adelaide dining car drinking coffee. The tablecloths had been scooped up – the Swiss woman's place was dotted with flecks of soup – and the tables re-set for the first breakfast sitting. Staggering slightly, the diners were making their way back to the lounge car to play cards or have a nightcap. Inside each of the couchettes the beds had been folded down and made up with monogrammed cream dunas. Minnie wondered if the Swiss woman would be able to climb into hers, and half-hoped she would have a restless night, for she had been demanding at dinner, asking for Bearnaise sauce to be removed from her steak though the menu clearly said *Filet mignon with sauce Bearnaise.*

Outside now the blackness was impenetrable and Minnie and Leannah's faces were reflected back to them: tired, but since they were young and fit, somehow elated. The sounds of the great silver train, which Minnie in odd moments tried to decipher and arrange in order and at which she always failed: the swish of air passing or being sliced through, the rails that seemed to lie waiting for the wheels, almost like an obeisance, even the civilised shudders of veneer and crockery, the glamour of creating night after night not just something powerful but an additional drama. Sometimes, Minnie thought, she knew what it was to be Jonah in the belly of the whale.

At the Melbourne Grand Hyatt Zoe Berryman was working at the reception desk, dealing with an early-morning queue of dark-suited businessmen. A trail of overnight bags and one or two tapestry-covered suitcases reached almost to the base of a ladder where a giant flower arrangement was being assembled. Zoe's private opinion was that it was hideous; ferns and gladioli, spears of flax attempted to raise it closer to the chandeliers, and after each descent of the ladder there was further head-scratching. On the ground floor Charlie the commissionaire would be reaching for a single long-stemmed rose to present to each female arrival. Sometimes a young woman would not know how to look, especially if she was trailing after a businessman old enough to be her father. And women on their own, for conferences, would often lay the rose by the guest book as they registered and collected their keys.

Zoe's manner was cool and businesslike, with a ready smile if one was required, but since there were sometimes queries or complaints she knew better than to appear fawning. But the early-morning queue simply wanted to exit: an exchange of credit cards and keys across the desk, the pushing forward of an account for signature. Sometimes one of the dark-suited ones would say, 'See you next month,' and Zoe would allow the corners of her mouth to curve in a smile of recognition.

A clutch of Singapore Airlines hostesses, closely followed by their dark-suited keepers – this was how Zoe thought of the short silent men who accompanied them – suddenly appeared in the lobby, trailing their overnight bags. The Singapore girls smiled and chattered like birds and several of the men in the queue turned to admire.

'A British pilot and a Singapore crew,' the man Zoe was dealing with said, leaning forward slightly as if he was confiding a secret. 'That'd be the ideal way to fly.'

'We love having them to stay,' Zoe replied. She had noticed before how seductive the slits in the uniform were and how the tiny waists invited the measurement of hands.

When the next guest stepped forward, Zoe patted the waist of her jacket as if she were frisking herself. At nineteen, her waist was only twenty-five inches, but compared to a Singapore girl she might have come from another planet.

The Swiss woman, Beatrix Geissler, accosted Minnie as she washed coffee cups in the tiny galley – once again Pedro was in evidence – and complained that she hadn't been able to sleep. It was a frequent complaint: the narrow little couchette bed, raised so high off the ground one needed a step to get into it, and once in it the option of lying on one's back or gingerly on one's side. The noise of the train, the rich meal consumed before retiring, made sleep difficult. Questioned, Beatrix Geissler admitted she had gone straight to bed after an unsatisfactory shower in the shower cubicle where the water flow had been erratic and it had been difficult to keep her balance.

Minnie's face assumed the look of concern and attentiveness that was now second nature. Further back another voice said: Never satisfied, probably frustrated, could circumnavigate the globe complaining.

'Would you like a cup of tea or coffee?' Minnie asked. 'Sometimes a walk through the train helps.' See how the other half lives, the voice said. 'Even a few turns down the First Class corridors.'

Soon they would be in Broken Hill and there would be the

chance to walk up and down the platform. Perhaps Beatrix Geissler would sympathise with the women who set up stalls with homemade pottery and bottles of preserves, rugs made of granny squares. Women with work-worn hands and lined faces, their sale items so modestly priced that most turned away. Minnie always tried to buy something from them.

She hung up the tea towel and walked through the train to the lounge car. A grass tree swayed in a pot and several couples were playing cards. Pedro was looking for a sweatshirt for an American woman. 'It looks kind of industrial,' the woman's husband was saying. 'Kind of like Pittsburgh.'

'The Pittsburgh of Australia,' Pedro agreed. He agreed with anything, it was the quickest way.

'Dirty weekend?' he said to Minnie when the sweatshirts had been debated and put back because of fear of shrinkage. The rich, it seemed to him, quibbled over everything.

Out on the platform in the sharp air which smelt faintly metallic, Minnie walked alongside the silver cars to stretch her legs. The Swiss woman was trying to take a photo and complaining she could only get a section of the train in. The contrast between the silveriness of the train and the brick and dust and slag of Broken Hill almost made Minnie's heart ache. And there, when she turned and faced the station, were the same sweetly complaisant women, who probably had to count every dollar, selling fresh scones and cookies, babies' bootees and matinee jackets, little packets of fudge. Minnie bought some fudge and a small furry cactus. Its soft gauzy surface was almost the colour of the train.

Minnie's boyfriend, Adam Scoular, lived with his widowed mother in a dark red brick house, almost the colour of rubies, in Iodide Street. Adam was studying mining and metallurgy at Newcastle University. His father had died in a shunting accident; Minnie had not asked the details, though his death still lingered in the too-neat house where even the sheets were ironed and tea towels folded with knife-edge creases. But his widow, Dulcie Scoular, who had gradually permitted Minnie the use of her Christian name – a sure compliment, according to Adam – was one of the sweet women on the Broken Hill platform. Minnie, when she stayed overnight, occupied a room with an old treadle sewing machine covered with a starched embroidered cloth. Adam was nearly as keen on the proprieties as his mother, though they clung together in the hallway, ready to separate at the sound of a step. And in truth, after a shift on the Indian Pacific, Minnie was pleased to sleep, nun-like, on a soft mattress in a real bed.

In the mornings Adam, Dulcie and Minnie sat in the yellow kitchen – painted the year before Dulcie became a widow – eating boiled eggs and rye toast and drinking endless cups of tea from a big yellow teapot shrouded in a multi-striped knitted cosy. Minnie thought of the Swiss woman being borne across the Nullarbor Plain, still complaining or sleeping better in her berth. Perhaps she would have made friends with another solitary woman Minnie had seated her next to in the Queen Adelaide: a mousy little German who told Minnie her father had left her a substantial legacy and now she was indulging her love of train travel, taking a new trip each year. And next Wednesday the Indian Pacific would pull in again at Broken Hill and Minnie would be transformed into what Adam considered a pawn of the capitalist system. He did not say lackey because he knew how hard Minnie and the staff worked. Nor could he not admire the train, its long silver length like a long silver glove or an arm in chain mail.

But today, late Sunday morning, the streets of Broken Hill were practically deserted. Only the Argent Milk Bar was open and even that looked half-hearted: a tired-faced girl was cleaning out the freezer. Singing issued from the open doors of Sacred Heart Cathedral as Minnie and Adam walked past; Minnie recognised the tune, 'Old Hundred', but the words were lost in a fervent rumbling.

Adam said nothing but pulled Minnie closer to him as they climbed steep Sulphide Street. She loved his saturnine good looks and that approaching him at a party had established an instant claim. She loved the idea that he discarded things and kept her in place. Only sometimes she wondered how central this position was, or if he was dangerously isolated. The hymns, for all their braying, sounded companionable, and Minnie, who was not a Catholic but knew some of the ritual from learning music from the nuns, guessed they would soon be exchanging the kiss of peace, hands snaking towards neighbours', and old miners with a crushing grip holding the soft hands of women who might wince. Adam's hand felt strong and powerful, as if it had not yet found its work. He had a tendency to clench his fists at his side when he was talking, not through any anger or tension but as if his hands felt comfortable that way. One day, Minnie thought, he will stop discarding beliefs, systems, injustices, and build. Already, imitating his mother, she had learned the value of saying little and making the few observations she offered potent.

She had pointed out the similarity that opposing sides soon took on, as if they were chess pieces, and he had listened to that, since they both played chess and Minnie could sometimes, but not often, win. And sometimes a person might set up opposing forces in their own nature, so a contest that was not present in the world could still exist. But this thought was ill-developed and needed more deliberation. She was thinking perhaps of Pedro Casado who confessed he had sabotaged every employment he had by an act of recklessness.

'Got through the week,' he had said to Minnie as he farewelled her, and she had called back, 'Fingers crossed.' It was as if he couldn't resist testing his charm to the limit to see what barriers it could lower.

Zoe Berryman came off her desk shift at the Grand Hyatt and walked through a green baize door and along a corridor. She removed her badge as she walked and began to unbutton her jacket. A motley crew lived behind the walls the public could not penetrate: one of the sous chefs was walking towards her, his hat bent and his face slumped and weary.

Zoe enjoyed the corridors, the behind scenes, as, as a child, she had enjoyed the backstage glimpses of a theatre where she had sometimes been taken to see her great-aunt in her dressing room. Her grandfather Rupert's sister, Sophie Berryman, had had a long career as an actress; she had graduated at times to a dressing room of her own with a mock glittery star pinned on it before sinking back into character parts and older women. Not that Zoe thought of the tired relaxed figures behind the soundproof doors of the hotel as lesser mortals: they were simply off duty and allowed to compensate for the vivacity demanded by an equivalent passivity.

In the staffroom – scuffed carpet and radiators in need of paint, old easy chairs – Zoe poured herself a cup of coffee and kicked off her shoes. The first weeks her feet had ached intolerably and she wondered if she might snap at someone paying a bill instead of patiently explaining the exorbitant phone charges or making an ongoing booking. But now she felt as strong as some small sturdy animal: a pit pony perhaps, or one that trotted ceaselessly in a ring while acrobats leapt on and off with extravagant gestures to hide an unvarying motion. And when her next shift came, Zoe loved the second before she swung through the baize door in the opposite direction, her head high, an eager but not too eager smile on her lips – she might be going to audition for a Singapore girl – and her eyes caught the massed colour of the latest huge floral offering. Sophie Berryman had sometimes had flowers in her dressing room and the sweet smell of roses and lilies mingled with powder and greasepaint.

Today Gina Giardina was working beside her: Gina who was bright and breezy, whose cheerfulness extended beyond the baize doors, who had been known to sing in the corridors until rebuked. Gina had worked in the Commonwealth Bank of Australia before coming to the Grand Hyatt, and queues of eyes regarding her were nothing. If Zoe's queue grew too long, Gina would beckon or lay a hand across her breast and call, 'Does no one love me?' Gina wore French perfume, bought at staff discount. 'A cloud of Arpège makes it hard for a man to dispute a bill,' she confided to Zoe, laughing. In the bank she had grown tired of asking, 'How would you like this, Sir,

Madame? Fifties, twenties?' Now she handed gold cards back to businessmen who scrawled signatures without looking; only the occasional one queried the wine on a dinner tab or whether he had had oysters as an entrée. And then Gina would lean forward, sorrowfully, as if she suspected the oysters had been bad or the businessman had tossed all night on his kingsize bed. 'Would you like me to remove the entrée?' she would ask. 'I would be happy . . .' But already the perfume was creeping forward, doing its work, and the little gold pen which Gina held out, for a signature could be expected from nothing less, and the hand with its signet ring, the white starched cuff with gold cufflinks showing, reached for it. It was all Gina could do to restrain from patting it with her fingertips.

Just a raised eyebrow in the next hiatus was directed at Zoe, but she knew the queue had enjoyed the performance and some of them, allowing their poker mouths to lift at the corners, might have contemplated complaining as well.

If Adam was frustrated by the sleeping arrangements imposed by his mother, or not imposed but decreed by himself, he showed no sign. When they were in Sturt Park, pausing in front of the memorial to the *Titanic* bandsmen, he took Minnie's hand and pulled it into his jacket pocket. Now she felt manacled and, because her hips were female, out of step. But it is the woman's nature to adapt, she told herself, as she walked with a slightly dragging step. Once she was back on the Indian Pacific she would adapt again, become the purveyor of cheer, able to deal with anything from inserting a film in a camera to finding a Panadol. Now she felt like one of the anarchists Adam had told her about. Sentenced to hang in a Russian forest, they had been taken in pairs to the gallows, all apart from one man who had waited behind so someone on the verge of collapse could take his place. Minnie forgot the crime they were accused of or whether simply being an anarchist was enough: she seemed to see the forest floor dappled in sunlight, with soft undergrowth and trees as in an English park. The gallows were in some deeper part of the forest and perhaps this last walk held some comfort or beauty. The woman who had gone with the despairing man, abandoning her own partner, might have held hands with him or made some remark.

They were on the other side of the park now and walking back towards Adam's mother's house. Under a red river gum Adam released her hand from his pocket and placed it on his shoulder. With his other arm he circled her waist. They kissed solemnly, as if, Minnie thought, they kissed the future. Adam's mouth was small but oddly passionate. She had read that somewhere: small mouths meant passion. Her own mouth was wide and curved up at the corners.

Back at Iodide Street Dulcie Scoular had set the table and was anxiously checking a dish of macaroni cheese which was being kept warm in the oven. Its crust of breadcrumbs and cheese was golden and the sauce was bubbling at the edges. 'My favourite,' Minnie said, as it was set down on a table mat on top of the checked tablecloth. But in her heart she longed for the Queen Adelaide dining room where the glistening white tablecloths were often stained at the end of a sitting and where one evening a man had upset a glass of red wine over a woman's white blouse. Minnie and Pedro had rushed for club soda and a napkin to sponge it, priding themselves on their knowledge. 'No charge,' Pedro had said when the man had offered to pay. And she thought of the little grass tree, swaying lightly in the lounge car, its strange dry trunk like an elephant's skin and its thin sharp fronds on which you could cut a finger. She imagined it travelling back across the Nullarbor, turning to the desert light or accommodating itself, as living things were supposed to do, to the light in the lounge car, the reflected flashes as the train sped through the night, the murmurs of voices, the clink of coffee spoons. It was strange, with Adam beside her, and a second helping of macaroni cheese which praise had compelled her to request, that one could long for something that was on the move. As if it were passing through time. She wondered if the Swiss woman had listened to the commentary and been soothed by it. There was an explanation of fertile and infertile desert, a line of longitude that no human courage could cross. She hoped the Swiss woman had stopped complaining.

Zoe Berryman's parents had drowned when their car ran off a bridge when she was ten. Her great-aunt, the actress Sophie Berryman, had become her guardian, having her to stay when she was not touring or conducting a discreet love affair. The cars drew up to St Mary's at mid-term breaks and long holidays and individual girls were borne off like cherished parcels. There were real parcels on the front seats, as if being cherished started instantly. Sometimes Zoe stayed behind. She had not wanted to be a boarder; she identified with her classmates who quarrelled with their parents over the state of their rooms or spent the holidays in sulks. At such times she missed her mother, and staying with her great-aunt, though she adored her, in a boarding house could not compensate. As soon as she left school she enrolled in a hospitality course.

The Grand Hyatt was Zoe's second hotel. She had been noticed on the desk at the Tilba, a boutique hotel on Toorak Road, by a friend of the personnel manager and her name passed on. The Tilba, with its small number of individually decorated rooms, gave excessive service and established a family atmosphere with its clients. In fact its guest list was rather static as reluctant guests departed after a week or a month to allow other aficionados to take their place. Though young, Zoe's manner was perfect for dealing with those who demanded discretion and luxury but also a certain intimacy. From behind her low desk with its spindly chair that might have graced a fashion showing, she rose, putting aside a folder, and held the proffered hand of an elderly lady in both of hers. A bellboy in a jaunty cap paused respectfully in a circle of monogrammed luggage, as if herding sheep. And in each room there were little touches, recorded in a register: a preference for blankets instead of a duna, a favourite chocolate mint or flower.

The Grand Hyatt was different: the number of staff, its layers of management through which Zoe intended to climb.

But the Tilba had served her well and her manner did not falter. The Hyatt's desk and the uniform were more mannish, the flower displays taller, but she did not allow herself to be intimidated. If she closed her eyes she could see her great-aunt curtseying deeply as if the audience were crowned heads, a bouquet clasped to her breast with the tenderness of a new-born child.

Minnie stood on the platform at Broken Hill and tried, as she had before, to work out what the first sighting of the Indian Pacific would be. She meant before its actual appearance. A car coming over a hill, observed by someone at its base, made a sliver-thin line of colour and then more and more was revealed. In the case of the Indian Pacific would it be a scintilla of silver? Something like the underside of a gum leaf?

If the platform was not full of people strolling and looking at the stalls – Dulcie Scoular was there with a new supply of knitting and shortbread – and if she was not wearing her uniform and feeling important and apart, she would have been tempted to lie down and press her ear against the platform to listen for vibrations. Adam had left in the early morning, easing himself into her bed, holding her tight in his arms, though he would do nothing more. And now she was to be wrapped around again in the train that had become something like a heart's desire.

But Minnie did not get to test which sliver of silver, which rippling movement of air above the tracks heralded the Indian Pacific on this clear bright morning. She was turned towards a stall that sold hard toffee and wondering if Pedro would like some, if she might hand it to him with a joke about keeping his jaws stuck together. She was even wondering if Pedro would still be there. Then the silver shape, or the segment of it that could fit against the platform, was there and the remainder just came to rest. A kind of awe came over the station as if, in a fairytale, a very large wish had been granted. Or, in an orchestra, the last note in a symphony had sounded, died away, and left, not silence, but a shimmering. Then the crowd pushed forward, the silver doors opened and Pedro was there, grinning.

Adam Scoular saw the Indian Pacific depart, snaking its way through mullock and tailings, as he paused on Crystal Street to roll himself a cigarette. Serves them right, he thought of the rich tourists, that they have to confront soil stained and spoiled as anything in Blake – 'satanic' was the word he meant. His mother would be packing up her useless offerings – over and over he had told her they were useless, that the First Class cars that came to rest against the platform had no need of such offerings, no one at that end of the train sat up all night or needed a granny rug to cover their knees. But, like Minnie, she insisted it was an event and, besides, she enjoyed the company. There are ordinary people on the train, Minnie informed him.

He was irked by the living arrangements at his mother's when he visited, by the need for Minnie to sleep in a separate room, but desire was no match for a deeper reticence: he felt there was honour involved in not disturbing the excessive neatness of his mother's home. Soon Dulcie would be going into the station cafeteria for a cup of tea with the other stall holders, spending the pathetic amount of cash on a lamington or a piece of seed cake. Then he reminded himself it was his turn to visit Minnie in Adelaide. She shared a flat with an insipid woman who worked for the International Arts Festival. A woman with a bland unmarked face like a new coin. Somehow Adam found that annoying as well.

Minnie and Pedro meanwhile were drinking coffee in their cramped staff quarters. Leannah and Jimbo were there as well. The landscape was moving sedately past the windows as if the train were bringing it to life. We are different when we are with people than when we are alone, Minnie thought. Pedro who had managed to hold his tongue on the return journey had been instrumental in persuading the Swiss woman and the mousy German to take the Ghan. The two women had finally teamed up after being seated together at dinner. Such a lack of elegance, Pedro thought, but as usual his charming face hid a sneering thought. The Swiss woman had bad teeth and the German a faint moustache. Pedro heard faint snatches of their conversation as he bent to remove their plates. 'Daddy,' the German woman was saying, 'had a strict routine. Every morning he read the paper for an hour.' And the world came to a standstill, thought Pedro, as he lifted the tray and smiled into two unresponsive faces. The galley was as hot as the engine room of a ship. Little eye fillet steaks were sizzling and the orders were piling up.

Philippa Cornford, the very good young woman who shared Minnie's flat and whose blandness was so irritating to Adam Scoular, was a temporary worker for the Adelaide Festival. Her role was lowly: she collected authors from the airport and saw to their needs in the Green Room. Platters of grapes and assorted cheeses, club sandwiches and crackers, coffee, tea, fruit juices and mineral water, because the authors preferred to graze. Nor were they particularly keen to meet one another as they sat gathering their resources before a reading or a panel. The panellists assembled and argued about the order in which they were to speak: this was more important than the content of their reading. Philippa decided they were competitive, even the quiet ones who acted graciously towards their fellows. On stage sometimes a quiet one underwent a metamorphosis that was startling. Just now Philippa was bringing a cup of filtered coffee to Laurie Andersson, the American novelist who, the day before, had confided she lived in a tiny hamlet with only a garage and a general store and not even a McDonalds. Philippa had tried to imagine the landscape as Laurie Andersson described it, flat and bleak, with ragged roadsides. The state was South Dakota; Philippa had read it was windblown with very few trees. It was the mention of the lack of trees that had caused Laurie Andersson – she wrote dense psychological thrillers which seemed sifted through elements: floods, snow and wind – to become friendly. Philippa didn't like to ask if she was homesick; perhaps she was pleased to be in a city with fast-food outlets, paved streets and elegant buildings. In return she had volunteered some information about Adelaide: the terraces which bounded it, a kind of neat closing off, like someone holding a ruler and drawing a line; the parklands outside the terraces, calculated to be the distance a musket ball could fly. Philippa never drove through this green space without thinking of Colonel Light and his calculations. 'Very interesting,' Laurie Andersson said, but Philippa could see she was just being polite. Probably one festival to a famous writer was just like another: hotels, readings, radio interviews. Yesterday Philippa had overheard an interview conducted on a crackly phone to a reporter in Launceston. The novelist's answers were courteous and considered, she even allowed a hint of laughter to show in her voice, but the minute the phone was set down she looked drained.

In her lunch hour Philippa walked down to the River Torrens. Cyclists were out on the cycle path, and joggers; a group of middle-aged women walked exaggeratedly swinging their arms. Black swans floated by; the bulrushes at the edge of the water waved.

Philippa walked on without thinking. In the afternoon there was another panel: the writers in it were known to be quarrelsome and had probably been chosen for that reason. It was highly likely the quarrel would begin in the Green Room. 'Thank you for your kindness,' Laurie Andersson had said to Philippa as she rose rather wearily from the comfortable chair in which she was slumped, and Philippa had replied, 'No problem', at which the American woman gave her a stare and then a smile.

There was a young man huddled against the wall of the boat shed. Philippa noticed him as she walked on, consulting her watch, for soon she must turn back. She walked to the rose garden and stood for a moment admiring the contrasting elements she always felt around roses: the dug-over soil in which not a weed showed, the gnarled and knobby stems, the thorns and then the blooms themselves. Suddenly she knew what they reminded her of: a fairytale, a castle approached by trial and pain. She stepped on the edge of the bed and put her nose into one of the blooms. At its base a label read: *Centenaire de Lourdes, 1958.*

The young man was still there when she walked back. Philippa stepped over the grass until she stood in front of him. 'Are you all right?' she asked. (Would you like a glass of water before you go on? she would say to a nervous author. Some were so nervous the mention of water sent them scurrying to the toilet.) The hands were removed from the face and it was revealed to be young and grimy. A blue bruise stood out upon a cheekbone.

'I'm hungry,' a thin voice said. It was almost expressionless. Hunger was a fact with the weightlessness of air.

'Wait here,' Philippa said. 'I haven't much time because I'm due back, but I'll bring you something. What would you like?'

But the hands had covered the face again as if the idea of a menu was too gross.

'Wait,' Philippa said again, and she began to hurry along the path.

Orange juice, she was thinking, a filled roll with ham and cheese and tomato, a packet of nuts and raisins, chocolate, some kind of snack bar for later. And fruit. A crisp red apple, a banana for potassium.

There was a coffee bar just over the bridge and soon everything was packed into white paper bags and then a carrier bag. Perhaps he will have given up, she worried as she hurried back, trying to still her breath. Her heart was racing in an absurd manner as if the bearer of gifts was the guilty one, the one asking a favour. And, true to his role, the young man kept his hands over his face and his hunched miserable pose even as she stood in front of him, wondering whether to take the paper bags out separately or to enumerate the contents or whether that would be an insult. 'I hope you like processed cheese,' she said finally, and the hands came away from the face and the low voice, so low she could hardly make out the words, said, 'I don't mind.'

Philippa put the bag down at his feet and walked away.

There seemed no etiquette for the receiving of necessities. She might have explained to him that her $20 had done its best to provide nutrition at short notice and he could save the apple and raisins for later. Her back felt stiff and her calves sore as she crossed the bridge a second time and blended with the lunchtime strollers.

Back at the festival four authors, two men, two women, were walking towards a panel on 'Dreamtime and the Modern Australian Novel'. Laurie Andersson was walking in the opposite direction. Unlike the panellists her face was open, relaxed. Her last appearance – a reading – was over. She caught up with Philippa.

'What is it?' she asked. She sensed something in the young woman had changed.

'I've just bought some food for a homeless man,' Philippa replied, not raising her eyes.

But Laurie Andersson, besides being broad was tall, and she looked into Philippa's face.

'And you feel undone by this?' she asked, as they stood at the edge of the path, and then, by unspoken consent, resumed their walk. 'I've several hours before I need to leave for the airport. Come back to the hotel with me and have a coffee. I'll say that I need you if anyone asks.'

But being seen in the company of Laurie Andersson amounted to permission and Philippa was glad to follow her through the doors of the Hyatt Regency, to wait in the lobby while the novelist went up to her room for a few minutes. She sat in a little half-moon chair, then jumped up and went to the cloakroom to wash her hands. Her face in the merciless mirror looked dazed – no wonder Laurie Andersson had noticed. She got back to her chair just as the novelist emerged from the lift with a small parcel in her hands.

'It's not very elegantly wrapped,' she said, setting it down on a little round table, 'and I don't want you to open it now. You've shown more interest than the other young people. Not that they haven't all been charming. I think you'd fit very well into South Dakota.'

The coffee came and some biscotti.

'You sound very fond of South Dakota,' Philippa said.

'I am,' Laurie Andersson replied, dipping a biscotti, 'but I'm not sure how long it can hold out. "Enjoy the rest of your day" will reach there sooner or later. Luckily most of the natives speak only in grunts, so it may not take.

'I'm very addicted to silence,' she went on, 'though you might not suspect it after these last few days. I shall be glad to get home and say nothing.'

'I think I like it too,' Philippa said. 'I can never tell if my words are sincere. They sound sincere at the time . . .'

'So now you're into action. One of those who think words need another dimension. So why did you stop for this homeless young man?'

'I don't know,' Philippa replied.

'In South Dakota when it snows and everything comes to a standstill, everyone seems brighter. Their eyes gleam when they tell you someone's trapped or cut off. We all get in extra provisions. I suppose your young man was surrounded by no such event, which made the giving of food seem more naked. Natural disasters are so useful . . .'

'I've read one of your books,' Philippa said hesitantly. 'It had a snow storm in it.'

'It was very useful,' Laurie Andersson went on, undeterred by the change of subject. 'It gave me lots of room for description. I went out into the fields and observed the hoar frost and I tried to describe the sound my boots made on the frozen ground. One thing just led to another.'

'I expect I won't see the young man again,' Philippa said. 'I expect he has a home.'

'You may need to look out for dependency,' Laurie Andersson said, as she got to her feet. 'Particularly if you gave him a very good lunch.'

Zoe stood at the reception desk taking keys and customer satisfaction surveys from departing guests. One woman had complained about the lack of hot water. 'Hot water in a luxury hotel should gush from the taps, not trickle,' she wrote. Another had complained about the diffuse lighting from lamps. When she first came to the hotel, Zoe too had felt awed by the great lamps in the rooms, worked by a control panel, the stark theatrical light of the bathrooms where makeup was re-applied and bodies scrutinised. The woman who had complained about the hot water probably went home to a house with poor plumbing and thought nothing of it. Some people considered hotels seedy, but most of the time it was quite ordinary. A few orgies might be going on behind doors with 'Privacy Requested', but couples were proud to give separate names when they registered. For every affair there were at least as many married couples attempting to refresh their marriages.

It was not the guests Zoe loved but the hotel itself. It was like a great stage set, full of gusts of life and then almost somnolent. It resembled the dolls' house handed down from her great-grandmother, Jane. The front with its bow windows and porticoed door opened like a book and the drawing rooms on the ground floor, the breakfast room and parlour were revealed, then the bedrooms on the first floor, rising to the maids' quarters under the roof. Zoe loved playing a part in it but she loved all the parts that made the whole. The cleaners pushing their carts of detergents and supplies, the rooms they could whisk through and others that looked like bomb sites, they were as much a part as the handing out of a complimentary rose.

Zoe wrote to her great-aunt on hotel paper and occasionally had a reply. *One day I'll pay a visit and surprise you,* Sophie wrote. *I'll register under a false name and wear a pompadour wig.* Zoe knew she wouldn't: clearly her aunt's career was in decline. She was touring with a second-rate company in New Zealand. The letter had been written on a wooden dressing-room table – little more than a long plank – under searching hot lights. From time to time Sophie raised her eyes to her reflection, which she gazed at dispassionately. *Little dust-covered, not quite alive cities,* Sophie continued on filched hotel paper from somewhere called Hamilton. *Rumpled fields with sheep on them like crumbs. An almost blinding green.* Still she had received red roses from a wealthy farmer at curtain call.

Minnie could tell Pip was upset when she got home to 20 Nile Street, Glenelg. There had been a bout of fervent cleaning: the ornaments on Minnie's dressing table had been lifted and put down on a polished surface. But the most obvious clue was the oven, its doors open to get rid of the chemical smell, its trays turned back to silver, its mottled sides gleaming.

'You don't mind?' Pip had asked when one of these moods was on her and they had been flatting together for a month.

'I don't mind at all,' Minnie had replied. 'But wouldn't you rather go for a walk?'

But Pip was on her feet all day at the festival, except when she drove someone to the airport. Even then she did not feel off duty until the author had passed through the barrier, usually without looking back. Most of the authors seemed flat and despondent, almost grudging as they left, as if they too would return to surfaces coated with dust, grimy ovens and resentful pets.

Slugman, the cat they had inherited, rubbed against Minnie's legs, aware perhaps that Philippa needed comforting but withholding it as a moral lesson. Minnie was not particularly fond of cats and she often felt she was being worked on.

Adam was arriving the next day and had promised to be in time for dinner. He had met Pip once and ignored her; she had taken the hint and pretended there was a movie she wanted to see. She had stayed out for hours, long after the film finished, drinking pots of tea in an all-night café. This time, Minnie thought, looking at the reproachful oven and fending off the circling cat, Pip should stay for dinner as well. Adam must see samples of all those who comprised society. He would require meat, which Minnie and Pip ate less and less. Serving in the Queen Adelaide dining room or producing platters of food for authors put them off. One night a week, Thursday, they dined on bread and cheese and an apple, as if to celebrate women need not cook.

'Can you make gravy?' Minnie asked, and Pip assured her she could. 'Philippa made the gravy,' she would say, if Adam was uncommunicative.

'I can go out,' Pip offered. 'There are still things on at the festival.'

'No, it's your day off. Stay.'

'If you're sure.'

Adam was in one of his moods. A visit to the Adelaide Gaol and then a walk along North Terrace had not soothed him; the wide streets, the delicate doll-sized gardens seemed the essence of snobbery. Why do you always have to have something to fight, Minnie thought, after he had hardly responded to her embrace. Now she was bending over the oven, poking a fork into roast vegetables, praying that the uncomplicated meal which demanded a complicated ending would come together. (The gravy was being kept warm in a little jug covered with tinfoil.) She didn't have the rest of the thought until Adam had thawed fractionally towards Pip and was describing Marx's tomb in Highgate cemetery where young people still came to pose, just as in Paris they visited the grave of Jim Morrison at Père Lachaise. The thought was – and for a moment Minnie wondered why clear thought always seemed to be required before she expressed her opinion to Adam – that if you were strongly for or against something it was a burden that weighed you down and you could never have a simple happiness. Pip had told her that some of the authors were like that, some even who were household names. No amount of fawning or signing or being whisked away to interviews or dinners could give satisfaction.

Adam had two helpings and praised the gravy, when Minnie reminded him. Then they ate apple shortcake with whipped cream, and drank coffee. Pip moved back and forwards clearing the table in spite of Minnie's protests that she sit down.

'Let her,' Adam said when she was out of earshot. 'She has a perfect servant mentality.'

'And you think I don't,' Minnie whispered angrily. Suddenly it seemed a chore to wind through the car of couchettes, to carry trays or make cups of tea in the night.

'Adam's a pessimist,' Minnie said, half angrily, when Pip appeared in the doorway, drying her hands on a tea towel. 'Which are you, Pip?'

'I like to act optimistically,' she replied, sensing the tension in the room. 'But I feel pessimistic underneath.'

'And Adam?' Minnie went on, as if this was a test he must pass. 'Is it to be half full or half empty?'

'Neither,' he replied. 'It's irrelevant. And if you ask me, it's a luxury to feel either. Either you're an optimist and you do good that no one wants but you're too blind to see it, or you use pessimism to let yourself off the hook.'

'So it doesn't do a blind bit of good? It doesn't matter that Pip here used some of her meagre salary to buy a homeless man lunch?' Minnie could feel the quarrel coming and she rejoiced.

'Not if you turn it into a memoir straightaway,' Adam replied. 'As seems to have happened here.'

'He's right,' Pip said. 'While I was walking to the coffee bar thinking what to buy I felt happy. Afterwards I just felt smug.'

'Well all I can say is it must be a sour thing to be a comrade,' Minnie stated. And she left the room.

In her bedroom she undressed, but instead of leaving her clothes on a chair she threw them on the floor. She didn't bother to remove her make-up. She lay on the farthest side of the bed with her back turned resolutely to the door. She knew Adam would come and she would be unable to avoid him: the bed was too small. And in spite of his antediluvian beliefs he was a good lover. But it was not a case of that, she thought angrily. As if love had to be won each time, each encounter. She remembered the single woman in the forest, going to her death. We are all alone, she thought, and tears ran down over her eyeliner and made a black smudge on the pillow.

A man died in 1428 and there was a bustle on the fourth floor. The hotel doctor was summoned and there was discreet opening and closing of doors. The doctor looked like a businessman. Maids coming and going in the corridors understood their role: a tray with a covered dish left outside the door was whisked away and the 'Do Not Disturb' sign removed from the door handle.

'That's the way I want to go,' Gina Giardina said to Zoe when they were walking along the corridor to the staffroom. 'A luxury room, a beautiful mattress, sound asleep flat on my back.'

But Zoe was thinking of the loneliness the man might have been feeling, for a hotel room, however luxurious, returned you to yourself. Lamps and luxury could not quite make up an identity.

'Perhaps he helped himself to the mini-bar,' Gina remarked. 'A last nightcap.'

In which case the little bottles of brandy or whisky would not appear on the bill. Already the room would have been stripped, a new crisp bottom sheet stretched taut, a new duna miraculously shaken out by one of the Filipino maids. Zoe had become friendly with one, Conchita Menezes, who worked on the fifth floor. She had marvelled at the way the kingsize duna was assembled, flung into the air like a shroud, then patted into place. 'I could do it in my sleep,' Conchita said. 'If only I could get some sleep.' Conchita had two small children who cried when she came to work on Saturday and they had to be left with her mother-in-law.

'I could babysit,' Zoe found herself saying one morning while she was seated in an armchair in Room 1521 while Conchita plumped pillows and replaced bath robes. She regretted the offer immediately, and Conchita, looking reflectively in the mirror she was polishing, beyond murmuring a vague thanks, said nothing more. It was two months later, when Zoe had forgotten her offer, that Conchita asked, very tentatively, if she would like to visit and meet the children.

The first thing Zoe noticed, as Conchita led her through the narrow hallway of the house in Dando Street, a hallway made shadowy by a stained glass panel in the front door, was that the duna on Conchita's bed was as unlike the Grand Hyatt as possible. Rich spicy reds and pinks and purples rose and were cooled by lime green and lemon scarves that trailed from the bedposts, while the fireplace mantel had been turned into a shrine with photographs and flowers and candles. Zoe turned, and two dark-eyed children, like dark-eyed pansies, were running towards their mother. When Conchita introduced them they placed their hands together and bowed and then spoiled the effect by giggling. Zoe tried to imagine an Australian child doing likewise.

'Ernesto is working,' Conchita explained. 'He apologises for not being here to welcome you.'

'I thought we might go to the art gallery,' Conchita said when they were drinking coffee. 'It is not something Ernesto enjoys and I don't like to bother him. I like looking at portraits and studying clothes.'

For a second Zoe wondered if Conchita intended her to stay with the children, but no, the children were to come too.

Faces were checked and hair brushed and they set off in Zoe's yellow Deux Chevaux. There was a great deal of adjusting of seat belts: Maria and Xavier Menezes together would have made one average-sized child. At the gallery the children held hands and didn't wander far. Xavier stroked a sculpture when a guard wasn't looking; he checked first, to Zoe's amusement. Conchita walked slowly from portrait to portrait as if trying to discover the essence of a Governor's wife or a captain of industry or a philanthropist. And Zoe was looking, as she always did in galleries, for a face that reminded her of her mother.

Pedro wrapped his arms around Minnie's waist as she bent over the sink in Car G. Two inches of coffee-stained water with a tired layer of suds held three coffee cups on their sides and a clutch of teaspoons. Exasperated, Minnie pulled the plug and ran fresh water. Even a first-time passenger should know what *Please wash your tea and coffee cups* meant. Straightening up, her hair swung against Pedro's chin and he made a soft growling sound.

'Lay off,' Minnie said, fishing for the last teaspoon.

'I'd be a better bet,' Pedro said in her ear. 'I've seen you with that sourpuss from Broken Hill.'

'He's not a sourpuss,' Minnie began.

'Probably a southpaw as well,' Pedro mused, refusing to unlock his hands which were now woven up like the church steeple game. So Minnie drew in her breath, inserted her hands between, and seized and bent back Pedro's two thumbs.

'Where did you learn that?' he asked, gasping. 'I can't stand women who fight.'

'Your kind never can,' Minnie said, reaching for a partly sodden tea towel. If there was anyone on this trip like Beatrix Geissler she might say a few words.

Minnie and Adam had made love, but it was an angry silent love as if each resented their responses. For a second an image had come to Minnie and distracted her, so she gave an impression of returning warmth. It was the statue of the Sacred Heart in the chapel of the music school where Minnie had been sent to wait when Sister Hedwig, already losing her memory, had double-booked. 'You can put your cardigan over your head,' Sister Hedwig had said, looking doubtfully at a Protestant. Minnie, when she was certain she was alone, had run her hand over the plaster heart, slightly raised, like a welt. On the red heart were brown thorns, like tiny train tracks. And now she was distracted again, and Pedro had placed a hand on her shoulder as if he was preparing to spin her in a dance. She jabbed him viciously with her elbow and he staggered back against the fridge, making the contents rattle.

They were speeding towards Peterborough. Yesterday one of the tourists, an American, had complained how hard it was to get a shot of a kangaroo, even if she had plenty of time to sight it. 'Like one of those vast cinema screens,' she had said, 'and then the kangaroo hops off.' Minnie had counselled patience, but she knew what the woman meant. Vistas opened and then subtly changed, surprising the watcher. A young man in a Dryzabone raincoat and an Akubra hat suddenly appeared boundary riding along a drive that stopped a few metres from the track. Minnie raised her hand to him and he waved back.

In her year on the Indian Pacific Minnie had come to love best the landscapes most people ignored. She had noticed a pattern of corridor-walking or visiting (for friendships were often formed only to be abandoned at the moment of debarkation): someone would mention Michael Palin for the hundredth time and a conversation would be struck up. But when they crossed the featureless Nullarbor Plain many took a nap or repaired to the lounge bar or examined the souvenirs. Sometimes when she walked through the corridors Minnie could hear the calm authoritative voice of the commentary which meant someone was attempting to marry the landscape to its history. It was a good commentary and some parts Minnie knew almost by heart. It did not presume that the listener would be overly interested, only gradually drawing them in. Those who had tried to farm the areas with unsustainable levels of rainfall were presented not as heroic but as having a certain naïve optimism. That was the thing about Australia and what Minnie would have liked to explain to her father. Australians looked for the best, even in defeat. The failed desert optimists were not just fools; their optimism added to the general pool and could be drawn on for other things. For a moment this made her feel more tolerant of Pedro Casado. He had already picked up and assimilated the national character.

Philippa's last days at the festival passed in a blur. There was tiredness after the first week, as if everyone was gathering breath. The authors who were collected at the airport seemed faintly resentful that so many events were over and discussed as triumphs while theirs were still to come. Distinguished authors had already flown back to America or Britain or the Caribbean. Philippa had assured one writer, known to be difficult, that they were saving the best for last. 'The last weekend is really the highlight,' she said, though she was far from certain.

'I was hoping to meet Caryl Phillips,' the disgruntled writer said, from the back seat, 'and now I find he has already left.'

An unproductive silence filled the car but Philippa was disinclined to point out features of the landscape: the Torrens, the famous oval on the other bank, Captain Light pointing a bronze finger on Montefiore Hill. At the doors of the Hyatt Regency she pulled the courtesy car in close to the main doors; inside she could see Hansie van Zom sitting at the festival desk. 'I'll just set you down here and your baggage will be attended to,' she said to the Nigerian who still looked sour.

As she drove off, Philippa unwound the window and tried not to think of the long conversation she had had with Adam after Minnie left to join the Indian Pacific. It was her morning off so it was natural she should sit drinking three cups of tea while Adam munched noisily through a bowl of cornflakes. At first there had been a silence between them, like the silence in the car with the Nigerian writer, but as soon as she had poured Adam a mug of tea, guessing a cup would not be to his taste, his manner had softened. Philippa was not to know that he found in her effacing manner, accentuated by the strain of being at the beck and call of writers, something of his mother's quiet movements. She took it for sympathy and soon they were discussing the problem of homelessness and whether her actions had been wise.

'You needn't have gone as far as the diet sheet,' Adam expounded, taking up a triangle of hot buttered toast and adding marmalade. 'Perhaps you're a bit of a goody-goody.'

Philippa found she didn't mind this: she had known at the time she was excessive. If there had been a diet sheet around she would have thrust it into one of the bags of food. The food pyramid, with lean meat and chicken at the top, pasta and pulses in the middle, and a positive cornucopia of fruits and vegetables at the bottom.

Then they got on to talking about whether good intentions counted for good ends and whether the end justified the means. Adam had a lot to say on this, and Philippa sat with her head resting on her hands, like a Picasso head, looking dreamily over the stained tablecloth – Adam had spilt some milk when he was pouring it into the cornflakes – and out through the steamed-up window to a patch of sky.

'If you concentrate too much on analysing the means you lose the end,' he was saying, as though adding 'analysing' somehow made it original, and Philippa certainly looked attentive. But in fact, her thoughts were somewhere subterranean, as if she were newly buried and was listening to the sounds of nature after the mourners had departed. If she ever got to know Adam she might tell him this, for it was a recurring dream. The feet moved off, their neat sharp sounds decisive as if everyone was wearing their best shoes, and then came darkness and silence. And then, out of the silence – while Adam went on talking, something now about the hardships of life in Broken Hill being outside the ken of most Australians, unless they had a sense of history – would there be other sounds, as minute as the movement of a root in the soil, a sudden spurt of water far below? Would one hear the grass stretching, the rain falling on it? Would there be anything from stars?

'Silver, lead and zinc,' Adam was saying, and Philippa wondered for a moment if she might be asked a chemistry question. 'What this country is built on, though no one wants to live on the site, unless it's to make a quick killing. If you could see that train going through and the stuck-up tourists getting off and looking at the stalls as if they were some sort of cute native flora, like a koala or a kangaroo . . .'

'I'd like to visit Broken Hill,' Philippa said. She felt perhaps she was not fully grounded. A mountain of slag or mine tailings might help. 'Then I needn't go around looking for strays.' It occurred to her that the term encompassed the authors.

On that afternoon's panel the Nigerian writer, ignoring the subject, 'Colonialism, Its Heritage and Effects on Commonwealth Writers', and the time limit – DO NOT EXCEED YOUR ALLOTTED TIME – had gone on for thirty-three minutes in a prepared rant about the wickedness of the white Commonwealth nations. The three other panellists, too cowed or polite to intervene, had looked hopelessly at the chair, a woman academic, as if waiting for a referee. 'A most interesting contribution,' she remarked when the Nigerian finally sat down and she had replaced him at the podium to introduce the final speaker whose time allotment was now seven minutes.

Already the audience was assembling for the next performance: three women playwrights discussing the role of women in the theatre. Philippa was replenishing the platters in the Green Room, ensuring the coffee was perked, filling jugs with water and slices of lime and mint. She avoided the Nigerian writer who now came triumphantly through the door with an entourage of supporters. What would Adam have thought of them, she wondered, lifting the clingfilm off a mound of club sandwiches. For she thought Adam, whatever his prejudices – and one might only be shown the depth of them as a kind of privilege – was at least his own person. The Silver City, the silver train passing through: if one side regarded it as a quaint throwback and the other as condescension, at least his attitudes added up. An image of a long wooden verandah came to her – perhaps it was the station in disguise: slatted boards scrubbed and made pure by shafts of light. At this very moment Minnie too was probably serving coffee, only, Philippa reflected, doing it with a better grace.

After the visit to the National Art Gallery, Zoe and Conchita found themselves becoming friends. Perhaps it was the quantity of lace collars and parasols they had admired together, the steadfast eyes of sitters in days before the camera who gazed at the artist, usually a FRA, as if their soul had finally reached the surface of their eyeballs.

Conchita and Ernesto possessed a spare room which Zoe was welcome to have in return for occasional babysitting. In fact the babysitting turned out to be quite seldom; it was more a case of accompanying Conchita on outings, being company in the evenings when Ernesto worked at his second job. Zoe's car had to be parked on the street for a few weeks until she found a garage to rent but no harm came to it and Maria and Xavier, who could kneel on the sofa in the front room, acted as watchdogs before they were shooed off to bed.

Her room, at the back of the house, looked out onto a small walled garden where Ernesto was attempting to espalier apples. Conchita had filled large earthenware pots with alyssum, pansies, white nasturtiums, parsley and ornamental kale. The walls of the room were a soft blue-grey, the colour of a bird's egg, and the drapes were Indian cotton. 'It's not permanent,' Zoe thought. 'One day I'll move on.' But it seemed as if in planning a career in hotel management she had not planned any further. Or she was imitating Sophie, so accustomed to living out of suitcases in borrowed rooms.

Sometimes when their shifts coincided Zoe and Conchita drove to work together. But once inside the plate-glass doors Zoe became management and Conchita, rising in the staff lift to the fifth floor, the stripper of beds, cleaner of handbasins, toilets and surfaces, noting when light bulbs needed replacing or collecting left items. Sometimes a luxurious bath robe would be missing, sealed in a client's suitcase and carried by a bellboy to a limousine brought up from the basement. Conchita would make a note for the housekeeper, and a letter on hotel note-paper would be dispatched with a bill if the item was to be retained.

Zoe meanwhile would be pinning on her badge, brushing the shoulders of her navy blue suit, checking the set of her collar and her makeup. As she walked the short distance to the desk she felt the planes of her face shift, as if the bones too were alert.

The last moment in the wings is the hardest, Sophie had confided. She was playing Lady Macbeth in an experimental theatre production. It was set in an old people's home: Lady Macbeth was dotty and Macbeth had Alzheimer's. Thinking of this Zoe's mouth moved in a smile and her eyes assumed an interest that might be solicitude or faint complicity, as she prepared to speak her first lines.

Minnie's father, the Count, sent letters, postcards, addressed to the Indian Pacific, though she urged him to desist. In some of them he addressed her as the Countess. It's not glamorous, she had tried to explain, but he knew his daughter better. Like Mr Bennet with his favourite Lizzie, he spent odd moments analysing her character as he never did with her older sister, Angela, whose consistency and steady progress through life – she was just engaged to someone highly suitable – was a barrier.

Weaknesses are what attract, he thought, lifting his pen from the back of a postcard of Pukekura Park, New Plymouth, New Zealand. Weakness was not the right word and not one he would use of his favourite child. More like a chink, a weakness in armour, a failure to safeguard the heel so an arrow could strike there. He thought sometimes that part of Irene's attitude to Minnie was not simply Minnie's more difficult personality but that she had returned to Australia. Their own trips back and forth, by sea and later air, had lessened until they finally faded. 'There's no one left, what would be the point?' Irene pointed out. 'A walk around a cemetery?' She was exaggerating of course: the family was not yet so depleted she would have to stay in a boarding house. And there were cousins in which traces of her loved sisters, the little core in the centre of her family, could be seen. But Teddy knew his wife was not sentimental, though Australians were expected to be that. They wear their sentiments on the surface, he thought, whereas we are undone by them when we discover they exist.

He picked up the pen again and placed the fine nib next to the last sentence he had written. *I suspect secretly you are acting like a countess. I know you don't take anything too seriously,* he added, *and that is good.* Not seeing that his words, like a word in jest, might soon be prophetic. *The Count* he wrote at the bottom, in the tiny corridor of space. Count Dracula or Monte Cristo.

But perhaps Dracula was truer: unknown to his wife he had already purchased a double First Class sleeper on the Indian Pacific for mid-September. He had casually asked about schedules in his last letter. *I won't get a break until October,* Minnie had replied, falling innocently into his trap. And he knew her roster from previous enquiries. She had sent an autographed dinner menu from the Queen Adelaide dining room. He had run his eye down it, making his choices already. If only she wasn't too surprised and dropped a tray of drinks.

Rosa Prouse had stayed on in the cottage in Nicholson Street after Lucien Humfress was committed to a private nursing home. His fame as an artist, based on the series of sleeping nudes and later extended to include sketches and working drawings, had reconciled him with his family. The nursing home at Kew was paid for partly from a trust, and the releasing of a sketch or two at judicious intervals paid the rest. The home, in its park-like setting, was nonetheless secure and patrolled at night by guards with dogs. None of these things interested Lucien, who in his lucid moments sat drawing on a large block of paper. He liked the nurses, less hurried than in the public hospital, and was forever urging them to remove their uniforms.

At first Rosa had visited once a week, but when, on three successive Thursdays, Lucien had failed to recognise her and, on the fourth, had asked a young nurse to ban this unknown woman from his room, she decided to go no more. On the journey back to Nicholson Street she chided herself for heart-lessness and found no defence but something in her character that was accustomed to discard what no longer served. Her chequered career had always involved an effort of brightness, as if the present moment was the one being concentrated on. How often in The Flying Worm had she walked to the stockroom to bring out a work for a client and then stood respectfully in line, waiting to add a word of admiration. Now she felt like not bothering, though she still housekept in a rudimentary way, doing the essentials. Some days she sat in her dressing gown for hours, leaning on the kitchen table, her hands wrapped around a mug of tea that had gone cold. If anyone came to the door – and she expected no one – they would see a middle-aged woman with uncombed hair. I could pretend to be sick, she thought, and the idea pleased her, for she imagined she could still act. Perhaps she should dress and take a tram and walk up the National Gallery steps again, reliving the night of the art award when she had finally emerged under the lamps to find Harriet and Garth waiting for her.

It was strange that the strongest most potent memories were not occasions but details: the cool air on her flushed face. She could see the dark clouds and patches of clear sky with stars, like the backdrop of an opera, the dew on the pavement as they waited for a taxi on Russell Street.

Though the little cottage on Nicholson Street was hers, once it was cleared of paintings, drawings, a few small sculptures which Lucien had regarded as experiments, Rosa had no desire to stay. She had catalogued Lucien's works for an exhibition he would never see and which she would not attend. Lucien's few decent clothes were packed and given to an op shop, his paint-smeared shirts and the straw hat he wore sketching in the garden burned. Once the paintings were gone the walls looked not merely bare but paltry; all the faults in the cottage had been hidden by colour, tall glass vases of flowers, towers of books.

Sometimes to get away from the diminishment of her life Rosa took a tram, riding it to the terminal, then paying for a return trip. She watched the crowds walking past on the pavements, the disturbance in the air as the tram rattled and shook, the cars that gave it a wide berth as they made their hook turns. After these trips Rosa returned to the cottage, refreshed. She made inventories, she wrote lists for herself, she phoned the Salvation Army to enquire if they accepted donations of furniture. When she was assured they did, she inspected everything with a critical eye: some pieces had borer but she had heard it was slow-acting. The rest was charming but easily replaced; she might let it all go. At night, though she had no destination in mind, she lay in her double bed, imagining it was her last night in Melbourne and tomorrow she would leave the key on the mat and close the front door. She would walk out without turning her head as she had done all her life. And where has it got me, she asked herself, allowing her face to relax in the dark and assume a grimace, or a tear to slide from an eyelid, or a smile she imagined was cynical. Still, the sale of Gertrude Street and the cottage plus the paintings she owned would be sufficient for a fresh start. It was not too late to re-create herself for a final time. She simply needed a new city.

On one of her excursions she got off the tram at Bourke Street and went into a bookshop. The *Lonely Planet Guide to Australia*: it might be amusing to see her country through the eyes of strangers. She bought a pottle of hot chips and a sachet of tomato sauce and sat in Grand Central Gardens. The chips were cold before she reached the bottom, just the right temperature for the semicircle of pigeons that assembled. The wind blew her fine dark hair with its badger's stripe of white and she turned her collar up. She ate about half the chips and threw the rest. The sunlight caught a chip in midair and it looked like a bar of gold.

At first Philippa could not reconcile Adam's wish to see her with his forthright views on social issues, his lack of compromise on workers' rights and nepotism in business. She thought it was pity and he was taking an interest in her because she was a weak creature, like a heroine in a novel.

Now the Arts Festival was over and all that remained was a T-shirt with the festival logo which she had no desire ever to wear again, she had gone back to work at St Ann's College. 'You deserve better,' Minnie said to her. 'You should use your festival experience to get into PR work.' But Pip, who could not quite meet Minnie's eyes – that lunch hour she had sat with Adam on the banks of the Torrens, not far from where the homeless young man had waited for his lunch to be brought to him – declared she needed a mindless job at present. Presiding over stainless-steel pans of scrambled or poached eggs, dried-up bacon with what looked like flecks of lint, gnarled sausages, spaghetti and baked beans, was restful after the authors.

And now Adam seemed to be taking charge of her life, lending her books, as if she were not already a reader, meeting her for coffee when he should be waiting for Minnie to return from the Indian Pacific. He still went to meet Minnie at

Keswick Station, and he sat down with them to eat the chicken fricassee Philippa had prepared. Minnie was tired and over-excited after the trip and full of descriptions of passengers and their eccentricities: someone had thrown a camera out on the tracks in exasperation and had to be soothed, and a very demanding Italian woman had complained the berths were too narrow for her to sleep with her husband. 'Why else did we take the train?' she demanded as her husband stood sheepishly beside her, pretending to examine the landscape.

'I nearly suggested they try showering together,' Minnie said, with a laugh. 'Or perhaps they could fly and join the Mile High club.'

Philippa saw a disdainful expression cross Adam's face and she quickly passed him a slice of bread. Perhaps I am not responsible, she thought unhappily. A silence hung between the reminiscences. Still, Adam would be leaving in the morning. Later she stood at the sink, soaking the dish that had held the chicken. Minnie had brought her an Indian Pacific sweatshirt. It was fine-quality cotton but Philippa liked it as little as the one from the festival.

Minnie had promised her parents she would return to New Zealand for a week of her holiday. Out of that, a day at either end would be taken up with travelling to and from airports. That left five days to play the dutiful daughter, to visit her older sister, now married and pregnant, to go driving with her father and avoid quarrelling with her mother.

'I dread it,' she said to Pip when her bag was packed. 'Why do we have families?'

When there was no reply, Minnie recalled Pip's mother had married three times and lived in Perth.

Even the sky was different over New Zealand. Over Australia it resembled flocks of half-starved sheep, but over New Zealand it was a fleecy shawl. Claustrophobia, Minnie thought, when the agricultural officials came through the aircraft to spray chemicals into the air. The hostess had explained the procedure in a syrupy soothing voice, but their faces were grim. Robots, Minnie thought angrily. Already she was thinking of her countrymen as more conventional, and feeling angry about it. There would be long discussions with her father about sport, since Minnie was his son-substitute. In attacking everything New Zealand, Minnie would simply make her mother feel more homesick and herself guilty.

But the visit began well. She got into a smaller plane, like a Babushka doll being disassembled, and soon she could see her father standing behind the barrier, looking faintly sheepish. 'Countess,' he said, and she said, 'Count,' as she laid her head against his chest. He looked older, a bit like a family tent that has discoloured with age.

'I can see the traffic hasn't increased to life-threatening proportions,' Minnie remarked when they were on the highway.

'But those that are on it are life-threatening,' her father replied. 'I hate to think what would happen to New Zealand if the place really filled up.'

'Can't bear to queue,' Minnie said, remembering her own behaviour. More than five people in a bank queue or a takeaway and she practically felt smoke coming out her nostrils.

'Backs against the wall before we begin to think of winning,' her father went on. It was their old game: describing their countrymen in one-liners.

And then Minnie described to him how in her first weeks in Adelaide she had walked from the youth hostel to a coffee shop and asked for a cup of tea. The girl, her own age, had handed over a polystyrene cup with the teabag dangling and asked if she wanted it left in or out. 'In,' Minnie replied, after a second's puzzlement, and the girl had indicated the milk jug and teaspoons. She had walked over to a round marble table at the window and sat sipping it for as long as she could make it last, for she knew no one in the city. But it had been a real exchange of equals, such as you were unlikely to get in New Zealand, she explained to her father, treating peasants and kings, or the Australian equivalent, with the same egalitarianism.

'Things under it, Countess,' her father had said. 'Darker things, I suspect.'

'Old pessimist,' she replied, as they turned in at the gate.

But Minnie's relationship with her mother, who was a real Australian, not a theory but a living and breathing person, was not so easy. Irene McAleer had found it hard to settle in New Zealand: she had found no equivalent egalitarianism, like the girl in the coffee shop, among the neighbours, though she had slowly made friends. When her husband had taken her on a trip to the South Island, to the Scottish-leaning city at the bottom of it, she had been appalled by the greyness of the buildings and the grim taciturnity of the locals. Shortly after they returned home she had taken her first solo trip to visit her family, to walk around the cemetery at Ouse and put flowers on the graves of her parents and Maud. And now the daughter who most resembled her in liveliness – her eldest child might have belonged in the southern city, so sunk was she in convention and matrimony – was here and they could not agree on anything.

At first there were photographs to show: Irene wanted a description of Minnie's Indian Pacific uniform. A group photograph was produced, with the silver train in the background. Irene's finger alighted on a tall blond man. 'He looks nice,' she said.

'Gay,' said Minnie, puncturing the interest. 'Common among waiters,' she added, increasing the gap between them. She knew her mother would not ask directly if there was anyone in her life.

'She doesn't want you to emulate her and be always between countries,' Minnie's father said later when they were driving to the supermarket with a list. 'I hear there's a flower trail,' he said casually as he locked the car.

'They put on extra cars,' Minnie said as she added little luxuries, Toblerone and Spanish olives, a pavlova in a box and half a pint of cream to the trolley. But the idea of crossing the desert to follow flowers made her feel angry. It was something to do with looking at a landscape for satisfaction. Bending over some hardy valiant sand-hugging flower, probably hideously coloured, and photographing it. Anyone would think the landscape was something to eat – and the little flicker of anger rose again, warming her and then dying away. So often it was her mother who produced it. Then she spent an absurd amount of time over the pavlova, whipping the cream into peaks, and covering the top with mandarin segments and slices of kiwifruit.

Rosa too was planning to take a trip on the Indian Pacific. It was among the pile of brochures she had sifted through one Friday night after she had ordered a skip to take the bottles and papers from Lucien's studio, the bottles evenly divided between wine and linseed oil, the old frames and mildewed canvases, the unusable tubes of cadmium white and burnt sienna. The stripping of the little cottage hurt her more than she could bear: the thought of Lucien in his bed with safety railings at Pleasant Acres filled her heart with pain. The four chambers of the heart and the pain passing from one to the other, though Rosa did not know how blood passed in the heart; it simply felt there was no egress and the pain filled and overflowed and filled again. But then, when she had made herself a pot of chamomile tea, and spread the brochures out, fan-shaped, on the table, it hurt because once she would have applauded Lucien's life, its wildness and disregard for convention, even this fine piece of escapism at the end.

Sometimes she swore he recognised her, closing his eye in a wink, as he had often done in The Flying Worm when he was banished to the stockroom in case he interrupted a speech or spilt wine over someone. And once, turning at the door of his room, and seeing his eyes removed from her and directed towards a nurse, she thought he was conserving his energy and making an effort where it counted. On her last visit she had handed him two miniatures of McCallum's whisky which he clutched like a child.

'I won't be coming for a while,' Rosa told the matron. 'I shall be travelling.'

'He is perfectly happy,' the matron said. 'Have no fears.'

'I might write,' Rosa offered. It was like a game of tennis

with the net down. At least by this evening Lucien would smell of whisky.

Adelaide, Rosa read, *is the opposite of a convict settlement. It has no buildings made from forced labour; it has an ease and grace which cannot be denied. Those who settled its hospitable plains came because they desired to do so.* It sounds like Salt Lake City, she thought, a beginning in smugness. But she knew that was not correct. And it was a pretty name.

When the chamomile tea was finished she got out her cheque book and bank accounts and looked at her balance. If the cottage sold – and she would leave a key with the agent while she was gone – she might be able to find a modest replica in another city. But she could not stay in Melbourne. Her faint notoriety had faded along with her appearance but she still felt it: she had been a woman on her own. She tried to remember if chamomile tea induced morbid thoughts as well as sleep. But before she slept she had decided to go First Class.

'Family is important,' Sophie said to Zoe when they were walking in the Royal Botanical Gardens, 'but it is not everything. If you are lucky it can be a base. You have relatives here, Zoe, if you wish to use them. There's your aunt Harriet, for one . . .'

'I know,' Zoe replied. But for the moment she felt content.

And, as if in illustration, a little group was approaching along one of the gravel paths. They all had high-bridged noses, deep-set eyes and no waists. Though they were looking at flowers and fountains, they seemed irritable. Zoe caught Sophie's glance and smiled.

'One of my sisters worked here,' Sophie went on, looking towards the great white pile of Government House. 'And one went to Kuala Lumpur. But I was too young to know them properly. It's your grandfather, beautiful Rupert, I remember most.'

They walked until they were tired, then Zoe took her great-aunt's arm and escorted her to a bench overlooking the ornamental lake.

Philippa Cornford sat at Adam's mother's kitchen table in Iodide Street drinking tea. Minnie was not mentioned. In any case Minnie was on the Indian Pacific, somewhere between Augusta and Pimba. Allowing for time zone difference, the passengers would be stirring in their sleepers, pulling up blinds and looking out at the landscape. 'So much of it passes in the night,' Minnie had said, 'and one of the surprising things is to open your eyes and see something totally different in the morning.' The fine foods in the Queen Adelaide dining room, the brandies and cocktails in the lounge car, tended to make heavy sleepers, disinclined to look out as the train ploughed through the night.

Dulcie Scoular was almost as silent as Philippa, passing cups and offering to make more toast. And Adam himself had a pro-prietorial air. She needs someone to look after her, he had said to his mother when she was making up the bed in the spare room. It was what his father had thought and now, twelve years a widow, Dulcie sat on the station platform with her friend Maisie, sharing a stall with pots of jam and little serviette-lined baskets of toffee and fudge, complicated knitting that suited no one on the train. Sometimes there was a raffle book as well, an amateurish affair made from a cut-down lined exercise book: the prize half a beast or $100 worth of petrol.

Dulcie Scoular was not sure of Philippa Cornford, though she was quiet and respectful and obviously kind-hearted. There had practically been a fight to do the few dinner dishes the night before, with Adam adjudicating. The idea of harems flashed into his mother's mind and she determined, when the occasion arose, to say a word in defence of Minnie.

Minnie at this moment was bringing a cup of tea to a woman in G11. She was not a young woman: her hair had a stripe of white but, even woken by Minnie's knock, her face had a lived-in spirited look as if she was quite accustomed to her morning face.

'I hope you slept well,' Minnie said, setting the cup of tea down on the little stand by the bed. No morning cup of tea was ever filled to the top.

'As well as I hoped,' the woman replied, and then smiled. 'I was listening to the noises of the train. And I discovered it is best to sleep on one's back.'

Minnie saw the woman again at the second breakfast sitting. She was with a Welsh couple and their overweight son. As she delivered sunnyside up, poached or scrambled eggs with bacon and sausages, she overheard the parents trying to interest him in the landscape. The woman Minnie had served tea leaned forward and asked the boy about Welsh trains and whether their tracks were as wide. The boy opened his mouth to insert a slice of sausage and his eyes flickered slightly. Uphill work, Minnie thought, but someone's got to do it.

Then the morning on the train began. Those who had breakfasted walked in the corridors or lingered looking out of the windows. The beds were unmade and folded away. In the lounge car, newspapers were unfolded and coffee sipped. Rosa, checking that her couchette had been attended to and her novel was placed on the little table by the window, walked from car to car to see how far she could go.

Adelaide was full of little gardens that seemed to froth. Their front yards were small but there were hardly any that were not packed and designed, even down to the last tendril, questing in air, of a climbing rose that had come loose from a trellis. Riding in a tour bus, Rosa chose one after another for herself, as if she were playing a childish game. Few of the chosen ones had 'For Sale' signs, nor did she expect them to: behind the garden borders fresh-painted doors with gleaming knockers hinted at contentment. And she liked the broad avenues, the way the stone buildings stood back from them as if they had room to breathe. Someone had taken space as a right and now it would take generations to fill it. Suddenly the little terrace houses seemed a reaction, a creeping together for warmth.

Rosa had thought about accommodation as the Indian Pacific neared Adelaide. She had listened to the commentary and read her book, *The Long View* by Elizabeth Jane Howard, and imagined a bed and breakfast guesthouse. But at lunch an

American woman had talked with such absolute conviction about the Hilton chain, as if the identical rooms were oases spread across the globe, that Rosa had returned to her couchette to make some calculations. The commentary was talking about the pioneers and their stubborn hopes to make the desert bloom. This did not make her stalwart and self-sacrificing; instead she had checked into the Adelaide Hilton, surrendering her bag to a bellboy, nodding, for had she not a great deal of hotel experience herself, at the commissionaire whom she decided was definitely in a class of his own. And now, each day after walking or taking a short tour – city environs, Haig's chocolate factory, cut-price markets – here she was among the lamps, almost tempted to run her index finger over a surface.

She sat at the writing desk and wrote to Harriet and Garth. *Tomorrow I will go to the bank and then a land agent. I don't know if Adelaide will suit me, or vice-versa. You know how I like chaos and there doesn't seem to be much of that here.* She lifted her pen from the page and wondered if chaos had to be created and some, like herself, had a gift for it. And if it was a gift did it last only for a section of one's life, a fact she had not considered up to now.

She would ask for an older agent, one who might understand her needs. *You might get one of these gardens under control yourself,* she wrote, *and enjoy the sort of superiority that goes with it.* For there had been a superiority: even the air had seemed controlled and tame. She couldn't get out of her mind the confidence of the last rose tendrils, like tendrils of hair around a face.

When the Indian Pacific stopped at Broken Hill on its westward journey, Minnie peered through a window to see if Dulcie Scoular was on the platform. But there was no sign of her sitting behind a trestle table, legs wrapped in a rug. One small mercy, she thought, for she felt Adam's mother was fond of her. But it would fade, as it must. Then she busied herself explaining to an elderly Dutch couple how long the Indian Pacific would be at Broken Hill and that they would have plenty of warning before it left. 'It's not very nice, is it dear?' the Dutch woman said as she carefully stepped down. 'Broken Hill. It's not very nice.'

And after the train it seemed to Minnie it wasn't. The hills of mullock and mine tailings, the naked reduced character of the place, even if some of its buildings had been lovingly restored, the pathetic quality of the stalls, even the assumed modesty had something false about it. For Adam had not been falsely modest when it came to desiring Pip.

'I suppose you think she matches the town,' Minnie had said.

'It's nothing to do with Broken Hill,' Adam had replied.

'It's everything to do with it. You're just too blind to see. Everything you believe in comes back to a pile of slag and being downtrodden.' She wasn't thinking quickly enough or she could have pointed out his mother's house was overheated.

'You've always hated the Indian Pacific,' she went on, voice lowered, as if it were an irreducible fact, that the rails that went through Broken Hill carried luxury as well as men to the mines. There was more than one set of rails at the station: she looked across them to the mullock piles and the cooling tower.

'It's not all that's come between us,' he said and left it at that.

On the next two trips Minnie refused to look at Broken Hill or get off the train. And when the silver carriages glided away she felt as if she was wiping the dust off her shoes.

Rosa, before Nicholson Street had been sold, took an option on an extremely beautiful small terrace house in North Adelaide. It had a lacy wrought-iron balcony and fence, an upstairs guest bedroom (designated for Harriet), a separate dining room with red wallpaper – this by itself had caused Rosa to go weak at the knees, though she kept her cool manner in front of the land agent. And at the rear, to her delight, there was a second narrow garden, like an echo of the front, but more shaded, less perfect, like the underside of a character that presents itself as sunny. A high wall sheltered the back garden while the front – a mere ten steps from door knocker to gate – was as public as a shop window. Some yellow roses climbing a trellis would have to go – Rosa detested yellow roses – but the rest was perfect.

She went back to the hotel, booked a flight, and instead of going to Nicholson Street, asked the cab to take her to Harriet's.

Her old friend had aged too – Rosa allowed herself this scrutiny since she had examined her own face in the bathroom of the Hilton before she left. A stripe of yellow from a lily she had stuck her nose into in Central Market marked one cheek, and her eyes had the wild look of someone who makes decisions too far ahead – the land agent must have thought he was dealing with a madwoman. Possibly he did not expect to hear from her again.

But Harriet, always slender, was thinner and her face had fine lines, hardly decipherable in a soft light. But in the north light, the dreaded artists' light, which Rosa knew so well, the cruel light in which faces, figures were examined with a cold detachment, Harriet looked frail.

'I'm having some tests,' she told Rosa, when the terrace house had been described. 'I may have something similar to my mother.'

'What is it?' Rosa cried. Instantly the little terrace house in Adelaide faded into darkness. She thought of the room in which Harriet was to stay. 'What is it? Tell me.' She wanted to kneel in front of her friend and hold her hands or undo her suitcase and tear the wrapping from the present she had brought, a mohair shawl from Myer's.

'Genetic,' Harriet said. 'Isn't everything in the end? Not just organs but the way we feel.'

'The way we feel? Do you feel that? What is the purpose of anything then?' But oddly Rosa felt slightly comforted for herself, as if a series of black clouds had ridden over the horizon.

'I'm not frightened,' Harriet was saying. 'The specialist thinks I just need to take care. Garth believes him, of course.'

'You must believe him too,' Rosa said, and this time she knelt in front of Harriet, close to the suitcase as if she was just about to open it, but it *was* kneeling. 'Belief must be genetic too.'

'But you can't pick and choose,' Harriet said, taking the shawl wrapped in tissue but not opening it. 'Belief mightn't be part of it. It makes everything so forgivable. I wish I could have seen it before.'

'Someone who has no need to forgive. And I could do with buckets of it. I suppose I always took refuge in drama.' The scene long ago, of herself, Harriet and Garth outside the National Gallery. Hers was the only nose in the air. And then Russell Street, the traffic and the street lamps, and further out little houses sleeping with their lives tucked up. Little genetic clocks ticking.

'It's lovely,' Harriet said, when the shawl was undone. She held it up against her throat and it caught the colour of her eyes, grey-green. The one who is ill has to lead, that was a new discovery. Her mother must have made it too. Sometimes Harriet thought of her when she went to bed early, a privilege no one now could gainsay. Garth pulled her close to him in the night; his body had thickened, he felt like an old bear. She had Garth, and her mother had a bolster and the spines of her accounting books.

'Do you think I should have worn a wig?' Irene said to Teddy at Central Station. 'What if Minnie is in charge of our coach?'

'What if she is?' Teddy replied.

He hoped she was; he hoped she might appear in the doorway and then stagger back with her hand over her heart as the Wallabies did when they played 'Advance Australia Fair'. But they made their double berth safely and sat side by side on what would turn out to be the bottom bunk, looking out the window, feeling the soft jolt as the Indian Pacific moved and then, Irene thought, seemed to slide out of the station. It was something to do with the silver colour: one expected a gliding motion. She avoided looking around too closely; when she had travelled by sea, seasickness had often forced her attention on a bed lamp or a rivet on the wall so she could keep control. Three days and three nights in this little space was ample time to explore every fixture. But Teddy couldn't keep still. He must go for a walk down the corridor and across the one part she was dreading: the maw where one carriage, silver or not, was coupled to another. There the wind blew, the walls rattled and swayed: a hellish few steps with luxury beyond. On a ship it was the dark patches in the sea that someone had told her represented deeps. There was a mirror on the inside of the wardrobe and Irene examined her face, brushed her hair, applied fresh lipstick. Then she took out the book she had purchased at the railway bookstore, *A Fence around the Cuckoo,* and put it down beside her on the seat.

Pedro and Minnie were in the staff quarters, Pedro removing a film from a camera belonging to a passenger and inserting another. The woman stood in the doorway watching and offering little phrases about her ineptitude and how grateful she was to Pedro who could obviously turn his hand to anything. Minnie was longing for the camera and film to be given back so Pedro could mimic the woman when her father's face appeared.

'Count,' she cried. The passenger looked around. 'What are you doing here?'

Then the camera was handed back and Minnie introduced Pedro to her father. 'I always call him Count,' she explained.

'And I call her Countess,' Minnie's father said. 'No particular nobility attached.'

'None at all,' agreed Minnie, 'though I don't see why titles can't be shared around.'

'Pleased to meet you both, I'm sure,' Pedro replied, easing himself out the door.

'Your mother's in our compartment,' Teddy said. 'Perhaps you could come along.'

'Certainly,' Minnie said and her voice, now the first astonishment was over, was becoming professional again. How would her mother look? Slightly accusatory or shame-faced, though it must have been her father's idea.

Irene, now she had the compartment to herself, was

beginning an inventory: she had read somewhere that children displaced from familiar surroundings must rapidly take their bearings and markings from the landscape. A tree, a stream, could become furniture. It was essential for her to know this little space in which she would spend three whole days.

So it was easy after all: her mother had her head in the wardrobe, contemplating how much to unpack, and Minnie could straightaway give advice about what to wear in the dining car and which sitting was the best. The ice was broken and the little compartment glowed like the Queen Adelaide dining car.

'You'll like the lamps,' Minnie said, 'and you can see your faces in the windows when it gets dark.'

'Something to look forward to,' her mother said, and Minnie could see she wanted to go on exploring. She and the Count exchanged a look over her head.

'I could be Count Pedro,' Pedro said later, 'if you'd prefer.'

'I wouldn't,' said Minnie. 'One count in the family is enough.'

Within three months Rosa was in possession of her Strangeways Terrace house. From Harriet she extracted a promise of a visit the minute she was unpacked. Harriet had demurred at first until Rosa reminded her of Mr Wu's flat above the shop, the mattresses on the floor, the nights contemplating the fruit-coloured walls. These walls, except for the dining room, were cream and the carpet a soft blue-grey. But when the furniture van pulled up none of the neighbours came out to look; there was just the movement of a curtain and a willowy woman took her poodle for a walk as if the van were invisible. Rosa, hair wrapped in a scarf and wearing what she considered her artist's clothes, stopped herself in time from raising a hand in greeting. Perhaps I have made a mistake, she thought. But if she had, it was too late. She looked angrily at the climbing roses, the unsupported tendrils resting confidently in the still air, and wondered.

In the afternoon, when the boxes were in the right rooms

and her bed was assembled and one of Lucien's *Nurse* paintings hung – she might hang a strategic nude to shock the neighbours – she walked until she came to the Central Market. At the entrance was a little coffee shop and a smiling Italian face that seemed to flirt. Rosa took her short black and sat watching crowds pour in and out, relieved at their ordinariness. At the fruit stall she bought apples, oranges, grapes. And she bought a postcard for Harriet: the Glenelg tram. *Don't leave it too long,* she wrote. *I hope the twins are looking after you.*

The twins were being remarkably good. Now aged fourteen years and five months they had a way of standing one on either side of Harriet as if they were props or bedposts. They positively beamed in their usefulness. They slipped an arm around her waist, one from each side, demonstrating the blessedness of the twin state. If Dr Oona could see them, Harriet thought, amused, she would say I am getting back a world. The periods in which they had denied one another's existence were obliterated. At night Harriet lay in bed thinking of miraculous stories of twins waking together on opposite sides of the world to a premonition or having identical illnesses. They might even marry at the same time, have children in the same year. When they were babies she had thought of herself; Dr Oona had probably considered her selfish.

Dr Oona's death notice had appeared after her burial, 'according to her wishes', so Harriet had been unable to go to her funeral. But she might, before she went to stay with Rosa, visit the cemetery mentioned in the paper. An attendant would be able to point out the grave.

Now Harriet found herself worrying about what the loss of a twin would mean to the survivor: the world that had once shut her out by its complicity she longed to have preserved. For Susannah and Samuel talked so easily, discovering coincidences as if they were expected. When Susannah had been keen on a boy called David, Samuel had fancied a girl called Davina.

'Both dogs,' Susannah said, and laughed. 'What letter of the alphabet shall we try next?'

'Don't,' Harriet laughed. 'Promise me you'll go for someone different.'

'I solemnly promise to date only girls from the second half of the alphabet,' Samuel said, laying his hand over his heart. 'Will that do?'

'And myself only boys from A to M,' Susannah piped up.

'But they'll probably have resemblances,' Samuel went on. 'One day you'll go for a man with a beard and I'll get a bearded lady.'

'Would you like a bedtime story?' Susannah asked one night. 'We could read you a favourite book. Sam could do the male voices. Or we could read alternate chapters.'

And that was how they began re-reading *Pride and Prejudice*: Sam, Susannah and Harriet sitting on the bed, the twins on either side of Harriet, passing the book across her body and Garth reclining languidly at the foot. In the end it didn't lend itself to voices, so they took it in turns to read a chapter. *His character was decided. He was the proudest, most disagreeable man in the world, and every body hoped that he would never come there again*, Garth read, with a slow dignity befitting Mr Darcy. With his free hand he squeezed Harriet's toes. The phone rang and he rolled off the bed to answer it.

'It's Rosa,' he said. 'Ringing from Adelaide. She says she's unpacked and she wants to know when you're coming.'

At Grand Final, when the streets were crammed with adults and children in club colours and scarves, the Hyatt's toilets were made available to the public and Charlie waved them in through the big front doors with the grace he would have accorded to a head of state. And in the evening the lounge bar was full of men playing backgammon, men in jeans and expensive boots, their shirts open at the neck. The Singapore girls and their escorts were in for another stopover; they moved twittering towards the bank of lifts.

'Penny for them?' Gina Giardina said, coming up behind Zoe.

'Nothing, really,' Zoe replied. 'I'm just tired.'

'Join me for a Chinese then?' Gina suggested.

'I think I'm almost too tired to eat,' Zoe said when, after inspecting several ox-blood entrances in Little Bourke Street and comparing prices on the menus posted outside – they could have been Royal birth notices, enclosed as they were in glass and elaborately framed – they settled on The Golden Dragon.

'You order,' Zoe said, 'and I'll just help myself from yours.'

So they ate Peking duck and drank iced water and hot green tea. But Zoe refused to open a fortune cookie, leaving it on her plate instead.

'You don't want to know what the future holds?' Gina asked. Hers had been innocuous: *Be cautious and wise to preserve tranquillity.*

'I'm more concerned that I've made the right choice,' Zoe said, pouring more green tea into her cup.

'You're tired of the Hyatt and all it stands for. Hand over the heart, American flag snapping, Charlie bowing, and behind the scenes we're run off our feet. Have you seen the pale faces of some of the cleaners? As if they've never seen the light.'

'I was thinking more selfishly,' Zoe admitted. And this time she tore open the fortune cookie with her fingernail. *Disaster is dispersed and the door of good luck opens.* 'I was wondering why all the choices we make, the passionate ones, are made on hardly any evidence and yet they influence our whole lives?

'It's not as if,' she went on, 'I've been particularly disillusioned by seeing behind the scenes, as you put it. I always expected that. I sort of rejoiced in it. Sometimes I think the cleaning staff pulling their vacuum cleaners and trolleys look like miners come up after a shift.'

'So you've been undone by romance,' Gina said, reaching her hand for the bill. 'Isn't that meant to be our fate?'

'And what's the fate of men?' Zoe asked, her voice rising a little and causing a young Chinese waitress to look in their direction.

'Oh, I think they have romance too,' Gina replied. 'But perhaps it comes later in their lives. And by that time most women have finished with it and become practical.'

Zoe was thinking of Conchita's face when she told her she was pregnant and would need the spare bedroom. The new baby was unplanned. The bright colours of the room, the shawls and drapes, had suddenly seemed to fade. Zoe had put her arm around her friend and let her cry quietly on her shoulder.

'Are you sure about the bill?' Zoe asked, as they stood at the desk together. The desk was tiny, taking up as little room as possible.

'You only ate a bit of duck,' Gina replied, and on the way back up Collins Street they linked arms. The wind was getting up and the flags in front of the Grand Hyatt snapped on their poles.

'Americans often have flagpoles on their front lawns,' Gina mused. And then she began to sing, as they reached the top of the slope, in a clear true soprano:

Australians, all, let us rejoice
For we are young and free

'Flower day tomorrow,' Zoe said as they strolled through the lobby.

'Flower day,' Gina echoed. 'How can we possibly wait.'

The next morning a huge arrangement was being assembled by staff standing on ladders and others handing up lilies and magnolia and tulips. Singapore grass and fan palm fronds rose towards the chandelier, and a little notice apologised for any inconvenience to the queues that were forming at reception. Guests waiting to go into breakfast watched from easy chairs, and lamps burned on low tables. Offcuts of leaves and twigs and less-than-perfect blooms lay around the podium to be scooped up and taken away.

With the morning Zoe's spirits had risen again. The high ceilings and the cool air coming through the doors as people passed in and out gave the foyer a transient air so she could almost pity those paying their bills or showing company cards, for surely no one returned to marble floors or opened a front door to such a floral display. Nor did anyone walk in quite this way in the streets. Sometimes Charlie with his welcome seemed like Charon the guardian of the Styx where the dead were rowed, with pennies to close their eyes.

When she came off her shift Zoe made her way to the fifth floor where Conchita was checking the mini-bar in 1579.

'Don't you sometimes feel tempted to swallow the lot?' she asked, looking at the row of little bottles like malevolent eyes.

'There's not enough gin here,' Conchita replied, and then she placed her hand over her mouth.

'I'll move as soon as you like,' Zoe said, putting an arm around Conchita's shoulder.

'I don't want you to move at all,' Conchita said. 'Everything was perfect, we were doing well.'

And now this unexpected gift, Zoe thought. As if a little fortune brings more and a little sorrow brings more too.

'How many more rooms have you got?' she asked, when Conchita stood up, arching her back.

'Four, after this.'

'Then I'll stay and give you a hand. As long as you do the dunas.'

After the first three-course meal in the Queen Adelaide dining room, the first night in her bottom berth, Irene felt herself beginning to relax. Whenever Minnie was in sight she felt a desire to fiddle or inspect: the nooks and crannies of their compartment or the cutlery in the dining car. As Minnie came towards them, carrying the soup, cream of asparagus, Irene moved the cutlery a little apart in case it should spill. Minnie noticed the gesture, the way her mother would never allow reciprocity, how everything had to be on her terms. Her father was leaning on the table on his elbows, engaging the couple opposite in conversation. Probably Michael Palin, she thought, as she smiled at her mother and set the soup down.

'Thank you, dear,' Irene said.

'The bed linen is lovely,' the woman opposite, from Aberdeen, remarked, and Irene nodded in agreement.

'Everyone likes the linen,' Minnie replied, handing the last two bowls, wondering which of her clichés would be required next.

Her father, who was into a discussion of gauges, only winked and touched her arm. 'Our daughter,' he said. 'Nothing familiar.'

Later Minnie's parents and the two Scots stood in the corridor, leaning against the walls and watching as the landscape rushed past, scrubby and flat with occasionally a kangaroo or wallaby disturbed, detaching itself from the monochrome surroundings.

'I suppose they grow used to the train,' Irene said, 'though you wouldn't think it by their panic.'

'It's probably the difference between theory and reality,' the Scotsman said. 'But I must say this reality has turned out to be something.'

Shortly after the men returned to the lounge car and the two women to their berths. Irene sat by the window for a long time with just a bedside lamp showing in the glass. Miles of scenery, even when she slept, would flow through her consciousness, for the train had made her aware of, was seemingly even protecting her from, a ribbon of time being stretched taut and cut. How the train rattled and shook, roared and panted, as if some great truth was not getting through. Irene undressed slowly, drawing the blind first so her figure was not reflected on the glass, and then raising it before she climbed into her berth.

Her hands stroked the monogrammed duna, and a pillow she didn't need lay at her feet. One day, she thought, as her hands seemed to be turning from stroking to plucking motions, this will horrify those around my bed; it will be as significant as a death rattle. The panting of the train had eased and Irene opened her fingers on the sheet as if a knife-thrower would throw knives between her fingers. She vaguely heard Teddy come in, the blind lowered, and felt whisky breath on her cheek. He noticed, though she slept peacefully enough, her hands were clenched into fists.

'Countess Minimosa,' Pedro said, as he, Minnie and Jimbo were laying the tables for breakfast after the second dinner sitting.

The door opened and a passenger with a camera appeared.

'The light's rather poor. You'll get a better shot in the morning,' Pedro said, lying through his teeth, but the passenger turned away, apologising.

'But we do have a countess,' he said, when the door was closed. 'Disguised as a skivvy.'

'Shut up,' said Minnie, 'if you don't want me to hit you.'

'Temper, temper. I thought sang-froid was the mark of the aristocracy.'

'Does the Count, your father, know of your romance with an anarchist?' Pedro asked as he checked a table. The breakfast settings were the most congested of all, and once you added eggs three ways, jugs of milk and juice, jams and honey, it was a wonder the guests didn't brawl.

'No, he doesn't,' Minnie replied. 'And since it's over, I can't see it's anyone's business but my own.'

'Still he looks a sympathetic kind of count,' Pedro said.

When Minnie didn't reply he added in a mollifying tone. 'Don't worry. I won't tell the papers. Your secret's safe with me.'

There was a letter in Zoe's pigeonhole at the Hyatt.

I'm retiring after this play closes, Sophie wrote. *And I think I might go and live in Wellington. It's a nice little city.* The wealthy farmer had turned out to be arthritic but there was a retired lawyer who was not too feeble. *I can hardly see to put on my makeup but it doesn't matter since he can't see me clearly either. You can't call it love but the two halved-creatures seeking one another still applies. I wish you love, my dear, and thank you for the pleasure you have given me. Visit me.*

Gina met her in the corridor, walking with trailing feet toward the baize door. She put her arms around Zoe.

'Stay with me,' she said.

Irene sat in the lounge car near the grass tree. She had reached out a hand to touch it and drawn back, surprised at the sharpness of its blades. Its thin trunk was set in bark. A primitive tree like a cactus, needing no one, expecting nothing, hoarding each drop of moisture, sometimes not even a drop but a kind of sweat such as might break out on a face. Still, in the lounge car the grass tree received plenty of air, for a window behind it was open a few inches and the leaves shivered and rattled.

'Would you like a coffee?' Pedro asked. 'Can I bring you anything?'

His head disappeared below the counter as he checked the number of Indian Pacific sweatshirts in stock. The most popular was off-white. Washes like a dream, he would say, though he had never owned one.

'There'll be a bus tour in Adelaide,' he said, when his head appeared above the counter again. 'Would you be interested in that? It returns you to the train.'

'I might just stretch my legs,' Irene replied. 'I mean in Adelaide. That's the one thing I miss. Being able to walk.'

'Would you like to come with me now?' Pedro suggested. 'I'm going to walk to the other end of the train. You could come as far as you like. See how the other half lives, or should I say reclines.' He was talking too much, as usual. Small wonder Minnie wanted to hit him.

But Irene got to her feet and he held the door open for her.

'I don't like the part where the coaches join,' she confided. 'I know it's silly of me.'

'That little strip of reality,' Pedro said, taking her arm. 'Perhaps I could go first and you could just keep your eyes on the middle of my back. I don't mind if you put a hand on my shoulder.'

'You're very gallant,' Irene said, and she smiled at his back.

They crossed the first divide safely: it was like a cauldron or a pit in the stage where a ghost enters or exits.

'Wiggle your hips,' Pedro instructed as they came to the single luxury couchettes. 'Like this.' And behind him, marvelling at him, Irene burst into a laugh.

Rosa made up a bed for Harriet on the ground floor but Harriet laughed and insisted on sleeping on the first floor in a room next to Rosa.

'It's the influence of Mr Wu,' she said. 'Now I always like to sleep up in the air. And to have the windows open.'

Harriet had travelled Economy Class on the Indian Pacific. It was only for one night, she told Garth, and she wanted to sit up. The seats reclined almost like a bed: the landscape rushing past, the stars, the companionship of other bodies. 'Are you sure?' he asked. And she hadn't fancied the Queen Adelaide dining room and a heavy meal late at night. By her feet a little plastic bag held a collection of pills: she walked to the bar and bought a bottle of club soda. And the man in the seat beside her was a mining engineer. He was reading *Cloudstreet* by Tim Winton. They discussed books and landscapes and at night, when the carriage resounded with snores and murmurings, half-drowned by the train, Harriet could see by the light reflected on the surface of his eye that he was awake. She pulled her blanket up to her chin and twisted her legs and thought of the kindness of strangers, and then of Rosa. She would thrust the little supply of pills at Rosa as soon as she got off so the visit should not be spent in worry and furtive observation.

And Rosa was as good as Harriet expected: a glance at the pills, the describing of them as an armoury, and they were forgotten. They climbed the stairs, a short flight, not to be compared to Mr Wu's, and sat propped on Rosa's bed drinking tea. A rose twined against the glass; Harriet could see its ferocious thorns.

'Just a week,' Rosa said. 'We could waste it.' It struck her as an extravagance, like being in a harem. Garth had insisted that Harriet fly home at the end of it.

Rosa poured more tea and they sat playing a game: Five Cross-your-heart Favourite Things. Rosa's were: thin spit-through bath towels which rasped when you dried yourself; rain-scented air; buckets of her favourite perfume, Cabochard; lighting a fire without assistance from green wood and old correspondence; making an origami crane for Mr Wu's anniversary, which she did every year and had told no one until now. They got sidetracked on Mr Wu and Harriet's Dr Oona. Harriet's were: red camellias on a green lawn; woodsmoke in autumn; getting slowly wet in a light drizzle; the desert; friendship.

The next time the Indian Pacific passed through Broken Hill Minnie got off and walked up the platform. At first she could not see Dulcie Scoular; then she saw her coming along the platform carrying a polystyrene cup of tea. 'You shouldn't avoid his mother,' the Count had said when she had told him about Adam. Privately he thought the young man sounded boorish. If Minnie had not spoken until they were on the Nullarbor Plain he and Irene might have paid more attention to Broken Hill.

Dulcie squinted at Minnie as if trying to place her, then she put her tea down next to a cake tin full of raffle tickets and petty cash and gave Minnie a hug.

'I thought you'd been ill,' she said. 'I've looked for you when the Indian came through.'

'I haven't been very well,' Minnie replied. 'Since Adam and I . . .'

'I'm angry with him,' his mother replied, looking at Minnie with kindly eyes.

There was no curiosity in her expression, just compassion. 'I hope he'll grow out of it, this chip on the shoulder. Because it's nothing to do with his experience. He's always been well provided for, and now he has his studies.'

'Whereas you,' Minnie began, and then didn't know what to say.

'One of the tricoteuses,' Dulcie Scoular laughed. 'All the knitting I've done would probably stretch from here to Adelaide.'

'Would you knit something for me?' Minnie asked impulsively. 'I'd pay you, of course. I could pick it up when the Indian comes through.'

'We could have a signal,' Dulcie said, her eyes smiling. 'I

could wave a handkerchief and you'll know it's ready.'

The passengers were climbing back on board, fussing with cameras, lamenting they couldn't get the full length of the train.

'Did you have a colour in mind?' Adam's mother asked.

'No, you choose,' Minnie said. Then she swung aboard and waved her hand.

Harriet and Rosa walked in Central Market and then took the tram to Glenelg. Rosa had bought a bus pass to take them to Rundle Mall or wherever they liked to stop. Harriet had bought a dress for Susannah and a book on great Australian cricketers for Samuel. The dress, a dusky pink, had a black hem inset with tiny mirrors. 'Like sitting on a beach after sunset and watching the stars come out,' Rosa said, and Harriet, who was thinking about the mirrors if the dress was washed, looked at her friend in gratitude. Rosa had always lifted her off her feet and set her down in a better place. The night at Mr Wu's when they had contemplated the multi-coloured walls – wasn't one almost this pink? – when her spirits had been about to sink, Rosa had rushed downstairs, shaking out the remains of her wages into Mr Wu's hand and brought back, in a silver bucket, all the leftover flowers.

And now, as then, the air streamed through the open windows, only the air in the tram was more like a whirlwind as the tram gathered speed and rattled through what Rosa pointed out was ordinary Adelaide.

'Whenever I feel confined by Strangeways Terrace I take the tram,' Rosa was saying. And Harriet had broken the ice there: one of the neighbours had waved when they were inspecting the garden which took just twenty-six steps, by Rosa's calculation, to circumnavigate.

The tram rattled to a stop at the end of Glenelg village, and Rosa and Harriet got down and walked leisurely towards the beach. The tide was far out and gulls and children clustered on the sand. A smell of chips and salt mingled with the scent of the sea.

'I think I couldn't live here without this,' Rosa said, running her fingers through her hair and throwing her neck back.

Harriet, whose back was aching, longed to lie stretched out on the white sand. Sometimes she wondered what it would be like to die: to be stiff and cold. Once she had dreamed she was looking down at her legs covered with cobwebs.

They moved down so the low wall was against their backs and the parcel with the dress made a tiny bolster for Harriet's back. 'I'll take you for tea at the Hilton,' Rosa said. 'When you feel like going back.'

'Are we dressed enough?' Harriet asked. Her eyes were almost closing.

'I know the commissionaire,' Rosa said. 'It's all a question of posture really. A good posture can take you anywhere.'

'Wake me,' Harriet said. The warmth was seeping into her bones, and though it would not be a proper sleep she knew she could doze.

Later, when they were rattling back on the tram, Harriet asked about Billy. Her voice sounded loud, as if everyone in the carriage could hear and the wind tore the words out of her mouth and flung them out the window onto dry lawns, dishevelled children and old parked cars. Occasionally they passed a jacaranda tree or a line of palms.

'I wrote to him on his wedding,' Rosa said. 'He sent an invitation.' She too was looking out the window. 'Better in the breach than the observance,' she said softly, and Harriet had to lean forward.

'He finally made his mother happy,' Harriet said. 'She had decided to keep all his postcards in a box and to send it to him after her death. She thought he could lay them end to end or use them as tiles. I think she wanted him to see all the phrases he had repeated to her endlessly over the years.'

'All that effort to obscure,' Rosa said. 'The poor woman must have been endlessly reading between the lines.'

'Oh Billy was better than that. There was nothing to read between the lines either. But I believe he did finally get to build a bridge somewhere. Billy's bridge, they call it.'

They were coming closer to Adelaide; primness and order were becoming apparent. The tram drew up opposite the Hilton and hid its face in a grove of trees. Rosa gave Harriet her arm as they got down and walked across the grass. Hugh, the commissionaire, was at the top of the steps, temporarily idle, though his face betrayed no trace. He caught Rosa's eye and winked.

Minnie left the Indian Pacific at Cook; her parents were bound for Perth and the flower trail. On their last night she sat with them in their berth and told them about Adam Scoular.

'There is no need, dear,' her mother said.

'Let her tell it if she wishes,' her father said.

In their marriage the roles were reversed: the Count was the talkative one, her mother silent and judicial. Minnie had never noticed it before.

'You always had a wild streak,' her mother said, 'but it concealed a good heart.'

Minnie looked at her in surprise.

'What your mother means is she was busy dealing with the wild streak,' Minnie's father said.

'I can speak for myself, Teddy,' Irene replied. 'Even if I speak less. You were not easy as a child,' she said, 'but I was not easy either. I took the line of least resistance.'

'You preferred Angela,' Minnie said, and the voice that spoke sounded like someone else, an aggrieved person, four feet tall.

'I'm sorry if all these years I've given you that impression,' her mother said. 'I felt your father preferred you. Sometimes he preferred you to me.'

'That's not true,' the Count protested.

'It is true,' her mother said. 'It's one of the reasons we are travelling to see these flowers. There's a survival element involved. I expect I shall learn something. Flowers pressed close to the earth, savouring a single drop of water.'

'I believe it is often dew,' Minnie said. 'Night dew.' She could have been reading the commentary.

'Whatever,' said her mother. 'Whatever it is, they treasure it . . .' She left the sentence unfinished.

'I'll bring some coffee,' Minnie said, 'and then I'll tell you more about Adam. Just the rudiments,' she added, when she was in the doorway, turning her head and looking back.

When she returned her parents were sitting close together and her mother had a rolled-up handkerchief in her hand.

Rosa and Harriet were drinking coffee in the foyer of the Adelaide Hilton and Hugh had presented them both, though they were not guests, with a long-stemmed carnation. They lay on the glass table between them, one magenta, the other a peculiar shade of orange. A group of Singapore girls stood near a nest of sofas, their bags at their feet.

'Those waists,' Rosa remarked. 'I could make three of them.'

'What does an old Singapore girl look like?' Harriet wondered.

'I expect there is quite a turnover. Businessmen must propose to them during flights.' She imagined them receiving folded notes with declarations of love.

'Whereas I have not behaved like a Singapore girl,' Rosa said, pouring more coffee.

'That innocent smiling, those wide eyes looking up, must stop somewhere,' Harriet said.

Really it was the expression of a child. Her own expression when she worked for Mr Worboys and later at the haberdashery or when she studied, even at Dr Oona's, was serious. How ridiculously serious she had been discussing the twins who were now such a comfort. She had found Dr Oona's grave, read that her second name was Eugenia. Beneath her dates an inscription read *We live our lives, for ever taking leave. Rilke.*

The Singapore girls departed in a twittering rush for their shuttle and Rosa beckoned the waiter for a liqueur.

'We'll take a taxi,' she said to Harriet. 'Or we can eat here, if you like. At the brasserie.'

'I think I'd like to see more of Hugh in action,' Harriet

smiled. 'He seems like a kindred spirit.'

The liqueurs came: Drambuie for Harriet and Benedictine for Rosa. Harriet thought she might not make it to the doors. Warm soft fire flowed down her throat; her heart felt warm and inflamed like a statue of the Sacred Heart.

'Do you think our lives are ordained?' she asked Rosa. 'Like tram tracks. We leap on or off or decide to walk alongside, but we go where the tracks go?'

'I once pulled myself up onto the St Kilda tram by holding onto a man's tie,' Rosa said. Her eyes were soft and dreamy. 'He looked surprised at first, as if I might garrotte him. Then he joined in and pulled me up by both arms. Perhaps he was the love of my life. If only I'd thought to fall against him.'

'So what did you do?' Harriet asked, though she already knew.

'Why I trod on his foot and stepped back, apologising profusely. I think I reached up to straighten his tie. A Singapore girl would have got his phone number.'

'A Singapore girl wouldn't have been able to reach his tie.'

'True,' Rosa said. 'There is some consolation in that.'

Minnie and Pedro were washing cups and saucers, glasses and spoons in the kitchenette of Car E. 'Please help yourself to tea, coffee and bikkies throughout your journey. If I have to say that again I think I shall choke,' Minnie said.

'Someone drank all the milk,' Pedro remarked, looking into the mini-fridge. 'You always get one.' Sure enough there was a milk-rimmed glass.

'Do you think there have ever been people elegant enough for this train?' Minnie asked, running hot water into the sink, then wiping and drying it until it shone. The scales seemed to have fallen from her eyes since her parents had gone. Her mother had embraced her on the platform at Adelaide, a hard fierce embrace. Her father had winked over her mother's back but she could tell he was pleased.

'We live in hope,' Pedro said, making a note of the milk. 'Perhaps one day there will be a mysterious veiled lady.'

'With an enormous amount of luggage,' Minnie went on. 'She'll never fit in a First Class couchette. You'll have to waggle your hips like a tart to get through the corridor.'

'It'll be worth it,' Pedro replied. 'She'll ring for me later.'

'And you'll tussle on that tiny bed.'

'She's already admired my hips, remember.'

'In the dining car I'll seat her next to that obnoxious Swiss family. The ones with Swiss bank accounts.' Minnie had overheard them say, 'Australians don't expect tips, so that's a saving.' No wonder they invented gruyère cheese, Minnie thought, as she went past. She must inform them they'd be safe in New Zealand as well. Two homes of the brave and the free.

'Come on,' said Pedro. 'I'll shout you a club soda.'

'Very generous,' said Minnie. 'And you'll bring back the milk?'

'You're not still thinking of that anarchist?' Pedro remarked as he led the way along the corridor. He swayed a little from side to side, experimentally. 'You must be over him by now.'

Rosa and Harriet sat side by side on their chairs at the Hilton. Their little table was cleared and fresh glasses of water brought.

'I don't think I can walk,' Harriet said.

'Then we'll eat here,' Rosa decided.

'I used to always have a book,' Rosa said, when they were seated at a not very conspicuous table in the brasserie. The waitress had given them a faintly enquiring look and Rosa had looked back firmly. If the Adelaide Writers' Festival had been on they could have pretended to be two distinguished lady authors. Then, Rosa suspected, they would have been shown a better table. But she was used to such tables, near a window with a view of a side street or close to the servery with its heat lamps warming dishes as they were set down. At least now I needn't look critically at everything in a hotel, she consoled herself, though she couldn't help inspecting the plates of food as they were brought.

For the rest of her stay she would cook for Harriet: dishes

that need not be disarranged because they would be artless. She would make chicken soup, and they could take a picnic to Glenelg and watch the sun set.

'Did you read or just pretend to read?' Harriet was asking, bringing Rosa back to the present.

'Not at first, I didn't. But after a while I forgot my surroundings. Sometimes a waiter would tell me someone had attempted to pass a note and been informed I was one of the staff. We used to laugh about it. And Lucien's family used to eat in silence with their books propped on special stands. They rarely spoke to one another.'

'Do you miss him?' Harriet asked.

'No,' Rosa said, spearing a morsel of fish. 'In a way he always belonged to his family. I really was, as he perceived, his nurse. And that's how he painted me.'

'And now you're nursing me,' Harriet said.

'No, I'm not,' said Rosa, and her voice sounded indignant. 'You are not to die and I am not going to nurse you.' She reminded herself not to make chicken soup. If anything happened to Harriet she would howl like a dog.

'I've got one of the paintings from the *Nurse* series,' she said, when their plates were cleared and they had waved away the dessert menu. 'I think of it as my life insurance. I'll show you when we get home.'

They came down the steps of the Hilton and got into a cab summoned by Hugh. Adelaide lay spread out in the dark, its lanterns glowing, its wide avenues speeding them towards Strangeways Terrace. Already to Rosa it was beginning to seem too undisturbed. In the little front garden the scent of roses was still heavy.

Adam Scoular's arrest for assault took only a sentence in the *Sydney Morning Herald* report of the Pasminco mine closure protests, and it wasn't until Minnie was back on the Indian Pacific that Pedro brought it to her attention. Wisely he made no comment. Among those detained, for resisting arrest, was a young woman.

'It must be Pip,' Minnie said. She felt pole-axed and could hardly go about her duties. She had never longed so much for the dreary landscape of Broken Hill to appear.

Dulcie Scoular, naturally enough, was not on the platform, but a woman from an adjoining stall told Minnie that Adam had not received bail but Philippa was staying with his mother.

'She always was a good comforter,' Minnie said, and the woman looked indignant.

'It was partly her fault. If she hadn't tried to join the picket line, it mightn't have happened. Then she fell and Adam waded in. Then, once started, his anger knew no bounds.' There was no time for more: the last passengers were climbing aboard.

'If you see Dulcie tell her I will write,' Minnie called as she began to run.

Pedro found her sitting in the galley, her head in her hands. If anyone came in they might think she was contemplating cleaning the sink. He couldn't think of anything to say. *Just deserts, had it coming.* With superhuman control he held his tongue. He put a hand on Minnie's shoulder and she shrugged it off. If only it hadn't been Pip, she thought. That was the trouble with good people: to maintain their goodness they left chaos in their wake. Like someone walking from a bathroom dripping wet and leaving footprints on the carpet. She needn't have feared the young man Pip had bought lunch would come back. He had probably eaten the lunch and fled. And Minnie had been on her guard lest he turn into a stalker! And now Dulcie Scoular would feel the whole thing was predestined. All that knitting, all that waiting on the Indian to pass through, that hopeful silver contact with the outside world had not been enough to ward off nemesis.

Minnie roused herself and walked through to the lounge car. The grass tree was shivering in its pot as several of the windows were open. A scent of dust and dry air filled the carriage. An elderly American couple were playing cards and a man in a safari suit was reading *Lonely Planet Guide to Outback Australia*. Minnie crouched down behind the counter and checked the supply of souvenirs without seeing them.

'The women who knitted in front of the guillotine,' Dulcie Scoular had said to Minnie once, when they had become friends. The relationship with Adam was already failing, though she couldn't bring herself to admit it. They were quarrelling about anger, the amount of it, and how far it should be allowed to spread.

'You use it as fuel,' Minnie had said to him as they trudged up Sulphide Street. 'It's not everything, you know.'

'You're just envious you haven't got any,' he had replied smugly.

'What do you know?' she had countered, and a tiny flame had shot into life inside herself, as if someone had clicked on a throwaway lighter. It reached her throat and then began a downward passage. Someone in the family had had it, she remembered her mother saying. Something about someone leaning on a fencepost, something about a horse.

'How does this compare to the Ghan?' The safari suit was standing by the bar.

'I'm sorry,' Minnie said. 'They're both wonderful. Different of course. I can give you a brochure. Or you might like to talk to Pedro Casado, he's been on it.'

She had never been so grateful for the sight of Pedro's face. He led safari suit over to a two-seater by the grass tree and began.

'Thank heavens,' Minnie said to him later. 'I might have had to go into the frying of emu eggs and the cooking of lizards.'

'I laid it on pretty thick,' Pedro said, and she could see his smile was not just a pair of well-shaped lips but infectious.

'Don't speak to me today, but we'll have a drink when we get to Sydney.'

Irene and Teddy walked among the wildflowers at Walyunga National Park. Hakeas, grevilleas, verticordias, triggerplants attached themselves determinedly to the earth, defiant as a skin rash. To Irene, who had a slight headache from the blinding sun, the flowers had a moral quality, a sort of reproach.

'It must be wonderful to see them under the stars,' she said to her husband and he took her hand, wondering that they could still surprise one another. 'I was thinking they're so fixed, so defiantly earthbound,' she went on.

'But perhaps they're not,' he replied, releasing her hand and putting an arm around her shoulder. 'They live so near the surface.' A kick from his shoe might dislodge something that had taken centuries to evolve. Tomorrow they would go to Foxes Lair Reserve to view endangered marsupials.

The little group in sunhats and dark glasses moved slowly on the dry paths. A man lay on his stomach to photograph a donkey orchid.

'What does it all mean?' Irene asked. 'We've come all this distance.' She had felt at home on the Indian Pacific, reluctant to leave.

'We can't know,' Teddy replied. 'I think Darwin said something about our brains not being adapted for it. We're just meant to be here and now.'

'And to think Minnie calls you Count,' Irene replied, and some of the tension went out of her face. She smiled. 'Whereas something more like a baboon or a gorilla . . .'

The man lying on his stomach, adjusting his light filter, looked up to see a woman past middle-age leaning into the embrace of a man.

Rosa and Harriet were back at Strangeways Terrace. In the morning Harriet would fly home to Melbourne. She had spoken to Garth, told him she had never felt so well.

The sky was bright with stars, the air still warm. Rosa dragged two old deckchairs out into the back garden. She took a shawl and a pillow for Harriet's head. They leaned back, side by side, slumped in the folds of the canvas. There were stars in clusters or side by side, like twins; there were some that were solitary. But what could be solitary in such a space? Harriet was thinking of Dr Oona.

'Do you still remember Mr Wu?' she asked Rosa.

'Not so much. But I love remembering his qualities, his

steadiness. All that patient labour, like the foundation of a house.'

They sat in a companionable silence.

'Who do you think is up there?' Rosa asked.

'Everyone, perhaps,' Harriet said. 'Out of sight, like behind an eyeball. Whole countries, centuries.'

'There's so much room,' Rosa replied. 'But it doesn't seem individual any more.'

'Do you think Billy will stay in New Zealand?' Harriet asked. 'Do you think he can be happy there?'

'He could be out looking at the stars,' Rosa said. 'Not much difference.' She was thinking of a hitch in a piece of fabric.

'I hope he's written to his mother,' Harriet said, but the languid way she lay back and the soft tone of her voice made it clear she suspected he hadn't.

Rosa had remembered something. She hoped she had the figures right. She arched her hands behind her head and looked up, as if speaking to the stars. 'Did you know,' she said to Harriet, 'that each one of us represents one out of 8.4 million possible mixes of our father's and mother's genes?' Finally she felt she had offered something back.

She turned her head and Harriet's quiet breathing showed she was asleep.

LISTENING TO
THE EVERLY BROTHERS

Elizabeth Smither

Elizabeth Smither is widely known as one of New Zealand's leading poets, but she is also a writer of short stories of the very finest quality. In this new collection, her fourth, Smither has produced stories that are witty and sharply observed and reveal her distinctive ironic sympathy with the lives of ordinary people.

'Though never in the least "poetical", these are a poet's stories. We are being directed to look through very clean, clear glass at retreating reflections we have up to now missed. A not-unusual situation, like an old woman's terror at finding herself in the clutches of a son who no longer loves her, is bared to the cruel bone. Two innocents playing with astrology as an aid to love are an examination of sweet experimental youth. As in her poetry, Elizabeth Smither celebrates the layers of oddness that lurk beneath the everyday. Sometimes her vision is as pure as Katherine Mansfield's.'

JANE GARDAM

'There is a secret in Smither's stories, something dry or black or wicked beneath a seemingly genteel, even prim, veneer. Darkly humourous and deeply felt, her stories reveal an infallible sense of the comedy of manners, of what is at once funny and bleak about the difference between what people say and what they mean.'

Harvard Review, CHRISTINA THOMPSON

Swim

Jackie Davis

'What will happen to me if you die?'

Maya is a young woman bringing up her child alone. Eight-year-old Charlie means everything to her. Then one day Maya finds a lump in her breast. She has to manage it all: her illness and treatment, her increasingly uncertain future as well as caring for Charlie. She must also face up to the biggest questions of all. There is one thing that keeps her going – she knows that at all times she can retreat to the local pool or slip into the sea, and *swim* . . .

This moving and haunting novel is Jackie Davis' much-awaited follow-up to the well-received *Breathe*. With this beautifully written second novel Davis confirms her place as one of New Zealand's most accomplished new writers.

'Davis is a gifted storyteller with the rare ability to capture raw emotions and present them in an unsentimental yet sincere fashion.'

The *Press*, STEVE SCOTT

THE SHARK BELL

Christine Johnston

'Go down to the beach, that's the way. Hang your feet over the chasm. Look up at the shark bell. Summon the shark. The sea is still and green and the waves flip over lazily. But the waves only represent the surface. Underneath it is seething with life . . .'

It is 1969. As summer approaches, Edmund longs to see a shark. Its coming will expose well-kept secrets – his mother's mysterious past, the terrible connection between his fascinating next-door neighbour Mr Zacek and the 'crazy' mother of his classmate Jake. Edmund's life is about to be changed for ever.

This new novel from Christine Johnston is about family secrets and shifting identities, about how we choose to deal with the past and how in the end, like the shark out in the bay circling beneath the waves, it must always be reckoned with.

'The writing is controlled and confident, and the sense of things gliding just below the surface is enough to keep the hairs on the back of your neck standing up throughout.'

North & South, JOHN MCCRYSTAL

Queen of Beauty

Paula Morris

Virginia Ngatea Seton leaves New Orleans, where she works as a researcher for an historical novelist, and returns home to Auckland for the wedding of her younger sister. Drawn back into the world of her Pakeha-Maori family, Virginia rediscovers many family stories and legends. She learns how the city of her youth has inextricably changed, as surely as the country of her grandparents is gone forever.

At turns haunting, moving and comic, *Queen of Beauty* spans three generations. Shifting between modern-day New Orleans and Auckland, as well as New Zealand of the 1920s and 1960s, it explores the fragility of truth, the elusiveness of the past and the burden it places on the living.

Queen of Beauty was the winner of the 2001 Adam Foundation Prize for Creative Writing. It marks the emergence of a unique and vibrant new literary voice.

'With its enchanting stories of friendship and love, Queen of Beauty *is a nostalgic journey into a lost world. While Morris writes with great affection and empathy for her huge list of characters, she never slides into the sort of cloying over-fondness that can tarnish so many novels of family legends.'*

NZ Herald, PENELOPE BIEDER